Special Thanks

My appreciation goes first to the Ultimate Creator for entrusting the "skeleton" of this story to me as I slept.

Thank you,

Cindy, Dagny ... all the friends at Writers' Bloc who have been a constant source of knowledge and support,

Mona, my always encouraging sister for your editorial help and advise,

Gayle, for your sharp eye, your encouragement and the perfect prairie photo for my cover,

Cissy, Beth and Maggie who couldn't wait for the next chapters to be emailed to them, and Sharon who insisted on hearing it all over lunch,

Katherine, my great-niece for being the lovely portrayal of my story's Catherine on the cover.

Bonnie, for all your support in actually getting it into print,

J.P. for putting it all together so beautifully,

The countless friends and acquaintances who have continually encouraged me in the writing of this book and anticipated its finally becoming reality.

Author's Note

I gained a new appreciation for the stalwart people who settled our West as I did research for this book, and yet my heart was troubled at the treatment of our Native American brothers and sisters in that process. I so wanted to re-write history adding compassion and understanding, commanding respect and fairness. Unfortunately we are powerless to change the past, but I trust we can learn from history to create a better future.

All of the characters in this story are fictional with the exception of one – our Heavenly Father. It is my greatest desire that every reader of this story will be encouraged to know His love and forgiveness and will be reminded that His grace is ever-present for all of us in our personal struggles - the changes in our lives.

Ellen Sherrill

Search for the Whole Heart:

Volume I

Change

CHAPTER 1

Fourteen year-old Catherine Sutherland was determined to reach the top of the trail. With only one step to go she lifted the front of her long skirt, grabbed the branch of a small tree on her left, and pulled herself up to level ground on the Missouri River bank. Winded from the climb, she stood with hands on her hips and lifted her flushed face to the cool river breeze. She breathed deeply, listening with closed eyes to the peaceful sound of the flowing water. The scene could have birthed a delight on canvas, the graceful woman-child with golden curls, her lilac dress alive in the breeze. But an artist would be challenged to capture the struggle of emotions on the pretty face that gave promise to striking beauty someday. The frown wrinkling her brow between those cornflower blue eyes spoke silently of the conflict in her heart. Her cheeks, tinged with color from the climb up the cliff bank, now glistened with tears she'd been trying desperately to withhold for the past hour.

"No, I can't do this! I cannot cry! I just have to think this through." Eyeing her favorite perch, Catherine found the familiar stepping stones and made her way up to the large, flat rock that jutted out over the water. It was a perfect observation point, not only for the river, but for the clearing below. Bunching up her skirt for a cushion she sat on the warm rock, hugged her knees to her chin and looked down to watch the busy scene she had just left.

A small white church was in the middle of the clearing, its cross-topped steeple identifying it as a house of worship. Cloth-covered tables had been set up on one side of the building where chattering women unloaded dishes of food. The wedding festivities would last into the evening as people ate, danced, and visited for hours. A group of men were gathered on the opposite side of the church near the wagons, and the smell of their cigars wafted over on the light breeze to mingle with the enticing aroma of the food. Excited children, free from school work and daily chores, were noisily setting up three-legged races and stickball teams.

Catherine struggled to organize the thoughts racing through her mind as she picked at the burrs clinging to her skirt. Somehow she would have to accept that her mother's marriage in that small white church today was a fact. But in spite of all those people celebrating the occasion, nothing about this day felt right to Catherine. She dropped her head to her knees in despair and silently prayed for strength.

"Heavenly Father, I guess I should be happy for Mama, but You know that I'm really not! I miss Papa so much. I'm trying to like Mr. McCloud, but he's a total stranger, and I don't know how to handle this!"

The tears now flowed unhindered as Catherine sat waiting for answers to the situation that lay ahead. She was so intent that she didn't hear footsteps, or see the wiry, brown-haired young man nearing the top of the trail.

"Hey, Cat," her brother, Jeremy, softly called with concern, using the nickname he'd attached to her when they were small. "I thought I'd find you here. Are you O.K.?"

He took the last few feet of the trail in one long stride and pulled himself onto the rock beside her.

Fighting another flood of tears, Catherine shook her head, and moved over to make room for her brother.

Looking out over the scene below, Jeremy echoed Catherine's previous thoughts, "I sure hope things work out better than I think they're going to."

They could see their mother in the church yard, smiling as she spoke with well-wishers who stopped to congratulate her. "She looks so pretty today," Catherine said.

"Yeah, she does. I wish Pa could see her," Jeremy said, then winced at the irony of his statement.

"That's O.K. It's just strange to go to your parent's wedding!"

"It sure is. But Cat, it's more than that. I haven't told you what I heard McCloud saying the other day when I went to get him from the saloon."

"You went to the saloon?"

"I had to. Remember last Saturday when Daisy was about to drop her calf and Mama sent me to get him?"

Catherine nodded her assent

"Well, I went to the mill where he was supposed to be buying supplies to repair the barn door. The men there told me he'd gone to Joe's Place. I had to get him, so I went to the saloon. It was so dark in there, but I heard his loud mouth as soon as I got in the place. He was bragging about what a deal he'd fallen into ... a pretty widow with a farm, and two snotty kids!"

"Jeremy, no! Did you tell Mama?"

Shaking his head Jeremy said, "I just couldn't. She thinks marrying this guy will make things better because he can work the farm." In frustration he clenched his fists. "She wouldn't have to do this if I could have done more! No matter how hard I try, I just can't do what Pa did!"

Catherine twined her arm through Jeremy's and laid her head comfortingly against his shoulder. Her heart ached at the pain in her brother's voice. She thought of the long hours he worked to tend the fields and livestock, all while keeping up with school work too. Ever since Pa had been forced to join that war that he was so against, things had been really hard. They weren't alone. The Confederate War had brought hardship to everyone. There wasn't a family she knew that had not lost loved ones, and hardly any soldier who made it home returned whole in body.

She'd never forget the day the two army officers came and gave her mother the letter saying that Pa had been shot in battle and had died of infection from the wound in his chest. Just weeks later the war ended, and the last of the hired hands disappeared in the night. Now things had reached the desperation point. She could understand why her mother would want to marry again, but not *this* man, Pollard McCloud!

"You don't like Mr. McCloud, do you, Jeremy?" Catherine asked.

Jeremy paused before answering, "I just can't figure him, Cat. Some days we work together just fine, and then at other times he looks at me like … I don't know … almost like he hates me. He's said some pretty nasty things."

"It's strange; he seems so nice around Mama," Catherine mused.

"I think he really cares for *her*," Jeremy stated, "It's us he would like to do without, and especially me.

Catherine was embarrassed to talk about her mother's relationship, but she had to know how Jeremy felt.

"Do you think she ... she ... loves him?"

They looked down at the group of men where their mother's new husband was blowing a stream of cigar smoke into the air.

Jeremy's gray eyes darkened as he compared Pollard McCloud to his gentle father. "No, Cat, I don't think she loves him. At least, not like she loved Pa."

Then turning to Catherine he asked, "How does McCloud treat you when Mama's not around?"

"I've never been around him without her. I don't think he's said a dozen words to me since he came."

"That's probably best. Just keep your distance, O.K?"

"That shouldn't be too hard. I can tell he wants Mama all to himself, and I'm afraid it's going to get worse now that they're married. We've lost Papa; I don't want to lose our mother, too. What are we going to do, Jeremy?"

With a deep sigh and feeling older than his fifteen years, Jeremy looked down at his pretty younger sister. Her blond hair fell about her shoulders in curls that defied control, framing a younger version of their mother's face. He'd always looked out for her, and now as her worried eyes searched his for answers, there was only one he could give.

"Cat, the only thing that's helped us make it since Pa left to go to the war, has been our faith in God. You know I don't talk about spiritual things very often, but that doesn't mean I don't think about them, or that I don't talk to God in my own way. I don't know what to expect with Mama marrying McCloud. I'm trying to sort it out too. Honestly, I've been mad at Mama for taking up with McCloud, but that's really not fair to her. I've been missing Pa so much

11

myself that I haven't given much thought to how lonely she must be and what a burden she's carried. I don't trust McCloud. I can't even tell you why, I just don't. But I know that God promised to be with us, so I'm going to do what I can to keep the peace and maybe it will all work out somehow."

Catherine stared at her brother in surprise. He had never talked to her about his relationship with God. They went to church as a family, but she hadn't been sure where Jeremy stood in light of spiritual things. For him to share feelings so personal was unusual. His words gave her courage, though, and she felt a surge of pride as she reached over to give him a hug. "Thanks, brother."

Now that he'd gotten all that off his chest, Jeremy felt a little sheepish. Rising to his feet he changed the subject, "Hey, where's David?"

"I don't know," Catherine answered, brightening at the mention of her best friend.

"I know he had to work at the shop earlier, but he was supposed to be here for the wedding. Something must have happened."

"Maybe his Pa will know," Jeremy said, speaking of the minister who had just performed the marriage ceremony for their mother.

"The way David likes to eat, I'm sure he has good reason to be late for that meal." Looking down, they could see people lining up at the food-laden tables. Catherine knew they couldn't excuse their absence much longer.

"For Mama's sake I guess we should try not to show how we feel about this."

Helping Catherine to her feet Jeremy agreed. "You're right, sis" He yanked one of her curls and tickled her in the ribs, "Let's go eat 'til we're stuffed and dance 'til we drop." Getting a head start he said, "Bet you can't beat me down the trail!"

With a toss of her blonde curls Catherine accepted the challenge, "O.K. buddy, you asked for it!"

Catching Jeremy off guard, she kicked him in the back of the knees, and as he crashed to the ground she raced down the trail to his cries of, "Cheat--er!"

*   *   *   *

There was something almost regal about the way Susannah carried herself. Even the years of hard farm life and the sorrow of a husband lost at war had not erased the beauty that came from within her. The pale blue gown she wore hung loosely on her now, but perfectly matched her eyes. Her blonde hair was pulled up and arranged into curls which were held in place with a mother-of-pearl comb.

She was Mrs. Pollard McCloud, as of one-half hour ago, and all these people had come to attend her wedding. Her heart was warmed by their generosity. Since few had money to spare, many of the wedding gifts were no doubt items the givers themselves had treasured.

"I wonder where my children are," Susannah thought as she accepted congratulations from another acquaintance. Trying not to be obvious, she casually looked around the church yard. Then movement on the hillside behind the church caught her eye, and at the top of the small cliff she saw Jeremy join his sister on the big rock.

She knew that beneath the taunts and sibling rivalry there was a deep bond between her children. Their drawing away from the celebration seemed to Susannah an indication of the distance growing in her relationship with them, especially with her son. From the church yard she couldn't define their facial expressions, but she could see the slump of Catherine's shoulders and the protective way Jeremy hugged her. "Oh, God, I hope I've done the right thing! I know they really don't like Pollard, but then, it's only been three years since Jim died."

The familiar pain struck her heart at the thought of her precious Jim. She hadn't allowed herself to put into words the fact she already knew; Pollard McCloud couldn't compare to James Sutherland. But then, few men could, and there certainly weren't any available in this area. The truth was that she could not keep the farm without a husband to work it. This plot of land had been in Jim's family for years and was to be passed on to Jeremy. Tears came to her eyes as she thought of how her fifteen year old son had tried to take on the workload of his father. After having so much responsibility for the past few years it wouldn't be easy for Jeremy to step aside and allow her new husband to be in charge. Pollard had been a complete gentleman in the few months she'd known him, but lately she had sensed the growing tension between him and Jeremy. She wondered what went on between them when they were out of her sight.

Suddenly, she was filled with fear. "Oh, God," she cried silently, "I didn't even ask you about this marriage, and now it's too late. If I've done the wrong thing, please forgive me and help us!" Watching her new husband as he laughed and talked with the group of cigar- smoking men, she thought of the day he'd first come to the farm. She'd been in the barn, milking Daisy ...

"That's a good girl, Daisy!" Susannah said, as she gave the cow an affectionate pat on the rump. She put away the milking stool, and shooed the kittens from her full pail of rich, creamy milk. Coming out of the barn she squinted

against the morning sun and was surprised to hear the sound of a horse's hooves coming down the path to the farm. She shaded her eyes with one hand, trying to identify the visitor as she held the pail of fresh milk with the other. The man on the horse was no one she knew. A myriad of thoughts bombarded her mind in an instant. The first was the rumor of renegade soldiers roaming the area, preying on helpless victims after the war. She was all alone here, her gun was in the house; if she ran to the house, she'd lose the precious milk ...

As if reading her mind the stranger stopped his horse from coming any closer. He spoke softly and removed his hat, "Mrs. Sutherland, ma'am?"

Surprised that the man knew her name, Susannah answered a guarded, "Yes."

"My name is Pollard McCloud. I'm looking for work in this area and I was told in town that you might need help here on your farm. I understand you lost your husband in the war, for which I offer my condolences."

McCloud's attitude was totally polite and he made no move to dismount from his horse. Susannah felt her heartbeat returning to normal as her initial fear faded. She managed to choke out a soft, "Thank you."

Susannah became aware of the weight of the full milk pail and shifted it to her other hand.

McCloud started to dismount, then stopped; "Mrs. Sutherland, if you'll allow me, I'd be glad to carry that as far as your porch for you." He smiled and Susannah was surprised at her thought that he was handsome. That brought a blush to her cheeks, and she became aware of her faded dress and fly-away hair. He hadn't offered to come inside; she felt he was trying to put her at ease. It seemed rude now to refuse his help.

"That would be nice, Mr. McCloud," Susannah said shyly.

McCloud quickly swung down from his horse and took the milk pail from her. As they walked toward the house he complimented her on the farm.

"It has so much potential," Susannah agreed, "But my children and I have not been able to work it like my husband did. The hired hands left as soon as the war ended so it has been a struggle." Turning to face McCloud she spoke frankly, "I can't deny that I need your help, Mr. McCloud, but I simply don't have the means to pay you."

They had come to the porch now and McCloud paused and offered his free arm to Susannah. She hated that she blushed again at this gentlemanly act. Resting her hand lightly on his arm as she walked up the steps she could feel the tautness of the muscles beneath his shirt sleeve. He'd certainly have no problem guiding a plow.

"Mrs. Sutherland, I think we might be able to work out the wage situation. If you don't mind my waiting here I'd like to talk further with you about it."

"Please have a seat Mr. McCloud. I'll put this milk away, and then we can talk. May I offer you a cup of coffee?"

"A glass of cool water would do for me, ma'am," McCloud said.

Through the kitchen window Susannah could see him as he waited, leaning comfortably against the porch railing and looking out over the farm. His auburn hair glistened in the morning sun, parted on the left side by a fresh-looking scar that she assumed was acquired in the war. McCloud

16

was broad shouldered, of average height and stocky build. His name was obviously of Irish descent. She'd heard of the Irish men's love of a fist fight, and found it easy to imagine McCloud in such a situation. He was clean shaven, his rugged features not particularly handsome until he smiled. And yet, Susannah thought there was something guarded in his green eyes. She took a quick look at herself in the old mirror above the washstand, dampened her hands and smoothed down the stray wisps of her hair. She went back outside with two glasses of water and offered one to McCloud. He sat in the big porch chair, leaving the wide swing for her.

"Thank you, ma'am," he said, taking the glass. "I've been taking a look at your fields and I think there's still time to get a crop in the ground for a fall harvest if we get started immediately. Do you have seed?" McCloud asked.

"Yes, fortunately, we do have most of what we would need, but Mr. McCloud, there's still the matter of paying your wages," Susannah said.

McCloud took a drink of water and leaned forward, twisting the glass in his hands. "Mrs. Sutherland, I hope you can understand this ... I need a place to settle down. Something about this area appeals to me, but there aren't a lot of jobs available. I can't say that I had much direction in my life prior to the war, but there's certainly not been any since then. As for money, I still have pay from the army that will meet any needs I have for a while. When the crops are in you can give me a percentage of the profits. Just provide me a place to stay and meals until then, and you've got you a hand."

"Unfortunately, Mr. McCloud, with farming there are no guarantees. As you know, there's the possibility of drought, blight from insects, any number of things that can determine the outcome. I can't promise that there will be any profit at all." Susannah said, "Are you prepared to work so hard with no guarantees?"

"Mrs. Sutherland, your land is level; soil in this area is generally rich. I believe we can produce a crop if Mother Nature will cooperate with us. If not, you'll have given me a place to stay, and I'll have helped you to some extent, so we can call it even. Do we have a deal?"

Thoughts battled within Susannah's mind as she weighed her decision. This man was a total stranger ... Without help she and Jeremy would not be able to get the crops in the ground in time ... As a widow there could be talk about her having a man living there ... Without a crop there was absolutely no prospect of keeping the farm ... What if McCloud didn't really intend to work, but just took advantage of her giving him a place to stay?... There was absolutely no one else to help ... McCloud seemed truthful and sincere... The war had taken so many of their men, and those who were left were struggling to get their own farms back into production ... Even if she could find help elsewhere, she had no money to pay wages ... She had no other choice but to try to save the farm for Jeremy.

Susannah stood and reached out her hand to McCloud. "It's a deal, Mr. McCloud. You're welcome to share meals with me and my family, but I don't have much to offer in the way of living quarters except the barn."

"It wouldn't be the first time I've bunked in a hay loft." McCloud stood and walked the few steps to take her small hand in his large one. "I have a few things at the boarding house in town. I'll get them and be back this evening. Tomorrow, I'll get started in the fields."

18

McCloud mounted his horse, tipped his hat to Susannah with a smile and rode back down the path. Suddenly feeling weak in the knees, Susannah dropped back down onto the swing and looked around her. How long had it been since she really noticed the condition of her front yard?

When Jim was alive it was beautiful with flowers. Weeds had now overtaken the bed, and the blooming plants that had survived showed distress from insects. But now she'd have help. Maybe there would be time for her precious flowers.

"Oh, God, I'll actually have help!" Covering her face with her hands she was unable to stop the deep cry that unleashed years of pent-up emotion. Sobs wracked her thin body as tears flooded her faded cotton dress; tears for the loss of the love of her life, for her children's loss of a father, for having to always be strong when she felt so inadequate, for the exhaustion that never left because the work was never done. Finally, feeling drained, but as though an incredible weight had been lifted, she rocked gently in the swing until suddenly she felt movement beside her. She opened her eyes as the large black and white cat climbed into her arms with a purr. Holding the familiar pet close, she stroked her shiny coat, and laughed out loud as the cat licked away the tears on her neck. "Hey, Puddles, you silly kitty!" Susannah protested. The cat meowed, eyeing her mistress with concern. Looking into the wide green eyes through the last of her tears, Susannah said, "Guess what, Puddles ... I have help!"

Susannah was checking her tomato plants for worms when Catherine and Jeremy arrived home from school. They were riding Midnight, the horse that had been

Jim's favorite. Catherine, carrying their books, slid down to join her while Jeremy took Midnight to the barn.

"Hi, honey, how was school today?" Susannah asked.

Catherine reached down to give her mother a hug. "It was good. I made an 'A' on my English test."

"That's great. Didn't you have a math test too?"

"You would have to remember that."

"Were you hoping I'd forget?"

Catherine grinned. "Not really, it wasn't that bad. I made a "B.""

"But you like to make 'A's.""

"Yep!" She watched as her mother pulled a worm off a plant and added it to her collection in an old pot. "Ugh! Do you like doing that?"

Susannah looked up and smiled, "No, but I like tomatoes, and especially tomatoes without worm holes!" She saw Jeremy approaching from the barn. "Hi, son."

"Hey, Ma," Jeremy bent down to wrap his mother in a hug.

"How did you do on tests today?"

"Good. My fair-haired sister is not the only one in this family who can make 'A's.""

"Well, I am very proud of both of you," Susannah said, rising to her feet. " I've got something special for you in the kitchen, as well as something to tell you, so why don't we talk for a bit before you start your chores."

Jeremy looked at Catherine with a questioning look as they followed their mother toward the house. She shrugged her shoulders and shook her head as if to say, "I don't know anything either!"

Susannah had made gingerbread, wrapped it in a dishtowel and placed it in the pie safe. When she opened it the sweet, spicy bread was still warm. Its aroma filled the kitchen as she poured Daisy's rich milk into two glasses.

Catherine and Jeremy were delighted at the special treat. Susannah waited until they were finished and then told them her news.

"There's a man coming to help us get the crops in. He's going to stay in the barn; but he'll be eating his meals with us here."

"How did this come about?" Jeremy questioned.

"Someone in town told him we had the farm and needed help. He was looking for a place to settle down, so he's agreed to work for his keep and a percentage of the crop's profits."

"What's his name? What's he like?" Catherine asked.

"His name is Pollard McCloud. He's about your father's age, not as tall. He was very polite and seems ready to work hard."

"What if the crops don't make a profit? How are you going to pay him then?" asked Jeremy.

"We discussed that as well. If that should happen, he agreed to still call it even and I won't have any further obligation to him. Mr. McCloud fought in the war too and mainly wants a place to start over." Susannah explained. "He seems to know about farming and feels we can get the crops planted in time for a fall harvest. Jeremy, you'll be the one working with him for the most part. How do you feel about it?"

"Mama, you know I'll do anything to keep this farm. Do you feel all right about being here with him while we're gone to school?" he asked with concern.

"Mr. McCloud was very much a gentleman when he came today. I didn't feel that I have anything to worry about.

"Well, we certainly do need the help. If he knows about farming and will work like he said ... I guess we'll see," Jeremy said tentatively. "I'll show him where everything is."

Standing at the window, Catherine saw a horseman coming down the path. "I think he's here now."

Susannah and Jeremy rose and went to the window. "Yes, that's him," Susannah said. "Jeremy, you might want to help Mr. McCloud clear out a space up in the loft. There's a mattress ticking in the linen closet, Catherine. He'll need that for bedding. I'll get blankets and a pillow after I introduce you to him. Oh, and Jeremy, he'll need a lantern. Bring one from the shelf on the back porch, and would you fill it, please?"

McCloud slowed his large paint to prevent raising dust as he neared the house. He rode the horse to the far side of the porch, dismounted and looped the reins over the porch railing. By the time he reached the steps, Susannah stood in the doorway.

"Hello, Mr. McCloud. Won't you come in? I'd like you to meet my children."

Removing his hat, McCloud greeted her, "Afternoon, Mrs. Sutherland."

"This is my daughter, Catherine," Susannah said, drawing her forward McCloud thought he was seeing a younger version of Susannah as he shook the hand the girl politely offered. "Miss Sutherland," he acknowledged.

Jeremy entered the room carrying the lantern and Susannah turned to introduce him. "This is my son, Jeremy, Mr. McCloud." When she looked back to McCloud she was puzzled to see his reaction. There was something in his eyes for an instant when he saw Jeremy, almost like recognition, but it was gone quickly as McCloud reached out to shake Jeremy's hand.

"Young man," McCloud said. "I guess you'll be the one to show me the ropes around here."

"Yes, sir, I guess so." Jeremy said.

"Jeremy will help you clear a place in the loft and fill this ticking, Mr. McCloud, and he has a lantern for you. I'm going to hang some bedding to air out and you can take it with you after supper. We'll eat in about two hours. Is there anything else you need?"

"That should do me just fine, Mrs. Sutherland.

Turning to Catherine, McCloud took the mattress ticking, "Thank you, young lady, it was nice to meet you."

"Jeremy," he said. "I'll get my things up to the loft and fix up my space later. I'd like to take a ride over the whole farm this afternoon if we have time before sundown. You can fill me in on what's been done."

"Yes, sir; just let me saddle my horse," said Jeremy as the two of them headed for the barn.

Susannah had been pleased to see the progress evident within just a few weeks of McCloud's arrival. As soon as Jeremy and Catherine got home from school Jeremy joined McCloud in the fields and the two of them worked until dark. On Saturdays she and Catherine joined them; evenly dropping seeds into the newly ploughed furrows and covering it carefully with several inches of the rich dark soil. At this rate it appeared they would indeed get all the crops planted in time for a fall harvest.

When supper was done Susannah found herself looking forward to time with McCloud. They discussed the work completed that day and the steps to be taken next. At first, Jeremy sat in on these discussions as Catherine washed the dishes, but then he began to find reasons to excuse himself and leave the two of them alone. Soon their conversations extended beyond matters of the farm and Susannah found that Pollard, as he had insisted she call him, could be quite charming. He had been so many places and seen so much. He made it all come alive to her, mentally taking her away from the exhaustion and hopelessness of the past few years.

McCloud treated her with the utmost respect, but she also knew instinctively that he found her attractive. Thoughts of Jim made her feel guilty for enjoying Pollard's company, but Jim was gone and the time had come to move on emotionally. Did she love Pollard McCloud? She wasn't sure. Her feelings for him were different from those she still held deep in her heart for James Sutherland. She and Jim had known each other all their lives. Their families were acquainted; there was nothing about him that Susannah didn't know. In contrast, she knew almost nothing about Pollard, even after spending hours in conversation with him as they shared their evening coffee in the old porch swing. Apparently, his father had died when he was very young, and there had been several stepfathers in the home. Any reference to his mother was tinged with disdain and Susannah knew not to question Pollard any further. He had told her that he'd been on his own since he was a boy, so undoubtedly he had experienced a very different life than she'd known.

Susannah was grateful to Pollard, both for his help on the farm and for making her feel alive again. Maybe it wasn't fair to marry him now, but she had been honest. When he told her he loved her, she could not tell him the same in return. He said he was willing to take the chance that he could win her love in time if she'd marry him. Regardless of her feelings, or the lack of them, she knew their relationship had come to a crossroad. Comments had made their way back to Susannah that people in the community had begun to question the respectability of his living there. They needed to marry, or Pollard should move on. The thought of carrying the burden of the farm alone again was terrifying to her. Perhaps the intimacy between them as husband and wife would bring more response from her heart. She remembered Reverend Winters' sermon that love was a choice. She could choose to be loving and kind to Pollard McCloud, and she would do her best to make this marriage work. Now, if only Catherine and Jeremy could accept it too, perhaps she'd stop feeling so torn between them and Pollard.

As though sensing her thoughts of him, Pollard turned and caught her eye across the church yard. Just then the fiddlers broke loose in a toe-tapping tune. With a smile he threw away the cigar and held out his arms, inviting her to dance. A glance aside assured Susannah that Catherine and Jeremy were there on the grounds now and had joined a group of young people gathered around the picnic tables. She knew the eager dancers would politely wait, since the first dance traditionally belonged to the bride and groom, "So it may as well begin," she thought, as she brightened the smile on her face and walked toward the man she had just married.

*   *   *   *

As Pollard McCloud walked out the double doors of the church with his new wife on his arm he wished he could whisk her away for at least a few minutes alone. Maybe something had changed in her heart toward him just by going through the ceremony. Was that possible? He had no idea, but he could hope. There wasn't to be any time alone, though. People couldn't wait to offer their congratulations, all strangers to him, but most of them familiar with Susannah and her struggle at the farm. All he could think right now was how badly he needed a smoke! In relief, he saw other fellows lighting up over by the wagons. As soon as he felt he could leave Susannah's side he joined them.

He was much more comfortable here, and the bridegroom jokes certainly didn't bother him. He loosened the collar and tie that he never expected to wear. But then, marrying a pretty woman with a farm that would be his as soon as the marriage was recorded in the county records was worth the discomfort. He knew Susannah's heart still belonged to her dead husband, but he'd change that. He'd make her love him! He was sick of hearing what a good man Jim Sutherland had been. It seemed like everyone who came to congratulate him on marrying the pretty Mrs. Sutherland just had to tack on, "It was a real shame- her husband dying- he was a fine man."

McCloud had no misgivings about himself. He'd done whatever he had to do to survive after he was forced out on his own as a kid by a mean stepfather. His mother stayed drunk so she'd probably not even noticed his absence. He had vowed that day that he would never again take a beating from anyone. He thought he'd met his match a few times, but the bitterness pent up within him fueled a

26

fire that made him a formidable opponent. At some point he'd learned he could influence people and used that to his advantage. Women generally found him handsome enough and what he lacked in looks, he made up with his own unique charm. Never in his life had he known love, and it hadn't mattered … until lately. Beneath his hard veneer an unaccustomed emotion had been stirred by the gentle goodness of the woman he had just married. He had not intended for this to happen. His plan had been solely to find Lt. Sutherland's widow, get her to marry him, and gain her farm in the process.

He remembered that night around the Union campfire as the tired and hungry soldiers pulled out the pictures of loved ones that gave them strength to keep fighting that miserable war. That was McCloud's first glimpse of Susannah. The Lieutenant carried the photograph in his left pocket, over his heart, but he didn't share it around the circle like some of the soldiers. He handled it as though it was breakable, something precious. McCloud couldn't resist wandering around behind the Lieutenant and looking down at the likeness of the beautiful, blonde woman. No wonder Sutherland treasured that photograph. There was something about her … so sweet and "pure," a word not normally in McCloud's vocabulary. It didn't surprise him either that a woman like this would marry the Lieutenant. McCloud didn't relish thinking of men as being honorable or good; that meant facing his own lack of character. But he'd seen evidence, time and again of Lieutenant James Sutherland's bravery and his care for the men under his command. McCloud was careful to never talk about the war to Susannah. She just thought it was because it brought back terrible memories. That was true enough, but mainly he was afraid that in the telling of circumstances he would say something to make her aware that he had known and served under her former husband. There was no reason for him to feel guilty. He had nothing to do with the Lieutenant's death. The war and fate had taken care of that. The only thing he'd done was to take the picture from his commander's pocket, and instead of putting it with the personal effects to be sent back to the deceased's wife, he'd kept it. He had carried it in his wallet ever since, but now that he was marrying Susannah he probably should put it in with his other belongings. He didn't think she'd be a snooping wife, but if she ever saw it, he didn't know how he could possibly explain having it!

Things had worked according to his plan- right up to this wedding. He still couldn't believe how easy it had been. He hadn't counted on falling in love, though. He had always considered men in love to be vulnerable, lacking in control. Now he was giving in to that son of Susannah's when he'd like to knock him across the barn, if for no other reason than he felt like the kid could see right through him. He almost "lost it" the first day he got there when the kid walked into the room. It hadn't crossed his mind that the son might look like the Lieutenant, so when Jeremy came in, for a split second McCloud felt like the dead officer was standing before him. As much as he hated to admit it, the boy was as straight an arrow as his father, and McCloud felt he was always being compared to the Lieutenant. And that pretty little daughter … it was uncanny how like her mother she looked. Before he got soft on Susannah he had thoughts of some fun in the barn with the girl, but his interest now was all in winning the heart of the woman at his side.

He wasn't sure he liked the changes that were happening inside him. He hated the idea that he needed this woman. He had never needed anybody! This was the first wedding he'd ever attended, but when Susannah walked down that aisle a few minutes ago, he thought she must have been the most beautiful bride ever. In that moment Pollard McCloud felt as though the locked entrance to an empty place deep within him had been flung open, and he realized how badly he wanted this woman to fill it.

"Do you, Pollard McCloud, take Susannah Sutherland to be your lawful, wedded wife?" The words of the preacher cut into McCloud's thoughts and he, more than anyone, had been surprised at the tremble in his voice as he said, "I do."

Now that he'd had his smoke and his nerves weren't quite so on-edge, McCloud was ready to get on

with whatever else had to be tolerated before he could take Susannah home and make her his wife for real. He wondered if the tension between him and the young ones would lessen now that he was there to stay. He'd just have to show them who was boss.

Just then the fiddles began to play, and McCloud glanced up to find Susannah looking his way. The unfamiliar lilt in his heart brought a smile to his face as he threw away the stump of his cigar and gladly went to dance with his bride.

*   *   *   *

"Why did Mr. Wentworth's watch have to stop working today, of all days?" David Winters questioned. He pulled down the window shade on the shop door, making certain the sign was showing "Closed."

"I should be at the church with Catherine!" he said in exasperation. But Mr. Wentworth was the president of the only bank in town, giving him a status not to be ignored. Silas Goodson, the owner of the Jewelry and Watch Emporium, had made a trip to buy supplies and wouldn't return until Monday. So David knew it was up to him to repair Mr. Wentworth's heavy gold timepiece. Irritated, he pushed back the shock of dark hair that was determined to fall over his eyes and went to work. There was no such thing as doing repairs in a hurry, especially on a fine watch like this one. The tiny gears had to be so carefully removed, cleaned, and replaced, that a watchmaker dreaded interruptions of any kind until the job was finished. Today, David's only intruders were his thoughts of being with the girl who had been his best friend

as long as he could remember. He was there for Catherine when her father died in the war and his heart had suffered pain equal to hers. He knew that things had become increasingly difficult for her family as they were unable to keep up production on the farm without her Pa. He also knew that she had faith that sustained her beyond any person of her age that he had ever known.

In the past few months David had begun to notice that Catherine was becoming a beautiful young woman and that had stirred him to begin thinking of their future. In two years he would be eighteen, and she sixteen, old enough to marry. He already knew a lot about watch-making, and lately he'd been learning to create molds and to design jewelry in gold and precious gems. For three years he'd been working with Mr. Goodson, one of the best in that field. His dream was to have his own business. Mr. Goodson was a bachelor with no family and treated David like the son he'd never had. He had hinted at the possibility of David's owning the shop some day, so David felt confident in his ability to provide for Catherine. They had never talked of marriage, they were still so young. But any mention of the future always included their being together.

As he carefully dusted and oiled the inner parts of Mr. Wentworth's watch David imagined his father performing the marriage ceremony for Catherine's mother and that man she was marrying, McCloud. Something about him caused David to bristle inside like Blackie the shop cat when a dog came in with its owner. Catherine felt her mother was marrying the man just to have someone to save the farm.

David tightened the tiny screws on the watch case and gave the face one last wipe to leave it clean and shiny. Setting it to the proper time he saw that he'd probably missed the whole wedding ceremony. He didn't mind that, he just wanted to be there for Catherine's sake. He grabbed his coat, put Mr. Wentworth's watch in his pocket to drop off on his way to the church and locked the door to the shop. Almost on a run, he grinned as he thought, "This is probably the only time I'll ever carry in my pocket a watch this expensive!

CHAPTER 2

The chirping of birds outside her window drew Catherine gently from sound sleep to the soft morning light. She lay perfectly still, trying to remain in her beautiful dream that lingered just this side of wakefulness.

She was walking through the fields with Papa, his big hand holding her small one. They were laughing together and his eyes shone with love. How important she felt, and how safe. Unaware that conditions were difficult and that the nation was split with turmoil, Catherine's young world felt secure.

Fully awake now, she could no longer hide from the reality that Papa was gone, and so was the security of her life.

Pulling the patchwork quilt over her eyes, she tried to go back to sleep, determined not to think about "things." Then suddenly, she threw back the quilt, jumped out of bed and grabbed her pink robe. How could she forget?

Today she and David were going to have the whole day together. Other than his coming by the school to make plans with her for today, she hadn't talked to him since Mama got married, and she had so much to tell him. At sixteen, David had completed all the schooling that was available in the public system. Reverend Winters was a university graduate so David had lessons with his father in the mornings and worked at Mr. Goodson's business in the afternoons. He and Catherine missed seeing each other everyday. His mother taught Catherine piano lessons on Friday afternoons, but David was usually still at the jewelry shop. Even on Sundays now, there was no opportunity for them to visit since Mr. McCloud insisted that they leave church immediately following the service. Today was special, though. She was going to make a picnic lunch, and they planned to ride on horseback to their favorite place near the river bluffs where they'd talk to their hearts' content.

Susannah looked up from the supply list she was making as she heard her daughter enter the kitchen. She smiled at the sight of Catherine's sleepy-eyed face surrounded by a cloud of tousled, blonde curls.

"'Morning, sunshine," she said, as Catherine bent down to give her a hug.

"Mama always smells so nice," Catherine thought, as she wrapped her arms around Susannah. "I dreamed about Papa," she said quietly.

Susannah reached up to gently pat Catherine's cheek. "Was it a good dream?"

Catherine nodded as she sat down at the end of the table. "We were laughing, and I was … happy." Catherine hadn't mentioned her father at all to Susannah since McCloud came into their lives, and she wasn't sure it was all right to talk about him.

"I'm glad you had the dream, honey," Susannah reassured her, "and I'm glad you told me about it."

"There have been times lately that I'd think of him, but I couldn't remember what he looked like. I was afraid I was forgetting him."

"Just keep thinking of the good times and of how much he loved you. You and Jeremy were his pride and joy.

"I still miss him so much," Catherine said softly.

"I know, I do too," and taking Catherine's face between her hands, she looked into her daughter's eyes. "I miss him more than you'll ever know, but life changes, and we … we change with it." Then, giving Catherine a quick hug, Susannah said, "Breakfast is on the stove, and you have a picnic lunch to get ready so we'd better stop moping around here."

The back door to the kitchen opened and stopping to scrape his boots on the mat outside the door, Jeremy came in. "Who's moping?"

"Nobody, nosey. Are you ready for breakfast?" Susannah asked her son.

"You don't even have to ask that, Mama." Catherine chided.

"Well, if you'd been feeding the animals since before sun- up, you'd be hungry too."

"I was getting my beauty sleep," Catherine told her brother with a toss of her head.

Looking at her tousled curls Jeremy grinned, "Well, 'looks like you need some more."

"Don't you come near that table until you wash up, Jeremy Sutherland," Susannah said in her sternest voice.

Catherine began to set the table as she quipped, "Why, Mama, I'm sure Old Pal just licked his hands perfectly clean."

Old Pal was Jeremy's aged dog that stayed at his side anytime he was outside the house. When Jeremy milked Daisy, Old Pal liked to lick up any milk that spilled outside the bucket.

"Well, Old Pal doesn't use lye soap, so that's not good enough for me." Susannah tossed Jeremy a clean hand towel as he made his way to the wash basin by the door. As she dished up the scrambled eggs, bacon, and homemade biscuits, she thought, "This is like old times." Since Pollard had come into their lives there was always tension when he and the children were together. She wished things could be different, but didn't know how to change them. At least this morning she could enjoy the time with Catherine and Jeremy. Pollard had left early to go to Independence to buy another mule and wouldn't be back for hours.

"What's that I smell in the oven, Ma?" Jeremy asked.

Before Susannah could answer, Catherine said, "It's Millie."

Jeremy looked at her in disbelief, and then at his mother, "Mama, you didn't...."

Millie was a blind-in-one-eye hen that Jeremy particularly liked. He opened the oven door to see the chicken roasting in the pan, surrounded by sweet potatoes lying on the oven shelf.

"No, Jeremy, that's not Millie. Shame on you, Catherine," Susannah scolded, trying to hide a smile.

In relief, Jeremy asked, "Who is it ... was it?"

"Just one of the hens I got from the Walkers last week."

"Good," Jeremy said, "I can't eat something I've called by name."

"Well, you're not going to eat that chicken anyway, it's for my picnic lunch with David," Catherine said.

"So you get the whole thing?"

"No, I'll probably get one piece and David will eat the rest."

Susannah laughed, "I don't see how that boy stays thin. He can really put away the food. I guess it's all going up instead of around; he's getting so tall."

"Well, I'm glad he's not here for breakfast, because I intend to finish off what you girls leave," Jeremy announced.

Catherine sat glasses of cool milk on the table and slid into her place as Susannah reached out a hand to each of her children. She didn't have to interpret the look she gave them before bowing her head to say grace. They knew she couldn't speak the words, but they were as thankful as their mother for this time without Pollard McCloud.

*   *   *   *

It felt good to David to be out on his horse … his father's horse, really, but he felt like Star was his. The beautiful chestnut mare always whinnied when she heard his voice and nuzzled his cheek with her soft lips as he stroked her neck. She seemed eager to be off this morning as well. He had to keep a tight rein on her until they had cleared the town traffic and rode out on the open road to the Sutherland farm.

It seemed ages since he'd seen Catherine. There had been no opportunity to talk at the wedding, especially with his getting there late. He hated that he'd not been there for the ceremony, but was relieved to learn that Jeremy had stayed beside her. Jeremy was a good sort, the kind of fellow you'd be glad to have as a brother … or a brother-in-law.

36

Ever since Catherine's mother had married that McCloud guy, David had been thinking about his and Catherine's future. He wanted Catherine out from under the man's influence as soon as possible. He was hoping to talk to her today about his plans for them, that is … if he didn't get "cold feet." Why was he so nervous about this? He and Catherine had always been able to talk about anything. "But this is different!" he argued with himself. Maybe it was a little premature to be talking about marriage, but they certainly didn't intend to be without each other in the future, so it was only logical to make plans.

David wasn't entirely comfortable with his new feelings; the desire to reach out and touch Catherine's cheek, and to stroke the softness of those curls. What would she say if she knew he was thinking about her this way? Maybe she didn't want things to change. For a moment, panic struck him and he was tempted to pull up on the reins and turn Star back toward home. He was nearing the turn-off to the Sutherland farm, so he slowed the puzzled horse, took a deep breath, and remembered the scripture he'd read last night that he felt had been placed in his Bible just for him. *"I know the thoughts that I think toward you, says the lord, thoughts of peace and not of evil, to give you a future and a hope.* Jeremiah 29:11.

David thought of Catherine's having to live in the unpleasant atmosphere created by her new stepfather. Surely that fell into the "evil" category. On the other hand, their childhood friendship had truly been a gift from God; certainly their future as husband and wife would be, as well. Perhaps that hope would bring Catherine the strength she needed to endure her situation for the next two years. With that thought, he was suddenly eager to see her. It only took a nudge to Star's flanks and they were off, leaving a trail of dust behind.

*   *   *   *

Catherine and David couldn't have asked for a more beautiful day. Gentle breeze toyed with a few thin wisps of white in an otherwise cloudless, blue sky. Even the sun withheld its heat for them as the mid-morning temperature remained pleasant. Catherine, riding Molly, their farm horse, had to concentrate to keep the picnic lunch balanced, but she was happy. As much as she and David had to say to each other, being together was enough for now, so they simply rode, only talking to point out something of interest along the way. When they reached the bottom of the bluff, they reined the horses to a halt and dismounted. They'd leave the animals here to graze and rest while they went on foot to the area they called their "special place." Catherine watched as David looped the reins over a limb and got out the feedbags of grain he'd brought for the horses. With the familiar toss of his head, he shook back the dark hair from his eyes. "He really *is* getting tall," Catherine noticed as she was reminded of her mother's words earlier that morning. He looked up then, saw her watching him and grinned.

"Has he always been this handsome?" she thought, as she smiled back. There was something different about him today. She couldn't pinpoint it, but somehow, he seemed older.

"Ready?" David asked, as he picked up the basket in one hand, and reached out to take hers with the other.

Once there had been a visible trail, but hardly anybody used it now. Rocks from above had broken loose and fallen, blocking the path and requiring more effort for David and Catherine to reach their destination.

Plenty of rainfall in the spring had fostered a generous supply of ground cover where soil lay between the limestone rocks. Pink buttercups flourished among the taller goldenrod, and white wild roses opened in full blossom to receive the morning sun.

They had reached the plateau from where they could see their destination below. Catherine and David stopped, as they always did, to marvel at the site. Surely God had personally planned this beautiful, natural sanctuary. From about twenty feet above them, a stream of cool spring water flowed from a fissure in the rocks on the side of the bluff, splashing into a small pool below. Flat rocks circled the pool, with a partial backdrop of cedar trees that gave a clean, crispness to the air. Wild violets and anemones grew between the rocks and onto the side of the bluff, kept fresh from the spray of the waterfall.

With a squeeze to Catherine's hand David almost whispered, "I think this is the most beautiful place in the world."

Catherine nodded her agreement.

They stood in silence for a few moments until the rumbling of David's stomach broke the spell, and they both burst out laughing.

"O.K., it's time to eat," he said as they started to pick their way down the path to the flat rocks below.

Catherine spread the tablecloth as David found the quart jar with strong, sweetened grape juice. He took it to the spring and filled it with the cold fresh water, shaking it to make a delicious drink. Catherine un-wrapped the roasted chicken and the two baked sweet potatoes that she'd sliced and filled with butter and brown sugar. She'd managed to save three biscuits from Jeremy's appetite, so she put two of those on a napkin for David and kept one for herself. David opened the small jar of homemade pickles, and their feast was ready.

Catherine nodded to David to say grace. As he prayed she was thinking how grateful she was to have a friend who loved the Lord as she did. Not many of the boys around her hometown of Lexington would have prayed in front of a girl, even if they were from church-going families. But David wasn't just the preacher's son; he was a Christian in his own right. That was the most important thing Catherine and David had in common. Catherine had experienced a personal relationship with the Lord Jesus at a very early age. She loved reading her Bible and found strength in it, especially after the death of her Papa. Lately, with the new stepfather at home, she needed that strength even more. Her attention returned to David's prayer:

" ... and thank You, Heavenly Father, for this day with Catherine in this beautiful place that You created, for the food You have provided for us, and for Your Presence in our lives. Amen."

"Amen," Catherine echoed. She handed David a knife to carve off pieces of moist chicken breast and asked, "How are things at the shop?"

"Great! Mr. Goodson's been teaching me more about designing jewelry. The next time you come into town you've got to see the bracelets I made. Mr. Goodson said they are good enough to go into the case. Hopefully they'll sell, because he's promised me a commission on them. I really like working with gold. You should see it, Cat, when you melt it down to pour it into the mold. It's so beautiful. I can understand why it's such a temptation for people to go west to find it."

"I heard Mama and Mr. McCloud talking the other night about how people are going west now to get free land, even more than to find gold. I felt like he was trying to find out if Mama would be willing to do that."

The bite of chicken and biscuit seemed to stick in David's throat. What would that mean for him and Catherine, for his plans for them? Taking a swallow of grape drink to clear his throat, he asked, "Do you think he was serious about it?"

"When Mama didn't seem interested, he didn't say anything else, so I guess not. After all, we've got the farm here, so we already have land."

"How are things at home? Is McCloud treating you all right?" David asked.

"It's always uncomfortable when he's there. Mama tries to make it up to us when he's not around, but things are really different."

"How is Jeremy getting along with him?"

"He keeps everything all bottled up inside for Mama's sake. When it's just the two of them working there at the farm, Mr. McCloud bosses him like he doesn't know what he's doing. I know that's really hard for him since he was doing the work long before Mr. McCloud came along."

"That's got to be rough for Jeremy. Maybe he'll unload some of it to another guy. I'll try to find a time to talk to him."

"I wish you would. He's got friends, but nobody that he talks to about personal things like this. He hardly even speaks to Mama anymore if Mr. McCloud is around. Mr. McCloud seems to be jealous of Jeremy."

David continued to eat as Catherine talked about friends at school and her concern about the more difficult mathematics they were studying. Could he bring up the subject of their future? That seemed so far removed from math problems. Still, he didn't know when they might have another chance to freely discuss something so important.

"Cat, I need to talk to you about something."

The different tone of David's voice caught Catherine's attention quickly. She saw the serious look in his eyes, and for some reason her heart began to beat rapidly.

"I've been thinking about us."

"About us?" she repeated softly, her eyes wide.

"Do you ever think about what our lives will be like in a few years?" he asked.

Catherine waited a moment before answering.

"I guess I just always think of our being together. I haven't thought much about what that really means."

Moving next to her, David took her hand in his. "I hadn't either until lately, really since your mother married McCloud. I don't like your being around that man. I don't have an explanation for it … just a feeling inside. It's made me start to think of what the future holds for us. I know it's really soon to talk about getting married, but I can't imagine spending my life with anyone but you. I'd like to think you feel the same way, but that's for you to say." His dark eyes held the question as he waited for her to speak.

Catherine had not expected this conversation today, but now that David had spoken she realized that her heart echoed David's love. "I can't imagine a future without you, either, David. How could I? You're the one I always turn to when I need someone. You've been "part of me" for years already. I know we're young, but I can't see how growing older could possibly change that."

David breathed a sigh of relief. "I'm thinking we'll have to wait for two years. You'll be finished with school, and I shouldn't have any problem supporting you by then. I'll be saving my wages during that time so we'll have a little nest egg to start with. Mr. Goodson is training me well. We may not be rich, but we'll be together, and you won't have to live under the same roof with that McCloud fellow."

Reaching gently to push back the blonde curls from her eyes, he said, softly, "Catherine Sutherland, you've been my best friend for most of my life … now will you be my girl?"

The love in David's brown eyes caused Catherine's to mist with tears as she said, "Yes, David Winters, I will."

She thought she knew everything about him, but she'd never imagined how it would feel to have his lips on hers. Surely there would be many kisses in their future, but none sweeter, or more sacred, as their lips met to seal their first vow of commitment to each other. She was certain that time stood still in their beautiful, special place as David took her in his arms. Softly he said, "Someday, when the time is right, I will ask you to marry me, but until then, remember that I love you, I'm praying for you, and I am always looking forward to the day when we can be together."

*   *   *   *

"Pollard, you're making me nervous." Susannah said to her pacing husband. "I know it's not like David and Catherine to be this late getting home, but they are both responsible children. I think it's too early to suppose there's something wrong."

43

Jeremy thought his mother sounded as though she was trying to convince herself, as well as Pollard. "Where are those two?" he questioned to himself. Any other time they'd gone riding for the day they'd been home before dark. If they didn't show up soon he'd saddle Midnight and go looking for them himself.

"Any boy having a girl her age out at this time of night is up to no good!" Pollard fumed.

"That's just not true with David, Pollard. He and Catherine have been the best of friends since they were small. He wouldn't do anything to harm her or to damage her reputation," Susannah said in David's defense.

McCloud stopped his pacing to sneer at Susannah. "You are so naïve, Susannah. The boy's *sixteen*! I know what sixteen year old boys do with girls, even your pretty 'Angel Girl,' any chance they get … and from what I've seen, preachers' kids are the worst."

Susannah tried to stop her ears from the vicious things Pollard was saying. What had gotten into him, anyway? He had come home from Independence without buying the mule he went after. He had obviously been drinking, but it was more than that. Even before they realized Catherine and David were late getting home there was an agitation about him that she didn't understand. He hadn't said what took place in Independence, but something had affected him.

Just then Jeremy moved quickly to the door and said, "I hear horses coming."

Susannah ran out onto the porch and sighed with relief as she saw Star and Molly round the last curve at a gallop. Catherine's curls blew behind her like a golden fan in the moonlight as she tightly held on to the picnic basket.

David began his apology even before they came to a halt beside the steps.

"I'm so sorry, Mrs. Sutherland. We went farther out than I realized and just lost track of the time. I didn't mean to worry you." David apologized. He dismounted and turned to help Catherine down.

Without warning Pollard McCloud burst through the door and was down the steps, grabbing David by the collar. "I'll have you know, this is Mrs. *McCloud*, you stinkin' son of a preacher! Who do you think you're fooling with your fancy talk? I know what you've been doing with this pretty young thing ... even if they don't believe it. I ought to beat the daylights out of you here and now! If she comes up expecting a kid there's not anyplace you can hide that I won't find you."

David was too stunned to speak. He drew Catherine protectively behind him as Jeremy and Susannah reached for Pollard on either side to restrain him.

"David, I think it would be best if you just leave now, son," Susannah pleaded.

"I swear it wasn't that way, Mrs. Suth ... Mrs. McCloud," David protested.

"We know, David, it's all right. Just go, we'll talk later," Jeremy stepped between McCloud and David, urging David to mount Star and leave.

Repressing his own emotions, David swung up onto Star and turned to Catherine. She seemed frozen in disbelief, her blue eyes wide with fear. All he wanted to do was take her in his arms and reassure her, but he knew that would only make things worse. He refused to leave her without something of their beautiful day to hold onto, though. He paused to look her full in the eyes, willing her to forget the ugliness of the moment.

"Cat, remember what I told you today ... I meant every word of it!" With a slap to Star's flank, the mare sprang into action and in seconds they were out of sight.

Susannah stood with her arm around the trembling Catherine as they watched David ride into the darkness. She didn't believe any of the things Pollard had said about

the two young people, but her insight as a woman and a mother told her that the relationship between Catherine and David had gone to another level since their leaving the farm that morning. She needed to talk to her daughter alone.

Pollard looked as though he wanted to continue with his insults, but the instinct that transforms mothers into formidable foes rose up in Susannah. Pollard saw it in her eyes and shut his mouth, slamming the door as he stomped inside.

Jeremy reached out to squeeze Catherine's hand. "Later, sis, I'll put Molly away," and taking the horse's reins led the mare toward the barn.

Susannah took the basket that Catherine was still holding as though glued to it. Placing it by the door, she guided her to the swing. "Let's sit here a while."

The gentle swinging soothed Catherine as Susannah held her daughter closely. When she was no longer trembling, Susannah kissed her on the forehead and asked, "Would you like to tell me about your day?"

Taking a deep breath, Catherine replied, "It was nothing like Mr. McCloud said."

"I know, honey, try to forget that. Now tell me what really happened."

Turning to face her mother, Catherine said, "Oh, Mama, it was such a beautiful day. We talked about our future for the first time. I'd never thought much about it; I just expect us to be together. But that means that we'll have to be married. I feel so young to be talking about things like this, but David says we need to plan ahead. He's going to save his wages for the next two years, and then he's going to ask me to marry him."

"And of course, you'll say, YES!"

"I love him, Mama. I always have, but after today, it's different."

"Catherine, David is a fine young man. You're both young, but I know there's always been a special love between you. That's not something that happens to everyone. It's a gift to be treasured. Keep it as pure as it is now and your marriage will be the greatest fulfillment of the heart that you could imagine. It will be everything that God planned for a man and woman to share together."

"He kissed me, Mama ... my first kiss," Catherine confided shyly.

Susannah hugged Catherine to her with a groan, "Ohhhh, my baby girl getting kissed! Where did the time go? I don't think I'm ready for this."

They sat swinging in silence for a few minutes. This time together had been good for both of them. "I mustn't allow Pollard to separate me from my children," Susannah thought, remembering with dread that she had an angry husband waiting inside. Pulling back to face her daughter Susannah said, "You're growing up, my sweet Catherine, and there's nothing I can do about it. But for now, you need to get a brush to those wild curls, and we both need to get some sleep. Tomorrow's Sunday, you know."

"Do you think I'll get to talk to David at church? He looked so upset when he left," Catherine asked.

"I don't know, we'll just have to see how things work out. 'See you in the morning."

"Good night, Mama, I love you."

"I love you, too, honey."

Susannah remained seated in the swing as Catherine went inside. The confrontation with Pollard had disturbed her far more than she showed outwardly. This kind of marital disagreement was something foreign to Susannah.

She and Jim had been so compatible, and they were both Christians. To them, there was nothing more important than keeping peace in their home - for themselves - and for their children. She was horrified at Pollard's outburst toward David and Catherine. Her concern had been for their safety when they were late getting home. But Pollard was furious! He was determined to make the situation ugly with his accusations of improper behavior on David's part. She thought it strange that Pollard would appear so defensive in Catherine's behalf when he hardly acknowledged her existence in the household. Who was this man she had married? What happened to the charming man who had entertained her every evening with his tales of far-away places? The man she had seen tonight was one to be feared. She was still curious to know what prompted his strange behavior when he arrived home from Independence.

Suddenly Susannah felt exhausted. Hopefully, Pollard would be asleep and she could avoid more confrontation. She simply did not have the strength for it. Quietly opening the bedroom door she was relieved to hear the heavy rhythm of Pollard's breathing which told her he was sleeping soundly. Without lighting a lamp she dressed for bed, gently slipped under the covers and was asleep within minutes.

CHAPTER 3

"**I**'m sorry, girl," David said to his horse as he rubbed her down and gave her extra feed. He'd ridden Star harder than ever before, pushing her to the limit from Catherine's home to his. If he could just ride fast enough, maybe he could leave behind the ugly words of Pollard McCloud that rang in his ears. His day with Catherine had been so beautiful. The expression of their love had been pure. Now he imagined it as beautiful crystal dashed into pieces by someone who had no sense of its value. If only he and Catherine were old enough to marry now! He could hardly bear the thought of her living under the same roof as that man, McCloud.

"Son, is everything all right?" Reverend Winters appeared in the stable door.

David knew his parents would be concerned about his arriving home late, as Catherine's mother had been. He was really sorry to create so much distress.

"I don't know, Pa. I'm sorry to cause you to worry. Catherine and I lost track of the time and distance today, and I was late getting her home."

"Was that a problem with her mother?"

"I'm sure she was concerned, but it was Mr. McCloud that flew into a rage. I really believe he would have hit me if Jeremy and Mrs. Suth … Mrs. McCloud hadn't stepped in."

"Why was he so angry? Did you explain the reason you were late?"

"I tried to, but he just accused me of all sorts of ugly things, of disrespecting Catherine."

The image of Catherine's face, drained of color, her blue eyes wide with fear, came to his mind. "Poor thing, she was terrified! Her own father was so gentle; he never yelled at anyone, then here's this man who married her mother, screaming at us, saying those awful things. I realize that he doesn't know me, but he's lived around Catherine long enough that he should know better than to think such things of her."

"There's a scripture that clearly explains that, Son. It's Titus 1:15, *Unto the pure, all things are pure: but unto them that are defiled and unbelieving is nothing pure; but even their mind and conscience is defiled.*"

"Well McCloud certainly showed what's in his heart and mind tonight."

"What did Susannah do?" Reverend Winters asked.

"She tried to stop him. I didn't feel she was angry with me, but she asked me to leave so McCloud would calm down."

"I don't think McCloud showed that side of his personality before he married her."

"There's no way she would have married him if he had, Pa. The man was violent. There's something about him that I know is not to be trusted. Jeremy feels the same way, but there's nothing he can do either," David said in frustration.

"Son, I know you care a great deal for Catherine and her family. We'll share this with your mother and make it a matter of prayer."

"I told Catherine I love her, Pa, and that I want us to get married in two years," David confided.

Reverend Winters placed his arm about his son's shoulder as they walked from the stable to the house,

"Catherine is a fine young lady, David, but two years can hold a lot of changes. Are you sure you want to make that serious a commitment with both of you so young?"

"You know how close we've been for years, Pa, That hasn't changed and it just doesn't leave a place for anyone else in either of our lives. We believe God has given us this relationship, and we want to honor Him through it."

Reverend Winters stopped as they came to the door of the house and looked at David with pride. "Son, a father couldn't ask for more than that. You make me proud. We'd better go in and let your mother know you're here. She's been keeping a plate of food warmed for you."

David felt better after talking with his father, and the mention of food was all it took to get him to hurry inside.

*   *   *   *

Jeremy didn't know how long he'd been there in the barn. He had never felt the kind of anger that seethed inside him now toward Pollard McCloud. Was this what the Bible meant about murdering someone in your heart? If so, he needed to do something to get rid of it. The situation tonight had revealed a different side of McCloud. Jeremy had no way of knowing the circumstances in the man's life that produced anger and ugliness to that degree, but he didn't want to contaminate himself with that kind of poison. That's exactly how it felt inside him, like a foreign substance that didn't belong there. He was shy about sharing his feelings, but he did everything he could to live his convictions.

Then a scripture came to his mind, Ephesians 4:6, *Be angry and sin not; let not the sun go down upon your wrath.* Jeremy knew that meant to deal with situations immediately, to not harbor unforgiveness, even until the next day. Obviously, that was the key to maintaining the inner peace that McCloud certainly did not possess.

"All right, God," Jeremy said with a deep sigh, and with that simple statement his obedient heart was flooded with peace. As tears flowed down his face, the bitterness within was gone, and gratefulness to a Father who would never leave him took its place.

Sensing the struggle of emotions in his young master, Old Pal curled up beside Jeremy on the hay and laid his head on his shoulder. Jeremy snuggled up to his familiar furry friend and both of them drifted off to sleep.

*   *   *   *

Catherine was exhausted, but lay wide awake as she re-lived the day. The time with David had been as perfect as a day could be. She'd never forget the sweetness of that first kiss if she lived to be a hundred!

Then the thoughts of McCloud's angry attack intruded on the pleasant memories. It was such a shock to her. She'd never seen anyone that angry. She knew her mother would be concerned about their being so late getting home, but she didn't understand her stepfather's fury. She didn't have a relationship with him, so the whole thing was puzzling. How would this affect her getting to spend time with David in the future? After McCloud's outburst this evening she doubted that he would be in favor of it. Could her mother withstand her husband's wishes if it came to that?

Catherine rose and lit the oil lamp on the nightstand. Then she opened her Bible to the book of Psalms. Her eyes fell on verse eleven of chapter five: *But let all those that put their trust in thee rejoice: let them ever shout for joy, because thou defendest them: let them also that love thy name be joyful in thee.*

Tears filled Catherine's eyes as peace flooded her heart. "Oh, Father, You always know what I need to hear. You know that David and I love You and want our relationship to honor You in every way. I'm not going to allow Mr. McCloud's terrible words to ruin this day because You know what really happened. Thank You for my beautiful day with David. Thank you for giving him to me. I know You have a plan for us, and You are able to fulfill it in spite of all the negative things that seem to be before us. Help me to trust You through it all. And please, Father, don't let David be hurt by the things Mr. McCloud said to him tonight. Amen."

Now that she was at peace, the exhaustion took over and Catherine barely made it back into her bed before sleep drew her into dreams of David and their special place.

*   *   *   *

Pollard McCloud was up and out of the house early the next morning. He didn't want to face any of the family after his behavior the evening before. What really confused him was the fact that he cared what they thought, especially Susannah. He had spent his life behaving as he pleased without any regard for others' opinions. He preferred it that way. This gnawing at his insides was an irritation he could do without. Hoeing around the newly grown plants was an appropriate task for his mood; he could direct all his pent-up frustration on the weeds.

He had told the land broker from Independence to come to the farm while the others were gone to church, knowing that was the only time he could be assured that none of them would be there. He'd planned to make up some excuse to stay home, so the argument with the preacher's son last night was all working to his advantage after all.

Stopping to take a rest, McCloud leaned on his hoe and looked out over the fields. In a way it was a shame to sell this place. Barring unforeseen natural disasters, the rich land should yield good crops if farmed properly. But he knew it would never be *his*. It had been the Sutherland farm from the beginning, and no matter how much hard labor and sweat he put into those fields, the place would still bear the Lieutenant's name. Jeremy expected to inherit it, but McCloud had other plans. He had spent hours talking with land grant officials in Independence about the availability of free land in various sections of the western territories. For the most part, a claimant had to get to the land, stake his claim, set up a simple dwelling and live there, making improvements as minimal as planting a vegetable garden. After the required time period the land belonged to the claimant, free and clear. That land would be in *his* name.

There'd be no shadow of the Lieutenant hanging over it. The money from the sale of this farm should be enough to set out from here with a top-notch rig, and how convenient for him that Lexington was just the place to get it.

McCloud was feeling better just thinking about his plans. He'd get Susannah away from the memories of that dead husband of hers, and young Susannah, as he had begun to think of Catherine, away from that preacher's-son boyfriend. Jeremy would be of use on the trip west, but he'd soon be old enough to file claim on land for himself. So what difference did it make that the kid wouldn't inherit *this* place? There was plenty of land for the taking. Only one more wagon train would be heading west before next spring, and one way or another, Pollard McCloud intended to be in it.

*　　　　*　　　　*　　　　*

Without opening her eyes Susannah knew morning had arrived. It was strange how one had that sense of something good to be expected or something negative to be dealt with, even before coming fully awake. The dread in her heart reminded her that things had been left unsettled with Pollard last night. Opening one eye, she saw with relief that he had already risen. Laying aside the bedcovers, she rose and walked to the window. She could see Pollard in the fields, hoeing as though his life depended on it.

"Good, I need some time to gather my thoughts before facing him," she said to herself.

Since this was the first disagreement between Susannah and her new husband, she had no idea what to expect from him. She could see now that too little thought had been given to how Pollard would relate to her children when it came to discipline. Jeremy and Catherine respected her authority, and other than procrastinating at tasks occasionally, they seldom gave her any reason to correct them. Certainly disobedience deserved discipline, but being young and thoughtless called for parental instruction, not abusive rage. The picture of Pollard McCloud's green eyes flashing with anger came to her mind. She hoped she would forget that. This was the man she had vowed to love, but the possibility of that becoming reality seemed far away.

She was glad it was Sunday. She needed to be in worship this morning, to feel the cleansing that came from the sacred music and to draw strength from God's Word.

Heading toward the kitchen Susannah paused to look in on her children. Only a few blonde curls showed from under the patchwork quilt on Catherine's bed. How had time passed so quickly that her precious little girl was already thinking of marriage herself? She was still so young and innocent of the ways of the world, but Susannah knew that the next two years would bring maturity. She, herself, had been just fifteen when she and Jim married. Jeremy was born a year later when she was sixteen, just one year older than he was now. Looking into his bedroom she saw that it was empty, his bed showing no sign of being used. She resisted the concern that instantly rose within her.

"What if Jeremy had left because of Pollard's actions?" Then vaguely she recalled his taking Molly to the barn last night as she and Catherine sat on the swing. Hurrying to the kitchen she slipped into her outside shoes and walked across the yard to the barn, accompanied by a bevy of chickens waiting for their morning feeding.

Quietly shooing the chickens away, Susannah stepped into the barn and waited as her eyes grew accustomed to the darkness. She saw Jeremy asleep on a pile of hay, curled up with his faithful dog, Old Pal. He looked so much like his father. For a moment Susannah felt she was seeing her young Jim again, and her heart stirred with emotion. Just then Old Pal raised his head to look at her with his soulful brown eyes as if to ask, "You want my boy?"

Walking over to them, Susannah said quietly, "Hey, 'Pal! Do you want to wake up Jeremy?"

Old Pal's eyes flickered with understanding. He rose slowly, his joints stiff with age and the chill of the morning air. With a soft whine he nudged Jeremy, who only turned over and continued sleeping. The dog then gave a soft bark and licked Jeremy's face. Quickly raising his arm in defense, Jeremy sat up, "Aaii, Pal, what are you doing, boy?" Sitting up, he saw Susannah, and then became aware of his surroundings.

"Good morning, son," she said with a smile. "Did you sleep well?"

Jeremy grinned sheepishly, brushing hay from his clothes.

"'Morning, Mama ... I guess I did." Then remembering the reason behind his coming to the barn last night, he asked with concern, "Are you all right? And Cat?"

Susannah pulled her robe tighter about her and sat down on the hay beside Jeremy.

"I'm all right. Catherine and I had a good talk last night. She's fine too."

"And McCloud?" Jeremy asked hesitantly.

Susannah took a deep breath before answering. "He was asleep when I got to bed last night and in the fields before I woke up. We haven't talked about what happened."

"I hope David didn't take those insults too seriously. He's really a good guy."

"David is a very solid young man. I couldn't talk with him last night, but I want him to know that I trust him with Catherine, that nothing has changed."

"But things *have* changed, Mama. Everything's changed with McCloud being here."

Susannah had no reply to Jeremy's remark. What could she say? It was true, but she just couldn't go there this morning.

Picking hay from Jeremy's hair, she said, "We'd better get moving or we'll be late for church. I need to get breakfast ready, and you have half a bale of hay in your hair!"

Jeremy stood and reached down to lend a hand to Susannah. As she stood to her feet she put her arms around her son.

"Thank you for all you do, Jeremy. I don't tell you enough how much I appreciate you."

"I love you, Ma," Jeremy said as his eyes moistened with tears.

"I love you, too, son. Please try to be patient as we work through all these changes."

Jeremy nodded his agreement as arm in arm he and Susannah walked from the barn.

*   *   *   *

The ride to the church was pleasant, but quiet. Nobody wanted to voice what everyone was thinking …

58

that they were glad Pollard had opted to stay at the farm this morning rather than attend church. It was strange though, how that seemed to strangle any other conversation as well. Jeremy pretended to concentrate on driving the team, when actually, the horses could have taken them to the church with no one at the reins. Catherine read her Bible in between wondering if there would be a chance to talk to David, and Susannah was recalling her conversation with Pollard an hour earlier.

When he didn't come in by the time breakfast was ready, she fixed a plate of food and carried it to him in the field. He was surprised to see her, and the fact that she brought him food totally disarmed him of any defense he had intended for his behavior last evening. Susannah couldn't help but be touched by the expression on Pollard's face. Had no one ever done anything kind for this man? Compassion beyond her own feelings welled up within her and she put her arms around him and simply allowed that gift to flow to this sad, empty man. To her surprise he clung to her, hungrier for the nurturing of his broken soul than for the food he had already forgotten in his hand. Moments later, Pollard had quietly spoken, "I'm sorry." She had smiled and nodded, "I know," and they both understood there would be no more discussion of last night.

Pollard told her he was not going to church with them, that he needed to work the fields, and Susannah accepted that without argument. So, just as they had done for the past several years, Susannah and her children made the Sunday morning wagon trip to the house of worship that had been the stabilizing center of their lives.

David had practically worn away the grass in front of the church, pacing back and forth as he watched for them. He didn't sleep well last night, wondering what took place at Catherine's home after he left. Finally, sheer exhaustion pulled him into fitful dreams of McCloud spewing ugly accusations at them. He was up before daylight and probably, for the first time ever, ready to go to the church before his parents.

Catherine had been watching for David too. As soon as they rounded the last curve she was looking between Jeremy and Susannah from the back of the wagon, hoping he would be waiting outside. That might give them time to talk on the way into the church. Then suddenly she felt shy. Yesterday had changed so much for them. She wasn't sure how to act now that they had confessed their love to each other and talked about such serious matters as getting married someday.

Susannah looked at Catherine and saw the changing emotions flitting across her face. It seemed she was reading her mind as well. "Catherine," she said gently, "He's still your same David."

Catherine hardly had time for that to sink in before Jeremy reined the horses to a stop and David was beside the wagon. She couldn't keep back the smile that began in her heart as she saw him. That was all David needed to assure him that she was well, and the grin she loved spread across his face. "How's my girl?" he asked, his brown eyes twinkling.

"Your girl is fine except she needs a hand down out of this wagon," Catherine quipped.

"You mean I can't just stand here and look at you?"

"No, Romeo, you can't! I've got to move this wagon," Jeremy called to him.

"Morning to you, too, Jeremy," To Susannah, David said, "Let me help you first, Mrs. Suth….McCloud."

60

"Good morning, David," Susannah gave him a hug as he helped her down from the wagon. "I hope you're doing all right."

David assured her that he was fine. Then he turned to Catherine and helped her to the ground. Jeremy flicked the reins and guided the team to where other wagons were already gathered.

Walking discreetly beside Catherine, David put her hand through his arm. Speaking so softly only she could hear, he said, "I want to give you a hug but I can't do that here. Did things calm down after I left last night?"

Catherine nodded, and just as quietly answered, "Mr. McCloud went inside and didn't create any more trouble. Mama and I sat on the swing and talked." Looking up into his face she said, "I told her about our day … the things we talked about. I hope that was all right?"

David smiled, "I told my Pa, too, is that O.K. with you?"

"I don't mind, I doubt that it was a surprise to either of our parents."

"No, they just think we're so young that we may not be ready for this kind of commitment."

Catherine was thoughtful as they walked toward the door of the church. "Doesn't 'commitment' mean that you make a decision to honor some sort of agreement?"

David nodded, "I'd say that's a pretty good definition of the word."

Catherine continued, "I really do respect our parents, David, and I value their advice to us, but it's hard for me to see our relationship as something we have to decide to honor. You are so much a part of me, and I'm part of you … what does that leave to decide?"

The sincerity in Catherine's voice touched David's heart. As he looked down at the pretty face turned up to his, her blue eyes deepened with the emotion behind her words, he could only say, "My sweet Cat … It's going to be a long two years!"

*   *   *   *

Pollard McCloud breathed a sigh of relief when he saw the wagon had rounded the curve and was no longer in view. He had told that broker, Dorset, not to come before ten o'clock, but Susannah was running late because of bringing him breakfast to the field. He still couldn't believe she had done that. His experience with women gave him good reason to think that an argument the night before would surely produce at least one day of a cold shoulder. But not with Susannah. Not only was she kind and sweet as usual, she had gone out of her way to do something nice for him when he'd been the one wrong. Now he really felt uneasy about his plans to sell the farm. How was she going to feel about him then? He'd have to convince her that it was all for their good as a family.

"Where was that Dorset?" McCloud lit his cigar and anxiously looked down the path as far as he could see. He wanted the land broker gone before Susannah and the young ones got back. This had to be a "done deal" when he broke the news to Susannah. She would never agree to it any other way. He wasn't sure what to expect from Jeremy. It would make it easier to get moving on preparations for the trip west if the kid didn't give him any flack. He'd really come in handy on the way, too. In spite of his age, Jeremy had carried the responsibility of a grown man, and he might prefer to stay around Lexington where he had friends and relatives. McCloud knew the biggest thing in his favor was Jeremy's loyalty to Susannah and Catherine. He'd just have to play on that if it looked like the kid wanted to stay behind. McCloud had talked to enough people in Independence to know that anything could happen along the trail. Every precaution had to be made to be as fully equipped for emergencies as possible. The fine line was finding the balance between having enough supplies and not overloading the wagons. He'd heard tales of the litter of household goods tossed along the trails to lighten the loads for exhausted oxen. He'd make sure their stuff was kept to a minimum.

McCloud was startled out of his thoughts by the sound of a horse and buggy rounding the last bend of the path to the house. He saw the short, round figure of Jonah Dorset holding onto the seat as a taller, thin man drove the horse furiously into the yard. McCloud stopped abruptly as he became aware that the rig was about to run him down.

"Whoa, horse!" the driver yelled, pulling on the reins.

McCloud stayed where he was until the horse and buggy had come to a complete stop. Both men straightened their waistcoats and hats, Dorset mopping the perspiration from his drenched face.

"'Kinda new at this?" McCloud asked the driver.

"I apologize, Mr. McCloud," Dorset said, "This is my partner, Parker Rhinehart. I'm afraid neither of us has much aptitude with the animal kingdom."

Anxious to have this transaction completed, Mc Cloud wasted no more time.

"Well, let's get started, Mr. Dorset. What is it that you want to see?"

CHAPTER 4

"I wonder what David's making me?" Catherine thought as their wagon bounced along the bumpy road to the farm. Without McCloud's pressuring them to hurry home after church, Susannah had taken advantage of the opportunity to visit with friends, allowing Catherine and David time to talk as well. Catherine was relieved to find that he had not taken to heart McCloud's ugly accusation.

"I'm making something for you at the shop, a surprise," he'd said. Then Susannah had come to tell her it was time to go, so she had no time to wheedle any more information from him. The twinkle in his eyes told her he was loving the fact that she'd have to wonder about his surprise.

Catherine's thoughts of David were interrupted by her mother's question, "Who could that be?" Catherine looked up to see a small buggy with two dark-coated men on the road ahead of them. They were obviously in a hurry, leaving a cloud of dust behind. The buggy hadn't been in front of them earlier, and there were no other roads intersecting this one for over a mile. That meant they had come from their farm. Jeremy turned to Susannah and a look passed between them that brought a chill to

Catherine's heart. Without saying anything, Jeremy flicked the reins and speeded up the horses' pace.

McCloud was entering the barn as the wagon rolled into the yard. Jeremy stopped at the house and helped Susannah and Catherine down from the wagon.

"Thank you, son," Susannah said quietly, and then, "Catherine, why don't you change your dress; you can help me with lunch."

"Yes, ma'am," Catherine replied, and went to change.

Jeremy drove the horses and wagon toward the barn. He unhitched the animals from the wagon and led them to their stalls. He tried to shake off the uneasiness that had come over him when he saw those men on the road. He knew they had come from this farm, and something wasn't right about it.

"Hey, Jeremy!"

Jeremy looked up to see McCloud standing there with feed for the horses. That was strange. McCloud had never helped him with the livestock. There was a nervous energy about the man that confirmed to Jeremy that something was going on.

"Thanks," he said, taking the feedbag from McCloud. Then nonchalantly, "We saw a couple of guys in a buggy out on the road ... 'looked like they came from here."

Jeremy couldn't quite read the expression on McCloud's face, but something was there, fear ... guilt?

"Oh, those guys? One tall, and one short and fat? Yeah, 'just a couple of city slickers looking for somebody. I don't remember the name. 'Guess I'd better go say 'hi' to your ma," McCloud said as he made his way out the barn door.

But McCloud didn't go to the house. He wasn't ready to face Susannah just now. Instead, he walked over to the corral and pretended to be checking a loose plank. He hadn't planned yet how he would break the news to her and the kids. He patted the pocket of his overalls that contained the check the land broker had given him. That brought a wave of excitement to him. He'd never had his hands on this much money in his whole life. This check was going to buy him a new future, land that had nobody's name on it but his, a place where he and Susannah could start fresh. She'd feel differently about him once they got away from here. He almost wished Jeremy *would* choose to stay in Lexington. He looks so much like his father, and that has to be a constant reminder to Susannah of the Lieutenant.

"Oh well," McCloud thought, "I'll treat him decent as long as I need him, and then make things so rough he'll want to leave!"

When he was sure that Jeremy had left the barn he'd go back there and start setting aside some things he knew they'd need on the trip west. It was really going to be a tight schedule, but with the outfitters being right here in Lexington he'd get started in the morning.

Sunday dinner was strange. Normally McCloud had nothing to say to Jeremy or Catherine at meals. The atmosphere was always tense. Today wasn't different in that respect, but McCloud's behavior certainly was. As though he felt obligated to keep conversation going, he talked of first one thing, then another. When everyone was finished eating, Catherine started to clear the table and

McCloud asked Susannah to join him in the porch swing. Jeremy stayed seated at the table as they left the room.

"I wish I knew what you were thinking," Catherine said to him in a loud whisper.

Jeremy looked up to meet his sister's eyes, and matching her tone of voice, said, "I wish I knew what was going on with *him*!" He motioned in the direction of the porch.

"Do you think it had anything to do with those men in the buggy?"

"Yes, I'm sure of it, but I don't know why."

Just then they heard Susannah cry out from the porch, "You did what?"

The two of them froze at the tone in their mother's voice. Something was terribly wrong. Jeremy reached out for Catherine's hand as they listened. They could hear Pollard McCloud as he tried to soothe Susannah.

"I did it for all of us ... as a family, Susannah. We need a fresh start away from here."

"But Pollard, this farm is the only thing Jeremy's father could leave him. Why do you think I have worked day and night for the past few years to hold onto it? How could you possibly do this without talking to me about it?"

"Because I knew you would react just as you have right now. Can't you see, Susannah, you're stuck in the past here. We can go west and get free land that will be ours ... the McCloud's. There's plenty of land for the taking, and as soon as Jeremy turns eighteen he'll be able to file claim on more land out there than he'd have here. The sale of this farm will give all of us a chance to better ourselves in a new world just waiting to be built."

Susannah's tone of voice was like steel, "You had no right to do this, Pollard McCloud! This was *my* land,

Jeremy's land! How did you manage it? Those men we saw, they had something to do with this, didn't they?"

Catherine and Jeremy stood immovable in the kitchen. They could hear McCloud get up and walk to the edge of the porch.

"Susannah, you know the law doesn't allow women to hold property. And Jeremy is still a minor. I don't know exactly how they worked it out, but yes, those guys were land brokers and they took care of all the legal details. All I know is that this check is good, and it's going to buy our future together."

"You have no idea what you have done to our future, Pollard," Susannah said angrily. "Marriage is based on trust, and I will never trust you again. I entered this marriage in hopes that we might possibly build a future. I thought I could learn to love you, but you are not the man you portrayed yourself to be. I can't undo what you've done, but I can assure you that you will never have my love!"

"Don't say that!" McCloud protested angrily. "We've had good times together. If you'd just forget your dead husband for one minute you might be open to being the wife that you promised to be at that altar."

"How dare you imply that I have not done my part in this marriage? You came here with nothing, and I trusted you with everything in my possession. You have betrayed me, Pollard. I wasn't going to tell you this just yet, but there's another very good reason I don't wish to take a months' long wagon trip ... I'm carrying your child."

"My ... child!" McCloud looked at her in disbelief. "A baby? ... I never thought..."

"Right now I'd give anything if it weren't true, but I'm sure it is. How do you expect me to make that difficult journey in a wagon expecting a child, Pollard? Have you heard how many women die giving birth on that trail? And how most of the babies never make it to three months of age? Is this what you want for your child? If you had discussed this with me before you acted I would have told you about the baby."

Jeremy and Catherine heard everything from the kitchen. Catherine's knees seemed to buckle, and she sat heavily in a chair.

"What does this mean for us?" Catherine wondered. Apparently they would have to leave the farm and go west with McCloud. What about her relationship with David and their future plans? And her mother was having a baby? "Oh, God, this is all too much at once!" Catherine dropped her head to the table in tears as Jeremy stood and walked slowly out the back door.

"Jeremy!" Catherine called to him, but he didn't stop. All his life he'd planned on someday owning his father's farm, and now that dream was gone forever. She couldn't imagine what he was going through, but she felt as though her own heart had been broken in two. What must her mother be feeling, knowing it was her marriage to McCloud that had allowed all of this to happen? ... David ... she had to talk to David! Surely he would have some way to make this better!

McCloud's angry voice interrupted Catherine's thoughts.

"This is how it's going to be, Susannah. As soon as the bank opens in the morning, I'm cashing this check. Then I'm going to the outfitters to get the wagon and supplies. Whatever personal things you want to take will have to fit into a couple of crates. There's no room in a wagon for a bunch of household stuff. It would never make it all the way to Oregon anyway. They say the trail is littered with perfectly good furniture that nobody wants because it's too big and heavy. I need every inch in that wagon for supplies. The oxen will have enough to pull without any unnecessary weight."

It was a moment before Susannah spoke. Catherine had never heard her mother sound so cold. "I have no place to go with my children, Pollard. If I did, there is no way I would embark on this crazy journey. But someday, somehow, you will pay for what you have done. I will do what I have to do, but don't ever expect me to be glad that you are my husband!"

McCloud's tone was hard and measured, "The wagon train leaves in two weeks. Do whatever you want with all your things, or leave them sitting here, I don't care. The brokers will move someone in here anyway to work the crops until they're harvested." Catherine could hear McCloud's footsteps as he moved closer to her mother; "It's not to your advantage to be hateful to me, Susannah. I've been known to keep a woman in line with the back of my hand. If that's what you want, I'll be glad to let you have it!"

"This can't really be happening," Catherine thought as she sat frozen in fear. She was relieved to hear McCloud stomp across the porch and down the steps. The screened door opened and a white-faced Susannah entered, practically collapsing into the nearest armchair. Catherine saw her through the kitchen doorway and ran to her, falling to the floor at Susannah's knees.

"Oh, Mama, what are we going to do?" she cried.

Susannah found enough strength to hold her shaking daughter closer.

70

"Sshh, child. We'll be all right. We'll do what we have to do."

"Do we really have to leave Lexington?"

With a deep sigh Susannah leaned back in the chair for support. "That's the way it looks right now, honey. This caught me completely off-guard, and there's not enough time to try to work out any other solution. I don't have any money except for the few dollars I've saved from selling the extra eggs. We'd have to leave the farm anyway when the brokers come to take it over, and Pollard has all the money from the sale. If we don't go west with him we'll have nothing at all. At least you will have food to eat!"

"But what about David … and our plans?"

"Oh, Catherine," Susannah stroked the blonde curls that she loved. "I'm so sorry. I don't know what to say. I know this will be hard, but not impossible. We will just have to pray that God will somehow work it out."

"I need to talk to David, Mama. Please let me go into town. He has to know what is going on."

"I can't let you go alone. Where's Jeremy? My poor, sweet Jeremy! How can he ever forgive me?" Susannah broke down then, weeping uncontrollably.

"Please, Mama, don't cry so hard," Catherine now tried to comfort her mother. "I'll find Jeremy. He'll be all right. He knows you didn't mean for things to turn out this way." Catherine went to the kitchen and brought her mother a glass of water and a towel for her tear-stained face. "Just stay right here; I'll bring Jeremy back."

Catherine went out the back door and stood looking about the farm for any sign of her brother. She knew he wouldn't be in the barn with McCloud. She started walking toward the fruit orchard and over a small rise, and then she saw Jeremy's horse, Midnight. The horse was saddled, so she knew Jeremy was there too. Running was difficult through the late spring growth, but it didn't matter. She could see Jeremy now, sitting at the edge of the pond with his head in his hands. Tears streamed down Catherine's face at the sight of her brother, his shoulders drooped in despair. "Oh God," she cried silently, "He didn't deserve this!"

Just as Catherine reached Jeremy she started falling to the ground, totally out of breath from her run. Jeremy heard her coming, stood and reached out to break her fall. He wasn't prepared for the force of her momentum though, and instead of stopping her, he found himself desperately trying to maintain his own balance. His flailing arms and legs tangled with the skirt of Catherine's yellow dress, and both of them went tumbling into the pond with a splash that caused Midnight to jump back with a whinny!

"Cat! You nut!" Jeremy gasped, both from surprise and the chill of the water.

"Why d-d-didn't you c-c-catch me?" Catherine gasped in return. Jeremy's hair was sticking straight up in back and mud was plastered down one side of his face and neck. "You look so funny!" she said between peals of laughter.

"I look funny?" Jeremy yelped, "You should see yourself!" Catherine's blonde curls were dark now with long, soggy masses half wrapped around her face. They both began to laugh hysterically until they got so chilled they knew they'd better get home. Leaving the pond was much harder than the way they entered it, though. It was impossible to get a foothold on the slippery bank. Every time they fell back into the water they started laughing again. Finally, Jeremy called Midnight to come close enough to the edge so that the reins fell within reach. He grabbed hold, Catherine pushed him from behind, and Midnight held steady until Jeremy managed to pull himself up to the dry ground. Now that he was out, Jeremy threatened to leave Catherine in the pond. She was shivering so badly that he didn't dare tease her for long, though. He pulled her out and they both mounted a not-too-happy Midnight and headed for the house.

It wasn't until they started back that they remembered McCloud's actions that created their situation. Catherine told Jeremy why she had come to get him ... to assure Susannah that he was all right. Not daring to go farther than the porch in their condition, they stood just outside the kitchen and called to her. Susannah's eyes opened wide at the sight of her two mud-soaked children, and her sad face broke into laughter too. As they told her how they happened to visit the pond, the three of them laughed together and it didn't matter at all that mud puddles covered half the floor of the porch that no longer belonged to them.

*   *   *   *

"I'll lock the door on my way out," Silas Goodson said to David, then paused at the doorway. "You know, son, I found years ago that sometimes it's better to get rest and then come back to work on a project. I usually ended up re-doing things I'd made when I was tired."

"I know, sir, but Catherine's leaving tomorrow and I have to finish this. I'm afraid if I don't work tonight I won't have it ready for her, and I'd never forgive myself," David replied.

The elderly gentleman looked with pride at his young protégé. They just didn't come any better than this one. He loved David like a son and had shared all his knowledge of this craft with him, hoping someday David might take over his business. He saw the heartache that Catherine's leaving had brought to David, and he was reminded of a lost love of his own many years earlier.

"I understand; just work slowly and carefully, and be sure to lock up when you leave."

David looked up from his work to the man he so highly respected.

"Thank you, sir … for everything." Mr. Goodson had allowed David to purchase the gold he needed for Catherine's gift at a price below cost and had given him a small, but quality diamond to place in the design.

Goodson nodded his acknowledgement as he put on his hat. "Good night, David; I'll see you tomorrow."

David was glad to be alone. These past two weeks had been extremely difficult, knowing that Catherine was leaving to some unknown place far away. He felt as though an actual weight had been attached to his heart, and sometimes it became so heavy he could only find relief in prayer. The gift he was making Catherine became even more important now that they would be separated. It would be a tangible reminder of his love for her. Mail delivery to and from the west was improving as railways increased, but stagecoaches still provided service for many areas. It would be months before Catherine would be settled and have an address, then weeks before a letter from her could reach him. It was possible that almost a year could pass before she heard back from him. These thoughts threatened to overwhelm him with despair, so he forced himself to focus on the work before him. He was finished except for the engraving and that had to be so carefully done.

"God, please help me to do this well, and to not think past tomorrow," David prayed as he picked up his tool.

*   *   *   *

Catherine entered the room that had been her bedroom all her life and closed the door behind her. She needed to escape from the people going through the house and yard, choosing items they wished to buy. As she looked at the bare room, she hardly recognized it. Even her bed was gone, sold to the Thomas family for their two little girls. She'd sleep on the floor tonight, her last night in the house where she was born.

"How could one's entire life be totally up-ended in two weeks' time?" she questioned.

She couldn't imagine what lay ahead for them in the months on the trail. At least McCloud was trying to make the wagon as comfortable as possible for her mother. It seems the idea of having a child had softened his attitude. It still didn't lessen the pain of his selling the farm, though. Catherine could tell that Susannah was performing the necessary tasks, but there was an obvious wall between her and Pollard McCloud.

Catherine could hear someone plunking out a tune on her piano. Tears stung her eyes as she heard her mother agree to a price. She thought of the many hours she had spent playing every piece of music she could obtain, loving the sounds and the feel of the ivory keys. The piano was a beautiful piece of furniture as well as a quality instrument. Papa had insisted on buying the best they could get. She thought of it as her legacy from him, as Jeremy's had been the farm.

Suddenly Catherine felt a surge of anger. "Is absolutely everything to be stripped away from me? From Jeremy? I hate Pollard McCloud!"

As soon as she said the words, Catherine wished she could take them back. There was no place for hate in the heart of a Christian.

"Oh, God, I didn't mean that! I don't want to hate anyone. I just feel so helpless. It seems that everything we love is being taken from us, and because we're young, there's nothing we can do about it."

She'd been so overwhelmed with leaving David and her home that all she'd felt was heartache. But now the thought of someone taking her beautiful piano, not knowing if she'd ever have another to play ... she couldn't just accept this like it didn't matter. She'd given away everything else ... the dolls she'd loved as a little girl, most of her clothing ... favorite things she'd kept for years. At least Mama had insisted that she be able to keep her music in hopes that someday she'd have a piano again. It fit into a leather satchel that didn't take up much space, so McCloud had grudgingly agreed to let her bring it. The music, her picture of Papa, one of David and his family, her Bible and a few items of clothing and extra shoes, were all Catherine would take with her.

"How am I going to make it without talking to David? Will I ever see him again?"

Catherine's anger, with no place to go, melted into despair. She wanted desperately to believe that David would be able to come west and find her, and then they'd be married. He had insisted that her leaving did not change their plans. But she was learning how uncertain life could be. The thought of the untold miles of wilderness that would separate her from David made it difficult to believe that even his determination would bring them together again.

"Catherine!" Susannah's call interrupted her thoughts. "There's someone here to see you."

Catherine used her skirt to wipe the tears from her eyes and opened the door, surprised to see her friends there.

"Sarah, Abby, Mary Beth!" Catherine hugged each girl in turn.

"We're really going to miss you," Abby choked.

All Catherine could do was nod her head. This was incredibly painful. She'd gone to school with these girls all her life. Next to David, they were her closest friends.

"We know you can't take a lot of extra things," Sarah said, with misty eyes, "But we wanted to give you something you can use on the trail."

Abby handed her a wrapped package, "You can open it now."

As she thanked her friends Catherine opened the package to find a journal with her name engraved in gold on the beautiful, rose leather binding.

"Oh, this is lovely, and so perfect!" Catherine exclaimed. She reached to hug them all at once.

"You can record your experiences on the trail. Maybe one of these years we'll be lucky enough to meet again and you can share them with us," said Mary Beth.

"And my mother made this canvas bag to protect it," Sarah said, handing Catherine a light-colored canvas pouch. The journal fit perfectly into the canvas as it folded to tightly secure the treasured gift. "We read about how people's things sometimes get ruined on the trail, going through rivers and rainstorms and such."

This act of thoughtfulness was just too much for Catherine. She could no longer hold back the tears as she hugged her friends again, trying not to think about the fact that she had no friends wherever it was that they were going. Susannah came to lend her support even as her own heart wept at her daughter's pain.

"Thank you for coming, girls. You couldn't have given Catherine a more perfect gift. You know how she likes to write. Sarah, please thank your mother for her kindness. We're going to miss all of you."

Susannah was thankful for the interruption as Jeremy opened the door and walked into the room. "Ma," he started to say, and then became aware of the four crying, teenaged girls. The look on his face clearly revealed his preference to be *anyplace else* at the moment.

"Jeremy, we're going to miss you too," Sarah had walked toward him, and only courtesy prevented his bolting back out the door. He muttered a quiet, "Thank you," and was greatly relieved to see that she, at least, had stopped crying. He didn't dare look at the other girls.

"Jay Bob asked me to give this to you," Sarah said, reaching into her pocket and handing Jeremy a knife. Sarah's brother had been christened James Robert by his parents, but with Jeremy's penchant for nicknames, he had started calling him "Jay Bob" years ago, and it had stuck.

Jeremy was touched by the gift as he recognized the silver inlaid ivory handle. It was Jay Bob's favorite pocket knife that he'd carried for years. Jeremy knew that it was special to his friend. Now he felt tears coming to *his* eyes. "Darn those girls; they started this!" he thought.

Finding his voice, Jeremy said, "Tell him thanks for me, Sarah. It's … real special. I'll take good care of it, and I'll think of him every time I use it." Then turning to his mother he said, "McCloud asked me to have you come out to the wagon when you get a chance." He nodded to Catherine's friends still standing with her.

"Abby, Mary Beth, thanks for coming … I gotta go." Jeremy tipped his hat to all of the girls as he hurried out the door.

"We've got to go too, Catherine. We need to be back before dark," Abby said.

"Tell your mothers I'll write when we get situated, girls," Susannah said as she headed toward the barn.

Catherine walked out with her friends, and after their final goodbyes she was exhausted. She was glad the familiar old swing was still in place on the porch. Puddles the cat came and joined her there as she rocked gently and looked around the farm. She wanted to etch this scene on her mind so she'd never forget this part of her life, at least the part before everything started to go wrong. And when, exactly was that? She was too tired to remember.

She saw McCloud talking to her mother, obviously showing her how he had arranged things in the wagon. He didn't raise any objections to taking the bed for Susannah's sake, and even though he had cut it down to fit into the wagon, it took up a lot of space. McCloud had bought so many supplies that they were taking the farm wagon as well, just to carry everything. He had rigged up a canvas covering for it, much like the one on the large wagon. It was imperative to protect the provisions from moisture.

Catherine had never given any thought to how much food one person ate in several months' time, but food was stocked according to the number of persons in the party. There would be very few sources of supply once they were on the trail. She certainly didn't think she ate a hundred and fifty pounds of flour in six months, but that was the amount calculated per adult. The twenty pounds of sugar, she might own up to consuming, though. From the multiple bags of beans and bacon, she had a good idea of what they would be eating for the next few months.

Now that the buyers had left, it seemed strangely quiet. The few chickens that would make the trip with them were already penned in a cage attached to the side of the wagon. Daisy would be going along to provide milk. Midnight and Flame were the only horses left, and once they got to Independence the mules would be replaced with oxen.

Catherine's thoughts turned to David. Where was he? He had said he was going to work frantically to finish her gift before she left. But what if they didn't connect in the morning? She couldn't bear the thought of leaving without seeing him again.

"Hey, move over," Jeremy shook the swing from behind as he jumped up onto the porch. He plopped down beside Catherine, almost sitting on Puddles, who meowed and gave him a green-eyed stare of indignation after landing on the floor.

Seeing Jeremy's dirty, wet- with -sweat clothing, Catherine moved as far away from him in the swing as she could.

"I hope you intend to clean up before we head out in the morning," she said.

"If you think I'm bad now, just wait 'til we've been on the trip for a few weeks. Just think, you'll be looking and smelling this good too!" he said with a grin.

He could tell by the look on her face that Catherine hadn't given any thought to wagon trail hygiene. She knew the washtub was packed in the wagon, but it hadn't occurred to her that there would be no water or privacy to bathe, and for months! She was definitely not prepared for this!

"Is everything packed out there?" she asked, changing the subject.

"All but the few things we need to take care of the animals in the morning."

"How are you doing with all this, Jeremy?" Catherine asked with concern.

As usual, Jeremy took his time to reply. "I guess God really does give the grace that's needed for tough situations, Cat. I don't think it's all over in my head, maybe I've just 'put it on a shelf' to deal it with later."

"McCloud should be easier to get along with once we get on the way."

"Yeah, I can handle him, though. I just don't let him get to me. I'm more concerned about Mama. She doesn't need to be making this trip in her condition."

"I can tell she's really tired, but she doesn't complain. I'll do everything I can to help her, but what if she has the baby on the way? I don't know anything about that."

"I guess we have to leave that up to the Lord, along with all the rest of this whole situation." Jeremy tousled his sister's blonde curls as he stretched his wiry frame. "Is there anything still here in the house to eat?"

"There's a chicken pot pie, some ham, fresh-baked bread and two cakes; the neighbors were nice to us today."

"I might wash up if you'd fix me a plate, huh, sis?" Jeremy wheedled.

"Only because I'm hungry, too," Catherine poked him in the ribs as they went through the door, the sound of their footsteps echoing through the empty house.

CHAPTER 5

"Whoa, Big John!" McCloud tried to calm the large mule as he set the collar over his head. For some reason the stock were on edge this morning. Maybe they felt the tension in the air, too. Well, it would be over soon. Within an hour they'd be out that gate and on their way, though McCloud didn't know what their final destination would be. The wagon train was headed to Oregon Territory, but he'd been thinking about other options. Truthfully, he had no desire to spend five or six months on a very difficult trek across rivers and mountains. It didn't matter to him where the journey ended as long as he had decent land in his name McCloud had heard tales of the greenhorns that came along on these wagon trains that created problems for everyone else. He had taken the time to learn what was needed and was well stocked with provisions and equipment for repairs. He didn't intend to be pulling someone else's load.

It would certainly be easier for Susannah if they could shorten this trip. He was concerned about how she would handle the rigorous journey in her condition. The past few years of working so hard on the farm had taken a lot out of her. He could tell that from the Lieutenant's photograph of her that he still carried in his wallet. They'd head west, but he'd keep his eyes open for any opportunity along the way that might suit his purposes better.

Now that railroads were expanding from both the east and the west to create unbroken transportation across the continent, fewer wagon trains were heading west, but untold numbers of pioneers had made the journey in the previous two decades. Certainly things had not gone well with all of them. McCloud was thinking it might be possible to pick up a place where some sort of shelter or house was already built, maybe one with a few improvements - a well, barns, pens for stock, etc.

He began one last check of the supplies he'd so carefully packed. The farm wagon would carry the tools and equipment. He had two, hundred-foot lengths of one-inch hemp rope, brake chains, a wagon jack, extra axles, tongues and wheels, wheel parts, axes, a handsaw, hammers, nails, knives, a sturdy shovel, several sizes of augers, canvas for repairs to the top covering, buckets and the extra food provisions. Saddles and bridles for the horses were placed on top of these.

The main wagon was the largest made, twelve feet long, but Susannah's bed took up half that space. Supplies would be stacked on top of it during the day and unloaded when they stopped for the night, at least until some of the stores were used up. He couldn't do anything about the rough trails, but he could bring the bed for her comfort.

The rest of the space was filled with bags of beans, rice, dried fruit, potatoes, flour, sugar, coffee, tea, spices and salt, saleratus for rising biscuits and breads, a keg of pickles, bacon and salt pork. McCloud latched down the locks on the storage bins on the side of the wagon where the cast iron cooking equipment, coffee pot and kettle were packed for easy access. Susannah's favorite rooster was already announcing the arrival of morning from the chicken coop attached to the side of the wagon. The all-important water barrel was secured with metal bands. McCloud checked it once again to make certain it was filled to the top and the tight-fitting lid was in place. Jeremy checked the lead reins for Midnight and Flame and the tether for Daisy.

Small trunks held their clothing, personal belongings, and the few household treasures Susannah insisted on bringing. She simply refused to leave behind the artful, hand-stitched quilts made by friends and relatives; they were stashed everywhere one could be squeezed in, even on the driver's seat for padding where Susannah would ride.

Inside the house Catherine was helping Susannah wrap the rest of the food the neighbors had brought, cutting up the ham to go with the morning's fresh biscuits.

"There's still enough food here for the rest of the day, so we won't need to cook a meal this evening," Susannah told her.

Catherine just nodded in agreement. She couldn't find words to speak. Everything was so strange. Even her mother's soft voice echoed in the empty room.

The food was wrapped and packed into two baskets. Susannah wiped crumbs from the counter and looked around the kitchen where she had prepared so many meals. Soon someone else would be cooking on her stove. She walked slowly through the house one last time. It had held so many wonderful memories for years, then one painful thing after another had happened to cloud those memories. She took a long, trembling breath and released it. Maybe it was time to let it go after all. Taking Catherine by the hand the two of them walked out and she closed the door. Jeremy was already on the seat of the farm wagon with Old Pal beside him. McCloud was pacing beside the large wagon, waiting to assist Susannah to her place.

When everyone was situated the men called to the mules to move forward. As the heavy wagon passed through the gate, Susannah looked straight ahead. Behind them, Jeremy quietly told his sister, "You know, Cat, one of these days I'm going to buy this place back. It may belong to those brokers right now, but someday it will be mine again."

Catherine didn't know what to say in reply. She had so dreaded this day. Now she just wanted it to end. As the house, barn and grounds became stripped of everything that had made the place "home," she felt her attachment waning as well. It didn't feel like home anymore, so they may as well leave. Her only concern now was that she still had not seen David. Surely he wouldn't allow her to leave without telling her goodbye. They would go directly through Lexington, though, so there was still the chance to see him.

"This is taking forever, Jeremy," Catherine complained. The thought of traveling for months at this pace filled her with dread. If their wagon always had to travel behind the larger one, she was going to be sick of the sight of it. They were finally coming into the edge of town when off to the side of the road she saw that David and his parents were waiting for them under a large oak tree. Reverend and Mrs. Winters were sitting in a buggy while David stood beside his horse, Star. When McCloud saw them he guided the mule team over to stop near them, and Jeremy did the same. The Winters now stood with David and called their greetings to everyone. Catherine was down from the wagon seat before David could get there to help her, running to meet him.

"I've never been so glad to see you in my whole life!" she cried as she threw her arms around his neck.

"Oh, Cat, I'm sorry I haven't been to see you, but I needed all that time to finish your gift," David said, holding her close. "My parents wanted to say goodbye to all of you, but I think mainly they came to talk with McCloud and your mother for a little while so I can have this time with you."

Catherine looked ahead and saw that the Winters' plan was working well. David's mother was giving Susannah a basket, apparently containing food. McCloud was talking with Reverend Winters, so she intended to take advantage of every minute of this precious time with David.

"So did you finish my gift?"

"I did."

"And are you going to give it to me?"

"I am," David said, taking her by the arm and leading her behind the wagon, out of sight of the others. "Actually, this is for both of us," he said.

He reached into his pocket and brought out a dark blue jewelry box which he handed to Catherine. She opened it and gasped in surprise at the exquisite gold heart. Then she saw that it was actually in two pieces, one on a fine chain. When fit together, the engraving read: "I love you with my whole heart." The heart was bordered with a raised design that represented the work of a skilled artisan. In the center of the delicate petals of a rose, a small diamond glistened in the morning sun.

"Oh, David, this is so beautiful! And you did this yourself?"

"Yes, but I want you to know that the diamond is a gift from Mr. Goodson. He asked me to give you his regards. He thinks a lot of you too."

"That was so nice of him. Please thank him for me, David."

"Look on the back," David said, and as she turned the heart over Catherine saw in very small, perfect lettering the words: "To Catherine, From David."

"Here, let me put it on you." David took the necklace and showed her that alone, her half of the heart read: "I Love You" on the front, and: "From David" on the back. He gently placed it around her neck as she lifted her curls for him to latch the clasp, and then took the other half of the heart for himself.

"Catherine, this half of our heart will be with me always. Someday, I'm coming to find you, and when we put these two pieces together again to make a whole heart, it will be time for our hearts to be joined as one, as husband and wife. Until then, every time you touch this necklace, know that you were in my thoughts every minute I worked on it, and I will be loving you every single day until we meet again."

David took her in his arms and held her, kissing her tenderly.

"This is 'home,'" Catherine thought, treasuring every moment.

"You have to send a letter to me as soon as you are settled so I'll know where you are. It could take months for me to get it." David said when he could bear to let her go.

"Oh! I forgot. I have a letter for you." Catherine told him. "It doesn't compare to this beautiful necklace, but I wanted to leave you with something you can read when you are missing me and know that I'm thinking of you." She handed him a letter from her pocket.

They heard a coughing sound that Catherine recognized as belonging to Jeremy. That probably meant he'd been sent to tell them it was time to get back on the road.

"Jeremy, come and see what David made for me," Catherine called to him.

Red-faced, Jeremy stepped around the side of the wagon. "Hey, David," he said, extending his hand, "I'm sorry to interrupt you two."

"That's O.K., Jeremy, we know it's not your fault," David said, shaking his hand.

"Look at my necklace, Jeremy! And show him your half, David."

Jeremy didn't claim to know much about jewelry, but even he could recognize the quality and beauty of David's work.

"Hey, I knew you tinkered around with watches there at the shop. I had no idea you could do work like this," Jeremy told him.

"Mr. Goodson's really taught me a lot in the past year about jewelry making. By the time Catherine and I get married I should be able to make a good living for her."

"Well, I hate to be the one to take her so far away from you, but we don't have much choice in the matter. Cat, McCloud's ready to get moving."

"David, maybe I could ride with you to the other side of town at least," Catherine said, trying to prolong the little time they had together. "Let me ask Mama. I want to show her our 'heart' anyway."

Susannah could see the glow on Catherine's face as she and David approached. She hated to be responsible for breaking them apart. The optimism of young love might hold onto the dream of being reunited someday, but Susannah knew that the reality of that happening was not likely. She'd never say that to her daughter, though.

"David, the necklace is absolutely beautiful. I am truly impressed," Susannah told him as she hugged him. "I'll miss you, son."

David had always liked Catherine's mother, and found it hard to say good-bye as he returned her hug. "I'll be praying for you to have a safe trip, Mrs. McCloud."

He turned to shake hands with Pollard McCloud and found that McCloud had busied himself with checking a wheel on the wagon. That was just as well, he really didn't want to talk to him, anyway.

"Mama, can I ride with David to the other side of town? Then I'll get back on the wagon with Jeremy," Catherine entreated.

"Go ahead," Susannah agreed. "Reverend and Mrs. Winters, thank you for everything you've done for us through the years, for the spiritual truths you have imparted to us, and for raising such a fine son. We'll write when we get settled."

"May God go with you, Susannah, Pollard. Our prayers are with you." They waved to Jeremy as his wagon approached. "Blessings, Jeremy, we'll miss you." Catherine hugged each of David's parents warmly before David helped her up in front of him on Star.

"I'll be home in a while," David said to his parents as Star fell into place behind the farm wagon.

Catherine wasn't complaining now about the slow pace of their progress. She was savoring every minute of her time with David, and every glimpse of her familiar home town. This might be the last time she'd ever see the courthouse column with the embedded cannonball, a memento from the battle fought here between the North and the South. If she did return to Lexington someday, things would be different. There was so much to be rebuilt after the war. Even now, the sound of carpenters hammering and sawing followed them as they made their way among the horses and wagon traffic through town.

The clerks from Russell, Majors & Wadell waved proudly to McCloud as they recognized the wagon and supplies they had sold him. They seldom learned the outcome of all these folk they outfitted for the trips west; sometimes they wondered how many of them actually made it to their destinations.

Too soon for Catherine and David, they reached the opposite side of Lexington where final goodbyes had to be said. David slowed Star's pace to have a time of prayer with Catherine, asking God to keep her safe and bring them together again in His perfect timing. With one last tender kiss he delivered her to her brother, turned Star quickly, and rode away at a gallop so she would not see his struggle for control.

Catherine had experienced the pain of separation when her father left for the war, and even more deeply when they learned he would not be coming home. But as she watched her handsome David riding wildly away from her, his dark hair flying, her heart felt as though it would break. She reached for the golden half-heart at her neck that would be her constant reminder of their love and clutched it tightly in both hands as tears streamed silently down her face.

CHAPTER 6

T his place is incredibly noisy and smells like a dozen barnyards all together!" Catherine wrote in her journal. Swatting at the fly that kept buzzing around her head, she stopped to look at her surroundings. As far as she could see from her perch on the wagon seat, there were wagons of every kind. Many of them were similar to theirs; others looked as though amateur carpenters had simply thrown boards together.

"Do people really think they can cross rough terrain and mountains with these things?" she asked herself. They must be the "greenhorns" McCloud complained about almost daily. In the week's time they had been here in Independence she had seen enough to know that his complaints were valid. At least once a day there was some kind of commotion created by men inexperienced in handling livestock and wagon gear.

The place was becoming an emotional tender box, simply from the tension of idleness. Most of these pioneers had come with excitement coursing in their veins only to park here and wait. Cramped far too closely together for comfort, tempers flared easily between people and animals alike.

It was difficult to know who was in charge. Money was paid to the company who sponsored the wagon train, but the wagon master who was to lead it had not yet arrived. McCloud threatened to strike out on his own if something didn't happen soon. That made Catherine very uneasy since McCloud had no more sense of where they were going than the entire group of greenhorns he complained about.

The mules had been traded for oxen, a team of twelve for the large wagon, and ten for the smaller one. Every wagon in the train was necessarily accompanied by a similar number of stock, and the gaseous smell of animal waste was particularly hard on Susannah in her condition. Camp rules stated that owners of the beasts were to help clean up the penned area each morning, but it didn't always happen that way. Jeremy and McCloud went at least twice a day to check on their animals to make certain they were fed and in condition to travel when the order came to pull out.

Catherine tried not to complain about her own boredom knowing there was nothing anyone could do. She had read more chapters in her Bible than she'd read the whole rest of the year. She wrote in her journal, but didn't want to use up the entire beautiful book before they got started on the trail. A letter to David was in progress as she added anything of interest that took place each day. Knowing he would be reading it as one letter she tried not to mention every time she wrote that she missed him terribly. When she thought of him, her hand would reach for the heart at her neck. She could close her eyes even now and see him promising to come and find her. Sometimes she felt comforted by those images, at other times they brought her to tears, and this was one of the latter, so she'd better not go there!

With a sigh Catherine put away her journal. Maybe she could take a walk around the inside row of the wagons. If her mother was feeling up to it, maybe she'd go with her. She swung down from the wagon, proud that she could do it without help, and walked over to the back of the larger wagon.

Susannah had the drawstring closure open for air to blow through the wagon as she sat on the bed. Jeremy had built a set of steps for easy access to the inside when the wagon was stopped. Catherine used them now to join her mother.

"Hi, honey, did you finish your writing?" Susannah asked.

"There's not enough new stuff happening to waste all my paper," Catherine moped. "Do you feel up to taking a walk with me?"

"I'd like that, but you know we can't leave the wagons unsupervised." Catherine had forgotten about the thievery that was such a problem. Even in broad daylight it was necessary to have someone at the wagons. McCloud and Jeremy had gone to a meeting of the men who were signed up for the train, so it was up to the womenfolk to stay with the wagons.

"I've been watching the children play and envying them because they have something to do. Would it be all right if I just walked down the row of wagons? Some of them are really a sight to see," Catherine said.

"I noticed some creativity out there, too. One wagon has so many things hanging all over it, you can hardly see any of the canvas top," Susannah said with a smile.

"Can you imagine how noisy it is to ride inside that with all those tools and pots and pans banging together?" Catherine cringed at the thought.

"I noticed that the man driving it looked to be as colorful a character as his wagon suggests. I think he must be a tinker or salesman of some sort."

"Another person who plans to get rich quick in the west, maybe."

"That could be true. You know, it will be time to start preparing something to eat soon. If you'd like to stretch your legs a bit you could take the bucket to that pump at the end of the wagon yard and bring me some fresh water to boil potatoes," Susannah said.

"Yes!" Catherine jumped up, bumping her head on the top of the wagon. "Something to do! I'll be right back." Taking the tin bucket from its hook near the water barrel, she started down the line of wagons toward the hand pump that supplied water to this part of the wagon yard. She dodged a little boy running after a crude ball made from rolled up strips of rags, and skirted a hop-scotch game marked out in the dirt by four dirty-faced little girls.

"I don't think Mama ever let me get *that* dirty," she thought. Then she remembered being covered in mud just weeks ago when she and Jeremy fell into the pond. She laughed out loud, thinking of how ridiculous they had looked. A baby girl sat digging in the dirt with a spoon, and hearing Catherine laugh, she looked up and squealed in delight. Catherine couldn't resist the pretty child and stooped to pat her chubby cheeks.

"Hi, baby," she smiled at the toddler.

The little one smiled back at Catherine and babbled a mouthful of indefinable sounds as she waved her spoon.

"You are so cute," Catherine told her, and looked around to see who might be caring for her. She met the gaze of a girl who looked to be about her age. Her dark hair was pulled back and fell below her shoulders in soft curls. With a shy smile she greeted Catherine, who couldn't help thinking what beautiful brown eyes she had.

"I think she's saying she likes you," the girl said, rising from the wooden crate where she'd been sitting.

"Well, I like her too. Hi, I'm Catherine. We're parked down the row there and I'm bored stiff."

"I'm Elizabeth. Everyone calls me Liz, and this is my little sister, Hannah. She's happy, no matter what's going on, but like you, I'm getting tired of this place."

"Maybe today the men will have some news about when we'll be leaving."

"I hope so, my father is really getting impatient," Liz said.

"I have a step-father, and he's getting pretty restless too. My mother is going to have a baby, and the animal smells here make it hard for her. She spends most of her time with a scented handkerchief at her nose."

"At least our wagon is far enough away that the smell's not so bad." Liz said.

"Do you take care of Hannah often?" Catherine asked.

Liz nodded, looking down at the baby still happily gurgling and waving her spoon. "I don't really mind, she's so sweet. My mother went to buy milk for her."

"Do you have other brothers and sisters?" Catherine asked.

"There's just my younger brother, Billy, but believe me, he's enough," Liz said. "Everything is a joke to him. He does help keep things kind of light-hearted, though. We came from the east coast, and the wagons moved so slowly, it really got boring."

"We're from Lexington, not that far away, but it was enough to make me know I'm not looking forward to months of traveling at that pace," Catherine confessed.

"Hello! I see my girls have made a friend," Catherine turned to see a smiling woman with Liz's dark hair and eyes.

"Hi, I'm Catherine. You have to be Liz's mother," she replied, offering her hand.

"I am indeed, Catherine. I'm Grace Tanner. I'm so glad Liz has met someone her age. She's been lonely on this trip." She shook Catherine's hand then reached down to pick up Hannah who had toddled over to her.

"I've really been missing my friends from home too," Catherine confessed. "I actually met Hannah before Liz. She's so cute I just couldn't walk by without speaking to her. You'll have to meet my mother. I know she'd welcome the company."

The mention of her mother caused Catherine to remember the purpose of her walk this direction. "Oh, I forgot I was coming after water for my mother to cook supper. Please, come to our wagon anytime. We're in space forty-nine. I have a brother, too, and even though I give him a hard time, he's really a nice fellow." She looked in the direction of their wagon and saw Susannah looking for her.

"Oh, my mother's getting worried about me, I've got to go. It was so good to meet you, Liz, Mrs. Tanner, and Hannah. I'll see you again soon."

Catherine impulsively reached out to hug her new friend. Grabbing her water pail, she waved to Susannah to let her know she was on her way.

As she pumped the water and carried it back to their wagon her heart was light. "What a difference it makes to

96

have a friend," she thought. Maybe Jeremy could be buddies with Liz's brother and they could all have fun times together. Surely it wouldn't be all drudgery for the next few months!"

*   *   *   *

Susannah and Catherine were finishing the preparations for their evening meal when they heard the sounds of men talking as they made their way back to camp. The tone of excitement in the air could mean only one thing … they would be moving out soon. Susannah looked up from her kettle to see Jeremy and Pollard McCloud winding their way back to the wagons.

She couldn't help but return the smile on McCloud's face as he lifted her and twirled her around. No matter what differences had been between them, everyone was thrilled to be "jumping off" from Independence and starting the journey.

"So when do we go?" she asked.

"In two days," McCloud answered. "We can finally leave this stinking place behind."

"Has the wagon master arrived?" Susannah asked.

"He got in this morning; 'Jackson' is his name. He said he'd been waiting to hear from his scouts that grass was high enough on the prairie to feed the stock. They could starve if the trains go out before there's enough growth for the cattle to eat, then there'd be no way to move the wagons," McCloud said.

Catherine stopped mashing the potatoes. Her blue eyes widened as she asked, "Then what would happen to the people?"

McCloud paused, then said, "Nothing good."

97

The reality of the hardship of the journey ahead of them had destroyed the lighthearted mood of minutes earlier. Jeremy quickly made an attempt to dispel the fear he could see on Catherine and Susannah's worried faces.

"Hey, Mr. Jackson just told us that because some of the loud-mouths were giving him a hard time about not being here sooner! He was trying to convince them that he knows what he's doing, and that's why he's the one in charge. He doesn't have any intention of leaving anybody on the trail."

McCloud added to Jeremy's comments. "He's going to inspect every rig tomorrow, and if they don't meet the standards, the people don't get to join the train. They have to qualify by having a sturdy enough wagon and supplies for repairs, and also enough in the way of food for every person in each party."

"Well, I feel better knowing that," Susannah said. "Catherine, why don't we celebrate with a jar of our home-canned peaches for dessert? Fellows, by the time you wash up we'll be ready to eat."

As she dished up potatoes, beans and salt pork in four tin plates she wondered how many meals like this she'd prepare before they could eat as they had on the farm.

She wouldn't even attempt a guess!

Chapter 7

"Look, Liz! Over there ... blackberries, and lots of them!" Catherine pointed to an area where purple-dotted vines stretched across and around bushes and rocks. It was early afternoon and the girls were walking behind the McCloud wagons. They alternated between families, a habit they had begun in the first few days on the trail. Their friendship had deepened quickly through hours of conversation. Still, boredom easily set in around this time of day and the sight of the berries was a welcome diversion.

"Do you think we could pick some?" Liz asked.

"I'll ask my mother if it's all right." Catherine said. When she looked into the wagon, she saw that Susannah was napping with little Hannah. As the families became acquainted Susannah had immediately grown attached to the Tanner baby. Grace Tanner walked the trail herself, but carrying a chubby toddler made that difficult. Hannah napped for hours in the afternoon, so Susannah kept her for Grace.

Catherine didn't like leaving the train without telling her mother. But she also didn't want to disturb Susannah's rest, so the girls decided to pick a few berries and then catch up with the train. They were certain they could be back before Susannah awoke. Catherine grabbed the water pail from the side of the wagon and the girls ran back to find their treasure.

The berries were full and juicy and sweet to the taste. At first, the girls ate almost as many as they dropped in the pail. The vines were heavy with fruit, enticing them from one area to another. When they filled the pail to the top, they started back to the wagon. They were surprised to find they had gone farther from the trail than they realized, and most of the train had passed them by. It was highly unlikely they would be able to catch up to the McCloud wagons until the train stopped for the night.

Catherine knew her mother would be frantic with concern. Liz was worried that Hannah had awakened from her nap and needed to be taken back to Grace. That was generally her job. The girls tried running, carrying the pail between them, but almost lost their prized berries, so they settled for walking as quickly as they could. The train ahead created a cloud of dust that made it difficult to breathe. With their bonnets pulled down for protection they didn't see Jeremy riding up on Midnight until he had almost reached them. He was leading McCloud's horse, Flame, as well.

"Hey, you two! You gave Ma a scare when she couldn't see you." Jeremy chided.

"Jeremy! I don't even care if you scold me … I'm so glad you're here," Catherine said, gasping for breath. "How did you know where to find us?"

"Billy saw you headed off the trail with the water bucket. He had noticed the blackberries, so he figured that's where you were going. 'Forgot the time, huh?"

"The vines were so full, Jeremy. We just couldn't bear to leave them there. It's been so long since we've had anything fresh. Mama was sleeping and I didn't want to wake her."

"We didn't mean to worry your mother, Jeremy. I hope she's not worn out from keeping Hannah," said Liz with concern.

"I think Hannah's still sleeping, but we'd better get back so Ma will know you're all right. One of you can ride Flame," Jeremy said.

Liz stood still, a pink flush rising up her face, "I, uh, I don't know how to ride a horse. We lived in the city."

Jeremy grinned, "Well, Cat knows how, so you can ride with her ... or ... with me." Now it was his turn to blush. Catherine thought she'd noticed a little interest between the two of them, but knowing Jeremy, she might have to help things along.

"Well, somebody's got to take the berries, so Liz, hold these while I mount Flame. Then give them to me and you can ride with Jeremy," Catherine said as she handed Liz their pail of treasure.

Jeremy held the reins while Catherine mounted Flame, then Liz handed the fruit up to her friend. Catherine carefully situated the berries in front of her then took the reins. Liz was completely red-faced now as she tried to figure out how to get up on Midnight.

"Here, I'll show you," Jeremy said. "I'll hold the reins. Reach up and catch a handful of the mane with your left hand, and use this stirrup as a step for your left foot." Jeremy held the stirrup steady for her.

"Hold onto the back of the saddle with your right hand, push up on your left foot, swinging your right leg over ... but try not to land too hard in the saddle."

Liz had never felt so incapable in her life, and she could have sworn there was real animosity coming from this horse to her. Lifting her foot high enough to reach the stirrup was quite a stretch, and as she tried to push herself up, Midnight moved just enough to make her lose her foothold, landing her soundly on the hard ground on her backside. Jeremy quickly bent down to help her.

"Are you all right, Liz?" he asked with concern, and then to his sister, "Cat, stop laughing!" He turned back to Liz and found her laughing too. He couldn't help but notice the way her brown eyes sparkled, and he thought she was the prettiest girl he'd ever seen sitting in the middle of a dusty wagon trail.

"I'm sure glad you didn't have the berries, because I really like berry cobbler," he said with a grin.

"O.K., let's try this again." He helped Liz to her feet and waited while she dusted herself off. Seeing a large rock nearby, he walked Midnight over to it, so Liz could use it as a stepping stool. This time she made it into the saddle, certain that this was the clumsiest horse-mounting ever!

"You make it look so easy," she said to Jeremy as he effortlessly swung up behind her.

"Lots of practice," he said. Liz sat stiffly, as if scared to death of the horse, or of being that close to Jeremy, or perhaps, a combination of the two. Jeremy had never been that close to a girl either. But Liz was really nice- as well as being pretty- and didn't giggle all the time like the girls back home. He'd have to think about this some more.

Susannah was watching anxiously for Jeremy and the girls from the back of the wagon. She gave a sigh of relief when she saw them approaching, then her eyes widened in surprise at the sight of Liz riding with Jeremy. Liz caught the look and blushed.

"Mrs. McCloud, I'm sorry we stayed so long. We saw the blackberries and wanted to get some. We lost track of time. I hope Hannah hasn't been too much for you."

Jeremy slowed Midnight to the pace of the moving wagon while Susannah assured Liz that Hannah had been asleep while the girls were gone.

Catherine pulled up on Flame and showed her mother the pail full of berries.

"Look, Mama, the vines were full. We just couldn't stop picking them. I'm sorry we worried you. We didn't realize how long we were there. Can we make cobbler in the Dutch oven this evening?"

"Cobbler is a wonderful idea, but girls, leaving the trail without my knowing, definitely was not a good decision. I don't think you're aware of the dangers involved in being off by yourselves like that. Let's make sure this is the last time this happens, O.K?" Susannah scolded, as the girls agreed.

"Liz, why don't you ask your folks to join us and we can have supper together," Susannah suggested.

"Did I hear something about eating?" a cheery voice called.

Liz turned to see her brother, Billy driving the team of the McCloud's smaller wagon. "I declare, Billy, you could hear talk of food a mile away!"

"I can smell it that far, too," Billy said with a grin. His skinny frame mistakenly gave the impression that he'd done without regular meals. His wheat-colored hair stood on end all around his head, and when he smiled, his green eyes turned up at the corners. Billy could find humor in even the most tedious tasks, so his good nature made him a welcome guest at any campsite in the train. When he brought out his guitar around the fire in the evening, he always drew a crowd.

"Thanks for taking the reins while I went after these girls," Jeremy said to him.

"No problem. These oxen and me get along just fine. If they get bored, I just sing 'em a little tune," Billy said.

"You got enough tunes to last till the end of this long trail, Billy?" Jeremy asked.

"Well, if I run out, I'll just make up some more. How 'bout a song about two foolish girls ..."

Making up a tune, Billy sang,

"Two girls pickin' berries got lost from the train,
The wagons kept a'rollin,' they were never seen again.
So now the tale is told about this section of the trail,
That two ghosts are seen a'cryin' with berries in a pail."

Just then one of the oxen turned his head in Billy's direction and brayed toward the sky. Everyone burst out laughing at the animal's response to Billy's song. Not to be outdone, Billy continued, "O.K., so you didn't like my ghost song. How 'bout this one, Mr. Bovin?"

" There once was an ox that was pulling on a load
He said to himself, I'm getting sick o' this road ..."

*   *   *   *

From his seat on the front of the wagon McCloud could hear the banter and laughter between the young folks. He didn't know why it irritated him. It irked him that

Catherine was riding his horse, too, which didn't make sense because Jeremy had asked permission before he took Flame. McCloud had decided it was best to stay out of any situations with Susannah's children after the fiasco at the farm with the girl and the preacher's son. He didn't want to jeopardize things with Susannah. He tried to see that she didn't work too hard; he didn't want her losing that baby. The trip was taking its toll on her, though. He could see it in her eyes, and the way she walked, as though it took all her strength to do the necessary chores.

With a deep sigh, McCloud looked away from the dusty trail ahead of him to the range of mountains he could see in the distance... The idea of traveling west was not nearly as romantic here in this dry, rough terrain as the thoughts of it had been back in Lexington.

It seemed to him that there were two states of condition on the trail ... boredom or crisis! They hadn't covered even a third of the distance, nor had they reached the mountain range where traveling could possibly be in the crisis state most of the time. There wouldn't be any going back then. He needed to make a change soon. Leaving the wagon train would mean losing the money he'd paid to sign up, but not even that thought was enough to make him want to stay the course. He couldn't talk about it to Susannah, though. He'd sold her farm to do this, and had moved her family away from everything and everyone familiar. Pride wouldn't allow him to admit it had been a mistake. But it wasn't over yet. From the beginning he'd hoped to run across some way to avoid making the whole trip west for land. Something would come up, and he'd be watching for it.

McCloud reached in his pocket for a smoke and saw the wagon master approaching on horseback. Thomas

Jackson turned his horse so he could ride alongside the wagon.

"Howdy, McCloud," Jackson tipped his hat.

"How's it going, Jackson?" McCloud returned.

"I think we've gone about as far as we should for the day. There's a good place to camp up ahead, plenty of wood and water, and some pretty good grazing too. The front wagons will reach it in about a half hour, so we'll stop there for the night."

"'Sounds good to me."

Jackson nodded and continued on to the farm wagon. He told Jeremy they would be stopping soon and tipped his hat in greeting to Susannah and Catherine as they rode in the back of the large wagon.

"Mrs. McCloud, Miss, 'hope you're doing well today."

"We are, Mr. Jackson. We'll be stopping soon?" Susannah asked.

"Yes, ma'am, we've made good time today, and there's a camp site ahead that's probably the best we'll see for a while," Jackson replied.

"You'll have to come by later this evening for some berry cobbler and coffee. The girls saw the vines full of the berries and couldn't resist picking some earlier."

"That's an invitation I can't refuse, ma'am. We don't get too many treats like that on the trail. But for now, I'd best be moving on down the train." Jackson politely nodded as he went on to the next wagon. He couldn't help thinking what a pretty woman that Mrs. McCloud was. He didn't remember her having those dark circles under her eyes when they started, though. It didn't look like she was taking this trip very well.

*   *   *   *

The rosy glow of the rising sun gave just enough light for Jeremy to see the words in his Bible.

"*O Give thanks unto the Lord, for he is good: for his mercy endureth for ever,*" he read aloud to Catherine. "*Let the redeemed of the Lord say so, whom he hath redeemed from the hand of the enemy. And gathered them out of the lands, from the east, and from the west, from the north, and from the south. They wandered in the wilderness in a solitary way: they found no city to dwell in.*"

"That sure sounds like us," Catherine said.

Jeremy continued, "*Hungry and thirsty, their soul fainted in them. Then they cried unto the Lord in their trouble, and he delivered them out of their distresses. And he led them forth by the right way, that they might go to a city of habitation.*"

"What Psalm is that?" Catherine asked. "I want to mark it in my Bible. I know it was written about the Israelites, but I believe it's for us too."

"It's Psalm 107, verses one through seven," Jeremy told her.

"*Oh that men would praise the Lord for his goodness, and for his wonderful works to the children of men! For he satisfieth the longing soul, and filleth the hungry soul with goodness,*" Catherine continued with verse eight. Then laying her Bible aside, she said thoughtfully, "You know, Jeremy, God really has been good to us on this trip. We haven't had any problems, even with our wagons and animals like some of the folks have. When I left David behind I didn't think I could ever feel happy again. I do miss him so much, but I'm not sad all the time. And I know you miss the farm and your friends too, but you don't seem to be terribly unhappy either."

"It's called 'grace,'" Cat," Jeremy said, "God gives us His ability to handle the tough things if we live for Him. He promised in *II Corinthians 12:9* that His grace would be sufficient for us, no matter how weak and incapable we feel in our own strength."

Speaking softly, Catherine said, "I think we really need to believe that for Mama. I can tell this trip is getting harder for her. She looks worn out all the time."

"I know. I saw that too. Just keep doing all you can to help her, Cat. There's not much I can do when we break camp. The chores with the animals keep me busy."

Their conversation was interrupted by a pleasant, "Good morning." Catherine and Jeremy looked up to see Liz, smiling as she held a cast iron skillet of hot, fresh biscuits with a thick towel to keep from burning her hands.

Jeremy jumped up to take it from her and sat it on their makeshift table. "Wow, this is a nice gift so early in the morning. Did you make these?" he asked.

"No, I have to confess, my mother made them. She appreciates your mother helping her with Hannah so she wanted to do a little something for her," Liz said.

"Well, I like that deal," Jeremy said, "Ma keeps Hannah, and we get the rewards."

"Only your share, buddy," Catherine warned him. She reached down to pick up their Bibles to put them away, and Liz noticed them.

"You were reading the Bible?" she questioned.

"We try to read every morning before we get started on the trail," Catherine replied. "We used to read by ourselves, but it's more fun to do it together. We really miss our church back home."

Just then Susannah stepped down from the wagon.

"Look, Ma, Mrs. Tanner sent us a skillet full of biscuits," Jeremy said. "Don't you think we need to eat them so Liz can take their skillet back?"

"You just hold your horses, young man," Susannah scolded him. "I'll have the rest of our breakfast ready in a few minutes. Liz, this is so nice of your mother; it cuts my cooking time in half. Tell her I really appreciate it."

"She appreciates your helping her with Hannah, too," Liz told her.

"Well, that is my pleasure. I think she's the happiest baby I've ever known. Would you like to have breakfast with us?" Susannah asked.

"Thank you, Mrs. McCloud, but I need to help my mother get things ready for the road," Liz said.

"I'll come to your wagon before we get started," Catherine said, "and thanks for the biscuits. I'll bring your skillet back then."

The morning chores had fallen into a routine. After breakfast, McCloud and Jeremy went to hitch up the animals while Catherine and Susannah packed up the cooking utensils and put out the fire. Taking one last look around to be certain they were not leaving anything behind, Catherine took the skillet and headed for the Tanner's wagon to walk with Liz.

It was a fresh, clear morning. Since the train was just starting, the air had not yet been filled with dust. Several species of wild flowers were in bloom, none of them familiar to travelers from the east.

"I wish we could keep some of those pretty pink flowers," Catherine said, pointing them out to Liz.

"I know, but they'd just wilt, and we'd have to throw them away. Mama said I can't use our water for flowers," Liz replied.

"I'll be glad when we get wherever it is we're going, and we won't have to worry about having enough water."

"Do you know where your family is going to settle?" Liz asked.

"I have no idea. I haven't heard my stepfather say. Honestly, I wonder if he knows. Jeremy asked him one time and he never gave a direct answer. He acted irritated that anyone questioned him, so we've never brought it up again."

"We're supposed to meet my uncle in Oregon City. He has some land picked out for us north of there. I sure hope your family will be close to that area."

"That would be great, but I don't know where we'll be. The scriptures Jeremy and I were reading this morning sounded just like us on this wagon train. It talked about God's people going through the wilderness with no city, but then the Lord led them the right way to the city where He wanted them to be."

Liz sounded thoughtful, "Catherine, you and Jeremy … you're … you're *real* Christians, aren't you?"

Catherine smiled. "I think that's the only kind of Christian to be."

"I guess that's true, but usually it's the adults who read their Bibles and talk about God. I don't think I know anyone else our age who does. I've heard you say other things that make me realize that you really have a relationship with Him."

"You're a Christian, too, aren't you, Liz?"

Liz paused a moment before answering. "If someone had asked me that question a few months ago I would automatically have said, 'yes.' But since I've met you, I know I don't have the kind of relationship with God that you do, and it makes me wonder if I truly am a Christian. I accepted Christ when I was young in my Sunday School class, but I'm wondering if I really knew what it meant."

"Liz, it's kind of like you and I meeting. If we'd never talked again since that day I stopped to play with Hannah, we could say we knew each other. But since we've had hours of sharing our hearts as we walk together, we have a relationship. God already knows everything about us, but as we read His Word … that's His way of talking to us … we get to know Him by listening to what He says in the Bible."

"So the more you read the Bible, the more personal relationship you have with Him …" Liz mused.

"I know a lot of young people don't really like to read the Bible, but for some reason, I've always loved it," Catherine said.

"I think God has a special plan for your life, Catherine," Liz said.

"I believe He has special plans for all of our lives, yours included, Liz."

"Well, I'm certainly glad it was in His plan for us to be friends," Liz said as she reached out to give Catherine's hand a squeeze. "I'll be thinking about this."

CHAPTER 8

The chestnut mare practically shivered with excitement as David swung the saddle onto Star's back. She knew this meant escape from the confinement of the barn and pawed the ground in anticipation.

"You're ready to go, aren't you, girl?" David said as he tightened the girth.

The horse reached around to nuzzle David's shoulder in agreement. Packing his lunch and a canteen of water into one side of the saddle bag and his Bible and writing materials into the other, David was all set. Swinging up into the saddle, he reined Star out into the early morning air. The streets of Lexington were almost empty at this time of day, and within minutes David and Star were headed toward the country.

Star willingly stretched out into a gallop and David was glad they didn't encounter other travelers that would slow them down. As the wind blew in his face, the heaviness he'd been feeling was blown away as well. He had expected to miss Catherine, but he wasn't prepared for the depth of loneliness that engulfed him at times.

Out of habit he had ridden the direction of the Sutherland farm. It would be interesting to see what was happening there. He reined Star to a slower pace as they neared the turn-off to the farm. He didn't go through the gate, not knowing how he'd explain his presence if anyone asked, but stopped a few yards short of it.

His heart ached as he looked at the house that had been almost as familiar to him as his own home. The place had an air of sadness about it. The porch swing where David and Catherine had spent many hours in conversation now hung uselessly from one chain. David could see that the crops were doing well; obviously someone was tending them, but around the house and barn there was no sense of life, no love. "Even the farm misses the people who belong there," David thought as he turned Star back to the road.

There was only one direction he wanted to go today- to his and Catherine's special place. Star still had some "run" in her, so David turned her loose and soon found himself at the bottom of the bluff. Tying the reins to a tree, he threw the saddle bag over his shoulder and left the horse to graze while he made his way to the beautiful pond and waterfall. Flowers still bloomed, though Catherine's favorite roses were gone for the season. David climbed up to the rock where he and Catherine had shared their last picnic. Stretching out full length on the sun-warmed ledge he took two worn letters from his pocket. He unfolded the first one, the letter Catherine had given him as they said their good-byes. He could have quoted it by heart, but reading the words in her handwriting always made him feel closer to her.

My Dearest David,
    It seems just days ago that we were making plans for our future. Then my life was totally upended and I found that, at

least for the present, I have no say at all in regard to my future. I never expected to be separated from you, my constant friend for so many years, and now the love of my heart. Every time I think of the time and distance that will be between us I feel that I have come up against an immoveable wall. That helplessness brings utter despair to my heart if I allow it to stay for even a moment. My only comfort is in knowing that our Heavenly Father has promised to work all things for our good. As I leave everything that has been familiar to me, I know I must remember that God loves me and will never leave me. Then I must remind myself that you, My Love and My Friend, hold me in your heart as I hold you in mine.

As difficult as the journey ahead may be, the hardest part will be not having you there to share the new experiences with me. Still, I will talk to you, My David ... listen carefully and surely you will hear the cry of my heart, even across the miles. Hear me when I tell you that I miss you terribly, that I love you still, and that I am waiting for you to bring me home to your arms.

With all my heart,
Catherine

The ache in David's heart was an actual physical pain as he carefully folded the letter and put it away. He picked up the second one, the only one he had received from Catherine since they left. She had mailed it the day they left Independence and he never tired of reading it. He could envision her blue eyes sparkling as she described the wagon yard there, and laughed at her tales of the colorful people around. It was wonderful to know she had met a friend whose family was part of the wagon train too. He'd heard tales of the difficulties of the trip, but surely it would be easier with a friend alongside. As he read the closing words of Catherine's letter he could feel her love for him. With a groan of despair he dropped his head to the rock and closed his eyes. It was in this very place that he had kissed Catherine for the first time, where they had professed their love for each other. For some time he lay there -- one with the rock-- and it was as though the love he and Catherine shared in that place had permeated nature and remained to bring healing to his aching heart.

If only he knew how she was doing. Catherine could be in great danger as he went about his daily routine and he would have no way of knowing. He prayed for her every morning and at other times when she was heavy on his heart; that was all he could do. David had never felt so helpless. Apparently, this was a time of learning to trust, to place whole-hearted confidence in God when there was nothing to stand on other than His promises.

David opened his Bible to the Psalm he'd been reading earlier that morning. It seemed so appropriate now. *Ps. 71:3 Be thou my strong habitation, whereunto I may continually resort: thou hast given commandment to save me; for thou art my rock and my fortress.*

"God, You are so faithful," David prayed quietly. "Thank you, Father." He carefully put away Catherine's letters and stood to stretch his muscles. He didn't need to see that the sun was directly overhead to know it was noon.

115

The familiar rumble of his stomach announced mid-day like clockwork.

His meal today didn't compare to the lunch he and Catherine had eaten there, but it would have to do. As David munched on his sandwich he thought of the things he wanted to write to Catherine. There wasn't that much to tell. He still studied with his father, went to church and to work. However, he could tell her how pleased Mr. Goodson was with the sales of the jewelry he was making. He had begun to study the craft, especially in regard to very old pieces. It seems he was developing his own style, blending ideas from antique designs with more up-to-date methods. His pieces were beginning to sell quickly now, and every commission was going into the bank for his and Catherine's future. She should be glad to hear that.

Finished with his lunch now and feeling light of heart, he pulled out his pad and pencil and began to write.

*   *   *   *

The bells on the door of the Jewelry and Watch Emporium jangled loudly as the door swung open. Silas Goodson looked up from the brooch he was cleaning. Two finely dressed women entered, one whom he recognized as Mrs. Evelyn Brunswick, a long-time customer. He knew that she spent part of the year in Lexington and the remainder in New York City, which she claimed as her home. He rose to greet her.

"Mrs. Brunswick, how nice to see you again. It appears that New York is treating you well."

Shaking the hand Goodson offered, Evelyn Brunswick replied, "It is indeed, Mr. Goodson, but it's nice

116

to be back in Lexington." Turning to the young woman with her she said, "This is my niece, Miss Charlotte Pendleton. She's here to keep me company."

"Welcome to Lexington, Miss Pendleton." Silas Goodson noted that the young lady had an air of confidence about her as she firmly returned his handshake. Appearing to be about seventeen, she was dressed in much the same modern style as her aunt in a full- skirted velvet dress of emerald green. Under her fashionable bonnet her auburn hair lay in curls about her face. Her smooth skin seemed never to have seen a day of sun, yet a glow tinged her cheeks that matched the life in her green eyes. "Striking," Goodson thought to himself.

"Since this is my favorite jewelry store I wanted to bring Charlotte to choose something as a reminder of her visit," Mrs. Brunswick said. "What would you suggest?"

"Well, young lady," Goodson said, walking behind the counter, "What is your preference? We have rings, bracelets, necklaces, brooches ..."

The jangling of the bells on the door interrupted Silas Goodson as David rushed into the shop. Excitedly he called to his employer, "We got the supplies from back east ..." He quickly stopped as he saw the two women. Their large hoop skirts practically filled the small shop. This type of finery was not often seen in Lexington, and David was embarrassed that he had entered the shop so crudely. Mrs. Brunswick, he recognized; the younger woman he had never seen. He had also never seen a girl her age dressed so elegantly. Trying to recoup some sort of composure David put down the package and bowed to the ladies.

"Good afternoon, ladies. I apologize for my ... my rude entrance."

"It was only 'lively,' not rude," laughed Mrs. Brunswick. "I believe you're David Winters?"

"Yes, how do you do, Mrs. Brunswick?" David replied.

To Miss Pendleton Mr. Goodson said, "David is my very capable--if loud at times-- assistant. A new supply of gems to work with always excites him as he is designing most of our jewelry now." To David he said, "This young lady is Miss Charlotte Pendleton, Mrs. Brunswick's niece."

"Mr. Winters, perhaps you'd like to show her some of your work. We'd like something as a remembrance of her trip to Lexington," Mrs. Brunswick said.

David could feel the heat rising up his neck and knew that he was blushing. He didn't understand why. He showed his jewelry often and didn't feel uncomfortable.

"I think I'd like to look at bracelets, Mr. Winters," Miss Pendleton said, taking charge of the situation as she gave David a warm smile.

David had the impression that not only was she aware of his discomfort, she was enjoying the fact that she was somehow responsible for it. Everything about her was perfectly in place and extremely attractive. Maybe if he hadn't come into the shop like a hawker pushing wares on the street he wouldn't feel like such a fumble-foot. "Just show her the jewelry," David said to himself.

There were six bracelets on the black velvet pad David set on the counter. Two were designs in gold only, the other four contained precious gems set in gold, each with its own unique design.

With a gasp of delight, Charlotte Pendleton's attention was completely absorbed by the sparkling pieces in front of her.

"Ohhhh, look, Aunt Evelyn! They're beautiful! I want to try them all."

"They are lovely indeed, Mr. Winters," Mrs. Brunswick exclaimed. "Your designs are unique."

"David has developed his own style. I can see in the future that people will be talking about wearing a 'David Winters piece,'" Mr. Goodson said.

David looked at Mr. Goodson in surprise. His employer was liberal with his praise and encouragement, but he'd never said those words before. Now David was really blushing. He wished Miss Pendleton would make her selection and go.

"Oh, I'm sorry, what was that?" They were looking at him as if waiting for an answer, and he'd been so lost in his thoughts he didn't hear the question.

Again, Miss Pendleton smiled as though used to men acting like idiots in her presence. "I was asking if you could shorten the length without losing the beauty of the design. I have very small wrists, Mr. Winters, and I couldn't bear the thought of losing your beautiful bracelet."

The piece she was wearing was David's favorite. Squarely cut emeralds graced the gold band, each held in place by graceful leaves of gold. The bracelet looked as though it was made to lie against Miss Pendleton's creamy skin. It was the perfect accessory for her emerald green dress.

"I believe I can remove almost an inch without changing the overall appearance," David said.

"Then this is the one I want," Miss Pendleton said convincingly.

"When can you have the adjustments completed, Mr. Winters?" Mrs. Brunswick asked.

David did a quick calculation considering work he already had lined up. It was now Monday ... "I can have it ready on Friday."

"Then we will see you Friday afternoon. Mr. Goodson, you have quite a treasure in this young man," Evelyn Brunswick said.

Charlotte Pendleton gave David one last smile from under her hat as she walked out the door. David had his hand in his pocket and on his watch chain he felt the gold half-heart that signified his love for Catherine. Strangely, he didn't feel like writing her about this sale.

CHAPTER 9

"Whoa! Whoa, there!" All the drivers shouted commands to their oxen as the wagons headed down the steep grade. Distance was needed between each outfit to prevent overtaking the wagon ahead, and hardwood brakes screeched as drivers strove to control their progress. Gravity gave a team relief from the weight of the wagon, but it took skillful handling on the part of the driver to prevent a downhill run-a-way.

At the base of this incline was the outpost where wagon trains normally spent a few days making repairs and re-packing cargo. When they moved out again they would cross the Republic River and immediately be in extremely mountainous terrain. This stretch of the journey placed the greatest strain on the wagons and equipment, so preventive maintenance was of the utmost importance.

Travelers looked forward to reaching the Republic River outpost because it was a stopping place for traffic going both east and west, and it also carried a limited quantity of supplies. Gold-seekers, trappers, and other travelers heading east arrived there ready for a reprieve from the rigors of the mountains behind them. They were hungry for news from home, especially about the political climate in regard to the western territories. People traveling west were eager to know if less strenuous routes with water and grazing had been discovered. Many carried precious letters for strangers either direction until they reached an area where postal service was in effect. This interaction between travelers created a social atmosphere of friendliness and welcome.

As he held his team steady Pollard McCloud's mind was busy at work. He needed to find a way to leave this train before it headed farther west. He had known they'd have to cross mountains. That had not concerned him; he grew up in an area considered to be mountainous back east. But those were no more than hills in comparison to the majestic peaks that lay before them. No, this was not for him. There had to be another way!

Maybe he was imagining it, but it seemed that Susannah was becoming more distant. He knew she had not forgiven him for selling the Sutherland farm, but it was more than that. He only hoped there were no problems with her carrying the baby. This past week she had insisted on walking when the going was rough for the oxen, but in the evening he could see that she was totally exhausted.

"Young Susannah," as he had begun to think of Catherine, did all the cooking now. She had matured on this trip. Any girlish roundness had disappeared, and she was strong and lean due to the miles of walking on a daily basis. She had been a pretty girl when they left Lexington. She was now a beautiful young woman. McCloud imagined that this daughter must look as Susannah had in earlier years, moving with that same graceful bearing as her mother. Still innocently oblivious to the admiring gazes of men on the train, all she thought about was that preacher's son back east. McCloud saw how many times she reached to touch the gold heart necklace that kid had given her. She was young and foolish enough to think that someday he'd really come looking for her.

"Whoa!" The oxen moved too quickly, closing the distance between them and the wagon ahead. McCloud figured he'd better concentrate on getting this rig down the hill safely, but when they got situated, he intended to do some talking to other travelers and see what he could learn. As determined as he had been to be part of this wagon train, he was now just as desperate to leave it.

*   *   *   *

"I haven't felt this good in months," Catherine declared, tossing her wet curls.

"I will never again take for granted the ability to bathe," agreed Grace Tanner.

"And to wash my hair," said Liz.

Susannah agreed, and baby Hannah just laughed out loud, her little face shiny clean as her dark curls quickly dried in the breeze.

Most travelers' favorite attributes of the Republic outpost were the simple bathhouses, one for men, and one for women. They were constructed so that fresh spring water was piped into stalls, providing a coveted place to bathe travel weary bodies. No one even complained that the water was ice cold, just gasped in delight to have fresh water flowing over their skin without restricting its measure.

"Now, if I can get my sheets laundered, I think I'll be in 'hog-heaven,'" Grace said, as they walked back to their camps.

As they passed other wagons on the way back to theirs, it was obvious to see that everyone had the same idea. Damp clothing and bedding were spread everywhere.

The trains didn't often stay in one place long enough to boil the laundry and spread it to dry, so everyone took advantage of the chance to start out clean again.

Since the kettles were filled with clothes, supper would be cooked in the coals of the campfires. The outpost had a supply of fresh potatoes so most of the travelers purchased a few to bake among the hot rocks of the fires. These would provide a welcome addition to whatever meat they roasted. It felt like a time to celebrate, so dishes were being prepared at many campsites using precious commodities that were saved for special occasions.

"Do we have enough dried apples for a cake, Mama?" Catherine asked.

"Yes, I think we still have enough," Susannah replied. "Just put them on to soak for a while, so they'll be soft enough for baking. I'll grind some fresh cinnamon."

"That sounds wonderful. We haven't had anything sweet since the berry cobbler," Liz said.

As they neared the wagons, Grace said, "We'll see you later. Liz and I have to get our laundry started."

"Come over for apple cake this evening," Catherine invited. "And tell Billy to bring his guitar."

"We'll do that, and we'll bring a dessert, too," Grace replied.

At Catherine's insistence, Susannah sat in a chair with her feet on a small crate. Lately, they had begun to swell toward the end of the day and keeping them elevated seemed to help. She would never say aloud how exhausted she felt. There was no point in complaining. Regardless of her feelings about the situation, they were on this wagon train, and she was carrying a child that was taking every last bit of strength from her. Susannah wanted to help

Catherine with the laundry, but simply didn't have the energy. What a blessing these few days at the outpost would be. Maybe she'd feel stronger since there would be no need to walk for miles, or even to ride in a wagon over ruts that jarred her to the bones.

As she watched Catherine stirring the pot of boiling laundry her eyes misted with tears. Her little girl had grown up and was working harder than Susannah had ever dreamed she would have to work. She watched Catherine wring out the hot clothes, her hands red from the heat, and the steam causing her hair to curl even more. What would David think if he could see this? Catherine had changed so much since she had left him there in Lexington. Only time would tell if their lives would ever meet again.

Susannah knew Pollard was concerned about her. He tried to get her to talk to him, but there just wasn't anything to say. She was too tired to protest his actions of the past or to talk of plans for the future. Every morning she prayed for strength for "this day," and that was all she had. Susannah could sense the unrest in her husband. She could tell he had not found this trip west to be as imagined. There was a sense of urgency about him since they arrived at the outpost that reminded her of his behavior prior to selling the farm. He was up to something.

*   *   *   *

"That's good enough," McCloud said to Jeremy. "I'll check that last ox; you can go ahead and take a break."

"'Sounds good to me," Jeremy said. "I'm ready to hit that bath house."

The two of them had checked the oxen's hooves, cleaning out small rocks and twigs that could potentially cause infection or soreness. Now McCloud wanted to make a round of the outpost without Jeremy. He didn't want to explain his actions, so he needed to get rid of the kid. It wasn't hard. The idea of a cold, soapy shower was pulling Jeremy like a magnet. It sounded good to McCloud, too, but first he wanted to check out the area. He might have to tell the wagon master the truth. Thomas Jackson was likely to find out more in his position than McCloud could learn on his own. The leaders of the various trains always got together and compared notes and information. He'd have to tell Jackson that he didn't intend to go on with the train in a day or two anyway.

McCloud saw him then, heading toward the corral. Riding his horse to the fence and dismounting, Jackson greeted him.

"'Evening, McCloud, how are your animals?"

"They're doing all right. A few of the oxen had picked up pebbles and such, but none seemed to have any real problems."

"Well, if you need it, the outpost sells a salve concocted by the Indians that heals up soreness in a hoof like magic."

"Good, I'll pick some up in case I need it in the future." Turning to lean on the fence rail, McCloud took a deep breath, "I do have a problem I need to discuss with you, though."

"What's that?" Jackson asked.

"I guess it's pretty evident that ... that my wife is ... is in the family way," McCloud said, awkwardly.

Jackson just nodded.

"We'd already planned to come west before we knew she was going to have a child, and she thought she could make the trip anyway. But she's not doing well; I can see her getting weaker all the time. Now we're headed for the worst part of the route where everyone needs to walk for the oxen's sake, but she's not going to be able to do that."

"If you don't mind my saying, so, McCloud, I did notice that she's not handling the trip well. So what do you have in mind?" Jackson asked.

"I need to drop from the train. I need to go another direction that is not so difficult. I know the government is granting land in Kansas too, and the plains would be easier to travel. I'm looking for a place we can settle, preferably where there would be some kind of shelter already built for my wife's sake."

"You know you'd lose the stake you put up."

"I expected that, but my wife's health is more important. I thought you might hear of something as you talk to other wagon masters over the next couple of days."

"The honest truth, McCloud, is that the remainder of this trip is no place for a woman in your wife's condition. If you're not dead set on making it to Oregon, I think you'd be better off looking for another option. I hate to lose you and that stepson of yours as part of the train, but I'll see what I can find out for you. I'd better get on around to a couple more wagons, but I'll let you know if I hear of something," Jackson said.

McCloud thanked him, gathered up his tools and headed back toward their wagons. He felt like a ton of weight had been lifted from his shoulders. He was excited for the first time in months. He wished he could talk to Susannah about this, but she'd ask a bunch of questions and he didn't have answers yet. It wouldn't be long though, he could feel it!

*   *   *   *

There was just enough light rising over the mountains for Catherine to see what she was writing. She had risen early, and remembering that the train was at rest for a few days, she decided to write to David. She described the Republic River Outpost and the view of the steep mountains that lay to the west. She knew he couldn't truly understand the delight they all found in the bathhouses, but she told him anyway. Trying to give him as many details as possible of her trip since the last letter, she avoided the difficult things, her concern about her mother's health, and fears about what lay ahead. She knew David would be excited to get her letter and she didn't want to fill it with negative things. She told him again how special it was to feel the gold heart at her neck, knowing it represented his love for her. She assured him of her love for him, told him she missed him terribly and lived for the day when he came for her.

Catherine sealed the letter and addressed it to David. Not knowing when she might find someone to carry her letter east, she wanted to be certain to have it ready.

As the sun rose, people were beginning to stir around the various camps. Since the train was not moving out there was no need to be up so early, but it was now habit for them to rise before daylight. Catherine was wide awake so she decided to start a fire at their camp and get breakfast started. McCloud and her mother would likely be up soon.

The wood was burning well and the coffee almost done when she became aware that a woman was standing beside the wagon. She seemed to be waiting for Catherine to notice her, rather than to speak out loud and wake anyone.

Catherine greeted her softly, "Good morning."

"Good morning to you, miss," the woman spoke quietly.

At a glance Catherine could see the worn look about the woman, not just in her clothing, but in her face, which showed the effects of hardship and sorrow. Compassion rose within her. She walked over to the woman and offered her hand in friendship.

"My name is Catherine Sutherland."

"Mine is Dorthea Gibson. I'm camped right behind you… there," she said shyly, pointing to a wagon close by, but not part of a train.

"Would you care for a cup of coffee?" Catherine asked.

Dorthea blushed. "Well, I must admit, that's why I came. I smelled your coffee brewing, and it's been nigh on a year since I've had real coffee. I'm ashamed to be a beggar, but not enough so to stay in my wagon and do without."

Catherine pulled up a camp stool. "Sit here, Mrs. Gibson, it will be my pleasure to give you your first cup of coffee in a year. I'll even have one with you."

Dorthea Gibson's face lit up as though she was as desperate for conversation as for the coffee. Catherine poured two cups of the dark brew, added rich cream and handed a cup to Dorthea.

"On the prairie we grind up all sorts of dried things and boil them to make a coffee substitute. Sometimes it's not so bad," she said, then took a drink from her cup.

"Oh, child, you have no idea how good this is to me." Tears came to her eyes as she again tasted the drink, "And to have cream ... this is heavenly!"

Catherine felt tears in her own eyes as she witnessed the tired woman's pleasure in a simple cup of coffee. She thought of the scripture where Jesus told his disciples that if they gave even a cup of water in His name, it would be as an offering of love unto Him. Surely coffee qualified too.

"It sounds like things have been difficult for you, Mrs. Gibson. Where were you living?" Catherine asked.

"My husband and I were some of the first to take advantage of the land grant in Kansas Territory. It's beautiful there in its own way, but the land is not as 'friendly' as all the advertisements indicated. We never had a single year's crop that brought in enough to get a good start on the next year. The winters are terribly cold, with snow and blizzards that sweep across the prairie for days, sometimes freezing the cattle right where they stand. Summers are hot, but wheat grows well there if you can keep the grasshoppers from eating it, or if a prairie fire doesn't burn it up."

Catherine could hear the despair in Dorthea Gibson's voice and understood now why the woman looked so defeated.

"Last winter my husband got caught in a snowstorm trying to gather the few head of cattle we had left. The storm had come up without warning, or he'd have gone after them earlier. He had frostbite so bad he lost three of his toes. His lungs were never right after that, and finally, he wasn't able to work at all. I think despair was the thing that killed him, though," Dorthea said, not even noticing that Catherine refilled her coffee cup.

"We had no money for supplies to see us through the hard times. We put everything we had into getting to Kansas, and into that first year's crops. We'd hoped to sell the wheat to make it the next year. That just never happened. Somehow, our three children have survived. I really don't know how. They haven't had food enough to eat on a regular basis in over two years." She paused and sat quietly as though lost in the grief of her children's suffering.

Catherine softly asked, "Mrs. Gibson, how is it that you are here?"

"I have people back east," she said. "One of my brothers is headed this way with four other families to go to Oregon Territory. My relatives pooled what money they could spare and sent it to me to come here and meet up with my brother's group. I got the cheapest wagon and team I could buy, and the rest of the money went on food supplies, but they're dwindling fast. I just need to hang on until my brother gets here. He'll have supplies enough for all of us 'til we reach Oregon. My nephews are big boys, and they'll help me get a farm going there instead of in Kansas. My sons will be big enough to help in a year or so, too."

"Well, I'm glad that you'll have family close to you." Catherine said.

"You have no idea how lonely the Kansas plains can be, miss," Dorthea Gibson said, her eyes still showing the depth of suffering she had endured.

Standing to her feet, Dorthea Gibson said, "Well, I'd best be getting back to my wagon. My little ones will be waking up soon and they'll be afraid if I'm not there."

"Mrs. Gibson, please bring your children and have breakfast with us this morning. My mother and stepfather will be up soon and I was going to start cooking for us. There's no telling when my brother will be up since he has the opportunity to sleep late, but my family would love to have you join us.

"Are you sure, Miss Catherine? I wouldn't want to use up your family's food."

"We are well supplied, Mrs. Gibson. Since there's no hurry to get moving today we intend to enjoy a hearty breakfast."

"Then I can't turn down a chance for my children to have a good meal. I'd be glad to help you cook," Dorthea said.

"How are you at making biscuits?" Catherine asked.

Dorthea's face brightened, "I once won a blue ribbon at the county fair for my biscuits," she said proudly.

"Then yours will certainly be better than mine. Why don't you mix them up and get them started baking. I'll fry the bacon and scramble the eggs while you get your children." Catherine pointed to a wooden crate nearby.

"All the ingredients are in this box and there's a mixing bowl and spoon," she said. "We have fresh milk cooling in the spring."

"My children won't know what to think of all this," Dorthea said, wiping a tear from her eye as she poured flour into a bowl. Deftly she worked the dough, shaping the biscuits to fit perfectly into the Dutch oven for baking, and then went to awaken her children.

Catherine began to slice bacon, twice the amount they normally used for their family. She broke two dozen eggs in a bowl and whipped them up to cook last. Digging into the box of preserves, she brought out strawberry and peach and a jar of grape. Thanks to Daisy, they had fresh sweet butter to put on Dorthea's prize-winning biscuits. It was beginning to feel like a party to Catherine.

The flap to the large wagon opened and Susannah and Pollard stepped down.

"Good morning, sweetie," Susannah said, giving Catherine a hug. Eyeing the platter piled high with bacon, she added. "My, what have we here? It looks like a feast."

"We have company coming for breakfast," Catherine announced proudly. "Our neighbors from that wagon over there," she said, pointing to Dorthea's rig.

"I saw them come in yesterday," McCloud said. "'Looked like just a woman and some kids."

"Her name is Dorthea Gibson. She's a widow with three children, coming from Kansas to meet up with family members going on to Oregon Territory. She's had a really hard time of things," Catherine said. "The way she talked, they haven't had a decent meal in a very long time. I just had to ask them to come for breakfast."

"I'm glad you did that; I haven't forgotten what it was like to have so little food to feed you and Jeremy," Susannah said quietly.

Catherine looked at her mother in surprise. She never knew her mother had struggled to feed them. They were too young to know, and Susannah never mentioned the sacrifices she made.

"Should we wake up Jeremy to get the milk and butter from the spring?" Catherine asked.

133

"I'll get it," McCloud offered, "Just let me pour my coffee first."

"Mrs. Gibson made the biscuits," Catherine confessed, pointing to the oven in the coals. "She told me she won a blue ribbon at the county fair for them, and as you know, mine still need a little perfecting."

Susannah smiled, thinking of the hard pellets Catherine had produced at her first attempt at biscuits. "Maybe you should ask her for some tips," she said, counting out plates and forks for the lot of them.

Catherine was pouring the scrambled egg mixture into the huge skillet when Dorthea and her children appeared. Catherine thought she had never seen such thin, hungry-looking children. Their clothing was made as presentable as possible for its worn condition. The boys had long ago outgrown their pants in length, but probably the lack of nourishment had kept them fitting at the waist. The little girl's hair had been neatly braided and the boys' hair had been dampened and combed to the side in an attempt to look their best. Susannah graciously went to welcome their guests as they stood shyly just inside the camp. Each of the children politely extended their hands to Susannah as she came to them, but instead, she gathered them in warm hugs.

"Welcome to our camp," she said to Dorthea as she put her arms around the woman. Seeing the desperation in Dorthea's eyes, she thought to herself, "I know that feeling!" She introduced herself and learned the names of Dorthea's children: Tabitha, Andrew, and George. They could hardly keep their eyes off the food.

"Shall I check the biscuits?" Dorthea asked.

"Please do, I think they should be done by now. The eggs are just about ready and the bacon's already cooked."

"And here is the cold milk and butter," McCloud said, walking into camp. "I swear that spring is as cold as any ice box!" One look at the hungry Gibson children was all McCloud needed to remind him of the many nights he went to sleep on some street corner with hunger pangs gnawing at his belly. He might not be the most honorable man alive, but he was surely not going to allow any kid to go hungry if he could prevent it.

"Here, Susannah, pour these kids some milk," he said, giving her the jar. Then handing each of them a plate, he said, "Come on, kids, let's eat!"

"Mister?" said little Tabitha, looking up at McCloud, "Can I say grace?"

McCloud stooped down to the little girl, and said, "Sure you can, honey."

Everyone stopped to bow their heads as the sweet little voice began:

"Dear God, thank you for hearing us last night when we prayed for food for today, and bless all these nice people for sharing with us. Amen"

Only the children had eyes untouched by tears as Tabitha finished her prayer and everyone said, "Amen." The adults stood aside and allowed the children to fill their plates with the fluffy eggs, bacon, and their mother's truly wonderful biscuits. Then Catherine gave them their choice of the fruit preserves and jelly, promising they could have all they wanted of them. Watching the children's delight as they drank the cold, fresh milk was as touching as Dorthea's joy over the coffee earlier.

"Undoubtedly, this family has been through more hardship than I can imagine," Catherine thought. Just then Jeremy rolled out of his pallet underneath the wagon. With sleepy eyes and tousled hair, he was embarrassed to see that they had guests.

Of course, Catherine couldn't pass up the opportunity to tease her sibling.

"This is my brother, Jeremy … in all of his glory. Jeremy, meet Mrs. Gibson and her children. This is Tabitha, Andrew and George.

Eight year old George giggled and said, "That's the way my hair looks when I wake up!"

"You mean I'm not alone, then?" Jeremy answered back. "That makes me feel better."

"You can comb it down with water," George advised him wisely.

"Except, as soon as his hair dries, it sticks up everywhere again," ten year old Andrew laughed.

"Now you're telling family secrets," Dorthea said.

"Why don't you comb your hair down with water as George suggested, Jeremy, and come eat. There's still food in the skillets," Susannah said.

Jeremy never needed a second invitation to eat, so he did as she suggested. He found an immediate rapport with the children, and laughed and talked with them as they ate. Finally, their stomachs were full for the first time since they could remember, and they were ready to play. After taking on a man's responsibility all through the trip, Jeremy was ready for fun, too. He romped and wrestled with the boys, and even Old Pal found the energy to play fetch with little Tabitha.

McCloud had not said anything, but he had been awake earlier when Dorthea Gibson told Catherine about her situation. He had heard the entire conversation, and now he wanted to know more about what she left behind.

"Mrs. Gibson, what did you do with your place in Kansas?" he asked.

"I simply rode away and left it, Mr. McCloud. I had no other choice," Dorthea insisted. "We were practically at the point of starvation, and out of every kind of supply. I sold the stock one by one, and then had no way to work the fields, even if I could have managed it alone. I sent a letter to my family telling them of my desperate situation and that's when they made the decision to help me come here to join up with my brother and his family. When I received their letter and the money, I barely had time to buy this wagon and supplies and travel here to meet him. He and his party should arrive any day now."

"Do you have plans to return to Kansas?"

"Sir, I would be completely happy to never see Kansas again. I know it has been a good place for some folks, but it was nothing but hardship for my family. It killed my husband. No, Mr. McCloud, I won't ever go back there." Dorthea Gibson said sadly.

"If you were there for a few years I'm assuming you had some kind of house or shelter," McCloud said.

"Yes, we built a sod house, pretty much like everyone else does there. And believe it or not, it was comfortable. I would have preferred it to be larger, but it was adequate. My husband built a small corral for the livestock with a lean-to on one side for shelter.

"Is there water nearby?"

"Yes, there's a nice creek that flows right through the land, and we managed to drill a well the first year we were there," Dorthea said.

"Is your paperwork clear on the property?" McCloud asked.

"Yes, Mr. McCloud, it is. The government requires tenure of five years, and we 'proved up' over a year ago."

"Where in Kansas is your place located?"

"It's in the southwestern corner of the territory. Not far from Fort Dodge."

"But aren't there Indians in that area, Dorthea?" Susannah asked. "I seem to remember hearing about problems with Indians in Kansas, in fact, isn't that the reason the forts are there?"

"Yes, the forts were built to protect trade along the Santa Fe Trail initially. Then when settlers began to come into the area, the soldiers started to patrol the areas within the fort's supervision to let the Indians know they are there. Most of the Indians are friendly, though."

"Did you see them?" Jeremy asked, "Did they ever come to your place?"

"We had visits from the Indians on several occasions. Their ways are totally different from those of the white man. It was their prairie, so they see no reason why they should not enter any dwelling there without so much as a knock at the door. I'll have to admit, that can be quite frightening! They are extremely curious about everything and almost always want food. I don't know anyone who has dared to refuse them, so I have no idea what their response would be to someone opposing them."

"Has anyone you know been injured or killed by the Indians?" McCloud asked.

"I heard of only one incident where the braves were quarrelling with a farmer who did not understand what they wanted. The Indians became more and more frustrated with him, but the poor man had no idea what they wanted him to do. He was extremely relieved when a scouting party of soldiers from Fort Dodge appeared, and the Indians mounted their ponies and rode away," Dorthea said.

"I would think that the more settlers that move into the area, the fewer problems they will have with the Indians," McCloud said.

"Some of the Indian nations have been willing to move aside and allow the white man to take over their lands. Others are not so ready to share. Much of the outcome of this situation will depend on how the government abides by the treaties made with those tribes," Dorthea explained. "I would say though, for my family, situations with the Indians were the least of our problems in Kansas."

Jeremy and the children walked up, red-faced and out of breath, and headed for the water barrel.

"We're thirsty!" George said, his eyes shining.

"Can I have milk?" Andrew asked.

"I think there's barely enough for a glassful left in this jar," Catherine said, 'but do any of you know how to milk a cow?"

Tabitha just shook her head from side to side.

Andrew spoke up, "I can remember watching my ma do it before our cow died."

"Well, would anybody like to learn?" Catherine asked, going for the pail.

All three children yelled, "I would!"

"Then come with me," she said to them, and to herself, "Boy, Daisy's going to love me for this."

Dorthea stood to go. "While Catherine's entertaining my children I'm going to get some laundry started. I can't thank you enough for the delicious breakfast, and it's been wonderful to have adult conversation. I'm sure you can see, my children haven't had this much fun in ages."

"Mrs. Gibson," McCloud said, "Why don't you and your children eat meals with us until your brother arrives? And you can make those biscuits anytime..."

"Dorthea, we'd love to have you," Susanna said.

"Only if you'll allow me to help cook and clean up," Dorthea said.

"Then it's a deal."

"I can get water for your laundry," Jeremy offered.

"Well, I certainly won't refuse that offer. What a blessing all of you have been!" Dorthea said appreciatively. "I'd best get my fire going now."

Jeremy left to get the water as Dorthea went back to her wagon. McCloud and Susannah were left alone.

McCloud took a deep breath then said, "Susannah, I need to talk to you … I don't want to go any farther with this train."

"Because of me? You don't think I can make it?"

"No, I don't. Some days you barely make it now, and the mountains are going to be even worse from here on out. The rivers that have to be crossed are dangerous. I don't want to lose you, and I don't want you to lose our baby. Even Thomas Jackson agreed it's no trip for a woman in your condition."

"You've discussed this with him?" Susannah asked in surprise.

"I talked to him last night. He understood, though he warned me it would mean losing the upfront money."

"You've been thinking about this for a while?"

"Yes, ever since I saw how hard it's getting for you. And honestly, I've had enough of crossing mountains and rivers myself. I just want us to get settled on a place of our own."

"Are you thinking of Dorthea Gibson's place in Kansas?" she asked.

"Susannah, it's everything I was hoping to find: a good sized piece of farm land, a house already built, a corral, a well."

"But Pollard, they had so many problems!"

"This morning I heard her talking to Catherine. She said they had no money to buy supplies when the first crop didn't come through. Farming is always going to be unreliable, you know that. You can't help the storms, the pests, the droughts, but sooner or later, things have to go right."

"But what about the Indians? Pollard, I think I would die of fright if they came bursting into our house! What if they decide not to abide by the treaties?"

"That's why the forts are built throughout the territory. Government troops are there to keep everything in order, and I'll do my best to see that Jeremy, or I, work closely enough to the house to see any Indians coming."

"Are you thinking that you'd like to buy the place from Dorthea?"

"Yes, I certainly think she'd be willing to sell it if she was ready to just walk away and leave it. Apparently, she's in real need of money, so it would be a good thing for her, too. If I can get it reasonably, we'd still have enough money left to buy seed for crops and some left over to last us until the crops start selling."

Susannah looked into the distance and saw the mountain range before them. She felt in her heart that if she attempted to cross those mountains, she would indeed lose the baby, and perhaps, her own life. The idea of Indians terrified her, but since Fort Dodge was nearby, surely they wouldn't be so much of a problem. She knew they had to make a decision quickly. The train would be moving out in a day or so, and Dorthea would be moving on with her brother when his party arrived. She turned to Pollard, who was waiting for her answer.

"All right, talk to Dorthea, and see what you can work out while Catherine has the children occupied."

McCloud reached out to give her a hug. "I'll make it up to you, Susannah. I'll get that place repaired so you'll be comfortable through the winter. Our baby's not going to grow up in a sod cabin. I'll start on a real house as soon as we get crops in the ground. I promise!" With excitement in his step he made his way to Dorthea's wagon.

CHAPTER 10

"I can't believe this!" Catherine cried in frustration. She and Jeremy had taken advantage of their trip to the spring for water to as an opportunity to speak freely to each other. "Everything is changing again."

"Let's sit here a minute, Cat," Jeremy said as they came to a fallen tree that made a perfect resting place.

Catherine continued her lament, "It was painful enough to leave behind my friends in Lexington -- to say nothing of David -- but now I have to lose Liz as well. I feel closer to her than any of those friends, I guess because we've been through so much together on the trail."

"I'm going to miss Liz, too, you know," Jeremy said, blushing.

Catherine's voice softened, "I know. It looks like you two are getting pretty close."

"She's the only girl that's ever interested me. I can't think of one thing about her that I don't like. If we'd gone on to Oregon I feel that Liz and I might have had a future together," Jeremy admitted.

"Have you thought of going on to Oregon with them? You know you're old enough to pretty much do what you want, and I'm sure Mr. Jackson would find a place for you on the train with someone."

"The thought crossed my mind, but if I were to go, *you'd* have to drive the team for the small wagon, and that could be disastrous!" Catherine grimaced, but knew what he said was true. "Besides, there's no way I'd leave you and Ma with McCloud. He's been pretty good on this trip, but I still don't trust the man. I've found he can be whatever he needs to be to make things work to his advantage."

With a sigh, Catherine admitted, "In a way, I'm relieved. Just look at those mountains, Jeremy. They're worse than the ones we've already come through, and those were bad enough. I'm not sure Mama could make it."

"She looks so much better with these few days of rest. I don't think the ride to Kansas will be as bad, so maybe she can gain back some strength."

"What are you going to do about Liz, Jeremy?" Catherine asked. "It was different with David and me, we'd been together for years, but you're just getting to know Liz."

"Well ... Cat ..." Jeremy stood and reached down to pick up the water pail, "I guess I'll pray about it."

＊   ＊   ＊   ＊

Liz and Catherine walked from the wagons to an area of the outpost humorously referred to as "The Dining Hall." Trees had been cut down to produce a clearing, and then used to make crudely constructed picnic tables. A rock fire pit near each table held ashes of the last user's cooking. Sunlight filtered through the shade trees, dancing on the table tops as the trees moved in the light breeze. Other than a single trapper and his dog on the far side of the area, the girls were alone. They sat down at one of the tables.

"All right, Catherine, I can't stand this any longer. What is wrong?"

Catherine had asked Liz to come with her, telling her that she needed to talk. From the expression on Catherine's face, Liz knew it was not some frivolous subject that was to be discussed. She had walked there without questioning Catherine, but now she had to know what was troubling her friend.

"My family is not going with the wagon train tomorrow." Liz's eyes were large with disbelief as Catherine continued, telling her of McCloud's concerns.

Liz seemed stunned into silence so Catherine continued. "We are now going to Kansas to a homestead that belonged to Dorthea Gibson, the woman in the wagon right behind ours."

"Oh, Catherine, how am I going to bear this wagon train without you?" Liz asked, her dark eyes filling with tears. "It's going to be so lonely ... *and boring.*"

"I know; I feel the same way. You're the closest friend I've ever had, Liz. We'll have to stay in contact with letters, even if it takes a long time to get them. I don't want to lose touch with you. We've shared too much," Catherine told her.

"I'm going to miss Jeremy, too," Liz said, the tears coming freely now. "He came by after lunch and asked if I could spend some time with him this evening. My mother said it was O.K."

"I don't know what my brother has to say to you, Liz, but whatever it is, you can count on it. I tease him every chance I get, but I will tell you this; he's as good a person as you could ever ask to meet on this earth. My mother says that he's just like our father."

"I believe that, Catherine. Both my parents have mentioned how impressed they are with him. I haven't had boyfriends, I just wasn't interested. But I see how Jeremy takes care of things like a man, and it makes me respect him."

"Some of those 'things' he takes care of are my mother and me," Catherine admitted. "I've told you about my stepfather selling our farm without telling our mother. Jeremy doesn't trust McCloud. He feels responsible for me until I'm with David, and hopefully things will be all right with Mama by then, but I honestly don't know how long that will be."

"How hard is it to wait for the one you love, Catherine?" Liz asked.

Catherine paused a moment before answering, "It's not easy. I miss David so much. But he's like Jeremy, good from the inside out. I'd rather wait for him and know that I'm marrying a man who will put God first, than to settle for another person just to have their company now."

"About putting God first ... Catherine, I want you to know that I made the decision to do that. I did accept Christ when I was really young. I was sincere, but I didn't understand that it was to be a relationship that grows. You and Jeremy have shown me such a great example of truly living for Christ, and that's what I'm going to do, too. I've made a commitment to read my Bible every day, and by the time we see each other again, I'm going to know a lot more about the things of God."

Catherine's eyes filled with tears of joy. "Liz, you will never regret this decision." Then the reality hit her that her friend would be leaving early in the morning as the wagon train moved out. She reached out to hug her, "Oh, Liz, what am I going to do without you?"

The girls clung to each other in tears for a few moments, then heard a familiar voice making light of their misery;

"I was sent a-lookin' for two purty girls,
One with a head full of flyin' yellow curls
The other one's hair was dark as the night
When I found her she was cryin' and really looked a sight!"

"O.K. Billy, that's enough," Liz said, wiping her tears away.

"Well, shucks, Liz, I ran into Jeremy back there, and I feel like cryin' too. He told me about y'all headin' to Kansas, Catherine."

Drying her eyes on her apron, Catherine said, "That's right, Billy, but I truly am going to miss your songs."

"Well, you won't have Liz bendin' your ear all the time, so maybe you can make up some of your own."

"They could never compare to yours, Billy Boy," Catherine said.

"I really was sent to find you, sis," Billy said to Liz. "Ma's tryin' to pack the wagon, and Hannah pulls stuff back out as fast as Ma puts it in. She needs you to keep the little squirt out of her way for a while. I've got to help Pa with the animals."

"Bring her over to our camp, Liz," Catherine said. "I know Mama would like to spend as much time with her as she can."

The three young people started back to the wagons. Everyone knew Billy and waved or called to him on the way. Catherine looked fondly at his grinning face, surrounded by the fly-a-way hair. "There's another fellow that's 'good to the bone,'" she thought, "I'm going to miss him too."

*   *   *   *

"It feels so strange to be standing here watching the wagon train pull out," Catherine thought. They had always been part of it. The outpost was barren as the last wagons began their forward movement. After three days of noise and activity, the quiet was almost eerie. There were still a few travelers here who were headed east on horseback or pack animals, but only the McCloud and Gibson wagons remained.

Parting good-byes with Liz and her family had been extremely difficult. Catherine and Jeremy watched them until too many other wagons obscured the view. They all felt a sense of loss for the depth of friendship that had formed so quickly between the two families.

It helped that Dorthea Gibson and her children were there. The difference in the widow's countenance was remarkable since obtaining money for her farm. Hope had replaced the despair that Catherine saw in the widow's eyes just three days ago. Dorthea had been able to purchase the food and supplies she needed but the families still cooked and ate together just for the fellowship. She had found a few items of clothing that fit her children from the limited selection at the outpost, and felt that she could now meet her family without the shame of poverty that had clung to them in Kansas.

Catherine saw that Jeremy had gathered his grooming tools and was giving Midnight the best brushing down the horse had known since they started on the trip.

She understood that time with his horse was a sedative to the ache in his heart from Liz's departure. How well she knew that pain. Catherine reached to touch the golden half-heart at her neck, and the longing for David welled up within her. She walked to the wagon and found her folder of writing materials. She could talk to him through her letters, even if she couldn't hear back.

"Mama," she said to Susannah, looking into the wagon, "I'm going to The Dining Hall for a little while to write." With all the wagons gone, she would be in view of their campsite while having some privacy too.

"All right, sweetheart," Susannah replied, "just stay close to this side so Jeremy can see you."

As she neared the closest table Catherine looked around. A gold miner with his pack mule was sleeping on the ground in one corner of the area, and a trapper with a stack of pelts was making coffee on a fire on the other side. She sat at the rough table, opened her folder, and began to think of what she'd write to David. How could she possibly explain how alone she felt? In her letters she'd never told him how really difficult things had been. She didn't want him to picture in his mind how she might look when covered in mud as she helped push the wagons through the deep ruts in the rain. Or how her feet were covered with blisters at times, and how dirty she was at the end of the day from the dust of forty wagon teams. She could tell David she already missed her friend whom she'd only known a few months, but he could not know what she and Liz had shared that brought them so close. At least Liz and Jeremy had that in common. In the future they would write each other, and when they mentioned things on the trail, the other would read between the lines and know there was much left unsaid.

These thoughts brought fear to Catherine's heart. There was more than distance growing between her and David now. Life experiences were changing her. She would never again take for granted a supply of water that flowed freely. Or the comfort of a bed, clean sheets on that bed ... the list was endless.

She dropped her head to her hands with eyes closed and tried to imagine what David might be doing right that moment. Was his life going on as it had when she was in Lexington? Maybe he was growing too. She had not believed that anything could change the way they felt about each other, but now she wasn't so sure. She was beginning to see how people could grow apart, not because they stopped loving each other, but because of the situations of life. If only she could be with David right now and put her fears to rest!

Catherine was so intent on her thoughts that she had not noticed the man approaching her until he spoke, "Ya sure are a purty little thing to be here all alone. How about some comp'ny?"

Startled out of her reverie, Catherine looked up to recognize the trapper who had been across the area. The man was far too close, near enough that she could smell the odor that accompanied his trade. Instinctively, she backed away, too frightened to speak. The man placed his hand on her shoulder.

"So you're a quiet one, are ya? Well, that's all right with me, we don't need no conversation for what I'm thinking."

He'd hardly uttered the words when a hand from behind him grabbed his arm on Catherine's shoulder and twisted it unmercifully upward behind his back. His eyes widened in fear as he felt the cold steel of a knife blade pressing against his throat.

"Is there anything else you'd like to say to this young woman before you die, you stinkin' trash heap?"

The young man had appeared and acted so quickly that Catherine barely had time to see that it was the miner who had been sleeping on the other side of the clearing. He hardly looked older than herself, his hair grown long and his face brown from the sun.

"I... I was just ... just bein' friendly... that's all. Ya wouldn't kill a man for that would ya?" the trapper stuttered.

His captor tightened his grip on the man's arm as the trapper gasped in pain.

"I don't think that's what the lady needed to hear. Do you want to try again or do I go ahead and slice your useless throat?"

"All right, all right! I'm sorry to 'ave bothered ya, miss. Now will ye move that blade off my neck?"

"I think I'll ask the lady first," the young man said, and then to Catherine, "Is that all you needed to hear from this scum, or would you like me to just finish him off?"

Catherine could hardly find her voice, but wide-eyed, she managed to squeak out, "Yes... No... I mean, it's O.K. Please, don't kill him!"

"Well, I guess you can thank the lady for saving your hide, which in my opinion is not worth even one of those you're packin.' I don't think this place is big enough for you and me and this lady. Get your stuff together and move out."

"But I just made a pot a coffee over there," the trapper whined.

"Then you should have darned well been over there drinking it. Pour it out and get on your way before I change my mind about bloodying my knife!" He removed his knife from the man's throat and released his arm, pushing the trapper in the direction of his belongings. Still grumbling, the smelly traveler emptied his coffee pot on the fire and gathered up his gear. When satisfied that the intruder was moving out of the area, the young man turned to Catherine.

"I'm sorry if I frightened you, ma'am. I only sound mean. I promise I've never killed a man in my life."

"Well, you were certainly convincing! I'm glad that man believed you, too. Thank you for helping me," and extending her hand, she said, "I'm Catherine Sutherland."

Bowing over her hand in a gallant gesture the young man said, "I'm Jonathan Chriswell."

"Cat, is everything all right?" Jeremy asked, walking up to the two of them. He'd been concentrating on his thoughts of Liz while brushing Midnight and didn't see what was happening with Catherine. When he looked up, he saw a young man shoving an older trapper away and then talking to Catherine. Jeremy dropped his brush and hurried to Catherine's side.

"Everything's fine now, Jeremy." Looking to her rescuer, she said, "Jonathan, this is my brother, Jeremy."

"Jonathan Chriswell," he introduced himself and offered to shake hands with Jeremy.

"Jonathan just scared away a guy that was being a little too friendly."

"It's actually kind of fun to play the tough guy every now and then," Jonathan said with a grin.

Jeremy smiled too, "Which way are you headed?"

"I'm on my way home back east. 'Been mining in California for a couple of years."

"Where is 'home,' Jonathan?" Catherine asked.

"I'm from Missouri, Saint Joe."

Excited, Catherine exclaimed, "We're practically neighbors! We're from Lexington. Jeremy, can you believe this?"

"That's great. I think we have some relatives there. My mother would know more about that, though," Jeremy said.

"Where are you folks headed?" Jonathan asked.

"Well, we started out for Oregon, but now we're going to Kansas. Our stepfather bought a farm there from the lady in that wagon over there," Jeremy pointed to Dorthea's rig.

Catherine thought of something. "Jonathan, when are you heading out?"

"I plan to get moving again in the morning. My animals needed a little rest after those mountains."

"Would you take a letter and mail it for me? My fiancé has no idea I'll be as close as Kansas. He was expecting us to go to Oregon," Catherine said.

"I'd be glad to take your letter. I have a sweetheart back home too. We'll be getting married soon. I did well enough in the gold fields to get us set up on our own."

"My boyfriend works with gold, but not while it's in the ground," Catherine said. "He makes jewelry."

Jonathan's eyes lit up. "No kidding? I was thinking I'd like to have our wedding rings custom made from some of the gold I found. Do you think he could do that?"

"He certainly could; David does beautiful work." Pulling her necklace from beneath her dress she showed it to him. "He made this for me when we left Lexington. He has the other half and when we get back together he's going to bond the two as one."

Jonathan stepped closer to get a better look at Catherine's necklace. He could see the quality of David's work. "This is beautiful, Catherine. I can see he'd have no problem making rings for us. You say he's in Lexington?"

"Yes, his name is David Winters and he works at Silas Goodson's Watch and Jewelry Emporium on the main street of town."

"Well, after I spend a few days at home, I'll take a ride over there and talk to him about making the rings. And I'll hand deliver a letter if you'd like. I know how special it is to get a letter from the one you love. I only got six from my girl in the two years I've been away. I know she sent more, they just never reached me. I guarantee you, though, I can quote every single word of those letters. There were weeks at a time that I didn't have anything else to read, just the Good Book and Janie's letters."

"I wish I could meet your Janie," Catherine said. "She's blessed to have you, and I know one thing, she'll be safe as long as you and your knife are around."

"Your knife?" Jeremy asked, looking at Catherine, then at Jonathan.

"Aw … nothing, Jeremy, you'd just have to have been here," Jonathan said.

"Jonathan, you must join us for lunch, and meet everyone else. We've kind of adopted the Gibson family, the people with the other wagon over there," Catherine said. "I owe you a favor, anyway."

"After eating my sorry excuse of cooking for two years I don't have to think twice about accepting your invitation," Jonathan assured her.

"We'll probably eat in a couple of hours, Jonathan; just come on over to our wagon whenever you're ready."

"Sounds good to me. Meanwhile, I think I'll go back and finish my nap that trapper interrupted."

"I just have to ask you something," Catherine said to Jonathan. "How did you know that guy was bothering me all the way across the clearing? You seemed to be sound asleep."

"Miss Catherine, gold miners are probably the lightest sleepers on the planet. There's as much thieving of gold in those mining camps as there is digging it. You learn to protect what you have and sleep with both ears open. It was nice to meet you; I'll see you for lunch," Jonathan said as he headed back toward his animals.

Catherine picked up her writing supplies, and she and Jeremy started back toward the wagon. "What really happened back there, Cat?

"Just what Jonathan said, that trapper was bothering me and Jonathan convinced him to leave," Catherine said with a smile.

"Cat," Jeremy stopped and took her by the arm, "Cat, you really need to understand some things about men. They are not all nice, in fact most of them are little better than animals. You … well, you're a very pretty girl. Your blonde hair makes you stand out in a crowd, and even if you're not aware that men notice you, they do. You have to be careful to not put yourself in a position where men could take advantage of you. Out here in this wild country some of these men haven't even seen a woman for months. No woman would be safe around them, and especially not a young, pretty one. Promise me that you will not go off alone again, even here at the outpost."

Catherine could hear the genuine concern in her brother's voice and see the intense expression in his gray eyes as he waited for her response.

"I promise, Jeremy. I won't invite trouble, or cause any worry for anyone."

"What if Jonathan had been like that other guy today? There's no telling what could have happened to you. Even though you were close to the wagon, you could have been taken away into the woods there in a few seconds. You would have been helpless against two strong men," Jeremy insisted.

"You're right," Catherine said quietly. "Can we just not say anything about this to Mama? We can truthfully say we met Jonathan at The Dining Hall and invited him to lunch. We don't have to worry her with the details."

Starting to walk again, Jeremy said, "I think that's best, too. Subject closed."

"I need more wood for cooking," Catherine told him. "Want to get it for me?"

"If you promise you won't forget to ask Dorthea to make the biscuits," he teased as he dodged her swing.

CHAPTER 11

D avid sat with his head bowed, listening to the choir's song of worship. The late morning sun shone through the stained glass windows of the small church, casting colored rays on people and furnishings alike. His father stood behind the pulpit ministering the elements of the Eucharist, and as the song ended, Reverend Winters began to speak.

"Our Lord and Savior, knowing the sinful heart of man, foresaw that in our weakness we would forget His divine work at Calvary. As exuberant as we might be at the time of our salvation, He knew that life would occupy us with its challenges, and the truth of His great sacrifice for us would be forgotten. Therefore He put into place this ordinance, the partaking of the bread and the fruit of the vine as symbols of His broken body, and of His blood that was shed. Each time we eat the bread and drink the cup, we remember that the stripes He took were for the healing of our bodies. We remember that His precious blood paid the price for the remission of our sins. This was His eternal covenant, His commitment to us."

Reverend Winters continued, "None of us are perfect, even after salvation. As long as we live in these earthly bodies we will struggle against this fleshly nature. But when we come to the Lord's Table, we are to examine our hearts and repent of anything in our lives that may not please our Savior. It is a time to renew our commitment to Him as we remember His covenant with us."

As his father spoke of commitment, David was reminded of the Sunday morning, months ago, that Catherine spoke of their commitment to each other, of how she and David were one at heart, and how that made commitment easy. Of course, she had no idea that her stepfather-- possibly when she was speaking those very words--was selling their home, and that David and Catherine's plans to always be together would be ripped to shreds.

The struggle that was plaguing David's mind began the day Charlotte Pendleton walked into his workplace. She was different than any girl he'd met in Lexington. He didn't love Catherine any less, but he couldn't deny that there was an attraction to this elegant, self-confidant young woman. Not only was she beautiful, she was witty and made him laugh. She had tried numerous ways to get David to spend time with her, but he had refused, so he wasn't guilty in being untrue to Catherine in that sense.

If only Catherine would appear at the door of this church today and never leave him. She was all he needed, but she wasn't here. And she wouldn't be here tomorrow, or the next day, or for nearly two years, and meanwhile, this angelic looking creature with red hair was tempting him with her laughing, green eyes. She had told him more than once at the shop that he was too serious. Maybe she was right. He didn't do anything for fun now that Catherine was gone. Their friendship had so filled his life that he hadn't developed close relationships with other young people. Now his fellow students had gone on with their lives, Catherine was somewhere unknown to him, and he was lonely.

The fact remained that he had a commitment to Catherine. And to be true to himself, he knew that commitment involved being faithful to her in thought as well as in action. Unless he severed that commitment, which he no intention of doing, he had no right to be thinking of how attractive Charlotte Pendleton was. He needed to have a talk with Charlotte about his reasons for refusing her company; he'd have to tell her about Catherine. That wouldn't be easy, but maybe she would keep her distance then.

Now that he had worked things out in his heart, David went forward to take the elements of the Lord's Table. Then he knelt at the altar and prayed:

"Heavenly Father, I had no idea of the weakness of my flesh. I repent of any thoughts that could be considered as unfaithfulness to Catherine. I love her with all my heart and never want to do anything that would bring hurt to her. I don't know how I'm going to deal with this loneliness for two long years. Show me what to do and how to please You as I wait for Your plan for Catherine and me to come to pass. And Father, I really need to hear from her. Please help her to get a letter to me so that I can know she's all right. Amen."

*   *   *   *

"I don't know how she does this," David thought to himself. Charlotte Pendleton had managed to catch him alone at the shop again. It seems she had a knack for knowing when Mr. Goodson would be gone. Well, maybe it was a good thing today, and hopefully other customers wouldn't come in until he'd told her about his commitment to Catherine.

"Have you made anything new this week, David?" Charlotte asked as she flashed her best smile his direction.

"I have several pieces that I've been working on, but I'm waiting for some new gems I ordered," David said.

"Well, I hope you get them finished soon," she said, coming over to the counter where he stood. "David, have you ever thought of having a show in New York?"

David laughed. "No, I can't say that I have."

"You know, you really underestimate your talent," Charlotte said. "As you might guess, I spend quite a bit of time in jewelry stores. I may be young, but I know good work and quality gems. I'm telling you, David, there's a market there for your jewelry that would make you *rich*."

She said that word as though it was the most important word in the whole world.

"I enjoy what I do, Charlotte, and I'm glad to sell my jewelry. I have plans for the money I make, but I'm not striving to be rich. In fact, I've been meaning to talk to you about this … sort of," David's confusion definitely confused Charlotte.

"What are you trying to say?" she asked

"Charlotte, I'm sure that you're not accustomed to fellows avoiding your company," he said.

"As a matter of fact, I think you hold the prize."

"Well, there is a reason for that. I am committed to another girl," David said, looking her squarely in the eyes.

This came as a surprise to Charlotte. "I've not heard of any girl or seen you with anyone," she said, as though not believing him.

"That's because her family left here several months ago for the Oregon Territory," he explained.

"Have you heard from her?" Charlotte asked.

160

"Only once, a letter mailed from Independence the day the wagon train moved out."

"David, the Oregon Territory is another world away. Surely you don't think the two of you will ever get back together. You're too young to sit here waiting for someone you'll never see again. You're not old enough to have *that* serious a relationship."

"You don't understand. Catherine and I have been the best of friends almost all our lives, and now we love each other with that same commitment. And yes, we do expect to be back together. My promise to her was that I will come to find her in two years, and we will be married. All the money I make from the sale of my jewelry goes into the bank for our future," David told her.

"But don't you get lonely?" Charlotte asked, coming seductively closer.

He moved to put distance between them again as he answered her. "I won't say that I'm not lonely. But it's Catherine I want to be with, the one who has shared my heart for years. The fact that I don't know where she is at the moment does not change that for me, or for her."

"How do you know that, David? There are no saints on this earth, not even your Catherine. She's probably already forgotten you!" Charlotte flung out hatefully.

David felt the sting of her words, seeing a new side of Miss Charlotte Pendleton.

Just then the jangle of the bells on the door announced the arrival of a customer. Charlotte turned her back and appeared to be looking into the case. The set of her shoulders was evidence to David that she wasn't through with this conversation.

"Yes, sir, can I help you?" David said to the customer who walked into the shop. Unconsciously he noticed that the young man was extremely tanned, obviously having worked in the sun for some time. His hair was to his shoulders, but he was neatly dressed.

"David Winters?" he asked.

"Yes, I'm David," he replied.

"Then I have something for you," and reaching into his coat pocket he pulled out a letter. "This is from your fiancée, Catherine."

"From Catherine? Oh, thank God! Thank you, sir! Did you see her in person? I'm sorry, I didn't even ask your name."

Grinning, Jonathan Chriswell introduced himself and began to answer David's questions.

"Yes, I did see your sweetheart, and she is doing well, other than pining over you. I ate a couple of meals with her family, and I'm telling you, the girl can cook. You're going to eat well when you marry her."

David was practically going in circles in the shop. "I can't believe this. I'm talking to someone who saw my Catherine!" He tried to calm down. "I apologize for my behavior, but I haven't heard anything from her since they pulled out of Independence. Where did you see her?"

In his exuberance David hardly even noticed that Charlotte angrily left the shop, slamming the door so hard the jangling bells swung wildly.

"Here, sit down. I'm going to have a million questions, Jonathan." David said.

"I'm not in a hurry, I can wait if you want to read the letter first," Jonathan said.

David thought a moment, then decided he'd wait and read it when he was home alone in his room. Besides, he wanted to hear everything Jonathan could tell him.

"I think I'll wait, I want to hear what you have to tell me. So where did you see Catherine and her family? Oh, how is her mother?"

"Mrs. McCloud is doing fairly well from what I could see. It seems it might not be too much longer before her child is to be born. She looked really tired, but Catherine and Jeremy said she was actually better than when they arrived there. The wagon train was taking a few days for rest and repairs before heading into the real mountains. We were at the Republic River outpost. Everybody stops there, going east or west, wagon trains, trappers, traders, and like me, miners."

"How did you actually meet Catherine and her family?" David asked.

Jonathon paused for a moment, not sure how much to divulge of the situation. He decided that if he were in David's place, he'd want to hear the whole truth, so he told David about Catherine's encounter with the trapper.

"Was Catherine hurt?" David asked with concern.

"No, not at all, David, and I think she was more afraid of me, the way I was talking to that guy, than she was of him. As soon as he was gone, though, I let her know it was just a bunch of hot air."

"How does Catherine look? Is she handling the trail all right?"

"Your Catherine is a beautiful young woman, David. If I didn't have my sweet Janie, I'd be trying to see if she wouldn't look my way. But I guarantee you, she only has eyes for you. Jeremy told me he made her promise not to go anywhere alone again. With so few women available out there in the wild, it's not safe for any woman. But Catherine is definitely a target with her blonde curls and pretty face."

"I pray for her safety, but I need to do it more often. I feel so helpless, not being able to be there with her."

"Well, there's some good news to tell you. I'm sure Catherine will explain it all in the letter, but I'll just tell you the best part ... she won't be as far away as you thought. There's been a change of plans, and they're on their way now to a farm in Kansas."

"Kansas? Why, Kansas?" David asked.

"I think a lot of it had to do with Mrs. McCloud's health. I'm sure Catherine will fill you in."

"I can't thank you enough for coming here and bringing me this information and this letter. You don't know how badly I needed to hear from her."

"Well, I think I do. I spent two years mining gold to get a nest egg for me and my Janie to be able to get married. I was determined we wouldn't start our life like so many couples do, with nothing. I wanted better than that for my girl. Like you, I went months without hearing from her, and I was just as excited as you were today when letters came. That's why I wanted to deliver it personally – to make sure it reached you."

"What was your destination back east?" David asked, "I'm sure you weren't planning to come to Lexington originally."

"No, but close," Jonathan said. "I'm from just up the road, at St. Joe. I took a couple of days to get rested up and to tell Janie to start planning the wedding, and then I headed here. I wanted to deliver Catherine's letter, but I also had another reason for coming." He pulled a small bag from his pocket.

"One day when I was out there mining, I was looking at the gold I'd panned out of a stream in the most beautiful place. I thought, this is what they make wedding rings out of, and it hit me. I want mine and Janie's rings to be made out of the gold that I found there. Someday, if I ever get the chance, I'm going to take Janie there to show her where our rings came from. Catherine told me you make jewelry; can you make those rings for us, David?"

"I would be so honored to do that, Jonathan. Is the gold pure enough?"

"This in the bag is. It came from a stream where the nuggets were ore free, the purest I found in two years of mining and panning."

"Do you have a design in mind?" David asked.

"My Janie did; she drew it out here, and these are the sizes of our ring fingers," he said, pulling out two short slips of paper and unfolding another with a drawing on it.

"Your Janie is quite a girl; she thought of everything. I hope I get to meet her sometime," David said.

"Maybe she can come with me when I return to pick up the rings. How much time do you need? I guess I should have asked that before we set the date. I sure don't intend to get married without the rings."

"I can have them for you in four days. I'm kind of stalled on making other jewelry right now because I'm waiting for some new stones."

"I should look at your pieces and buy one for a wedding present for Janie. I hadn't thought about that, but she deserves something for waiting for me for two years."

"Well, here they are, everything in this case is my work, but my employer makes beautiful jewelry too. You might prefer something of his."

"I kind of feel a connection with you, David, and besides, if I buy from you, it goes into your kitty for you and Catherine."

David laughed, "Jonathan, I can't thank you enough for coming here. Even if there'd been no letter, just to talk to someone who was with Catherine has meant so much. Say, can you have dinner with my parents and me? I know they'll be excited to meet you, and my mother is a great cook too."

"Sure, I'd like that. I do want to get back on the road to St. Joe tonight, though."

"All I've been asking about is Catherine," David said apologetically. "How is Jeremy doing?"

"That Jeremy is a fine guy. I really liked him. It seems he was beginning to get kind of sweet on a young lady who went on to Oregon, so he doesn't know how that's going to pan out," Jonathan said.

"And their stepfather, McCloud, how's he?"

Jonathan paused a minute before answering, "You know, that guy's kind of a strange duck. He didn't say or do anything I could put my finger on, but my gut tells me he's not true blue."

"Well, there's good reason for that. The farm he sold here to finance their trip west was to be Jeremy's inheritance from his father. McCloud sold it without a word to Jeremy or his mother."

"Well, that makes Jeremy an even better man than I thought. I didn't pick up on any resentment from him toward McCloud."

"That's just the kind of guy he is. Well, I'd better stop asking questions and let you pick out something for Janie. I'm going to straighten up here so I can close up."

David's heart was light as he finished the closing chores and locked up the shop. He felt Jonathan would be his best friend forever for bringing him news of Catherine and the letter that he could feel in his pocket. He couldn't help looking upward and saying in his heart, "Thank You, Father! Once again, You have been faithful!"

CHAPTER 12

Things had become busier around the outpost again. Dorthea Gibson's brother and the four families with him had rolled into camp yesterday afternoon. Catherine couldn't help but rejoice at Dorthea's happiness to see her loved ones, but their arrival meant that in a matter of days Dorthea and her children would be leaving. Catherine tried to avoid the painful thought that she would very likely never see them again. Tabitha clung to her like an adoring younger sister, and Jeremy had taken on the task of keeping Andrew and George occupied with various activities as they all waited those few days with little to do.

The children would now be part of a whole new family. Dorthea's nephews were fun-loving, respectful, young men. They would be a great help to Dorthea as she started a new farm in Oregon.

"It's just nice to see things work out right for someone," Catherine thought wistfully as she watched Dorthea and her family. "I wonder if it ever will for us."

McCloud asked everyone that came into the outpost for information regarding the route to Kansas. Apparently they would need to head southeast to Fort Hayes, further south to Fort Dodge, and from there to the property McCloud had purchased from Dorthea. The trail was not frequented with many travelers like the Oregon Trail, nor was it as defined. Dorthea had been extremely brave to tackle that journey alone with her children, but God had been gracious and sent help to accompany her.

"God will take care of us, too. I'm sure of that," Catherine thought. She hoped they could leave for Kansas before Dorthea and her brother's group left. The idea of being left behind and watching loved ones leave again left a sick feeling in the pit of Catherine's stomach. She was so tired of telling people good-bye. It was amazing how quickly relationships formed here in the west. She thought of Jonathan. They only knew him for two days, yet she and Jeremy both felt they had gained a brother. She was glad she could send her letter to David through him.

Catherine saw McCloud walking back toward their camp. She recognized the spring in his step that meant he had news that pleased him. She looked up expectantly as he came closer.

"We'll be heading out in the morning," he said, excitement in his eyes. Seeing Susannah in the opening of the wagon he told her the news.

"There's a caravan heading southeast that's taking workers to lay the railroad tracks. They just came in, and will be pulling out in the morning. Soldiers from Fort Hayes are coming to escort them, and I've received permission to travel with them as far as they are going in our direction."

The women both breathed a sigh of relief.

"Tell Jeremy to tighten up everything in his wagon. I need to go to the outpost store to pick up a couple of things. I'll buy whatever I can get in fresh produce that will last a few days; we may not see any for a while."

Jeremy, Dorthea's boys and all her nephews appeared then, proudly lifting up the strings of fresh trout they'd caught in the mountain stream. Apparently they'd all have fresh fish for dinner this evening.

"Maybe this sense of excitement is what feeds McCloud's need for change," Catherine thought. She couldn't deny that she felt it too, even while confessing to fear of the unknown situations that lay ahead. It did provide the energy to get things done, and she had plenty on her list.

*   *   *   *

Catherine and Jeremy were both awake before sun-up. She wanted to be finished with the morning meal earlier than usual since everything had to packed away for traveling. Jeremy got the oxen yoked before McCloud stepped out of the wagon, and even Susannah appeared rested and ready to begin their journey to Kansas.

Things were taking place on the other side of the outpost too. The caravan of railroad workers was buzzing with activity. Catherine was surprised to see that the majority of the workers were Chinese, their dark braids hanging down their backs. The army escort had arrived just minutes ago. What an impressive sight they made as they rode into the outpost with the pink dawn of the rising sun as their backdrop. They sat proudly on their fine horses, their uniforms gleaming with gold buttons that sparkled in the morning light. Catherine felt she should stand at attention as they passed with the Stars and Stripes blowing in the wind, and it brought tears to her eyes.

"This is not the time to be sentimental," she told herself as she went back to her cooking. Perhaps it was silly, but she had felt like wearing one of her better dresses today instead of those she'd worn most of the trip. They were so faded. Today felt like a new start, and that deserved a better dress. She picked her favorite, a lilac one, and a fresh apron so she wouldn't get her dress soiled while cooking. She had showered at the bathhouse last night and washed her hair, wondering how long it would be before she'd have that luxury again. Her blond curls were falling softly about her face, and the glow of excitement tinted her cheeks a rosy hue beneath the golden brown of her skin.

"You look especially pretty this morning, hon," said Susannah as she put an arm around Catherine.

"I just felt like celebrating this next phase of our journey, I suppose," Catherine said. "I have another surprise too."

"Can I know what it is?"

"I'll only tell *you*. I've been watching Dorthea make her biscuits and I think I've figured out her secret. So I made the biscuits this morning and we'll see if anybody notices the difference."

"Well, I will never tell. And Dorthea won't be here to say anything either. She thought it would be easier for you not to have her bunch to feed this morning since we'll be heading out so soon afterward. She promised they'll be here to see us off, though. If you don't need my help I'm going to pack away some things in the wagon."

"I have it down to a routine now," Catherine said. "I'll call when breakfast is ready."

Susannah went to the wagon as Catherine laid strips of bacon in the cast iron skillet. She looked up to see two officers from the escort walking directly to their camp.

"Good morning, miss," the senior officer said, and both tipped their hats to her.

Catherine felt timid before the officers. They looked so regal.

"Good morning to you, sir, uh, both of you … sirs." She knew she was blushing.

"I'm Colonel Edward Dawson, and this is Lieutenant Samuel Rushing. We'll be leading the escort for this caravan and have been informed that your party is going to accompany us for part of this trip. Is Mr. McCloud here?" Col. Dawson asked.

"He and my brother have taken the water barrel to the spring to fill it, but they should be back any time. I'm Catherine Sutherland, Mr. McCloud's step-daughter," Catherine said. "Would you like to wait here for him?"

"We don't want to impose …" Col. Dawson said.

"It's not an imposition at all, Col. Dawson. I have a fresh pot of coffee made; don't tell me you're going to refuse that," Catherine teased.

"I think I'd have to start an uprising if he did, miss," said Lt. Rushing, "It smells wonderful."

"We would greatly appreciate a cup of coffee, Miss Sutherland." Col. Dawson replied. "We started out quite early this morning without any."

"Then welcome to our parlor and choose your own crate," Catherine motioned to the circular area around the fire where wooden crates supplied seating. As she gave the coffee to the officers, she couldn't help thinking she was glad she'd dressed up a little this morning. The two officers were both handsome men, though very different in appearance. Colonel Edward Dawson was the taller one, slender, his face as perfect as a Greek statue. His hair was dark blonde with highlights from the daily exposure to sun. Though he exuded the confidence of one in command, Catherine noticed that his blue eyes were warm and he smiled easily.

Lieutenant Rushing was not as tall as his superior officer, but his broad shoulders and sturdy build also gave the appearance of one to be obeyed. His hair was black, his eyes a deep hazel. They sparkled when he smiled, giving the impression of a man who enjoyed making others laugh, yet the strength of his jaw beneath the trimmed sideburns reminded Catherine of her father.

"Oh … my biscuits! Excuse me, please," Catherine hurried to grab a hot pad and uncover the Dutch oven. With great relief she saw she'd caught them just in time to prevent their being overdone. She was thrilled to see the biscuits had risen high and fluffy, just like Dorthea's. Now if they'll just taste the same. One look at the bacon told her that rescue was needed there. She hurriedly put down the biscuits and grabbed the long fork to turn each slice, painfully aware that two finely uniformed army officers were observing her every move. What happened to her morning? Just a half hour ago she was feeling on top of the world. Out of the corner of her eye she saw Jeremy and McCloud coming, carrying the heavy water barrel between them.

"Thank Goodness, they're here, I mean, my step-brother and my … I meant to say, my step-*father*, and my *brother* … they're here … uh … over there. Would you care for more coffee?" Catherine stuttered.

"That would be great, but why don't I get it? You seem to have your hands full getting breakfast there," Col. Dawson said, struggling to hold back the smile that made its way to his eyes in spite of him. He poured coffee for himself and Lt. Rushing and sat the pot back on the coals.

"I'm sorry if our being here makes you uncomfortable, Miss Sutherland. But I'd be really disappointed if you ran us away. We haven't seen a pretty lady cook breakfast in a very long time, and you're a sight for sore eyes, " the Colonel said.

"You'll know that's a fact when you meet our cook, miss. He's five feet tall, bow-legged and missing most of his teeth. And his cooking's nothing to brag about either," Lt. Rushing said.

"We're going to be seeing a lot of each other on the trail ahead, so you may as well get used to us being around," Col. Dawson said with a smile.

Catherine relaxed then. In site of the imposing uniforms and titles, they were just men, hungry men, at that.

"Then why don't you gentlemen stay for breakfast with us," Catherine told them, "and I'll let you decide if I can outdo your cook. My stepfather is on his way over, so you can take care of your business with him. I just have to cook the eggs and we'll be ready to eat."

"I saw your biscuits in that Dutch oven, so I'm not going anywhere," Lt. Rushing said.

"Good morning, officer," McCloud had entered the camp and extended his hand to Col. Dawson, whom he recognized as being the superior officer.

"Mr. McCloud, I understand you're to be part of the caravan that we're escorting. How many wagons…"

The next couple of hours passed so quickly. Breakfast was over and not one biscuit was left. The officers assured Catherine that she had outdone their cook, hands down, and that they looked forward to sampling her efforts again in the days ahead. Both of the handsome soldiers were pleasant and witty. Catherine had to admit, she had enjoyed the bantering between them, Jeremy and herself. McCloud was surprisingly quiet, ate his food and excused himself to tasks. Susannah was glad to see Catherine smiling again. There had been enough sadness lately.

Information was exchanged with Dorthea to stay in contact; hugs and words of appreciation were shared, and soon they were on the move. Catherine was surprised to see that their wagons had been given the forward positions, since this train was originally intended to transport the railway workers.

"See the benefits of a good meal, Cat?" Jeremy said to Catherine as she rode on the driver's seat beside him. "Those poor Chinese guys get to eat our dust, and all because of a pretty smile and a skillet of biscuits!"

Catherine, for once, couldn't think of a retort.

"How'd you get Dorthea's biscuits? She wasn't there 'til later," Jeremy said.

"I'll have you know, Jeremy Sutherland, *I* made those biscuits."

"*No!*" Jeremy looked at her in disbelief.

"*Yes*! All on my own. I've been watching Dorthea."

"Well, I guess you know, you started something."

"Don't think you're going to get biscuits everyday. I think I'll use them as bait for when I want something from you," Catherine teased.

"You'd really do that to me?"

"To you and maybe some officers I know, too," Catherine said wickedly as Lt. Rushing pulled up beside them on his horse.

"Is everything going all right, Jeremy? Miss Sutherland?"

"Officer, my sister has just confessed she intends to dangle a pan of biscuits before our noses the next time she wants favors. Isn't bribery against the law?" Jeremy quipped.

"It is indeed, and if she persists in this behavior, it may be necessary to seize her and force her to ride alongside me so that I can prevent any more such acts," Lieutenant Rushing said with a fake frown.

"I confess, officer, I'm an incurable reprobate. You may as well take me," Catherine said.

"In that case I shall return shortly with a horse, wicked woman. I'm not sure I can produce a side saddle, though."

Catherine laughed, "I grew up on a farm, Lieutenant; I wouldn't know what to do with a side saddle."

Lt. Rushing grinned, "Don't go anywhere, I'll be back in a few minutes," and rode away toward the army supply wagon and extra horses. Soon he was back, leading a pretty, dark mare.

"All right, you miscreant, I'll ride ahead and dismount, and when your wagon gets to me, jump, and I'll catch you," he said.

Catherine saw the Lieutenant waiting and tensed to jump from the moving wagon. What if he didn't catch her? With her heart in her throat she jumped and found herself held firmly in the strong arms of the officer. With sparkling eyes she looked up at him, "That was fun!"

Still holding onto her, the Lieutenant grinned and said, "It was indeed."

"I think I should get on my horse, now, Lieutenant," Catherine said.

"Ah, yes, the horse," he said, releasing her. The way Catherine swung up into the saddle, in spite of her dress, left no doubt that she was comfortable with horses.

"Just one thing, before we ride, Miss Sutherland ..."

"Please, if you're going to be my captor, call me Catherine."

Sam Rushing looked up at the young woman smiling down at him, her hair like a halo of curls framing the most beautiful face and laughing blue eyes he'd ever seen. Something akin to a pleasant pain hit his heart. He took a deep breath to make up for the one he had just lost.

"Pardon me, Miss Catherine, but I do believe our positions have been reversed!" He turned quickly and mounted his horse. "What I was going to say is that the only way I got permission from the Colonel for you to ride with me, is to have your promise that you won't ride off from the train, and that if I instruct you to get inside the wagon you will go immediately ... Promise?"

"I promise, Lieutenant."

"Please, call me Sam. I don't mean to put a damper on the joy of our ride, but the reason we soldiers are here as an escort is that there have been a few incidents with unfriendly Indians recently. Indians are intrigued with blonde women, as are most of us men, and they love to convert them to squaws. So stay close to me, and if we suspect any problems I'll see you back to your wagon. You should cover your head with a scarf, if possible and preferably, stay completely out of sight. I talked to your stepfather about this in regard to your mother as well. It wouldn't matter at all to them that she's about to have a baby. They'd raise him as an Indian chief and flaunt him to the Great White Fathers!"

Catherine recognized the seriousness of Lt. Rushing's warning.

"Lieutenant ... Sam ... I assure you I have no desire to become an Indian squaw. I will keep my horse as close to yours as you tell me to, and I'll dive headfirst into that wagon at the first sign of trouble. I have to tell you, the Indian situation does bring fear to my mother and me. We know there are hardships on the trail; we've learned to deal with that, but we don't know what to expect from the Indians."

"Quite honestly, Catherine, the army doesn't either. I know that's not much comfort, but it's the truth. The tribes react differently to our being here, and even the same tribe may be friendly one week and hostile the next. The problem lies in communication. We don't understand them and their ways anymore than they understand ours."

Sam had guided them into a position where there were soldiers ahead and behind them, and now their horses fell into a pace that kept them abreast with the other riders as they talked.

"I know my family is coming to take possession of land in Kansas that just a short time ago belonged to the Indians. It makes me feel badly. And yet, the area where we lived in Missouri once was occupied by Indians as well. I suppose because they had been gone for years by the time I was born and lived there, I just never thought about it. I'm not knowledgeable enough to know what should be done, but it seems so unfair that we white people are pushing the Indians from their lands all the way from the east to the west coast. Have they no rights at all?" Catherine asked with concern.

"They are continually being forced to give up more and more of their lands. Treaties are signed, supposedly giving them some rights, or at least promises of payment and benefits." Lowering his voice, Sam said, "It probably is not good for me to be heard saying this, but I am not aware of any of those treaties that have been totally kept by our government. The Indians then react in the only way known to them, they go to war; they take what they want from whomever they can because that which was promised was withheld."

Catherine could see that this subject troubled Sam deeply. He seemed to be searching for words to express his feelings, so Catherine rode silently beside him.

"Last winter we were ordered to an area where an uprising had been reported," he said. "The Indians had been moved from their lands where they were accustomed to growing certain types of vegetation. Those plants, their food, would not produce in the new soil and climate. The people were near starvation. They had been restricted by the government from following the buffalo because it meant leaving their territory, so they were without the meat that they normally cured and ate most of the year, too. Money and food had been promised to them. Through the scheming of the Indian agents who handle those things and line their own pockets, the pitiful supplies sent to them were molded or dried up, and most of them, totally useless. Many of the people, especially the children, were sick from lack of nourishment. There's no telling how many died."

Catherine could see the compassion in Sam's eyes as he continued, "Is it any wonder that their braves are angry and take food from the white men's farms? Catherine, this whole situation is so one-sided. There seems to be no one who stands up for the Indian. I'm not certain that any person, or even an organization of people, could stand against the tide of the white man's greed and hunger for land. There seems to be no satisfying it, and I'm sure what you said is exactly true; this taking of land from the natives will not cease until it consumes all this territory to the Pacific Ocean itself!"

The passion of Sam's feelings was mirrored in Catherine's face as he looked at her. Those blue eyes that had been full of laughter were now as saddened as he always felt when he allowed his thoughts to dwell on the Indian problem. He certainly had not intended to make their ride one of despair, though.

"Catherine, I am so sorry. I had no intention of getting into the depths of my feelings about this situation. I have chased away your beautiful smile and most likely ruined your day."

"You have not ruined my day, Lieutenant, and I assure you, my smile is nearby. I needed to hear the things you said, and I admire your compassion for these people. You've given me insight that I may need someday," Catherine told him.

"Well, at any rate, I would prefer to change the topic to something more pleasant, such as how you came to be on this wagon trail to Kansas."

"I'm afraid that would be another tale of despair, Sam; one that is certain to make me lose my smile." Catherine said.

"I am so sorry, Catherine. I didn't mean to intrude. I'm coming up with a total zero on conversational skills today." Sam said apologetically.

"Please don't feel badly, Sam. It's just that our story is ... how shall I say it? Very complicated. Perhaps I'll share more of it another time."

"I promise I won't ask again. If you want me to know, you can tell me. Anyway, it's rather exciting to be spending time with a 'mysterious woman.'"

Catherine giggled, "That's certainly not a title I ever expected to have been given."

"Well, it is very fitting. I assure you, in my two years of being in this wasteland, I have never before come to a campsite where a golden-haired angel in a lilac dress was cooking food fit for a king, and yet no one knows how she came to be there."

"Miss Sutherland, is Lieutenant Rushing treating you well?" Catherine and Sam looked up to see Col. Dawson.

"I just may have charges to bring against him, Colonel. This officer has called me wicked, a miscreant, and now a mysterious woman," Catherine said with a pout.

"Well, I would be interested to know how you could provoke all that in less than two hours on horseback, Miss Sutherland, so rest assured, I will thoroughly question the Lieutenant in regard to his dubious opinions of you. In the meantime, Lieutenant, your services are needed at the front. Lest we incite jealousy among the other soldiers by allowing you to have the sole responsibility of protecting Miss Sutherland, we will take turns enjoying her company as long as she chooses to put up with us," Col. Dawson said.

"Then I leave you in good hands, Miss Catherine; it has been my pleasure to protect you," He tipped his hat to Catherine with a smile. She couldn't help thinking how handsome he was.

"Lieutenant, we'll 'noon' in about an hour. You can give the order to stop when you see an area that will accommodate our train," Col. Dawson said.

"Yes, sir," Lt. Rushing said with a salute. He tipped his hat to Catherine, then turned his horse and rode away.

"How are you doing, Miss Sutherland?" Col. Dawson asked. "I hope the ride is not too tiring."

"Not at all, Colonel, it's a beautiful morning, and Lieutenant Rushing was charming company," she replied.

Col. Dawson raised an eyebrow, "Charming, you say? I'll have to ask him where that fits into being protective."

"Well, if it makes you feel better, sir, I find your company most pleasant too. I'm really quite grateful, in fact. My dearest friend on this journey went on to Oregon Territory, and without you and the Lieutenant, I'd have only my brother for companionship. For all his good qualities, he might have something to say once or twice an hour, and I know he's sick of hearing me talk."

"We certainly can't have him being ill, so it looks as though we'll need to rescue him on a daily basis. Are you comfortable riding that much?"

"Colonel, this pretty mare is far more enjoyable than a bumpy wagon seat. I grew up riding on the farm so I'm quite comfortable on horseback. To save our animals, I walked on foot for most of the journey from the east, so this is luxury for me."

Col. Edward Dawson looked at the beautiful girl riding alongside him. The idea of her walking the difficult trail for months on end was unthinkable. There was a grace about her that implied royalty. With a little imagination one could see her dressed in finery and commanding obeisance, just by her presence. Or in a more relevant setting, walking into an officer's ball and capturing the eye of every man in the room, escorted by himself, of course.

"Colonel Dawson?" Catherine was looking at him with a puzzled look.

"Miss Sutherland, I'm so sorry, for a moment there I was lost in thought. Did you ask me something?" Catherine thought the Colonel was actually blushing.

182

"No ... but you were looking at me strangely."

"I do apologize! It's just that I'm still trying to digest the fact that this lovely creature has found her way to the untamed west and is actually riding with me, gracing me with her smile that would melt any man's heart," Dawson replied.

"And you fault Lieutenant Rushing for being charming!" Catherine teased.

"Miss Sutherland, I fear I must limit your protective care to the two of us lest my entire company be reduced to a group of drooling schoolboys," he replied.

"I think you greatly overestimate my influence, but tell me about yourself, Colonel," Catherine said, wanting to divert the conversation. "Where was your home before coming west?"

"I grew up in Boston and graduated from West Point in '66. My first assignment was a command at Ft. Larned. Soon afterward, the Eastern Division of The Union Pacific Railroad began construction parallel to the closed Smokey Hill Trail. The Army was sent here to protect the workers due to unrest with the Indians and needed a base of operations. So the old Fort Fletcher was reactivated, and renamed Fort Hays in honor of Brigadier General Alexander Hays who was killed in the Civil War."

'So you've spent your entire military career on the frontier. How do you feel about that?" Catherine asked.

"I suppose my feelings are mixed. The loneliness of the west, especially the absence of the fairer sex," he said with a smile, "is extremely difficult to adjust to in the beginning. After a few years of this open country, though, most of us feel cramped in civilized territory. I do think the officers who have wives to brighten their lives bear up under the strain of the west much better than those of us who are bachelors. So please don't be offended by the attention your presence has generated. We are simply delighted to have your company. I'm afraid when you reach Fort Hays you will be inundated with requests for your time. There are at least a dozen single officers there, not to mention the enlisted men, who will clamor to be first in line," Col Dawson assured her.

For the first time today Catherine thought of David. Her hand automatically went to her neck where she could feel his necklace beneath her dress. It had been so pleasant to interact with these officers, and yes, their compliments made her feel pretty and alive. She felt years older than the girl who had kissed David goodbye just months ago, vowing to love him until they were reunited. The last thing she needed now was the attention of dozens of men! She hadn't thought of her playful conversation with the officers as being unfaithful to David, but would she have related to the men in the same way if David were present? No, she was sure she wouldn't, and they would have treated her differently too. Somehow she would have to correct the direction these friendships were headed.

Col. Edward Dawson wasn't sure what happened in this conversation. His beautiful companion was now somewhere else in her mind. At a loss for words he rode without speaking, but Catherine didn't seem to notice. It was with relief that he heard the order coming from the front that the train would be stopping for the midday meal and to rest the animals. Rushing was right; she *was* a mysterious woman!

"Are you ready for a break, Miss Sutherland?" he asked.

Catherine smiled, back from wherever she'd gone, but something had changed. "You know, Colonel, I think I am, and I'm sure this pretty mare is too. Do you know if she has a name?"

"I don't know, but as the chief officer of this escort I officially grant you permission to name her whatever you please. Do you have something in mind?"

"Not yet, I want to think about it," she replied.

"Take your time, my lady. We'll be here a couple of hours before getting back on the trail. I know you were cooking this morning for your family, do you do that all the time?" the Colonel asked.

"My mother helps with preparations that she can do from a chair. I try to do everything else."

"I understand. After eating your cooking, I don't think your family would care to join us more than once a day for our cook's fare, but if you could endure it at noon, it would keep you from having to get out all your equipment and preparing a midday meal," the Colonel said.

"Oh, my! The benefits of this escort just keep coming," Catherine said, reaching her hand to him. "You are a kind and thoughtful man, Colonel Edward Dawson."

Dawson reached across the space between their horses and taking her small hand in his he bent and kissed it lightly. Though he dared not speak his thoughts aloud they were no less sincere, "Catherine, my queen, I am forever at your service."

CHAPTER 13

The days on the trail had fallen into a pleasant routine for Catherine. Each morning either Col. Dawson or Lt. Rushing appeared at her family's campsite with the saddled mare which was commonly referred to as "Miss Catherine's Horse," even though Catherine had officially named her "Pansy."

Jeremy said the officers flipped a coin to see who shared Catherine's company first! The losing officer exchanged places with the winner mid-morning, and they repeated the same routine in the afternoon. The long hours of conversation gave her a great deal of insight into both these men. Their company was not only entertaining; she learned much about living on the frontier from their conversations about army life and dealing with the Indians. She shared stories of her childhood in Lexington, and they talked about their boyish escapades. Catherine grew fond of each of them. She felt their good natured bickering over her company was due more to the fact that she was the only young woman on the train than to genuine interest, yet she knew that deep friendships were being formed. She tried to keep an emotional barrier in place to separate her friendship with them from her feelings for David. Still she found herself feeling closer to these men every day, and farther from David.

When Catherine asked Jeremy how things were left with Liz in light of their relationship he told her they had agreed to write each other. Liz had given him an address in Oregon City that held mail for travelers, and she was to send mail to him at Fort Dodge. Some other girl might have encouraged Jeremy to live his own life, but Liz respected his determination to fulfill what he considered to be his responsibility. In the meantime, they would use this period of separation to get better acquainted through letters.

Liz and Jeremy made the decision to trust their hearts to God. If the feelings that had just begun for them were truly in God's plan, then that love would grow in this time of waiting. If other people came into their lives and found places in their hearts, they would recognize those relationships as meant to be, and just be thankful for the friendship they had experienced with each other.

Catherine was amazed at the wisdom Jeremy so often showed in times of decision. He had just turned sixteen last month on the trail. But Godly wisdom was obviously no respecter of age. She knew Jeremy prayed about things and God gave him answers. She decided she hadn't been praying enough about her future. It would be at least another eighteen months before David came for her. That seemed like an eon; one bleak beyond description. Very soon her family would leave this escorted train. Her entertaining, adoring officers would be gone, along with her idle, fun days. She remembered the look in Dorthea's eyes that first morning they met as she talked about the loneliness of the Kansas plains. Panic rose in Catherine's chest as she saw her future through those eyes … lonely, worn out from the dry, hot winds, and as faded in spirit as her sun-bleached dress.

"God, please, no! Surely You have something better for me than this," she prayed silently, as tears flowed down her cheeks.

She had forgotten that Sam was riding beside her. Now that they had talked for weeks, there wasn't as much small talk going on, and they often rode companionably in silence. He was aghast to look up and see that Catherine was crying.

"Catherine! What's wrong? …I'm sorry, maybe I shouldn't ask … It's just … is there anything I can do? Here …" Sam handed her a clean handkerchief.

Catherine tried to laugh it off. Wiping her tears she said, "Oh, Sam, I'm just a silly girl."

"I know I've called you a few things since we met, but "Silly Girl" is definitely not one of them," he insisted. "Would it help to talk?"

"Maybe it would, but there's nothing you can do to change things," she said, with a fresh rush of tears.

"Now you *are* talking silly. Don't you know I am Lieutenant Samuel Rushing, World Changer? Now tell me what you need changed to do away with those tears, and I will move heaven and earth to make it happen," Sam insisted.

"I was just thinking that in the next two days we will be leaving this train and heading to Fort Hays. After that, we will go on to Fort Dodge and then to the farm my stepfather bought. The previous owner's description of the place makes me think it's the last place on earth I would want to live. The loneliness she described was unbearable. They worked night and day there just to survive, and never made a profit. Until today I hadn't stopped to think what that will really be like, and now that I have, I'm wondering how I will ever bear it!"

188

The agony in Catherine's voice was more than Sam could bear. "Here, come this way." He led his horse and Pansy off the trail to the shade of a large tree. Dismounting, he looped the horses' reins to a branch, then reached up to help Catherine dismount. He enclosed her with his arms and in spite of all her intentions; she gave herself to his embrace. Her tears dampened the front of his uniform as he held her, stroking her hair.

"I can't bear seeing you so unhappy. Catherine, I was joking earlier, but the truth is ... I *can* change things. You don't have to go to that God forsaken place. I know this is not the right time or place, and certainly this is not the way I intended to say these things, but ... I love you, Catherine. I have absolutely adored you from the first day we rode together. Marry me, love. I know the life of a soldier's wife is not the easiest, and you deserve so much more, but at least it's better than the picture you painted of your future there. And I promise, you will never be alone except for the time I have to be away on duty. I can't bear being separated from you now as it is!"

Sam lifted her face to his and kissed her forehead. "Marry me, Catherine." Wiping the tears from her cheeks he covered them with gentle kisses as his fingers caressed the lines of her face, her throat. "So sweet ... so beautiful." He traced the outline of her full lips that beckoned him with their sweetness. Finally, he could bear it no longer, "Oh, Catherine!" he cried as he pulled her to him and covered her mouth with his.

"This is wrong ... I love David!" Catherine's head screamed, and yet she found herself returning Sam's kisses. She needed his nearness, and David was so far away. She felt so alone, so empty, and Sam was here, loving her ... wonderful, sweet, funny Sam. She loved him, too ... in a

189

different way. She couldn't fight any longer. The world around them ceased to exist as Sam kissed her gently, time and again until she felt she'd cry for the sweetness of it. Then his lips possessed hers in way she had never experienced with David. This was the kiss of a man, a kiss that reached to the depth of her. It was so easy to surrender to its beckoning, to lose herself in Sam's strong arms, in Sam's love for her.

"No, Catherine! This belongs to David!" The voice within her brought her back to reality.

"Sam, no, I'm sorry. I can't do this!" She pulled back and turned away from him.

"Catherine, what is it. I didn't mean to offend you." His eyes were filled with distress. "I didn't mean to get carried away ... I just love you so."

Catherine turned back to face him, "Sam, it isn't your fault. It's mine. I should have told you already ... I'm committed to someone ... a young man back east."

"You're committed ... Catherine, what exactly does that mean? Are you betrothed?" Sam asked.

He looked up to see the last of the wagons carrying the Chinese workers passing by. Drat the timing! He had to get Catherine back on the trail. It wasn't safe to be out here by themselves, and as badly as he wanted to finish this conversation, he wasn't going to take a chance on their lives.

"Catherine, we have to go back to the train immediately. But we'll talk when we get back on the trail. I just want you to know that I meant every word I said to you." He helped her mount Pansy, swung up onto his horse, and they rode until they arrived back where they had begun.

As they passed Jeremy's wagon, Catherine waved briefly, seeing his puzzled look. She didn't even glance at McCloud, but Sam noticed his angry expression as they rode to their place in the line. It might be wise to keep an ear open to what went on at the McCloud camp tonight. He had bad feelings about that guy.

Sam knew Catherine well enough by now to know that she did not want to resume their conversation. This was going to drive him crazy, thinking about what she said; "I'm committed to someone, a young man back east." Undoubtedly, she had a boyfriend back there; that shouldn't be a surprise. Maybe it was a kid thing that she'd outgrown since leaving there. He knew she was young, but she was mature for her age. She already took care of household chores like a married woman of years. He knew she liked him, at least she had before today, and she had certainly returned his kisses. Then she abruptly pulled away and brought his world crashing to an end with her declaration of a commitment to another man.

Catherine sneaked a sideways look at Sam as they rode. She knew he was confused. He had to know she enjoyed his kisses. She blushed remembering that. Then she had told him there was another man. How was he supposed to reconcile those two things when she couldn't do so herself? She believed his declaration of love. She'd seen it in his eyes numerous times. He wanted to marry her! Oh, God, what had she gotten into? What had she done to him? Could she be so certain that David was still waiting for her? What if she refused Sam's offer, then months later learned that David had gone on with his life with someone else? She could love Sam. She already loved so many things about him.

But she'd been loving David for years. If only she had some kind of confirmation that he still loved her. And yet, she did. It was on a chain around her neck where it had been since the day she left Lexington. She remembered the love in his eyes as he told her the necklace was to be a tangible reminder of his love for her. He knew she would not be able to hear from him by letter for many months, even a year or more, but when she felt that necklace she was to remember that his love was there. David was not one to break a commitment because it was difficult to keep. She thought she was not either, yet how easily she had laid aside that commitment for a few moments of comfort in Sam's arms. Now there was no way to avoid hurting Sam. She already had. She could see it in his eyes. Nothing was gained by this situation today; she had been untrue to David, her comfortable and fun relationship with Sam was ruined, and she still faced the lonely prairie.

"Sam," she spoke to him now, and as he looked into her eyes he saw a resolve that caused him to dread whatever she would say next.

Catherine told Sam of her years- long relationship with David, of their profession of love to each other and their plans to marry in two years. She explained how McCloud's deceit had brought them to this trail now, separating her from David.

"I had no idea how difficult it would be to never see him, or to hear his voice telling me he loves me. Our relationship had never been tested by separation, or by other wonderful people coming into our lives. But as I told you, Sam, I am committed to David, as he is committed to me. I hope you can forgive me for today and understand that I was not being false with you. I felt your love, and my response to that love was real. It was so comforting to be in

192

your arms, but I had no right to be there. Can you possibly understand this, and can you forgive me?" Catherine asked.

Sam looked at her with sorrow in his eyes. Sorrow for himself, certainly, but also for Catherine and the situation that circumstances had created for her.

"My sweet angel," he said with a sigh, "after having those few moments with you today I envy your David even more than ever. I wonder if he knows what a wonderful woman he has waiting for him. And as long as you're waiting, I really hope he is, too. If I someday learn that I have given you up for nothing I will be most upset. In fact, I intend to stay in touch with you to see that he shows up, and if he doesn't, will you be glad to see me?" Sam asked with a wistful look.

"Sam, Sam," Catherine smiled at him, "I will always be glad to see you."

*   *   *   *

The day Catherine had been dreading was here. The road to Fort Hays went south, and the caravan still had further to go in a northeasterly direction to reach the railroad construction site. This meant that her family would have no more military escort as they headed for the fort. Catherine hoped that the road's proximity to the fort would be sufficient reason to be problem-free. Edward's reports had shown no incidents with Indians in that area.

Catherine dreaded having to say goodbye to Sam and Edward. Apparently Sam had told his superior officer of her relationship with David, and Catherine could sense a difference in his attitude. He was still attentive and gracious, but there was a reserve that told her he respected her boundaries. Catherine was so thankful that Sam did not hold a grudge against her, but kept being her sweet, funny friend. She would never forget these two officers; they had made this part of the journey, not only bearable, but enjoyable for her. Col. Dawson hated for Catherine to work hard setting up her cooking apparatus every evening, so he hired a couple of the Chinese workers to help his cook and insisted that Catherine's family take all their meals with the escort. That had improved the caliber of meals served, saved Catherine work, and also saved the supplies that her family would have used. Now she would go back to being the hard-working cook and chore-keeper of the family without the special favors bestowed at the Colonel's command.

Edward came to their camp first. He had paperwork for McCloud to give to officials at the fort, and assured them they would be able to stay there for a while if they needed to do so. He was a true soldier, but saying goodbye to Catherine was nearly his undoing. As she warmly embraced him, he so wished the competition would all disappear. He kissed her on each cheek, and took one last look at her blue eyes. "She'll always be my queen," he thought.

Sam appeared shortly after Edward left. He looked so sharp in his uniform, tall and handsome. His eyes showed the lack of sleep, though, as he had tossed and turned all night in dread of this day. He said his goodbyes to the McCloud's and Jeremy, then took Catherine by the hand.

"Come over here, mysterious woman!" He ordered, drawing her away to a place away from the others.

"Why do you call me that now? You know all my secrets," she laughed.

"There's one I don't have an answer to."

"And what is that, Lieutenant?"

Sam looked down at her with love in his eyes. Softly he said, "There's got to be some secret to learning to live without you. Otherwise, I don't think I'll make it."

"Oh, Sam," Catherine said, taking both his hands in hers. "I'll never forget you."

"But you'll never marry me either as long as your David is hanging on. But just in case that doesn't work out, I want you to know that I'll be waiting for the next eighteen months to see if this guy shows up. Until I know that you've married him, my heart belongs to you. If you ever need me, Catherine, all you have to do is get the word to me. If I'm not stationed here, they'll know where I've been transferred, I'll make certain of it." He gave her a quick hug and a kiss on her forehead. "I love you, Catherine," and with a sharp turn about he strode away without a look backward.

* * * *

Catherine was sitting in the back of the large wagon with Susannah. She'd ridden with Jeremy until they stopped for a short noon break, but joined her mother when they started again. She suddenly realized she hadn't spent much time with her mother lately. Edward and Sam had occupied her time, and Susannah had been staying close to the wagon and in bed as much as possible. From the size of her abdomen, it shouldn't be much longer before the baby came. Catherine still had the secret fear that Susannah would go into labor in some secluded place, and she would have to deliver her younger brother or sister.

195

It was incredibly lonely to be on the road without others. Catherine hoped they would indeed reach the fort this evening. She hated the thought of their having to camp alone at night.

Catherine had not told Susannah about her time off the trail with Sam, not that she didn't want to talk to her about it, there just didn't seem to be any time.

"Mama, is it possible to love more than one man at the same time?" she asked.

"Well, I once knew a lady who swore that she deeply loved four men at once, so I suppose it is," Susannah said. "She said they were all different and she loved all of them differently. She wouldn't marry any of them, since she'd have to give up the other three."

"I think I can relate to that," Catherine said. "My case is different, though. I do want to marry, and I can only marry one. I guess I thought that loving David would prevent my having feelings for any other men. And yet, I do have feelings for Edward and for Sam. They are both wonderful, kind, thoughtful, fun … all the things I like about David, but so different from him and each other. I really believe that I could be happily married to any one of these men. I suppose it's good that I have a commitment to David, because that settles it."

"Does it, Catherine?" Susannah asked. "You and David were so young when you made that commitment. You're still young, but you've grown up a lot in less than a year. You have no way of knowing what is happening in David's life. Is he also growing as a person? Will the two of you be at the same place emotionally at the end of these two years? Will situations cause either of you to break that commitment somehow? Will your heart go its own

196

direction in spite of your commitment? People don't decide to fall in love, Catherine, it just happens."

"What should I do, Mama?" Catherine asked.

"The heart is such a strange thing, Catherine. It doesn't have to stop loving one person to start loving another. I don't know that we'll ever understand it. That's why it's so important to bring the Lord into our relationships; to guard our hearts so that we only truly love the one He knows will follow His plan for our lives."

Catherine was taking in that thought silently when they heard:

"Whoa! Whoa, there!" They could hear McCloud calling to the oxen. Then they heard Jeremy calling his team to halt too. Catherine went to the front of the wagon to see why they were stopping. All she could see at first was an Indian pony standing almost in the trail. Jeremy jumped down off his driver's seat and was headed on a run to the right.

"Catherine!" he yelled, "Bring towels!"

"What is it? What's wrong?" Susannah asked in fear.

"I don't know, Mama, Jeremy just yelled to bring towels," Catherine said as she pulled three towels from a box. The step wasn't in place so Catherine had to jump to the ground and barely landed on her feet. She headed the direction she'd seen Jeremy run and then saw an Indian lying on the ground. One of his legs was broken so badly that the bone protruded from his skin and blood was pouring onto the ground around him. As she came closer Catherine could see that this was a teenager, probably Jeremy's age. He had to be in excruciating pain, but he did not cry out. Only a moan came from his lips as he tried to rise from the ground.

"No, friend, lie still," Jeremy said to him, pushing him gently back. He quickly placed his hand on the leg where blood was freely flowing.

"Catherine," he said, in a controlled voice, "quickly take my belt off and hand it to me." He took one of the towels and placed it under his hand, then continued the pressure on the boy's leg.

Catherine was shaking as she unbuckled Jeremy's belt and pulled it free of the loops. She held it out to him and he told her to put her hand exactly where his had been and to press firmly. She did so, and Jeremy quickly put the belt around the boy's leg above the wound and made a tourniquet. They were both relieved to see that the blood flow was greatly reduced. Now they had to deal with the broken bone. The eyes of the boy looked to Jeremy and then to Catherine, as if pleading for relief.

"Cat, just stay here with him while I get some boards to splint that leg." he said.

McCloud stepped forward then, "Why are you even messing with a lousy Injun? Let his own people find him. We don't have time to deal with this trash. We've got to get to the fort."

Jeremy looked at McCloud for a short moment and said, "Yes, we do, and he's going with us." Then he started for his wagon at a run to get the boards.

Catherine looked at the boy and saw him writhe in pain. Instinctively, she reached out and took his hand. "I am so sorry ... so sorry!"

The boy gripped her hand so tightly it hurt, but Catherine didn't care. That was the least she could do. Jeremy came back with the boards and leather thongs to secure them. He also brought a blanket.

"Cover him up, Catherine. He's going into shock from losing so much blood."

The boy was shivering as Catherine tucked the blanket around him and pushed his hair back from his forehead.

"Do you speak any English?" she asked. She wasn't sure if the nod was in answer to her question, or if it was another chill.

"What is your name?"

Between chills he spoke, "Runs … Like … the … Wind."

Jeremy looked up at Catherine. He saw that she was thinking the same thing, that this young man would more than likely never live up to his name again. As Jeremy placed the board beneath the broken leg the boy shuddered in agony.

"Cat, when I have to pull this leg back into place enough to splint it, it's going to hurt worse than you can imagine. He'll probably pass out."

"Here, Catherine," Susannah was there now with a wet towel which Catherine took and squeezed a few drops of water into the lips of Runs Like the Wind. Then she gently wiped his brow, as he whispered, "I … thank … you."

"Wind," Jeremy said, addressing the boy. "I'm fixing to have to hurt you really bad. It's gonna hurt me just as bad to do it to you, but I have to get this bone back into your leg before we can splint it up and get you to the fort."

The boy nodded that he understood, "My …knife .." he asked.

Jeremy reached to the scabbard at the boy's waist and brought out a knife.

McCloud stepped forward again. "What are you doing, giving him a knife?"

Jeremy ignored his stepfather, covered the blade with one of the towels and helped the shaking boy place the knife between his teeth.

"Pray, Catherine," he said. Then carefully checking the tourniquet again, and gently lining up the rest of Wind's leg, he gave one quick jerk and the bone was back within the general area of where it belonged. The young native gave only one large groan as he bit into the knife, and then wilted in a dead faint. Jeremy put away the knife that had fallen to his chest.

"We need to move him to the wagon while he's still out; he won't feel the pain then. We've got to get him to the fort as quickly as possible. We shouldn't be that far away now. Does he have any more belongings other than the horse?"

"I don't see anything else around. But the horse has no reins, so I can't lead him," Catherine said.

Her quick look about the area told the tale. A large rattlesnake lay mangled on the ground a few feet away. Apparently the horse had been spooked by the snake and had thrown it's rider, breaking the boy's leg.

"I'll have to put a rope around his neck, but first we need to get Wind moved. I'd appreciate it if you'd help me get him to the wagon," Jeremy said to McCloud.

"I don't want him in my wagon!" McCloud said.

"I'm not putting him in yours, he's going in mine," Jeremy said, "and don't you even try to say that wagon belongs to you. It was on my farm long before you stole it."

Everyone stood still in shock. Jeremy had never said a word to Mc Cloud about taking his farm. He'd also never stood up to him before. McCloud turned around and walked back to his wagon, speechless. Jeremy grinned, and then turned to Catherine.

"Cat, I'm gonna need you to ride with us and stay close to Wind. All the stuff's flat in my wagon so we can lay him right on top. I'll pull up closer and the two of us can get him in there since Mr. McCloud finds helping so distasteful." Then to Susannah he said, "Ma, we could use some pillows to prop that leg. I'm going to be traveling as fast as these oxen will go, and it's going to be a rough ride for him."

"I'll get them," Susannah said, heading for her wagon.

"Cat, stay there with Wind in case he regains consciousness," Jeremy said.

Susannah was there with pillows as Jeremy pulled his wagon as close as possible to the injured boy. He brought a large board that he gently slipped underneath Runs Like the Wind.

"I'll get this end; you get that one," he said to Catherine. "Up on the count of three … one … two … three." Carefully they lifted the unconscious boy and walked the few steps to the wagon. It was difficult actually getting him on top of the cargo, but Jeremy climbed inside and gently pulled the board up into place. They pushed pillows beneath and all around the broken leg, checking again to make certain the tourniquet held.

"Catherine, take this, he'll need it when he wakes up," Susannah said, offering her a glass jar filled with water.

"I've got to get his pony," Jeremy said, grabbing a rope from the side of the wagon. Thankfully, the horse didn't resist as Jeremy slid the rope around his neck and led him to the back of the wagon. He tied the rope to the wagon with a quick knot and climbed into the driver's seat.

Catherine was sitting beside Runs Like the Wind.

"Ma, I guess we'll see you at the fort when you get there." Jeremy said.

"God go with you," Susannah said as she looked at her children.

"O.K., Cat, we're moving," Jeremy said, "Git up!" He called to the oxen.

"Find us when you get there, Mama!" Catherine called. She hated leaving her mother standing there in the middle of the trail, looking after them. Heavy with child, Catherine knew Susannah could not travel at the pace they would be moving, but it was the loneliest feeling she had experienced in all her goodbyes.

*   *   *   *

"Catherine! Wake up!" Susannah was shaking her shoulder.

"Oooh, Mama! Can't I sleep a little longer?"

It was so late last night when they got to bed. The frantic ride to the fort with Runs Like the Wind had jarred every bone in her body. The young Indian was in and out of consciousness, groaning with pain. Catherine continually spoke encouraging words to him when she knew he could hear her, and held his hand when the waves of pain washed over him. The doctor at the fort said he would not have lived much longer had they not reached the fort at that time. Catherine and Jeremy had waited in the outer room of the doctor's quarters to learn the outcome of the examination, and so Runs Like the Wind would not feel alone. Jeremy's tourniquet was the most important factor in the rescue, the doctor said. Had the wound continued to bleed as badly as when they found him, he would have been dead in minutes, for a major artery had been severed.

A kind sentry showed them to quarters where they could sleep, but neither of them could rest until they knew their mother and McCloud had arrived. Catherine was relieved beyond measure when she saw them coming through the gate of the fort. They were given quarters as well, but it was after midnight when everyone was situated. And now her mother was waking her up so early!

"Catherine, I'd let you sleep, but there's someone here to see you."

She was immediately awake, "Who is it?"

"Runs Like the Wind and his parents," Susannah told her. "His father is apparently a very important chief."

Catherine jumped out of bed and threw on her clothes. Thank goodness, she'd placed them over the chair last night so they'd be less wrinkled. She washed her face in the bowl on the nightstand and brushed her hair, pushing her curls into place.

Susannah smiled approvingly. "That's the best two-minute toilette I've ever seen." Moving toward the door she said, "We'd better go. Jeremy's already there."

As she opened the outer door of the building Catherine gasped in surprise. In front of the building a large group of Indians stood waiting for her. If Jeremy had not been standing there with them, smiling, she probably would have slammed the door and run back inside in fear! Runs Like the Wind, with his leg in a cast, was lying on a travois attached to a horse that would pull him back to their village. Standing beside him was the most impressive man Catherine had ever seen. Taller than six feet, the chief wore a fringed leather shirt and leggings. His feathered headdress flowed down his back almost to his knees. Everything about him exuded power and authority, but his handsome face was kind, Catherine thought. She could see the resemblance between father and son.

Runs Like the Wind's face broke into a shy smile when he saw Catherine. His father took a step forward and almost bowed. Catherine walked to him and extended her hand. His huge hand grasped hers firmly, but gently.

"I am Catherine," she said.

"I am Chief Black Horse," he said. "I have come for my son. I give many thanks to you and to your brother. You save life of Runs Like the Wind."

"Chief Black Horse, I am honored to meet you. Your son is the bravest man I have ever met. I am glad to see him doing well."

"White man's doctor say leg maybe no more good for running," the young Indian said, his eyes troubled. "I heard you pray to Great Father for my life, and my life saved. Will you ask Him for my leg to run again?"

Tears came to Catherine's eyes as she took Runs Like the Wind's hand in hers.

"I promise you I will pray to the Great Father for your leg to run again."

Chief Black Horse turned to Jeremy, "You great friend to my son. Chief Black Horse will not forget. You now 'White Brother' and he handed Jeremy a leather cord with a beautiful, polished stone. "This my sign to all red men ... you are White Brother to Black Horse and Runs Like the Wind."

Jeremy placed it around his neck and shook the hand of the chief. "It is a great honor to be White Brother to you, Chief Black Horse, and to you, Runs Like the Wind. I hope someday to see you run." And with a grin, he said, "Maybe we race, you and me."

All of the Indians laughed.

Runs Like the Wind turned to Catherine, "White Brother call you 'Cat.' Is O.K. I call you, 'Yellow Cat?'"

Catherine was delighted. "I would love that, Runs Like the Wind, 'Yellow Cat.'Yes, that's me!"

Runs Like the Wind spoke shyly to Catherine, "Yellow Cat very kind, beautiful here," he moved hand in a circle over his face, "and here," he said, touching his heart.

Chief Black Horse spoke again, "My son's mother bring gift for you," and a beautiful Indian woman stepped forward. Her smile and the warmth in her eyes made Catherine want to hug her, but she didn't know if that would be acceptable in Indian culture. The woman held out to Catherine a beautiful white leather throw. The hide was soft and supple, the edges lined with a fine fringe.

"I am Rippling Brook," she said. "May this bring comfort and warmth to you as you brought comfort to my son." She laid the beautiful gift in Catherine's hands and solemnly pressed her cheek to Catherine's, first one side, then the other. It was a sacred moment, as though she was being received into this tribe; and maybe she was; all the Indians cheered!

Catherine had the urge to introduce this lovely native woman to her mother. She turned to Susannah and called her to come forward.

Susannah felt awkward in her condition to be the center of attention, but as Catherine introduced her to Rippling Brook she sensed the bonding of one mother to another.

"Your son was so very brave last night, Rippling Brook," Susannah said.

"Both your children bring honor to you, Susannah," Rippling Brook said as she held Susannah's hands in hers. "May the child you carry here, be as they are." She placed her hands on Susannah's abdomen and looked into Susannah's eyes in unspoken communication that only they understood.

Black Horse spoke something quietly in his language to Runs Like the Wind. They both looked in the direction where Pollard McCloud stood. The younger man gave the slightest negative shake to his head. Only Jeremy heard him say to his father,

"No help White Brother. Has black heart."

CHAPTER 14

"I love what money and influence can do!" Charlotte Pendleton said, looking at the flier in her hand. Propped with a half-dozen pillows in a huge mahogany bed, she was picking at the breakfast tray in front of her and gloating over her success. Her auburn hair tumbled girlishly about her face and onto the shoulders of her white lace nightdress, giving the impression of sweet innocence. Her thoughts, however, were closer to those of a mythical siren using her charms to seduce men for her own purposes.

"David Winters," Charlotte read aloud from the flier, "the latest in the Majestic's entourage of first-class jewelers, will be in our east salon on November 10th for the most exciting show of the year. Mr. Winters has been the rage of the fashion critics with his style which has been called the "contemporary antique" look. The private showing for 'Invitation Only' guests will begin at 10:00 A.M, with doors opening to the public at 1:00 PM. Be one of the first to own this new artist's work; it is certain to become a classic!"

Pushing aside the tray of half-eaten food, Charlotte sunk down into her pillows and looked at the ceiling. Now that she had David in New York City, on *her* territory, she definitely had the advantage. For months now her primary mission in life had been to make him forget this Catherine girl. It irritated her no end that she had not yet been able to accomplish her goal. She was accustomed to men bowing to her wishes. She had yet to meet any girl whose charms exceeded her own, and especially one who had been absent for the better part of a year. But David was not like other men. While his strength of character was the thing she found most attractive about him, Charlotte hated that it was keeping them apart. She was determined to break down those barriers.

She remembered the day in the jewelry shop when that long-haired young man brought the letter to David from his Catherine. Just thinking of his joy and excitement lit that small flame of jealousy that began to burn every time Charlotte thought of it. David had totally forgotten she was there. She knew in talking to him later that he was hardly aware that she had left in a mad rage, slamming the door as she went. That was a mistake, showing her anger like that. She'd have to be more careful to control her temper. This was a game, and as in any game, strategy was the key to winning.

Obviously, being beautiful, charming, and witty was not the winning strategy in this situation. Charlotte came back to her aunt's home that day determined to find the course of action that would accomplish her goal. One thing she'd proven already, the more she used the seductive approach, the more David withdrew from her. All right, she'd be his friend … for now. And as his friend she would pull strings to put him in her favor and in her debt, and then go from there.

That afternoon she had written a letter to her father. Her Poppy would do anything she asked, he always had. Her mother had died when she was born and her father had spent her lifetime trying to make up for the loss by granting

Charlotte's every wish. This would be a small thing for him. As the president of the most prestigious bank in the city he was a powerful man in the business world. All he had to do was say the word and it was done. Charlotte and her aunt Evelyn had already discussed the prospect of having Poppy pull a few strings in David's behalf, so this was a good time to proceed with that. His bank carried the loan on the Majestic building, the most elegant shopping location in New York. Its various salons offered well-coffered clients the very latest in anything fashion had to offer. A showing of David's jewelry there could thrust his career into unbelievable places, and a few words from her Poppy could land that showing. She knew the manager of the exclusive jewelry salon would be concerned about the quality of David's work. It was practically unheard of for an unknown artist to show work there. She would have to convince both Poppy and the manager that David's work was of the caliber to which their clients were accustomed. That meant sending them the pieces she'd purchased from David; she'd borrow Aunt Evelyn's as well, so there would be samples enough to prove his talent. She had no doubt they would be impressed.

Her plan had worked beautifully. The salon manager was extremely pleased with David's jewelry, and intrigued that someone so young had developed skills of that quality with a style of his own. With a clientele of wealthy young ladies, an equally young, handsome artist could be a drawing card that would benefit his salon for a long time to come. The fact that Martin Pendleton's daughter was behind this artist guaranteed that at least twenty-five or so of her acquaintances would be there making purchases. He had nothing to lose. He wrote a letter to David, but sent it through Miss Pendleton as he had been instructed, inviting the young Mr. Winters to a showing at the Majestic in November.

Charlotte smiled, remembering the day she took the letter to David. She had waited at the tea room across the street until she saw Silas Goodson leave the Jewelry and Watch Emporium. She knew he went to the bank on Wednesday afternoons. She'd made it her business to know. That was the only way she could talk to David alone because he wouldn't meet her anywhere else.

She'd been as nice and caring as any friend should be and told David she had good news for him. She gave him the letter and he read it. He was genuinely surprised and thanked her. Then to her amazement he had said he'd pray about it! She had expected more appreciation from him. Obviously, he didn't realize what an opportunity this was. Mr. Goodson, though, knowing the industry, had been duly impressed and told David that this could be the chance of a lifetime. Then David had begun to show some excitement. He was concerned that he couldn't get enough pieces produced in time to make a really nice showing, but he went to work immediately and had produced a small, but imposing portfolio.

Now he was in New York City. She would show him her world, convinced that once he saw the grandeur that could be his David would never want to go back to his small home town. Surely then he would forget the girl named Catherine who was lost somewhere in the west.

She had insisted that they travel from Lexington to New York together. She couldn't help but notice the glances their way. She was used to attracting attention herself, but she had to admit that she and David made a handsome couple. He was dressed more stylishly than she had ever seen him in the shop. He shyly admitted that his father had taken him to purchase new clothing suitable for the city. His dark hair was nicely groomed, but still that lock in front insisted on falling attractively down over his forehead. The new suit accented his broad shoulders and slender waist. When he smiled his dark eyes lit up from within, making him one of the handsomest young men she had ever known. She couldn't wait to show him off to her friends.

Charlotte had offered David the hospitality of her father's home, but he had insisted on acquiring his own room at a hotel near the Majestic. He'd still need her, though; he was totally out of his element here in the city, and she'd be here beside him, smiling and encouraging him until he realized he couldn't live without her! Convinced now that she was in control of things, Charlotte jumped out of bed. She wanted to take special care with her appearance today. Many of her friends and Poppy's acquaintances would be at the private showing and she intended to sparkle as brightly as any of David's gems!

* * * *

David breathed his first deep breath since he'd left his hotel room that morning. It was 5:00 PM and his showing was done for the day. The initial excitement had ebbed, and a new feeling of confidence had taken its place. His jewelry had received raves from friends and acquaintances of Charlotte and her father, people who were accustomed to purchasing fine jewelry as nonchalantly as they ate their fine dinners. A wave of appreciation swept over him. He'd been keeping his distance from this charming and attractive girl, but it seemed that she finally understood his relationship with Catherine and genuinely wanted to help him get a start in the jewelry business. He still wasn't comfortable staying at her home, though, and was glad to have his own room. David had never rented a hotel room before and thought it was quite expensive just for a place to sleep. Charlotte laughed and told him that was the lowest priced hotel in the area that could be considered a decent place to stay.

His jewelry was now under lock and key and the building was guarded at night. Most of the pieces he brought had been sold today, but were left for him to display tomorrow to procure more orders. He was going to be busy beyond belief when he got back home. He had stopped taking a salary from Mr. Goodson because his time at the shop now was spent primarily in doing his own work. David felt he should be the one paying for the use of the space and equipment, but Mr. Goodson would hear none of that. He was thrilled to see David's success, even if it meant losing him to bigger things.

As he stepped out of the Majestic to walk back to his hotel, the sights and sounds of New York City enveloped him. He never dreamed he would be here and couldn't have imagined a place so large with so many people. And the buildings! The tallest building in Lexington boasted of three stories, and here buildings were so tall they called them "skyscrapers." He had no idea how many stories they contained. And not only were there marvelous things above ground, just this year a new form of transportation had been completed that ran a type of streetcar in a tunnel under the ground.

A uniformed attendant opened the hotel door for David as he arrived there. He stopped at the desk for his room key and was handed a message from Charlotte. In his room he read the note which stated that she and her father would pick him up at 7:30 to go to dinner. He'd planned to dine alone, spend a quiet evening, and get to bed early, but apparently that would change.

He hadn't expected to see Charlotte until tomorrow. She had left the showing with a friend whom she introduced as Alex Caine. The thought provoked a negative feeling about the man, but David didn't remember why. He had been so busy with clients he'd not given much attention to Caine other than shaking hands when they were introduced.

Taking off his suit jacket, David sat down on the bed and tried to recall what had triggered those impressions. He remembered noticing a quick change in Charlotte's expression when she saw the man; she seemed uncomfortable that he had come. He was a colleague of her father's she said, as she introduced him to David. Caine, probably in his thirties, was impeccably dressed in the latest New York menswear, his hair just as neatly groomed. But his eyes were those of a man who bent rules, a man who could be dangerous if crossed. They held a mocking expression as Charlotte introduced him to David. As he remembered the situation now, David recalled the man's attitude with Charlotte. She tried keeping her distance, but somehow Caine managed to be close to her with a possessive touch, looking at her with the same mocking smile in his eyes. There had to be some sort of history here, David thought.

He lay back on the bed and suddenly a longing for Catherine flooded his emotions like a wave. Tears filled his eyes as he wondered where she was and what might be happening with her. For years they had shared everything about their lives, and now he had so much to tell her and no way to reach her. She could never imagine that he would be in New York City, showing his work in a fancy jewelry salon. He knew she had a multitude of things to tell him too, and he so badly wanted to be with her, to see her blue eyes sparkle as she told him every detail of those things. How would they ever catch up? There was so much to say already and they had another year to go before they married as planned. At least, the sale of his jewelry was going to provide them with a good start. The sales from today alone, plus what he already had in the bank, would be almost enough to buy them a small house, and he still had tomorrow to go. How he wished he could tell her that! He walked to the window and looked down from his sixth floor room at the busy New York street. People lined the sidewalks, most of them hurrying home from their days' work. It seemed so impersonal from where he stood, yet he knew that each of those people represented lives that were filled with joys, problems, heartaches, and needs, just as his was. The great comfort was in knowing that God knew each of them. He knew everything about those problems, and He loved every single person and promised to be there with His grace. That included Catherine and him. God's grace was for them too.

Kneeling beside the bed, David poured out his heart to his Creator one more time, asking for the grace to make it through this time of separation from Catherine and for peace for his lonely heart. Soon the familiar assurance came and his thoughts went toward the evening. He really didn't want to go to dinner with Charlotte and her father, but in light of what she had done for him, he knew he should go. Right now, he had time for a nap, and as he drifted off to sleep, his last thought was, "Catherine, if you can hear me ... I love you ..."

*   *   *   *

Dinner with Charlotte and her father was, to David's dismay, a large dinner party. He was introduced to several of her father's business associates and their wives. Two of the ladies had been at the private showing of his jewelry. Three of Charlotte's closest friends were there with escorts, and David was somewhat surprised that Alex Caine was present as well. Seeing that Charlotte had indicated to David to take the seat at her left, Caine moved to sit at her right. That did not go unnoticed by Charlotte's father and David noticed a tightening of the older gentlemen's jaw and an expression in his eyes that David couldn't quite define.

It was evident that Martin Pendleton was a man of influence in New York City. The preference given to him wherever they went spoke loudly of that power. And yet, when it came to Charlotte, the man practically melted at his daughter's wishes.

Alex Caine was keeping Charlotte occupied, intentionally, David thought. Two of her friends tried to draw him into discussions pertaining to jazz artists and entertainers, and found it quite amusing that David was unfamiliar with the famous personages.

Then the conversation turned to David's reason for being in New York. The women who had purchased jewelry today complimented his skills again and told him how eager they were to see more of his work.

"Just what are your future plans in regard to your business, Mr. Winters?" Martin Pendleton asked.

"I prefer that you call me, David, sir, if you don't mind. I started making pieces for the small shop of my mentor, Mr. Silas Goodson, and my work began to do well in that area. Then your gracious daughter instigated this situation here which has been more than I could ever have dreamed. Quite honestly, sir, I have been so busy with the creative aspect that I've not had time to think of the business end."

"That is a common fault among artists, David," Pendleton said, but in a kindly manner. "However, if an artist is to be successful, the business aspects must not be ignored. Nor should they be trusted totally to a person without your own supervision. Many a talented person has lined the pockets of unscrupulous managers only to end up penniless themselves."

"Thank you for that advice, sir. I have every intention of sitting down with Mr. Goodson when I return to Lexington and drawing from his years of experience," David replied.

Alex Caine spoke, addressing David directly for the first time, "If you're looking for a manager in New York City, that is my field of work, Mr. Winters. I'm quite familiar with the largesse of the market here and could quite benefit your company." His voice and eyes still had that mocking tone, and though Martin Pendleton did not say anything, David caught the quick, disapproving look he sent across the table.

"Thank you, Mr.Caine, I appreciate your offer," David said graciously, although his face reddened, knowing he would never enter into a business agreement with Caine.

Dinner was finally over and David learned that the evening included a concert by a popular musical performer. He excused himself as the group proceeded through the large hotel and went in search of a men's room. The door to the concert hall was closed when David returned, and he felt it would be rude to open it in the middle of the performance. He really had no desire to be there anyway, and preferred to be back in his hotel room. He decided to walk around the lovely hotel, taking in the details so he could describe them in his next letter to Catherine. He walked out onto a porch with huge columns. Plants and beautiful flowers were attractively displayed along the wall of the building, with marble statues placed throughout the courtyard. A small waterfall added to the beauty of the surroundings with its sound of gentle rushing water. It reminded David of his and Catherine's special place where he had told her he loved her and kissed her for the first time. There was a small table to the side, almost secluded by the potted plants and trees. David sat there, wishing that Catherine could be there with him.

Suddenly, the sound of voices came from behind him. He recognized the man's voice as that of Alex Caine.

"Come here, you wench! I've been waiting all evening to get you alone!"

David recognized Charlotte's voice as she said, "Alex, stop it. I told you there wasn't going to be anymore of this!"

"So you think you can just cut me off that easily?" Caine asked. His laugh had a vicious sound. "You know that would mean denying yourself, too."

"I told you it was over between us," Charlotte said.

"It's never going to be over between us, baby. Not as long as I want you. And you know that nobody makes you feel the way I do," Caine said.

"Alex …"

In the silence, David wished he could disappear into the air. He was not intentionally eavesdropping, but to show himself now would be an embarrassment to both

Charlotte and himself. He didn't think it would matter to Caine.

"Ahh, that's my girl … see, you can't do without me anymore than I can stand to be without you. We're two of a kind, Charlotte. If your daddy thinks that sending you off to some two-bit town is going to keep us apart, he's mistaken."

"Alex, I don't want to be on his bad side. I stand to inherit a lot of money someday, and I'm not going to risk that. You know he would never approve my marrying you."

"Maybe not now, but there's got to be a way, I just haven't found it yet. I don't intend to spend the rest of our lives having to sneak you into my hotel room through the back door. Now kiss me like you do when that door closes behind us."

"Alex, stop it! I told you, it has to be over. I'll admit, I have no resistance when you're with me. That's why you have to stay away!"

David could tell that Caine had walked a few steps away from Charlotte.

"Well, this is something new … what's going on? … Oh, I see … it's the pretty boy with the bangles, is that it? Don't tell me you've fallen for a kid from some small town."

"David is not a kid. Unless you think I'm one too. We're the same age, which, if you'll remember, you and I are not. Poppy says you're much too old for me, and that's one of the reasons he wouldn't approve our relationship."

"Older men marry younger women all the time, Charlotte. Your sweet Poppy is afraid I'll get my hands on his money … that's his one big reason for cutting me out! But back to your pretty boy … did he take you out to fine places in his hick town? Or maybe for drives in the country, since that's about all they have there?"

"No, David and I never went out together."

"Well, how did you get so chummy ... enough so that you got your Poppy to drop a word to the salon manager at the Majestic for him to show his wares there?"

Caine laughed his sarcastic laugh. "Oh, I get it ... this was all your plan to get him to fall at your feet. My, my, you finally met a man you couldn't wind around your little finger!   Oh, my wicked Charlotte, don't bother denying it. I told you, we're two of a kind!"

David could hear Caine quickly walk back to Charlotte and he heard her gasp in pain. "Alex, you're hurting me!"

"Let's get one thing straight, Charlotte, either you're mine, or you're nobody's! Is that clear?" Caine's voice was cold as steel, leaving no question as to the meaning of his words. Then David heard his footsteps walking quickly away. The sounds of Charlotte's soft sobbing wrenched David's heart, but he knew he couldn't let her know he'd heard the conversation between her and Alex Caine. He felt sick. So the opportunity to show his work had not been because of its quality, but because a powerful man had spoken a few words at his daughter's request, and made the doors swing open. All those sales to Charlotte's friends and her father's acquaintances ... were they part of the plan too? Had he been played for the fool? That's exactly how he felt.

David heard Charlotte walking back toward the hotel hallway. He'd wait for a few more minutes, then leave. He didn't want to face her again until he'd thought this thing through.

When he felt enough time had passed for Charlotte to return to the ballroom, he walked back to the hotel foyer and left a message with the concierge for Mr. and Miss Pendleton that he was not feeling well, and had gone back to his hotel. He hailed a cab, returned to his room and closed the door, relieved to be alone.

To bring clarity to his jumbled thoughts, David tried to take this situation back to its beginning. That had to be the day Charlotte came into the shop the very first time. Every visit thereafter she made him aware of her interest in him. The day he told her about Catherine, she was angry, and especially when Jonathan brought him the letter from Catherine. David had no desire to make Charlotte feel badly, but he couldn't contain his joy over hearing from Catherine. Within two weeks Charlotte had brought him the letter from the manager of the jewelry salon at the Majestic. He didn't know enough about these things to know that the letter should have come straight to him from the company. The fact that Charlotte brought the invitation proved that she had indeed set it up, and Alex was probably right, a word from her father was all that was needed to open that door. However, David also knew that a place like the Majestic had a reputation to uphold, and that his work would not have been allowed there had it failed to meet their standards. He truly believed that the women's admiration for his work was genuine, too.

So what was it Charlotte expected from him now? Did she really think that because she had helped procure the show for him that he would forget about Catherine? He felt pity for her. She was a spoiled, little rich girl, one blessed with all other outward graces as well. And yet she was like a lovely, empty, perfume bottle, promising delights from within, but having no fragrance to share with the world. She would always be dependent on money and power to give her what she wanted without something inside her to attract the true gifts of life. David could only be thankful that God had protected him from the entrapment of her attentions. When he looked at her now, he didn't find her beautiful at all.

*   *   *   *

As David looked out the train window he was relieved to see that all evidence of city life was now gone. Only fields and country farmhouses dotted the landscape as the churning wheels of the train devoured the steel tracks before them. This was refreshing to David's soul. He'd be perfectly content to never see New York City again. He just wanted to get home and start to work. He'd always be grateful for the good that had come to him from this trip, even if it had not produced the effects that Charlotte had intended for her benefit.

David had gone to the Majestic early yesterday morning. He needed to have a private conversation with Mr. Dubois, the salon manager, before the doors opened for the last showing. David felt he had to know the extent of any deception in this situation and how it would affect his business. To his relief, the gentleman had been discreetly forthright with him about the initiation of his being there.

"Mr. Winters," he had said, "I won't deny that this showing of your work began in a manner slightly irregular to our normal procedures in procuring a new artist's work. However, you need not think that this irregularity has anything to do with the success of this showing. Your work must take sole credit for this. Every compliment you have received is duly earned. I would like to contract with you to provide pieces to us on a regular basis with the rights to be the exclusive purveyor of David Winters jewelry in New York. Would you be interested in this proposition?"

David was overwhelmed. "Mr. Dubois, I'm at a loss for words. This is unbelievable!"

"I have no intention of taking advantage of your youth and inexperience in this type of transaction, so I will allow you to take the contract with you and have your own advocate approve or adjust it. I would suggest that you allow me to set the prices, because yours were far below the true value of your work, and you deserve more. Needless to say that will increase my profits as well," Dubois said with a smile.

"Sir, I can't thank you enough for this opportunity. I will do my best to continue to develop the finest pieces for your establishment."

"Of that I have no doubt, Mr. Winters," Dubois rose to shake David's hand. Then with a look at his watch he said, "It's ten o'clock ... let's go sell jewelry!"

The showing had gone well yesterday too, even better than the first day. There were more customers present that came as result of the notices from the Majestic. David was pleased, knowing they were not associated with Charlotte or her father. He left with an empty jewelry case, a hefty check, and a list of orders that would keep him busy for weeks. Mr. Dubois' contract was in his inner jacket pocket as well.

Charlotte did not make an appearance until the afternoon. She stayed at the showing but didn't talk much to David, making small talk with clients in her charming manner. When closing time came she asked if David would have dinner with her, and assured him there was no party attached this evening. David felt he could not refuse, so he went with her to a small restaurant not far from the Majestic. Conversation was mostly about David's impressions of New York City. Charlotte was disappointed that he did not share her love for the fast-paced lifestyle there. They were having dessert when an older gentleman and his wife recognized Charlotte and stopped to speak to her.

"Well, if it isn't the pretty Miss Pendleton! How are you dear?" The gentleman bent to give Charlotte a kiss on the cheek.

"Hello, Charlotte! You look beautiful," his wife told her.

"Hello, Judge Joe … Mrs. Edith … It's good to see you," Charlotte said

"How's your father, dear? We really need to have you two for dinner soon," the Judge said.

"And you should bring this handsome young man, too," the judge's wife said to Charlotte, admiring David.

"I would love to do that, but I'm afraid he's leaving to go back to his home town in the morning. David, meet Judge Josiah Sutherland and his wife, Edith. They've known me all my life. This is my friend, David Winters, who's been here showing his jewelry at the Majestic."

"Oh, yes, I received the invitation to the private showing, but I had committee meetings for two days that prevented my getting over there," Edith Sutherland said. "I'm so sorry to have missed it, was it a success for you?"

David had stood to greet the couple as they stopped at the table and shook hands with both of them. "Yes, indeed, Mrs. Sutherland, it far exceeded my expectations."

To the judge he said, "Sir, I'm very close to a family by the name of 'Sutherland' from my home town. Would you by any chance have relatives in Lexington, Missouri?"

The judge placed his finger on his chin in thought, "Lexington?.... You know, I think I might, young man. If I remember correctly, my grandfather's brother moved that direction when it was opened up for settlement years ago. I recall my grandfather talking about letters from him, telling about the rigors of the frontier. Well, that's hardly frontier anymore, but you know, it's quite possible that your 'Sutherlands' just might be my relatives. What did you say your association with them was?"

"Catherine Sutherland is my fiancée, the girl I intend to marry," David said.

Charlotte looked up at David in disbelief. The silence that followed was extremely uncomfortable. Female intuition led the older woman to take her husband by the arm saying, "Joe, we really have to be going. Charlotte, it was so good to see you. Say 'hello' to your father for us. Mr. Winters, it was a pleasure to meet you."

The judge said, "Young man, I wish you well with your jewelry business, Charlotte, dear, hopefully we'll see you soon."

Charlotte and David spoke their goodbyes as well and David took his seat. Charlotte's face was flushed as she toyed with the dessert on her plate.

"I can't believe you are still hanging on to that idea of marrying *Catherine!*"

She spoke the name with a mocking tone.

"Charlotte, what made you think I had changed my mind? I've been very clear to you about my relationship with Catherine."

"What relationship?" she exploded. "She's not even there!"

"Catherine would be with me if she could be, and I would be with her if it were at all possible. The situation is beyond our control at the moment, but that does not change our love for each other," David said.

The polished, in-control Charlotte Pendleton suddenly felt as though all her worldly possessions had little meaning. Tears came flooding to her eyes as she covered her face with her hands. "I just wish it was me you loved."

David had the feeling that these were the first genuine words he had heard from Charlotte Pendleton, and compassion moved his heart.

Placing his arm about her, he spoke gently, "Charlotte, I will forever be grateful to you for all you've done for me. But for years before you came to Lexington, my heart has belonged to Catherine. We feel that God put us together to use our lives for Him in some way in the future. This separation is temporary. It has been very difficult, but we will be together again and our love will be even stronger for having been apart."

Neither Charlotte nor David was aware that Alex Caine had walked up behind them. Already frustrated that no one would tell him where Charlotte was, he had settled for dining alone at the restaurant where they frequently ate. Then he saw them, Winters with his arm around Charlotte, talking intently as she cried, probably because the guy was going back to Lexington. Caine was furious! He cursed and fought back the desire to grab Winters and beat him to a pulp!

Forcing himself to control his anger he walked over to them, only to hear David telling Charlotte that their love would be stronger for having been apart. "Excuse me," he spoke with sarcasm, "for interrupting your tender moment."

David saw the fear in Charlotte's face as she heard Caine's voice. She pulled away from David and grabbed her napkin, dabbing at her face.

"I thought you and I had plans for dinner tonight, my dear," Caine said in a mocking tone. "But I see I've been jilted in place of your lover boy."

David stood to face the older man, "Sir, you have a wrong impression …"

Caine would not allow David to finish. Stepping almost into David's face he spoke with such venom that David could feel the evil about him, "*No, You* have the wrong impression, boy! Charlotte Pendleton belongs to me, and she's leaving with me now!" He grabbed Charlotte roughly by the arm, pulling her to her feet.

Just then, the owner of the restaurant approached the table. Not wanting to offend regular, influential customers, he was hesitant, and yet for the sake of other clientele he had to defuse whatever was happening here.

"Pardon me, Miss Pendleton, is there a problem?" he asked quietly.

"No, Henri," Charlotte told him. "Everything's fine, we were just leaving." She picked up her purse and looked at David. Caine still held her by the arm. "I think I'd best go with him. Goodbye, David."

"Goodbye Charlotte, Thank you for everything," David said, feeling helpless to change the situation.

"May I have the check, please? he spoke to the restaurant owner.

"It has already been taken care of, sir."

"Then thank you, and good evening," David said and walked out of the restaurant.

CHAPTER 15

Soldiers with horses ready to mount stood casually around the three wagons which would head south to Fort Dodge. McCloud and Jeremy were making last minute checks on their wagons before heading out on the trail. The third wagon was a supply wagon transporting needed items from one fort to another.

Catherine sat on the seat of Jeremy's wagon with Old Pal at her side. Several of the unmarried soldiers were milling around, hoping to make conversation with her. Col. Dawson had been right when he warned her about the attention her presence at Fort Hays would bring. Catherine had enough frustration in her life in regard to men, so she had done her best to stay out of sight and unavailable the few days they were there. Soon they would be moving out, and if things went as planned, they should be at Fort Dodge in two days. Another few hours' travel should bring them to Dorthea's place, as she still thought of it. Without having seen it, she couldn't bring herself to think of it as her new home.

Colonel Edward Dawson's kindness continued to follow them, even in his absence. The papers he had sent to the fort were authorizing a delivery to Fort Dodge at whatever time the McCloud party needed to go that way, therefore guaranteeing an escort for Catherine and her family. They were also to be supplied with food for the road that would make cooking unnecessary for those two days. Catherine was touched again by his thoughtfulness. She sincerely hoped that he would soon meet a woman who would love him as such a man deserved to be loved.

The sound of the bugle announced that it was time to mount up and prepare to depart. McCloud and Jeremy took their places and lined up their teams. Soldiers went before the train and behind it as well. Those remaining in the fort stood on either side to wave goodbye to Catherine. She smiled gratefully at them and thanked them for their kindness to her and her family.

The commanding officer for this journey was Lieutenant Gregory Bronson. He frequently made this run between the two forts and was familiar with every mile of the trail. He said they would undoubtedly be bypassed from time to time as traders frequented that section of the Santa Fe Trail. The merchants were traveling at the fastest speeds their animals could take them, all eager to get their wagon loads of goods to their destinations without Indian problems or thieves along the trail.

Susannah's condition was of major concern to everyone. The doctor at Fort Hays had examined her and said she could go into labor at any time. Catherine was hoping that would happen while they were still at the fort, or that they could remain there until the baby came. However, every day was of essence now in regard to traveling. Autumn had arrived with its nostalgic changing of colors in foliage. Nights were especially cool and daytime temperatures were pleasant. Sometime soon, the cold winds would find their way south, possibly accompanied by snow and ice. To be on the road with Susannah in that condition was unthinkable; they needed to reach their final destination before weather added more complications. They would move at a slower pace to lessen the effects of the rutted trail for Susannah, so they could expect two day's travel time before reaching Fort Dodge and medical assistance. Extra padding had been placed on the bed in an attempt to ease the jarring, but there was no way to prevent it altogether.

They had been on the trail now for at least an hour and neither Catherine, nor Jeremy, had spoken a word. Not that this was unusual for Jeremy, but for Catherine to be quiet that long usually meant troubled thoughts that Jeremy was sure he'd hear about soon enough.

Catherine realized now that she had become quite spoiled to the company of Edward and Sam in the previous weeks of their traveling south. Now, bumping along on the wagon seat with her silent brother it was hard to stay in a positive frame of mind. Catherine had this sinking feeling that everything good in her life had either already taken place or was so far in her future that it could take years to attain. She was finding it really difficult to stay encouraged spiritually without attending church. It meant taking total responsibility for one's spiritual life and being disciplined enough to read her Bible and pray without the help of anyone else. She hadn't realized until this journey that the opportunity to meet freely with others in worship was a precious privilege. No wonder the pilgrims were willing to cross an ocean, risking their lives, for that right. It just occurred to her that she hadn't given much thought to what might be available in the way of church meetings when they arrived at their destination.

"Jeremy", she said, breaking their silence, "What are we going to do about church out here?"

"That's a good question, Cat," he replied. "One day when I was fishing with Andrew and George I asked them if they went to church. They said there weren't any churches, but sometimes people got together and read the Bible and sang, and George said there was always a lot of good food. I told him that was my kind of church."

"I wonder if there are any preachers out here."

"'Seems I've heard of circuit preachers who go from place to place and hold services for people. They must set that up in advance so people will know when and where to gather."

"I'm just realizing how much I took Reverend Winters and our church for granted. I've missed it so much," Catherine said.

"I have, too, Cat, far more than I expected. We'll have to ask around and see what's available in the area where we'll be."

"Who will we ask? The way Dorthea talked there's no one within miles." The thought of it brought tears to Catherine's eyes. "Oh, Jeremy, I don't know if I can stand this."

"Hey, sis," Jeremy reached out and tousled her curls. "Don't give up before we even get started on this deal. God's going to take care of us. And anyway, you still have the best big brother in the world to yank your curls." he said with a grin.

Catherine couldn't help smiling. There was no way she was going to say it to Jeremy, but she really was extremely grateful to have him around.

Just then they saw Lt. Bronson ride up alongside McCloud's large wagon and talk to him for a few moments. Then he made his way to them, informing them that the train would stop in a few minutes at a pleasant watering place. They'd have lunch and a short rest and be back on the trail in two hours.

"Thank you, sir," Jeremy replied. "I'll watch up ahead."

As the Lieutenant rode away, Catherine said, "He's a nice officer."

Jeremy smiled. "Yeah, Edward handpicked the soldiers he wanted to fill this escort. Just in case you haven't noticed, sis ...every one of them is married ."

Catherine laughed, "That's Edward. It's no wonder he's the commander. He thinks of everything!"

They could hear the sound of the bugle signaling the train to stop, and soon they were off the trail in a shaded area. A small stream provided water for the animals, and in spite of the changing season, there was still green grass for them to graze. Within a half hour the soldiers in charge of the food had set up a make-shift table spread with fresh bread, fried chicken that was cooked that morning at the fort, canned baked beans, and a variety of fruits.

Catherine went to check on her mother and was concerned by the strained look on Susannah's face.

"Mama, are you all right?"

Trying to put Catherine at ease, Susannah patted her hand. "I'm O.K., honey. There's just no way to get comfortable when you're in this condition."

"Do you want to leave the wagon to eat something?" Catherine asked. "The soldiers have a nice lunch set up out there, and it's such a pretty place."

"A change of scenery from this wagon would be wonderful, but the energy it takes to get up and down those steps seems more than I can manage right now," Susannah said with a tired smile.

"Then I'll bring you a plate; you have to keep up your strength," Catherine said, rising to leave the wagon. "I'll be back in a minute."

McCloud was coming to see about Susannah as Catherine left. Stepping up into the wagon, he too, was concerned about her tired appearance.

Taking her hand, he said, "Susannah, you don't look well. Be honest with me, what's happening here?" he asked with concern.

"Pollard, I don't want to alarm Catherine; she's been terrified all along that she's going to have to deliver this baby. I am lying here praying that doesn't happen, but the truth is, I'm having mild labor pains now."

"Oh, God, Susannah! What kind of time frame are you talking about?" he asked, visibly alarmed.

"It's hard to tell. I was in labor for two days before having Jeremy. Of course, he was my first, and I was so young. Catherine was born about eight hours after labor started. Of course, I wasn't bumping along a wagon trail at either of those times, so this could be a completely different story."

"What do I need to do to be prepared?" he asked. "Lt. Bronson has already told me that the train can stop immediately if you should go into labor."

"I have clean linens, towels, scissors, everything that might be necessary in that basket," Susannah said, pointing to a basket within easy reach. "I have covered everything to keep it free from dust as we've traveled. If I feel we should stop I'll let you know, and you'll need to build a fire and boil water as quickly as possible."

"I am so sorry things worked out this way, Susannah," McCloud said, hanging his head.

"We can't change things now, Pollard; we just have to make the best of the situation. Now go get some lunch before Jeremy eats it all."

Kissing her on the forehead, McCloud said, " I promise, I will do my best to get you to Fort Dodge, if this little one will just wait a while."

"Well, babies are notorious for coming at the most inconvenient times, but at least, we're prepared," Susannah reassured him.

McCloud left as Catherine appeared with two plates of food.

"I think I should ride in here with you from now on, Mama," she said, handing a plate to Susannah.

"Well, I'd love to have your company ... Oh, that looks good," Susannah said, in response to the food. "Edward's men did well."

They were back on the trail in less than the two hours Lt. Bronson had mentioned. McCloud had shared with him Susannah's condition, and they agreed to increase the pace of the train as much as they could without making it extremely uncomfortable for her.

Catherine sat on the big bed with her mother, trying to write in her journal. After hitting a bump that caused her pencil to mark from the top of the page to the bottom, she decided that what she wrote would be unreadable anyway, so she put it away. Propping pillows at the end of the bed, she sat facing Susannah.

"Mama, how do you feel about our ending up in Kansas instead of Oregon? Are you disappointed?"

Susannah waited a moment, thinking of her answer. "No, I can't say that I am. Since I had no desire to go to Oregon in the first place, it really doesn't matter."

"Do you think one place would have been better for us than another?"

"Only the Lord knows that, Catherine. In Oregon we would more than likely have had heavily wooded acreage to clear in order to plant crops. That's extremely hard work. In contrast, many homesteads on the Kansas plains may not have a single tree on their 640 acres, according to Dorthea."

Thinking of her home in Missouri where in her younger years she had climbed trees along with Jeremy and played in their shade, Catherine couldn't imagine living without trees.

"Life here is really going to be different, isn't it?" she said, more as a statement than a question. Susannah had her eyes closed and Catherine noticed she'd fallen asleep. That was good; her mother needed the rest. The steady pace of the wagon had relaxed Catherine as well, so with a yawn, she snuggled down into her pillows and drifted off for a nap.

Susannah dozed only a few minutes before she was awakened by a slow, dull pain that started in her back and moved around to grip her abdomen. She was relieved to see that Catherine was sleeping soundly. The last thing she wanted was a teenaged daughter hovering over her in fear. She lay still, concerned that activity on her part would hasten the pains that were coming with regularity now, though still far apart.

"Heavenly Father," she prayed silently. "You promised to be our ever-present help in time of trouble. I fear that I am in that category now. I confess, I was not happy when I realized I was carrying this baby, but I've come to love it, in spite of everything. I ask you to keep this little one safe. If it's to be born on this wagon trail, please let me deliver it without problems. Give me the strength I need, and if Catherine has to do this, help her too."

Almost three hours later, Catherine woke with the feeling that something was wrong. Becoming aware of her surroundings she sat up and looked at her mother. Susannah's forehead was beaded with perspiration and her face showed the evidence of pain.

"Oh,my! Is it the baby?" she asked, dreading to hear the answer.

"I'm afraid so, Catherine, but it's all right. We're going to do this together," she said in a calm voice.

"Do I need to tell McCloud to stop?" Catherine asked frantically.

"I really expect Lt. Bronson to stop the train soon, anyway. This is about the time we stopped yesterday, so I'll wait a few more minutes. I heard him tell Pollard that we would spend the night at a small way station, so hopefully we'll be there soon. I would definitely prefer to be there than out here on the trail," Susannah said.

"Do you think someone will be there who knows how to deliver babies?" Catherine asked hopefully.

"I would like to think so, but Catherine, listen to me; if we have to do this alone, I will guide you through it. Remember, I've done it twice before. It certainly wouldn't be the first time a woman gave birth in a wagon on the trail."

Before Catherine could answer her, they heard the sound of the bugle announcing their stop.

"Oh, thank God!" Catherine cried, and moving to the front of the wagon she called to McCloud that the baby was on its way.

Moving his team quickly to a halt just past the way station, McCloud jumped down from the driver's seat and hurriedly stepped up into the wagon to see Susannah.

"Pollard, see if there's a fire there to heat water, and ask if there might be a woman who could help us," she said.

McCloud almost ran into the simple building and was relieved to see a fireplace burning with a low flame. To the roughly clad man inside he announced, "My wife is having a baby in the wagon. Can we use your fire to heat some water?" And looking around, he asked, "Is there a woman here that could help?"

The man obviously didn't trouble himself for other people's situations. With hardly a glance upward from the trap he was oiling, he drawled, "Wood's a'side the buildin' and water's out yonder in the well. Ye kin hep yoursef. Thar ain't nobody here but me, and I ain't deliverin' no baby."

Behind McCloud, Lt. Bronson appeared, "Luther Johnson! Get up off your lazy rear, and go get water for this man, or I'll tell the commander what a useless twit you are. You'll be looking for a real job so fast your head will spin!"

The man jumped to his feet, "Well, I didn't know they wus with *you*, Lieutenant! Yessir, I'll get some water." He grabbed a pail and started toward the door.

Lt. Bronson looked in the direction of rooms to the side, "Are any of those rooms decent enough for a woman to use?" When the man stammered with no real answer, the Lieutenant said, "Never mind, I'll check them myself."

A quick inspection of all three small rooms proved negative. With disgust Lt. Bronson said, "Mr. McCloud, the bedbugs and lice would carry off your baby as soon as

Mrs. McCloud gave birth in one of those beds! I suggest you make the best of the situation in the wagon. Is Miss Catherine capable of helping with the birth?"

"We're depending on that. I hate to admit it, but I'm totally helpless in this situation," McCloud admitted.

"Well, build up that fire and get some heat going so the water will boil. I'll check with Mrs. McCloud. I assisted with a birth once when the fort doctor was away, so I do have limited experience with the process."

Jeremy came in with an armload of wood and laid it near the fireplace. McCloud found a poker and stoked the coals to life, adding more wood to the fire. He put an empty pot on the tripod, ready to receive the water that Luther Johnson was getting.

"I'm going to check on Ma," Jeremy said to McCloud and hurried out the door. As he came to the wagon, he called to see if he could enter. Susannah told him to come in.

"Hi, honey," she said, reaching out to take his hand.

"Ma, are you all right? Is there anything I need to be doing?" Jeremy asked, his eyes filled with concern.

"Really, these things just have to run their course. I should be in labor for a while, and then the baby will come. Just pray that everything works out well for us," Susannah told him.

Jeremy reached down to wipe her brow. "I'll be out there praying. Cat, I don't know what I could do, but if you need anything, call me."

Catherine looked pale and frightened. "I guess later we'll need the hot water, but I'll let you know when it's time."

Jeremy started down the steps as Lt. Bronson approached. "Can you ask your mother if I could have a word with her, son?"

"Yes sir," Jeremy said and went back into the wagon. "Ma, Lt. Bronson would like to speak to you."

"Certainly, tell him to come in," Susannah.

"Hello, Mrs. McCloud," Bronson said softly. "I know you've been through this before, but in much better circumstances, certainly. I wanted you to know that I've had some small experience in bringing a child into the world, and though Miss Catherine is with you, if you need my help, you only have to call. Meantime, I'm going to see that my men get set up for the evening meal. I'll make sure Mr. McCloud gets some food in him; he's looking kind of pale."

"Thank you, Lieutenant, I appreciate your offer, and we will send for you if Catherine feels it's too much for her."

With all the men gone now, Susannah instructed Catherine to get the basket with the clean linens, scissors and a gentle soap. There was a small wash basin too, and Catherine made a place to sit it near the bed.

"Now what do we do?" she asked.

"About all we can do now is time the interval between the pains and how long they are lasting. The time between the pains should get shorter, and the length of the contractions should be longer as the time for birth gets nearer."

Susannah handed a pocket watch to Catherine. "All right, the contraction is starting now ... note the time, and I'll tell you when it stops."

Catherine's hands were shaking, but her eyes were glued to the watch as she listened to Susannah's breathing become heavier. "All right, it's over." Susannah said.

For the next hour or so, Catherine continued to time Susannah's contractions as they became stronger and closer together. When she had a moment to think her own thoughts, she was praying silently, "Oh God, please help. I am so afraid!"

Knowing the situation in the wagon the soldiers had been respectfully quiet, everyone hopefully listening for the sound of a baby's cry. Jeremy and McCloud were taking turns pacing the length of the wagon and back. Suddenly, the noise of an approaching wagon and team startled everyone. Soon voices laughing and talking loudly were heard ... women's voices! To the amazement of the entire group, a large wagon filled with women pulled up to the way station and stopped. One after another the women got down from the wagon as the men stared. The frilly, revealing dresses quickly identified them as "ladies of the evening." The last woman to emerge was obviously the madam of the group. Dressed more appropriately than the rest, she looked about for someone in charge among the gaping-mouthed men.

Lieutenant Bronson momentarily found his tongue and stepped forward. "Hello, ma'am, I'm Lieutenant Bronson," then unable to think of another thing to say, he just stood there.

"Good evening, Lieutenant. My name is Emeline Carter. My girls and I are on the way to Dodge City where I intend to open an establishment. However, we were not aware how far we'd have to travel. I'm hoping that this place has sleeping quarters and food available."

"Miss Carter, I wouldn't set foot in one of those rooms for all the money in Dodge. As for food, our cooks are preparing supper for this bunch, and you and your ladies are welcome to dine with us."

Emeline Carter looked at the six women, "How about it, girls, does that sound good to you?"

"Yes! We're starving!" All the girls exclaimed their assent, giggling among themselves as they noticed the camp full of men.

Before the arrival of the newcomers, some of the men had found comfortable places to stretch out on the ground and had been dozing while the cooks prepared the evening meal. None of them were sleeping now! The ladies walked about, needing to "stretch their legs," and exchanging greetings with the soldiers.

The Lieutenant cursed under his breath, "What did I do to deserve this duty? I've got a woman having a baby in the wagon and a camp full of whores! I'd rather fight Indians any day!"

Just then, a low cry was heard from the wagon. McCloud, Jeremy and the Lieutenant turned their attention that direction. Emeline Carter noticed their expressions of concern and looked to Lt. Bronson with a questioning look.

"Miss Carter, Mr. McCloud's wife is about to deliver a baby in that wagon. We were attempting to get her to Fort Dodge where a doctor is available. However, it appears the little one may come this evening."

"Is she in there alone?" Emeline asked.

"No, ma'am. Her teenaged daughter is with her, understandably scared out of her wits," Lt. Bronson confessed.

Emeline Carter suddenly seemed the commanding officer instead of Lt. Bronson. She quickly removed her outer jacket and began rolling up her sleeves. "I'm assuming someone has water heating on the fire? Get it ready for when I call you." To the girls flitting about the camp she said, "Girls, I do not have time to be concerned with you, but there is to be *NO* working at this campsite tonight ... Is that clear?" She panned the group, getting the nod from every girl. "I'd better not hear of one skirt being lifted above an ankle! And Lieutenant, if you'd corral them over into one area after supper, I'm going to deliver a baby." With that statement she strode to the wagon and stepped up to the back flap.

"Mrs. McCloud!" she called. "May I come in?"

Just the sound of another woman's voice brought instant relief to Catherine and Susannah.

"Yes, please do!" Susannah called to her.

When Emeline stepped into the wagon Catherine knew her prayers had been answered. There was such an air of confidence about the woman. Her pretty face was surrounded by a cloud of dark hair, coiffed in the latest fashion high on her head. She moved with ease in spite of the cumbersome looking dress.

"Hello, ladies, I'm Emeline Carter. I understand we have a little one on the way."

"Miss Carter, you have no idea how glad I am to see you!" Catherine said, almost dropping to the bed in relief. "I'm Catherine, and this is my mother, Susannah."

"I don't know where you came from Miss Carter, but you were definitely heaven sent," Susannah said weakly.

From that point, Emeline took charge of the situation, encouraging Susannah as to when to push with the contractions, instructing Catherine to get the hot water. In less than an hour after her arrival, a tiny baby boy came screaming into the world in a covered wagon on the Kansas prairie trail. When she was certain Susannah was doing well, Emeline and Catherine bathed the baby and dressed him in the small gown from the basket. Then she showed Catherine how to wrap him snuggly in the square blanket. He was still crying with the fearful wails of a newborn, so Emeline held him close and rocked him in her arms.

"Shhsh, now, little one," she said softly, patting his diapered bottom. "You're O.K. now." As she looked down at the new miracle of life and touched his velvety cheek, his little hand slipped free of the blanket and five tiny fingers latched onto hers. He seemed to snuggle up against her body and contentedly began to doze off. Suddenly, Emeline Carter was no longer in Kansas, but in a shoddy house of prostitution in Boston. The baby she held in her arms was her own, a baby girl, the only one she would ever birth. The man who controlled her brought in a quack doctor to make certain of that. She'd only been allowed to hold the baby for a moment, but in her mind she'd named her "Lila, Lila Rose." Then her baby was taken away. They didn't call it *selling* babies, but that's what it was. Emeline knew the little one would have a life far better than she could have given her, but that fact never filled the empty void inside.

"Miss Emeline, how can we ever thank you?" Catherine's voice brought her back to the present situation.

"This is the most fun I've had in a year, girls!" Emeline said, and handing the baby to Susannah, "Meet your mama, little one."

Susannah kissed the baby and smoothed the red-blonde fuzz on the top of his smooth, round head. "He's so pretty, but smaller than Jeremy and Catherine. I guess we

242

should let the men folk know everything's all right now. Catherine, would you like to call Pollard and Jeremy?"

Catherine took the wash basin to empty it as she went. She didn't have far to go to find the men. She told them Susannah was waiting for them. Emeline was right behind her, leaving room in the wagon for McCloud and Jeremy to go inside. As she and Catherine stepped forward, the entire camp broke out in a cheer!

Emeline took Catherine by the hand and raised their hands up together as winners of an important event, "It's a boy, a healthy baby boy!" she announced. Another whoop went up as the men came around to congratulate them for a job well done.

"I hope you left us something to eat, fellows," Emeline said. "I'm starving! How about you, Catherine?"

"Now that you mention it, yes, I am too." Catherine admitted. She wasn't quite sure what all those women in frilly dresses were doing there, but it really didn't matter. Her mother's baby was here; they were both fine, and God had sent help … just in time!

*   *   *   *

Realizing that this was a special, private moment for Susannah and Pollard McCloud, Jeremy waited outside the wagon for McCloud to go in to see his son for the first time. McCloud stepped to the bed and bent down to see the tiny face showing from the white bundle in Susannah's arms.

"Pollard, meet your son," Susannah told him, looking tired, but happy.

McCloud gently touched the baby's face, "Gosh, Susannah, he's so tiny. He's beautiful! Is everything there … all his fingers and toes?

Susannah laughed. "Yes, they're all there, but he is small, probably because of the rough months I've had on the trail. But don't worry, he'll catch up. Do you want to hold him?"

McCloud said, "I think I'd better wait a day or two. I have to get used to this. We've got to name him, though. I hadn't even thought about that. How do you pick a name for a baby?"

"Well, you can name a child after someone in your family, after yourself, or someone else you love or respect. Or you can simply choose a name that you like."

"There's not one person in my ancestry that I'd want to name anyone after," McCloud said."

"I've always like the name 'Jacob.' We could call him, 'Jake.' How do you feel about that?" Susannah asked.

"Yeah, that's good … Baby Jake … but we have to have another name too, don't we?" he asked.

"Pollard, I just thought of something. Emeline Carter's being here to deliver this baby was an answer to prayer. I don't know what we would have done without her. What about naming him Jacob Carter in honor of her?"

McCloud spoke the name, "Jacob Carter McCloud. Yeah, I like the sound of that; it's got a nice ring to it. So, is that all you have to do to name somebody?"

"We'll need to register his birth with whatever records the territory has. It probably would be a good thing to write up something and have Lt. Bronson sign it as an official witness. Why don't you call Jeremy in to meet his little brother, then we'll tell Miss Emeline."

McCloud stroked the baby's head then reached down to hug Susannah and the baby altogether. "I'm so glad you're all right, Susannah!" Surprised to find tears in his eyes he quickly wiped them away. "I'll get Jeremy," he said.

Jeremy was eagerly waiting close by. "Go see your little brother, boy," McCloud told him.

"It's amazing that something this small can be a real person with everything that works," Jeremy said as he looked down at Baby Jake. He was so relieved to see that his mother had come through the ordeal, and now it was behind her. Jeremy held the baby and laughed at the way the baby squinted his little eyes as if trying to identify his older brother.

Catherine appeared at the flap of the wagon with a tray of soup, bread, and hot coffee. "Miss Emeline said it would be good for you to eat something if you feel up to it, Mama."

"That sounds good, I could use some nourishment. Let me get situated here." Susannah sat up straighter so she could accommodate the tray in front of her. Catherine set it down for her then held out her arms to Jeremy. "O.K., it's my turn to hold him. What are you going to name him?" she asked her mother.

"Pollard and I decided to name him 'Jacob,' just because we like the name, and 'Carter,' after Emeline since she delivered him. So he's 'Jacob Carter McCloud,' or 'Baby Jake' for now."

"Oh, Mama, I love that, and I know Miss Emeline will. Jake really seemed to like her, too." She looked down at the baby in her arms and felt she had never seen anything so beautiful, or so helpless.

"Jeremy, would you ask Miss Emeline if she'll come here. I want to tell her we're naming Jake after her," Susannah said. "Catherine, do you know how it is that Emeline happened to be here?"

"I don't know, Mama. I was in here with you when she got here. I just know there are a lot of pretty girls with her, all dressed in fancy clothes."

"Oh," Susannah said, just, "Oh."

"Well, how are Mama and baby doing?" Emeline said, appearing in the wagon.

"Thanks to you, we are doing well, and I appreciate the soup. I feel stronger after eating." Susannah told her. "Sit here, Emeline, I want to tell you something."

The dark haired beauty sat on Susannah's bed. "All right, Susannah."

"Pollard and I are so very grateful for your being here and for your willingness to help in our baby's birth. Things may have turned out all right if you had not come, but they were certainly so much better with you here. We've decided to name our little boy 'Jacob', and call him 'Jake' for short. His middle name will be 'Carter' in your honor."

Emeline just looked at Susannah for a moment, and then tears filled her eyes.

"I could not be more honored, Susannah, but …are you sure you want to do this?"

Susannah looked at Catherine, "Honey, would you give Baby Jake to Miss Emeline and take this tray back for me?" Catherine handed the baby to Emeline and took the tray, leaving the wagon.

"Are you thinking that I might not want to name Jake after you if I were aware of the profession you're in?" Susannah asked Emeline.

"That's exactly what I'm thinking," Emeline said.

"Well, that has nothing to do with the kindness you have shown me, so it doesn't bother me at all," Susannah assured her.

"Then I would love for this baby to carry my name," Emeline said, looking down at the tiny, sleeping child. Without looking up, she softly said, "I had a baby once."

Susannah, sensing this was a confidence rarely shared, reached out to touch Emeline's arm and said, "I'm so sorry."

After a few minutes, Emeline asked, "Where are you going to be settling?"

"We've bought a place somewhere east of Fort Dodge," Susannah replied, then told her about meeting Dorthea and how they'd come to buy her farm.

"I hear that is a hard life, Susannah," Emeline said.

Susannah smiled, "It's been so long ago that my life wasn't hard, Emeline, that I can't even remember it!"

"Susannah ..." It seemed Emeline was about to say something then changed her mind. "If you ever need anything, if Catherine or Jeremy or this baby, ever need anything, please let me know. I will be in Dodge City." She smiled and jokingly said, "I won't be hard to find."

Handing Baby Jake back to his mother, she rose. "I need to see that my girls are behaving and see what kind of bedding arrangements the Lieutenant has come up with for us. It's been a long day, and we'll be back on the road in the morning."

"Good night, Emeline. Thank you again for everything. We'll see you before you leave, won't we?" Susannah asked.

"I wouldn't think of pulling out without one more look at my namesake!" Emeline said as she left.

*   *   *   *

Luther Johnson swore his way station would never be the same. When he looked outside the next morning there wasn't a bush within sight that wasn't wearing a petticoat, lacy bloomers or some other ruffled unmentionable! Since the girls weren't allowed to ply their trade just yet, they decided to take advantage of Luther's good well and wash out a few things. Of course, those few things multiplied by six made a *lot* of things. Luther just shook his head, turned around and closed his door, and didn't open it until those "gol-darned women" had left.

Lt. Bronson tried to keep an eye on the activities of his men, and had to agree that all of them being married made his work a little easier. Had the girls broken Emeline's rule and thought to entertain a soldier or two, he was certain the other men would go back and tell their wives, who in turn would tell the wives of the wayward men. Only God knows where that would lead. Already, he could imagine the righteous indignation on the faces of those proper wives when they heard their husbands shared a camp with a handful of "Fallen Angels" last night!"

Normally, the transport trips between forts were uneventfully tedious with only an occasional Indian sighting to break the monotony, but this one would be the talk of the fort among the ranks for a long while.

Emeline Carter was eager to get to Dodge, so she and the girls would be on the road as soon as their laundry dried.   Catherine couldn't help but like the laughing, playful beauties, and the sight of all their under things everywhere was one she would never forget. Jeremy was the only single man in the camp, other than the hiding Luther Johnson. Now, it was his turn to get the attention, as Catherine had at the fort.

"Jer-a-mee! Will you check this wagon wheel for me, sweetie?"

"You're sooo strong, Jeremy. Would you move this heavy trunk for me, pretty please?"

"Do you need more coffee, Jer-a-mee? Is there anything you need, honey?"

"You're the handsomest guy I've seen in this place, Jeremy. Will you come to see me when we get to Dodge?"

Finally, in desperation, he went to Susannah's wagon.

"Ma, can I please hide in here for a while? My only other option is to join Luther in the station house, and I really don't want to do that."

Susannah laughed, "Is my brave son afraid of a handful of women?"

"Well, I never met women like these ... I mean, they're nice, but ..."

"I agree," Susannah said, "You're probably better off in here. Will they be leaving soon?"

"I heard Miss Emeline telling them they had a half hour to get all their clothes off the bushes and back in the wagon, so I guess that means they'll be gone then."

Baby Jake was awake so Jeremy entertained himself with talking to him for a few minutes. Emeline Carter came to see the baby one last time and to tell Susannah goodbye.

"So this is where you went to escape, Jeremy," she said. "How's our Baby Jake this morning? I didn't hear any crying in the night, did you and he sleep well?"

"He woke up to feed a couple of times, and that was it. I actually had the best night's rest I've had in months," Susannah said.

"Well, my girls are all in the wagon. If I don't get out there, they'll be piling out again, and who knows how long it would take to get them rounded up." Emeline hugged Susannah and bent down to kiss the baby. "My sweet little namesake, take care of him, Jeremy," she said with a pat to Jeremy's back.

"I will, Miss Carter," he assured her.

"Remember, I'll be in Dodge," she said as she stepped down from the wagon.

Outside, she hugged Catherine and shook hands with McCloud and Lt. Bronson, climbed up on the driver's seat beside the girl who was handling the team, and off they went in a cloud of dust. The sound of the girls laughing and talking slowly faded and the soldiers went back to their conversation around the coffee pot.

The Lieutenant thought it best to stay put another day for Susannah to gain strength since the weather seemed to be in their favor. The men played cards, napped, and took turns fishing with a couple of poles they borrowed from Luther who now dared to show himself since Emeline's girls were gone.

Catherine took advantage of the time to do laundry herself, thinking how boring hers was in comparison to the garments that had been spread about the bushes just recently. It had been a while since she'd had to cook and she found she missed it. Besides, that, she wanted to make sure she hadn't lost the touch for making those fluffy biscuits, so she told the cooks she'd relieve them from duty that evening. It felt good to be busy again. "One can take just so much pampering!" she decided.

CHAPTER 16

Almost as soon as the wagons were out on the trail after leaving the way station, there was a visible change in the terrain. Hills now melted into slopes as the land became flatter. Trees were scarce except where several had been deliberately planted to create a stand against the wind. None of the descriptions Catherine had heard could truly describe this wind! With only the grasslands in its path, it seemed that the world of Kansas was at the mercy of this untamable force. It could be one's sweetest friend in its milder disposition, blowing the tall grasses so gently that they appeared to move in waves as the ocean. But when angry, it beat upon the land, man, and beasts like the breath of an enormous giant bent on destroying everything in its path.

All the men wore handkerchiefs over their faces as the wagon train moved toward Fort Dodge, a necessity to prevent filling one's lungs with the blowing dust. Traveling in Susannah's wagon, Catherine had closed everything tightly, hanging extra cloth coverings at each end to act as filters against the blowing sand for the baby's sake. Still, when they arrived at the fort, she spent at least two hours carrying the contents outside and shaking out the sand.

As soon as the animals were situated, Jeremy sought the postal clerk. He had instructed Liz to write him there at Fort Dodge. When he asked if there was mail for

"Sutherland" he was handed two letters, one to him from Liz, and one to Catherine from David. Jonathan, the gold miner, knew that Fort Dodge was a U.S. mail depot and had told David he could send letters to her there. It was her first communication from him in seven months, and after she danced around in excitement for five minutes or so, she sat down to read it. She had re-read it so many times since then that she could practically recite it from memory. His familiar handwriting brought joy to her heart and seemed to speak the words to her from the paper.

My Dearest Catherine,

You can only imagine my elation when Jonathan walked into the shop and handed me your letter. I assure you; I made a complete idiot of myself! When I came to my senses and apologized for my craziness he told me about his lonely days mining in California and how he'd been just as excited when his letters from Janie came. By the way, I did make their wedding rings. They turned out beautifully. Janie came with Jonathan to pick them up; she is a delightful girl. I hope that someday we can all be together for a visit. We certainly will have plenty of stories to tell.

Jonathan told me how the two of you met. The only thing he regretted is that you were frightened. He got a real kick out of scaring that trapper silly.

Gosh, Catherine, where do I begin? I have so much to say to you, but here I've already written half a page and I haven't said "I love you!" Catherine, My Love, I miss you so very much. Truly a piece of my heart is gone with you and I will never be whole until you bring that part of me back again. I love you as much in your absence as I did when we were together. I speak it to the wind at times, hoping it will find its way to the windy prairie and you will hear my voice as the breezes caress your golden curls.

I was delighted to learn that you are in Kansas, and not so far away as Oregon. Jonathan told me what it's really like to be on a wagon train, and I was in torment for days, wishing we'd been old enough to start our life and spare you that hardship. I finally had to give it to God as I have so many times since you left. I do pray daily that you will have the strength you need to endure.

My father asked me to teach a Bible class to the younger people of our church. That has been really good for me. It keeps me reading my Bible, and I have been amazed at how the Lord emphasizes things to me as I read, making me know what to teach. All of your friends miss you almost as much as I do and send their love to you and Jeremy, too.

I really miss your brother. I was so distraught at the idea of your being gone that I failed to realize what a big part of my life Jeremy filled. Please give my regards to him and to your mother. She had not given birth at the time Jonathan was with you; so hopefully, you have good news to write me about the baby.

Now for my most exciting news that impacts our future. Two months ago a young woman came into the shop and bought a bracelet. She liked my style and bought several other things over a period of time. She is not from Lexington, but was visiting a relative here. Her home is in New York City. She is a regular customer at a very elite shopping outlet known as the Majestic and contacted the manager of the jewelry salon about my work. She showed him the pieces she had purchased, and he has now invited me to have a showing of my work as their newest artist. Mr. Goodson said it is highly unusual for this to happen for someone so young and has encouraged me to pursue it. I leave in a week and have been working day and night to have a decent portfolio to take with me. My bank account for us has been growing nicely already, and this should only increase it further!

I have never been to New York City, as you know. I think I'll try to do more observing than speaking. There is a hotel near the Majestic where I shall stay for those three days. I promise to try to absorb everything I see there so I can write you about my impressions of the city.

I must get back to work on jewelry. I so wish you could see the work I am doing. Someday I will make you the most beautiful things of all. I still carry my half of our heart with me at all times, just as I carry you in my heart. May God keep you in His care until we meet again.

I love you, My Catherine, with my whole heart,

David

Catherine carefully folded the letter, pressing it to her lips as she always did. How could she ever have had doubts about his love for her, or of her love for him? She'd never known how precious words written on paper could be. What hope they carried! The reassurance of David's love brought strength to her, somehow enabling her to face her future on the Kansas prairie with hope.

Catherine realized that she was tired. Tired inside. The physical rest each night restored her body, but there had been little refreshment for the inner person. Then suddenly, it became clear to Catherine ... strength for that part of her being came from reading God's letter of love to her. As David's words brought strength to her mind, God's words, the assurance of His love for her, strengthened her spirit. Life on the trail these past few weeks had robbed her of the ability to have her regular time of devotions. She knew that time with God was special, and she hated missing it; but she hadn't truly understood that strength to endure the situations of life came from that fellowship with Him. Catherine felt she could relate to the Psalmist as he said in *Psalms 63:1, "O God, thou art my God; early will I seek thee, my flesh longeth for thee in a dry and thirsty land, where no water is."*

As she looked about her Catherine thought, "This certainly qualifies as a 'dry and thirsty land.'" She was riding on the wagon seat with Jeremy, who was quiet, as usual, probably lost in thoughts of his letter from Liz. So Catherine prayed silently,

"Heavenly Father, I'm sorry I have been missing my time with You. I feel so empty without Your Presence. I am weak without Your strength. We will soon be at the end of this journey, but from what I see around me now, I will need You as never before. This journey could have been so much more difficult than it was. But You have been with us all the way. Now, we will need You in this next part of our lives, and because You have proven Yourself faithful, I know You will be with us here, as well. Keep my David safe, too, I pray. Amen."

Peace came to Catherine then. As a spring released comes to fill a dry well from within, the joy and strength of God's Spirit rose within her, bringing refreshing. She had been told that prairie dwellers insisted that the wind sang at times. As she watched the tall grasses bending in the breeze, she was certain that she heard that song.

Up ahead, Pollard McCloud was looking at the directions given to him by Dorthea. According to her map, they should soon be approaching a road where they would need to turn left to travel east. She said it should be marked with a sign saying, "Spearville." He could hardly believe that their journey would soon be over! It seemed he'd been driving oxen forever. He was so eager to get to his new place and begin to work on it. Dorthea had warned him not to expect too much, so he was trying not to get his hopes up. His first concern was that the sod house would be livable for Susannah.

The few dwellings they had seen along the way were made of sod, one story, almost always square, ugly buildings. Lt. Bronson had told McCloud that even some of the original fort structures in Kansas had been made of sod because there were no trees for lumber. Thinking of the Lieutenant, McCloud realized that he had missed the company of the officer and the friendly men of the escort. These miles from Fort Dodge were the first that his two wagons had traveled without company. Maybe the lonely feeling of this prairie would get to him too. He was glad there were five of them in the family. It might make the house pretty crowded for a while, but he and Jeremy should be able to enlarge it. After all, it was made of prairie sod, and there was certainly no shortage of that. Looking around, one could see for miles with no house or structure in sight. Some emigrants lived first in dugouts, actually digging out the side of a rise in the ground or ravine, creating a cave. Those were easy to miss if you were looking for the dwelling. Sometimes only a stovepipe was visible above ground from a distance. Usually, a door of some kind was built across the front, but often had to be made of buffalo hide for lack of wood.

McCloud wanted better than that for his little son. He'd gone all his life without having any idea how a person could care for someone as much as he did that baby. He was actually uncomfortable thinking about it. This kind of emotion was a new experience for him, and it would take some time to absorb.

Up ahead, he saw a board, hopefully, the sign he was looking for. He slowed the team, and as they approached he saw that it read, "Spearville," with an arrow pointing east. After rounding the turn, McCloud checked Dorthea's directions again. His place should be four miles straight ahead on this road. For all he knew, this might be his own land he was looking at now. He would have to walk it off from the house, using the markers Dorthea's husband had put in place to identify the property lines.

His property; he loved the sound of that. His nomadic lifestyle before settling down with Susannah would never have provided a place he could say was his. McCloud never once considered that he had taken what rightfully belonged to someone else in order to get his property. As long as no one else brought it up, he could live with it just fine.

A small board on a stake could be seen up ahead. McCloud knew it should read "Gibson," marking the path from this main road to the house. He stopped the team as they came to the path, which was hardly visible from the road. The lack of use in Dorthea's absence had allowed the prairie grass to reclaim much of its territory. McCloud reached down and pulled the board from the dry ground. He'd repaint it, "McCloud" just as soon as he had the time. As he climbed back onto the driver's seat he called inside the wagon, "Susannah, we're here, get ready to see your new home!" Then he called, "Git up!"one last time to the oxen, and the wagon began to move toward their final destination.

The grass was tall on either side of the wagon path. If Catherine had been on foot it would have reached almost waist high. She had to admit, there was a beauty about it, and the sky was enormous and blue. The roof of the house could be seen now, much like all the other sod houses they had passed. Then suddenly, it was in plain view.

Catherine had never felt such a sense of desolation. It was easy to see why Dorthea had looked so beaten down. The only two windows in the house were on either side of the faded wooden door. There had once been oiled paper covering them, but it was now torn and blowing in the wind in jagged strips. The small fenced area, which had served to corral animals at one time, was badly in need of repair. A lean-to had been erected at the end of the house, but had also suffered from damage by strong winds. Evidence of previous attempts to make the ground yield crops lay in dried stubble in fields around the house, with the plow left sadly defeated in the lean-to. Catherine tried to find something positive in this picture of despair; at least there *was* a house there, and they wouldn't have to build one. Thinking of their comfortable farm house in Lexington, her heart sank. "God, You're really going to have to help Mama!" she prayed under her breath.

McCloud had put the steps in place at the back of the wagon and reached up to help Susannah down. She handed Baby Jake to him, and then looked around at the scene before her. She stopped on the first step. The thought flitted through her mind; "If I don't step foot on this place and claim it as mine, then it will not be my lot in life." She was tempted to step back inside the wagon, as though that would reverse this movement of her life toward the place before her. Instead, she stood motionless, her eyes sweeping the faded, dry, scene. Then she looked down at McCloud holding the baby and tears began to flow soundlessly down her cheeks.

"Susannah! Please, I know it's not much now. But I'm going to make it better, just give me a little time!" McCloud pleaded earnestly. "Just look around … as far as you can see; this is ours."

Susannah did look around, and then took the remaining steps to the ground. Catherine felt cold chills as she watched her mother and saw the same, lonely look of despair in her eyes that had been in Dorthea's.

Jeremy couldn't bear seeing her disappointment. "Ma, we'll have this place looking great in just a few weeks. Cat can help you plant flowers in front of the house, and it'll feel like home. This place is just lonesome since there's been nobody here. But we're here now; we'll get it cheered up again!"

Susannah took a resigned breath and said, "Well, let's go see what the house has to offer."

They walked to the door of the sod house. There was no doorknob, only an eight-inch board nailed to the frame and pulled down to prevent the door from opening. Since McCloud was holding Baby Jake, Jeremy stepped forward, turned the board and the door swung open. He stepped inside, and before his eyes could adjust to the darkness he heard the soft rattle that signaled him to quickly step back. The snake struck, hitting the tip of his boot before escaping rapidly out the door as it slithered between Susannah and Catherine. Catherine hardly had time to shriek and grab Susannah before McCloud ordered them to get back, not knowing if there were other such unwelcome guests to appear. Like a flash of lightning Old Pal was after the rattler, and moments later proudly held the dead snake up to Jeremy like a prized offering.

Jeremy leaned against the side of the soddie, white-faced and short of breath, as everyone expressed their concern for his safety.

"Jeremy! Did it bite you? Are you sure?"

At first, he could only shake his head and point to his boot. "Whew, what a welcome to our new home," he said when he could catch his breath. He looked down at his boot where two fang marks could clearly be seen. "You don't suppose venom can soak through leather, do you?"

McCloud handed the baby to Susannah. "I think I'd better get something to use as a weapon before we try this again," he said, and went to the supply wagon for a hoe and a pistol.

"Wait out here," he said, "I'll go in and make sure it's safe. A few moments later, he stepped to the doorway. "The only squatters we have now are spiders. Jeremy, if you'll get me a broom I'll sweep down the cobwebs. Maybe after we move in they'll prefer to take up housekeeping somewhere else."

Jeremy went to get the broom, and Susannah walked back to sit on the steps at the wagon. She had been up very little since the baby came, and the close call with Jeremy had drained her of the strength she had. Catherine sensed this and took Baby Jake from her. Totally oblivious to all the drama around him, he slept peacefully.

Apparently McCloud felt that a little more sweeping up inside might give Susannah a better first impression of her house. She and Catherine watched as clouds of dust and debris went flying out the door.

In spite of her exhaustion Susannah couldn't help laughing as she said to Catherine, "This is probably the first time that man has ever used a broom."

"O.K. I think that's about as good as it's going to get," a red-faced, dusty McCloud called to them.

This time their entrance to the cabin was uneventful. It was sixteen feet in length and twelve feet wide, with the fireplace on one end wall. By the time they moved the furniture and crates of food supplies inside, there would be very little space left. Susannah and

Catherine were glad to see that Dorthea had left her small stove there. Catherine had learned to cook on the trail over a fire, so now she'd have to learn to use a stove. She was delighted to have a real oven now. Dorthea told them that the fireplace alone was inadequate to heat the cabin in extremely cold weather, so the stove would help provide warmth.

The sod structure had a damp, musty smell that they would find ever- present. The two small windows were the only source of light, causing it to be dark, as well. McCloud had included window panes in his supplies, so hopefully, they had survived the rough journey without breaking.

There was evidence that Dorthea had attempted to make the place livable. A sleeping loft had been built over the end of the room opposite the fireplace. From just past the cooking area to the back of the cabin, the walls had been covered with the pages of a women's magazine from back east. Dark rings marred the print here and there, proof of water that had seeped through the sod in a previous rain. Simple, faded curtains hung at the windows. Susannah feared they might fall apart if laundered. The idea of laundry brought the subject of water to mind.

"Pollard, we should check the well," she said.

"It's more than likely going to need priming after not being used for so long," McCloud said.

"I'll get a bucket of water from the barrel," Jeremy said.

They walked out to the pump with its faded red handle. Dried strands of grass had blown up all around it. McCloud cleaned it off, and poured in the water. It took a few pumps of the handle, then clear, fresh water poured from the spout of the pump. That felt like a victory, and a cheer rose involuntarily from all of them. Water was the sustenance of life, and the scarcity of it on the trail made this even more precious.

"Shall we start moving things in?" McCloud asked Susannah.

"I don't think I'm up to it this evening, Pollard," Susannah said. "Catherine and I need to do more cleaning before we get everything in there, so I think we'd better stay one more night in the wagons."

Jeremy had slept on the ground under his wagon the entire trip, but his encounter with the rattler had made him leery of being on the same level with others like it.

"I think I'll take my bedding and sleep in that loft tonight, just in case the snakes object to our being here," he said.

"I've got enough buffalo chips to cook out here, Catherine said. " I think we could use some of Dorthea's biscuits this evening," to which Jeremy heartily agreed.

As she kneaded the dough Catherine thought, "Sometimes we make foods to celebrate special occasions, but at times like this, there's little to celebrate except the food!"

CHAPTER 17

"Here, Catherine, I found another red ribbon," Susannah said, handing the narrow satin streamer to her.

"Oh, good, I need more bows," Catherine said

Somehow they'd managed to find room enough to put a tiny tree in the cabin. None of them knew what kind of tree it was, and it was a far cry from the evergreens back home, but it was a tree, nonetheless.

Jeremy had run across the seedling as he was riding Midnight and couldn't resist bringing it home. Maybe it was childish, but it just wasn't Christmas without a tree, whether in Kansas or Missouri. They hadn't brought any decorations west with them, but Cat was creative; he was sure she'd come up with something, and she did.

Catherine had made ropes of beading from salt dough and painted them with red paint she found in McCloud's supplies. Then looking among her few belongings for things she could use as decorations, Catherine had found her hair ribbons. She certainly had no occasion to be wearing them now. She cut several of the ribbons into smaller pieces, and tied brightly colored bows on the sparse limbs of the tree. The last addition was her favorite … the gingerbread people. Susannah mixed the dough and Catherine cut out gingerbread boys and girls, baked and frosted them. They too, hung by ribbons on the tree, and would be eaten on Christmas Day. The finishing touch was Susannah's lacy white handkerchief, made into an angel, and placed on the top of the tree. Catherine stood back and looked at her handiwork.

"I know it's a far cry from our previous Christmas trees, but I think it's beautiful," she said.

"It is indeed, honey. It brightens up the whole cabin," Susannah told her. Even Baby Jake smiled his approval when they held him up in front of it.

There had been so many adjustments for everyone in these past few weeks. As glad as they were that their traveling in the wagons had ended, it was hard to get used to being in one place and in such close quarters. There had been other people around them for months. Now they only had each other.

The lack of privacy had been a major adjustment. Pollard and Susannah's bed took up most of the space on one end of the cabin. Catherine slept in the loft above them. Jeremy had opted to sleep out in his wagon for the first few weeks, but night temperatures often dropped below freezing now. It became necessary for him to bring his bedroll indoors to sleep on the floor in the kitchen area. There had been no time to cut sod to build an addition onto the house. Other things had taken precedence: repairing the corral and the lean-to to protect the animals, and breaking up as much ground as possible. This alone was a chore that took a very sharp plow blade and a full team of oxen. The wheat had to be planted one week following the first frost, so Jeremy and McCloud had gone to work immediately on the fields, working from daylight to dark preparing the hard soil.

Dorthea had told them about the bitter cold. She warned them of the possibility of being snowed in, and said they would need enough fuel to last as long as they were snowbound. Since there was so little wood available, Catherine and Susannah were cooking with buffalo and cow chips. Catherine took it upon herself to walk the grassy plains and gather the dried chips from cattle herds that had been driven across the land, and from the buffalo that had roamed freely for so many years. As she concentrated on filling the burlap bag, she didn't realize that she was going farther from the house. After a while she looked up and could see nothing but grass and sky. It was as though the house and all her family had disappeared. Panic rose in her chest, and she turned back to run the direction from which she had come. To her relief, she had walked over a slight rise which caused the house to be hidden from view. It was frightening to feel she was totally alone in this vast sea of sky and grassland, and yet there was a sense of freedom at the same time. "Getting used to this place is not going to be easy!" she said out aloud.

Susannah and Catherine had taken inventory of food supplies that were left from the journey and made a list of things they needed to purchase. They were in much better shape in regard to food supplies than they expected to be. This was due to Colonel Edward Dawson's kindness in insisting Catherine's family eat with the army escort for two weeks. Still, with no fresh produce available for months, these supplies would not be more than they needed. Thankfully, the chickens had safely made the journey in their cage on the side of the wagon and were again laying eggs. Daisy, the cow, was producing more milk now that she had plenty of good grass and was not walking a wagon trail.

The crops were in the ground now, and there was nothing to do but wait. Even Catherine had helped

McCloud and Jeremy with the planting. They had been careful to place the wheat seeds exactly the correct distance into the earth. Strong winds could blow away the topsoil and take the seeds with it if planted too close to the surface. If buried too deeply young plants seem to lack the strength to push their way to the surface. There hadn't been time to break up enough ground to plant as large a crop as they'd hoped. Still, if this planting produced a successful yield, they should have enough profit to start the new, bigger crop for next year. Buying the land from Dorthea had taken a large sum out of the money McCloud had planned to use to tide them over until the farm began to produce. They would have to be as frugal as possible.

The bright spot in everyone's day was Baby Jake. He hardly ever cried, only enough to alert someone to his needs, and when fed and diapered he returned to his good humor. The fact that the baby was still sleeping much of the time gave Susannah the opportunity to rest at intervals as she needed. He was smiling now and seemed to know each of them as they talked to him. That one little smile of recognition and the wave of his small hands was enough to make any of them forget their struggles.

Jeremy built a travois like the Indians used and rode for miles around in search of wood for fuel when the snows came. He brought home anything that could be burned. Sometimes roots protruded from dried up creek beds and he used his hatchet to chop them from the soil and added them to his stash. He was deeply concerned about their ability to keep the sod cabin warm enough through weeks of really cold weather. They didn't have much in the way of extra clothing, either. They had brought so little with them in order to conserve space for supplies. Jeremy was reminded of God's promise that since He fed and cared for sparrows, He would certainly feed and clothe His people.

As Jeremy rode, he thought about Liz and the letter he'd received from her. The wagon train had arrived in Oregon, but not without problems. In crossing a turbulent river one family lost their wagon altogether, and a man was drowned. Liz's family was doing well, though. Her parents, little Hannah and her brother, Billy, were adjusting to their new life there. Liz described Oregon as the most beautiful place she'd ever seen. As Jeremy looked about him, it was hard not to feel envious, or to wonder if he should have gone on with them to the northwest. But he knew he couldn't have done that. He still was not certain in his heart that things were well with his mother, and until Catherine was safely with David, Jeremy wouldn't feel free to go on with his life. He really didn't mind the solitude of the prairie. Being a quiet person himself, it was peaceful to him. However, he was very concerned about their lack of proper shelter for the animals. He didn't know how the animals could survive a really cold winter without a barn. "Just another thing for God to take care of," he thought.

Jeremy had allowed Midnight to graze and drift since he had no particular destination in his hunt for fuel. He was careful to keep his directional bearing, though, or otherwise he might never make it back home. Midnight was walking alongside what appeared to be a shallow, dry, creek bed that circled around a rise in the ground. As he followed the curve, he was surprised to see a man hoeing a garden! The man saw him at about the same time, and surprise broke across his face as well. Jeremy smiled and waved, and the man waved back. Laying down his hoe he walked to meet Jeremy and Midnight.

"Hello! Welcome to my little plot of land. I'm Owen Heldman." The tall, lanky man extended his hand to Jeremy as he smiled with pleasure at the sight of a visitor.

Jeremy dismounted and shook Owen's hand. "I'm Jeremy Sutherland. My mother and stepfather bought the place a few miles to the west. I was out scavenging for fuel. I wasn't aware there was anyone living anywhere near us."

"My wife and I got here too late to build a sod structure, so we will go through the winter in this dugout," he said, pointing to a ravine in the dry creek bed. Jeremy then noticed the stovepipe above ground. "Come and meet my wife," Owen said.

"I've never seen inside a dug-out," Jeremy admitted.

Owen smiled, "We hadn't either until we got here. Other than being dark, it really isn't too bad, at least for me. Of course, I spend my days outside. I think it's harder on Martha."

Jeremy followed Owen around to the other side of the ravine where he could then see a wood framed doorway and a shelter that extended out over the door for a few feet.

"Honey," Owen called as he opened the door. "We have company."

"Company?" a woman's voice cried, "Well, praise be!"

"Martha, this is Jeremy Sutherland. His family has moved into the place up the road a few miles. Jeremy, this is my wife, Martha."

"My, my, it is so nice to see another soul! Do come into our humble dwelling, Mr. Sutherland. Have a chair there by the table. I have some coffee on the stove."

Jeremy's eyes were still adjusting to the darkness, but he could see that Martha Heldman had the face of an angel. If he had asked to see a picture of "goodness" he thought it would certainly be this kind woman in her blue checked apron. Her eyes crinkled up when she smiled, giving her a friendly, mischievous look. Curious about the dugout, he looked around and was surprised to see that it was set up very cozily. There were almost as many pieces of furniture in this dwelling as in their sod house. Rag rugs covered most of the dirt floor and there were even pictures somehow secured to the dirt walls.

"Please just call me Jeremy, Mrs. Heldman. Your place is quite nice. I must tell you, my mother and sister will be delighted to know there's another woman within a few miles."

"Oh, Owen, did you hear that? Other women nearby!" And to Jeremy she said, "I've been telling him that I was starved to talk about recipes and sewing."

"And I told her I didn't know a thing about those subjects, so she'd better pray for some female companionship," Owen said with a smile.

"Well, Christmas is only two days away. Why don't you come and have Christmas dinner with us. My mother and sister would be thrilled, and I know my stepfather would welcome having someone other than me to talk to. I have a baby half brother that's less than two months old, and he's pretty much the center of attention in our household," Jeremy said.

Martha sat cups of coffee down before Jeremy and her husband. "I can't believe it, women and a baby, too! We can go can't we, Owen?" Martha pleaded.

"Well, I have to admit, I wasn't looking forward to spending a lonely Christmas day here," Owen said.

"What can we bring, Jeremy?" Martha asked

"Now, you're getting me into the recipes. I'm sure that whatever you have to bring will be just fine. Come in the morning and we'll have the day to spend together."

"What is your mother's name? And your sister's? I know I won't think of another thing until I get to meet them," Martha's eyes shone with excitement.

"My mother is Susannah McCloud," Jeremy said. "My sister's name is Catherine, but I've always called her 'Cat.' She's a year younger than me, so we've always been close. Our mother just married Mr. McCloud about a year ago, and now they have Baby Jake. We barely made it here in time to get a wheat crop in the ground."

"Sounds like you arrived a couple of weeks before us," Owen said. I wasn't able to get ground broken in time to get any wheat planted, but I've got some winter vegetables that might survive if it doesn't get too cold."

"I've heard how bad the winter can be here, and I'm sure not looking forward to it," Jeremy said. He drank the rest of his coffee and turned to Martha, "Thank you for the coffee, Ms. Martha. I've been gone for quite a while, so I think I'd better be getting on home. My mother still worries about me."

"If you'll go along by the creek bed for about a half mile the opposite way than you came, it will take you right to the road which leads straight to your place. That will be easier on your travois than the rough ground, too. By the way," Owen said, "We have plenty of wood. I brought a lot of rough boards thinking I could use them to build a temporary house, but I've decided that building a soddy in the spring will work better, so we intend to use it as firewood. I'll put a few pieces on your travois and bring some more when we come for Christmas."

"What a blessing that is!" Jeremy said. "I've really been concerned about keeping the cabin warm enough for the baby, especially when the snow comes."

"The Lord always provides, doesn't He?" Martha said.

"I can't even tell you how good He has been to us, Martha," he said, shaking her hand, "I'll look forward to seeing you and Owen on Christmas day." Jeremy said, following his new neighbor out the door.

Following Owen's directions, he was home before he knew it. He was surprised at how light-hearted he felt after meeting the Heldman's. He knew his mother and Catherine would be just as excited to know that another woman would be coming to their place.

"God really did make people to need each other," Jeremy thought as he rode into the drive with his travois full of wood.

*   *   *   *

"I'm still having a hard time believing this." Susannah said to Catherine as she poked stuffing into the cavity of a large bird. "We haven't had turkey for so long, and then one shows up just in time for Christmas dinner!"

"It's kind of like God sending the animals to Noah's ark," Catherine replied.

"But with a totally different outcome for the turkey," Jeremy said with a grin. It really did seem like a small miracle. He had come back to the cabin from hunting quail, and had just leaned his gun against the wall of the house to begin cleaning his catch. He looked up to see a large wild turkey slowly walking toward the house, as if to say, "Here, I am, I've come for your Christmas dinner!"

Jeremy wasted no time reaching for his gun in case the turkey changed its mind. Now Mr. Tom would make a very special meal, especially with company coming.

When Jeremy told Susannah and Catherine that they would have female companionship for the holiday, they were thrilled. Even McCloud seemed pleased to have company coming as Jeremy told him about meeting Owen and Martha Heldman. He hoped the neighbor might have answers to some of his questions about growing crops in the area.

Catherine was already thinking ahead to after dinner and celebrating Christmas. She suddenly missed her piano with a longing so intense that it hurt. From the time she had been old enough to learn the simplest carols, she had played Christmas music as part of their family's celebration of the day. Well, at least they could sing the familiar songs.

Susannah had put the dried cranberries on to soak last evening, so Catherine was adding sugar, and would cook them for a few minutes to make cranberry sauce. She had already made an apple cake. Potatoes were boiling to be mashed, and the smell of the turkey filled the small dwelling. The last to be baked were the yeast rolls, which at present were rising in their pan over on the dresser for lack of space in the kitchen area.

The men could hardly bear the closeness of the cabin. Tormented by the smells of the good food cooking, they opted for the outdoors. The weather itself felt like a Christmas gift. It was crisp and clear, the sky as blue as mid-summer, without a snow cloud in sight. Jeremy hadn't thought about playing horseshoes since they'd left Lexington; there really hadn't been time to play anything. But this was Christmas. For the men there would be no work beyond caring for the animals. On this day, the women had the brunt of the labor, but loved it, anyway. So Jeremy went to gather the horseshoes and stakes and set up the game.

McCloud was about to throw the first pitch when they heard the sound of a wagon coming. Soon the Heldmans rounded the curve with Martha waving cheerily as soon as she saw Jeremy and McCloud. Owen grinned his greeting as he reined his horse to a stop. Jeremy went over to help Martha down from the wagon as McCloud greeted Owen.

"Oh, Jeremy! It's so good to see you again. Merry Christmas!" Martha said, giving him a hug as though they'd been friends for years.

McCloud came and shook hands with Martha and introduced himself. By then Susannah and Catherine had come from the cabin, eager to meet their new pioneer sister.

"Welcome to our home, Martha," Susanna said, opening her arms. "I'm Susannah, and this is my daughter, Catherine."

Martha Heldman returned Susannah's hug, tears filling her eyes. "Oh, you have no idea how happy I am to meet you … to know you're here. And Catherine," turning to Catherine, she hugged her too. "You're both so beautiful. Oh, my, we've just begun, but I think this is the best Christmas ever!"

Owen was lifting covered baskets from the back of the wagon.

"Are you ready for these, now?" he asked.

"Oh, yes, I'm so glad to meet these ladies, I forgot about the food. Ladies, this is my husband, Owen," Martha replied.

Susannah and Catherine shook hands with Owen and welcomed him. Jeremy offered to move his wagon.

"I'd better get back to my cranberry sauce before it scorches," Catherine said, hurrying back inside.

Susannah and Martha followed, each carrying a basket.

"I didn't know what to bring; Jeremy wasn't any help when I asked him. So I baked a pecan pie and sweet potatoes, and brought a couple of different kinds of my pickles," Martha said.

"Oh, that's wonderful, Martha. We didn't have any sweet potatoes, and we haven't had pecan pie since we left Lexington," Susannah said.

Baby Jake was just waking up as they walked inside, fussing slightly to let Susannah know he'd prefer a dry diaper.

"Oh, the baby! How precious. I haven't seen a baby in six months. My, the things we take for granted before we no longer have them," Martha said wistfully.

"Meet Jacob Carter McCloud, Martha, or Baby Jake, as we call him. I'll change him, and then you can hold him while I cook," Susannah told her.

That arrangement worked well for everyone since there was little room to work in the kitchen space. The conversation never stopped between the women; there was so much to learn about each other. By the time the dinner was ready, they had become fast friends. Since the weather outside was beautiful, and room inside the cabin was so scarce, they decided to move the table and chairs outdoors. The men, too had become quickly acquainted as they enjoyed the friendly competition of the horseshoe game.

As she looked at the beautiful feast on the table before them, Catherine could only have asked for one thing more … that David was here to share it with her. At the thought of him she reached to touch the necklace around her neck. For just a moment she stopped and tried to imagine what he was doing right then. She knew that his mother cooked turkey for Christmas too. They'd have all the baked goods and side dishes and David's favorite cornbread dressing and gravy. There would be gifts under their beautifully decorated tree that they'd open after dinner. Then his father would read the Christmas story, and they would bow their heads as he prayed a prayer of thanksgiving for the gift of Jesus Christ to the world. Tears welled up in her eyes, re-living the times she had shared that special day with David and his family. But this was a special day, too. God had sent precious new friends to share it with them, so she wasn't going to be sad. Catherine was beginning to realize that she had a choice when it came to emotions; maybe that came with growing up, or with learning to trust everything to the Lord. Anyway, she was choosing to be glad on this day, to celebrate the good in it. That certainly felt better than moping around and wishing things were different. She smoothed her curls and removed her apron, and then joined her family and friends for their first Christmas dinner in Kansas.

*   *   *   *

Owen and Martha smiled and waved as their wagon rolled out the driveway. Saying goodbye had been hard for the women, and especially so for Martha. Knowing she was going back to the lonely dugout with only her husband for company, she found it difficult to keep the smile on her face.

276

Catherine and Susannah were more appreciative of each other as they watched the Heldmans leave. Susannah put her arm around Catherine's shoulder as they stood watching and waving as long as they could see their new friend.

"I'm so glad I have you here with me," Susannah said to her daughter.

"Oh, Mama, I can't imagine being without you!" Catherine said as she hugged her mother in return. "Do you think we could go to see Martha at her place sometime?"

"I'd love to do that, but from now until spring we will have to be careful of the weather. The soldiers said the winter storms come up so quickly without warning. We definitely don't want to get caught out in that," Susannah answered.

As though hearing her words, a chilling wind blew across the homestead. The sky that had been so clear earlier was now darkening with clouds that moved swiftly across the sky.

"I think I'll milk Daisy early today," Catherine said.

"All right, honey, that's probably a good idea with this weather moving in," Susannah said. Jeremy and McCloud had already gone to tend the rest of the animals for the evening.

By the time Catherine finished the milking, the sky was covered with ominous looking clouds and the winds had risen even more. She shivered with cold as she walked slowly back to the house, not wanting to spill any of the precious milk. Susannah's exhausted body had simply not produced enough nourishment for the baby and he was drinking Daisy's milk from a bottle now.

The cabin seemed to radiate the good feelings of the day. The aroma of food still permeated the air. Catherine decided to climb up into her loft and write in her journal. As she wrote about meeting the Heldmans and how they had enriched this Christmas Day, she stopped to think about the reasons the couple had come to Kansas.

Martha had told their story as Catherine and Susannah prepared the meal. She said that neither she, nor Owen, had been married until a year ago. She'd almost given up on finding a husband until she met this tall, gentle man. Even though they intended to begin by farming and getting settled here in Kansas, they had really come to eventually start a church and be pastors.

That calling on Owen's life was evident today as he read the scriptures telling of Christ's birth. He so beautifully expounded on the love of God the Father in sending his Son to earth to live as a man so He could redeem mankind. Catherine had glanced at McCloud. It was evident that Owen's remarks had moved him in some way. There was sadness there, as though he might think this wonderful gift of salvation was for others, but not for him.

Hopefully, they'd get together for more Bible studies in the spring. Catherine could hear the wind howling louder. Jeremy put more wood on the fire and then pulled back the curtain to look outside.

"Well, I guess this is Mother Nature's payback for giving us such a nice day earlier," he said. "It's snowing!"

Throughout the night the winds blew and the snow fell. But the cabin was warm, its inhabitants were well fed, and Christmas had been wonderful.

CHAPTER 18

"Come on, ox!" Jeremy pulled on the animal in frustration. The bitter cold went through his coat and chilled him to the bone. The lack of hay had forced them to allow the cattle to graze for whatever food they could find, but it also meant having to keep an eye on them. This one had wandered into a creek bed that previously had held just enough water from melting snow to create a mud bog. The ox would die if Jeremy couldn't get him freed from the mud and back to the shelter of the other animals before nightfall. The combined body heat of the small herd helped them combat the freezing temperatures.

"Push now, boy!" Jeremy encouraged. The animal gave one last great effort, and to Jeremy's relief managed to get its footing on solid ground. Looking at the mud-covered animal and down at his own spattered clothing, Jeremy remembered the day he and Catherine had fallen into the pond and looked much as he and the ox did today. He couldn't help smiling. That seemed ages ago, but not even a year had passed. This had to be the longest year of his life. Without doubt this was the worst winter he'd ever experienced. He would be so glad to see spring with its warmer temperatures.

"I think Christmas day was the last time I felt warm," Jeremy thought. The weather had stayed cold since that first snow came. The temperature had seldom risen more than a few degrees above freezing. He was so thankful for the wood Owen had given them. That had made it possible to keep the fire going in the cabin, even if it wasn't as warm as they would like.

Baby Jake was doing fine, though. It was Susannah Jeremy was concerned about. A few days after Christmas she had developed a fever and congestion in her chest that brought on times of deep, wracking coughs. She had taken the various home remedies they'd brought from Missouri and would seem better for a while. Even at the best times though, she was never completely free from the cough. Jeremy could see that she tried to hide her problem from the rest of the family, suppressing the cough when at all possible. Without making an issue of things Catherine began to take on the cooking again. She enjoyed it, and it gave her something to do. Jeremy had insisted on milking the cow to keep Catherine from having to go out in the ice and snow. They were doing everything they could to protect Daisy from the cold because her milk was Baby Jake's only food now. McCloud had enclosed the lean-to for the cow, using the canvas wagon cover as protection from the wind As if appreciative of her special treatment Daisy faithfully kept producing rich milk.

As Jeremy and the ox approached the cabin McCloud was carrying a pitchfork of hay over to Daisy. He shook his head as he saw the muddy ox.

"Found a bog, did he?" he asked, his breath freezing in the air.

"Yeah, I thought for a while I'd have to leave him there before I ended up in it myself." Jeremy said.

McCloud threw the hay over to Daisy then turned to Jeremy with a serious look on his face.

"Jeremy, I'm going to make a trip to Fort Dodge. I'm extremely concerned about your mother. I'd rather the doctor examined her, but there's no way she could make the trip in this cold. I'm hoping the doctor there will give me medicine that can help her cough," he said.

"Do you want me to go?" Jeremy asked.

"No, I think she'd feel better knowing you're here," McCloud said.

"Are you going today?" Jeremy asked.

"Yes, I don't see any evidence of a snowstorm coming … some rain, maybe. I should be able to make it on Flame in a couple of hours," McCloud said.

"I'll keep an eye on things here. Would you mail some letters for Cat and me and ask if there's any mail for us?"

"Yeah, I'd planned on that already. 'You want to saddle Flame for me while I put on some extra clothing? I'd like to get started right away."

Jeremy nodded his agreement. "I'll bring him up to the door and bag some feed for you to take for him, too," he said as he headed toward the corral.

Susannah's face lit up with relief when McCloud told her he was going to get some medicine for her. Then it clouded with concern.

"But Pollard, the weather. Are you sure you can make it through safely?"

McCloud knelt by the rocker where Susannah was holding Baby Jake.

"Yes, the sky looks fairly clear. The wind is up, as always, but I think I can get to the fort in about two hours," he said.

"Well, don't try to come back tonight. Stay until morning," Susannah said with concern.

"I will. I'll start back tomorrow after I pick up a few supplies," and seeing the expectant look on Catherine's face, he said, " If you have any letters going back east, I'll take them and ask about mail for you and Jeremy." He bent to give the sleeping baby a kiss on his head and one to Susannah, too. Rising, he said, "I've got to put on some extra clothing. Jeremy's saddling Flame for me."

Within minutes he was gone, riding into the cold wind. Susannah called Catherine and Jeremy to her, "We need to pray that Pollard will make this trip safely," she said. As they bowed their heads Susannah prayed that God would be with Pollard, and that the doctor would have medicine that would strengthen her. She ended her prayer with, "and Lord, it would really be nice if there were letters for Catherine and Jeremy!"

*   *   *   *

Knowing there was the possibility of receiving mail from their sweethearts had lifted both Catherine and Jeremy's spirits. They pulled out their old childhood checker game and set it up on the kitchen table. Apparently, a thunderstorm had moved into the area and now it was raining outside. That could mean the sod roof leaking if the rain lasted for any length of time, but that didn't dampen their enthusiasm, or their sibling rivalry.

"You still can't beat me, you know," Jeremy taunted Catherine.

"You're talking like I've *never* beaten you!" Catherine retorted.

"That one time doesn't count because David was giving you tips," he insisted.

282

As Susannah rocked Baby Jake and listened to Catherine and Jeremy, she enjoyed having this time alone with her children. The thought made her feel guilty. For all his wrong-doings, Pollard had worked hard since they arrived in Kansas, and did everything he could to make things better. Even now, he was enduring bitter cold to get medicine for her. Because of these things she appreciated him, but never had her heart loved him like he so wanted to be loved. Maybe if he had done things differently in the beginning, if they were still at the farm in Lexington, perhaps she would have eventually been able to love him. Selling Jeremy's birthright had placed a barrier across her heart that refused to let him in. Now, here they were, in the freezing plains of Kansas in a sod house that would undoubtedly begin to leak water through the roof at any time. Her body was giving out on her. If the medicine Pollard hoped to bring to her did not do wonders against this thing in her chest …

Susannah's thoughts, and the bantering of Catherine and Jeremy, were interrupted by the sound of a horse and wagon outside. As Jeremy looked out the window they heard Owen Heldman calling, "Hello! It's us, the Heldmans!"

Jeremy rushed to the door and opened it. A gust of wind blew rain into the room as Owen and Martha came inside as quickly as possible.

"We're so sorry to drop in on you like this!" Martha said, as she stood, dripping wet from riding in the rain.

"Nonsense! Come in, both of you. Are you all right?" Susannah asked, standing now with the baby.

"I really hate to be dripping on your floor," Owen said apologetically. "Apparently this storm dropped quite a lot of water further north and the creek bed alongside our dugout now has water running almost up to its banks. Our little dirt home has about a foot of water in it."

"I'm so sorry to hear that, but you know you are welcome here with us for as long as you need to stay. You have to get out of those wet clothes, Martha, you are shivering!" Susannah said with concern. "Catherine, put on some coffee to warm them up. Do you have any dry clothing with you, or do we need to find something here?"

"I'm hoping the things we packed are still dry," Owen said, lifting the small case in his hand. "We wrapped them in oilcloth."

"Let me see, dear," Martha said, her lips blue with cold. She opened the case and found that the extra clothing they'd brought had indeed somehow managed to stay dry. Now they faced the question of modesty and how to change clothing in one room with others present!

Thoughtfully, Susannah took charge of the sensitive situation. She laid Baby Jake on the bed and went to the dresser. Opening a drawer she brought out a large sheet.

"Catherine, when you finish getting the coffee started, come and hold one side of this sheet. Jeremy, you can hold the other, and we'll give Owen and Martha some privacy to change their clothing there in front of the fire." She also handed them towels to dry off.

"You'll never know how much we appreciate this, Susannah," Martha said. "I don't know what we would have done without you. We don't even know where another neighbor might be this side of Fort Dodge."

"What about all your nice things in the dugout?" Jeremy asked. "Will they be ruined?"

"We really don't know what to expect, Jeremy, since this is the first time we've had to deal with this. I'm thinking now that building the dugout so close to the creek bank wasn't a good idea," Owen said. "When water started coming in I put the furniture up on blocks of wood. I'm hoping that will save it. Martha's rugs on the floor will have to be taken out, washed and dried."

"O.K. I'm ready," Catherine said. She and Jeremy took ends of the sheet and stood with their backs to the fireplace, giving the Heldmans their own little room to change.

Within a half hour they were all sitting around the table having coffee and a light supper of leftovers.

"I can't tell you how much we enjoyed being here for Christmas Day," Martha said. "I think about it every time I feel lonely, and the memory drives my sadness away. Knowing that you're just a few miles away, even if we're all snowbound in our places, helps me not to feel so isolated."

"We feel the same way, Martha," Susannah said. "Catherine and I often talk about that day."

"Owen, I'd like to know more about how you decided to come to Kansas to be a pastor," Catherine said.

"That's kind of a long story, but let's see if I can give you the high points," Owen said. "I guess it really started a number of years ago. I began to feel the calling toward ministry. I developed a love for the Bible; I was quite happy to be alone and just read for hours.

"For some reason I read everything I could find in the papers about the settling of the frontier areas, and especially, Kansas. One day as I was reading, I suppose I had a vision, as it's spoken of in the Bible. In my mind I could see lonely people on scattered homesteads, much like both of ours. These people were hungry, not only for natural food, but for the Word of God. I saw that in their struggles to tame the new country, they needed strength from the Lord as much as they needed physical strength. I didn't hear an audible voice, but I heard in my spirit, "Owen, you have what they need, take it to them!" From that point on, my heart was set on coming here. Shortly afterward, I met Martha and knew immediately that she was to be my companion.. When the crops come in we will share all we can with those who have needs, and will travel as the circuit preachers did to bring the Word of God to the pioneers."

"Well, you have certainly been a blessing to us," Susannah said.

Catherine sat quietly, thinking about the things Owen had said. He and Martha were so sure of God's plan for them. Knowing His will for one's life would prevent going in wrong directions that might lead to a totally different outcome than God intended. But it also meant trusting Him to carry out that will when it seemed that things were going terribly wrong. That was where she found herself now. It certainly didn't look like God was in charge of things, but then, her vision was limited. She would simply have to trust that a God who already knows the future was certainly capable of guiding her life to fulfill His purposes.

*   *   *   *

Morning came with a clear sky. It was still cold, but the winds had died down and it was actually pleasant outside. Catherine and Martha carried out bedding that was wet from the leaking sod roof and spread it on the corral fencing to dry. They mopped the rough wooden floor that Susannah was so glad to have. Most of the pioneers lived with hard dirt floors. Martha covered hers with rugs, but she could only imagine the mess she'd have after their dugout flooded.

"When you are finished there, I think we should be heading back to check on things, hon," Owen said to Martha.

"All right, dear," she answered. "I just want to have a word with Catherine."

Drawing Catherine aside she spoke softly, "Catherine, I'm concerned about your mother. Owen and I will be praying for her. If you need me for any reason, just send Jeremy to get me, all right?"

The concern in Martha's eyes caused a flash of fear to race through Catherine's heart. "Do you think she's going to be all right, Martha? Surely the medicine McCloud is getting for her will help."

"I'm sure it will, sweetheart. I just wanted you to know that I'll be here if you need me," Martha consoled her. They turned to walk back toward the house.

"Owen, you can put our case in the wagon. I'll just say my goodbyes to Susannah and be right out."

"It was so good to have you here again, Martha, although, I hate that it meant having a flood in your dugout," Susannah said as she hugged her friend.

"It was a lovely visit, dripping roof and all," Martha laughed. "We'd better get back and see what kind of mess we have waiting for us now. I just have to hug and kiss Baby Jake one more time," she said, as Susannah handed the baby to her. The little one gurgled and smiled at Martha, who squeezed him in delight and kissed his chubby cheeks. Then handing him back to his mother, she said, "Susannah, I've told Catherine, if you need me, please don't hesitate to send for me."

"Thank you, my friend," Susannah said quietly.

"I know Owen is anxious to get back to our place, so I'd better go. Thank you for rescuing us and give Pollard our regards," Martha said, going out the door.

Jeremy stood talking to Owen by the wagon as he waited for Martha.

"Oh, Jeremy, I'm so glad you happened onto our place that day," she said as she hugged him goodbye. Owen helped her up to the wagon seat and then climbed up himself.

"Come whenever you can; we'll be thinking of you!" Martha called as the wagon moved on out onto the road.

Catherine and Jeremy stood watching them go. "Why does it feel so lonely when they leave?" Catherine asked.

"I guess because they just don't come often enough," Jeremy replied.

"Do you think it will always be this way, with so few people around? Will it ever be populated like it is back east?" Catherine wondered.

"Probably so," Jeremy said. "The government is advertising the cheap land and wherever people can get land, it will eventually be filled. Things will be easier as more people come. Businesses will start up, then schools will be built, churches, too. The railroad tracks are being laid so fast they will soon reach all the way to the west. Then people won't have to make the hard trip across the country in wagons."

"So we're the ones who had it the roughest, huh?" Catherine smiled. "But Jeremy, just think of all the fun they'll miss ... eating dust for twelve hours straight, hunting buffalo chips for cooking ..."

"And don't forget the boredom of looking at a dozen oxen's rear ends for seven months straight while your own gets bruised to the bone bouncing on a wagon seat!" Jeremy added.

"Well, at least when our children complain, we'll have our stories of hardship to tell them," Catherine said as they headed back to the house. She threw back her head and began to sing lustily, "I'm a pioneer woman, I'm as strong as they come, I rode that wagon trail … "

Her song ended abruptly as Jeremy clamped his hand over her mouth, "That's enough, Billy!" And they went into the house laughing.

Pollard McCloud returned to the homestead in mid-afternoon. He brought two bottles of medicine for Susannah. He also brought mail, several letters, in fact. Catherine had two from David, one from Liz, Jeremy had two from Liz, and they received a letter to both of them from the young people at their church.

While Catherine and Jeremy went off to read their letters, Susannah told Pollard about the Heldmans coming for the night. He told her about his conversation with the fort doctor and gave her instructions from the doctor for taking the medicines. He couldn't carry much in the way of supplies since he was traveling by horseback, but he'd picked up a few things, including a new bottle for Baby Jake. They'd only had one for him and if that got broken, they'd be in trouble.

McCloud didn't want to alarm Susannah, but he felt he should tell her what he'd heard at the fort in regard to Indian activity in the area. Things had been peaceful for a while, but the bad weather had created hardship on the Indians. With the restrictions placed on them by the government they were not allowed to move to places where things might be better for them. Whole tribes were hungry. And they were angry with the white man's government for putting them in this position. There had been several incidences of raids on area farms. So far, no one had been injured or killed as long as they gave the Indians the food or animals they wanted.

"We need to tell Catherine and Jeremy," Susannah said, with fear in her eyes.

"I'll talk to them when they come back inside, and I'll also try to make sure that either Jeremy or I stay in view of the cabin with our rifles at all times. They assured me at the fort that they have increased the details going out on patrol, especially where homesteaders are living," Rising, McCloud said, "I need to check Flame's hooves. Just before getting here he seemed to be favoring his left front leg … probably has a pebble in the shoe."

"All right," Susannah said. As he left she closed her eyes and laid her head against the back of the rocking chair. "Oh, God, will there never be peace?"

CHAPTER 19

"David!" Hearing his name, David turned to see Sarah and Abby waving at him from across the church yard. He waved back and started toward the girls. "Hi, Sarah, Abby," he said as he reached them.

"Have you heard from Catherine?" Sarah asked first, then Abby questioned, "Do you think she and Jeremy have received the letter from all of us?"

"I don't know if they got the letter, and I haven't heard any more from her," David said. "I know it takes a while for mail to reach the fort, but then I don't think they get there very often to pick it up. That means she doesn't get to send mail to me very often, either."

"We miss her so much and I know you do," Sarah said. "Sometimes I think about her and wonder what she's doing right that moment."

"She doesn't complain in her letters, but from what she tells me, I know her life is very different than it was here, and I know it's not easy," David said. "I'm really concerned about them making it through the winter."

"Is it colder there than it is here?" Abby asked.

"From everything I've heard, it's far colder there, and they have a lot of snow- sometimes blizzards that last for days," David replied.

"I know she would love to be here for your Bible studies. I've been meaning to tell you how much I've enjoyed them, David," Sarah said.

"We're all loving it, and even Jay Bob's coming regularly ... that's a miracle!" Abby said. "You break things down to our level and I always understand what you're teaching."

"I think I'm enjoying it more than anyone," David said with a smile. "I believe God directs me to the topic and the scriptures to teach about, and I study them. But then when I get started with the teaching, it all really comes alive for me, and by the time I'm finished I feel as though I've had the best time of my life!"

"You make us feel that way too, David. Why do you think our class has grown so much since you started teaching us?" Abby asked.

"Yoo-hoo! Girls! We're ready to go!" Sarah's mother called from their wagon.

"We've got to go, David; let us know if you hear from Catherine," Sarah said as they made their way to her family's wagon.

"Bye, girls, I will," David waved to them. "See you at Bible study."

David's parents had been invited to have Sunday dinner with a family in the church. David was invited, too, but he chose to spend some quiet time at home. He'd ridden Star to church, so he put his Bible into the saddle bags and swung up into the saddle. His mind was still on the conversation with Sarah and Abby about Catherine. He couldn't explain it, but he felt concerned for her safety. He'd planned to make himself a sandwich when he got home, but instead, he went to his room and knelt by the bed.

"Father God," he prayed, "Please be with Catherine and her family right now. I have no idea what is going on in Kansas, but You know everything that concerns her. Be her shield against any evil that might come her way." Immediately David thought of the scriptures in Psalms 91:1&2 : *He that dwelleth in the secret place of the Most High shall abide under the shadow of the Almighty. I will say of the Lord, He is my refuge and my fortress; my God; in him will I trust."*

He rose and opened his Bible to this passage and read the entire Psalm, building his confidence that God was able to protect Catherine.

"Lord, I pray that every word in this scripture will cover Catherine and her family, and I trust her to you now. Amen."

       *   *   *   *

The next morning David went into the shop early. He was working on a new design for a necklace that he wanted to add to the pieces on display at the Majestic. He was amazed at his success there. He really couldn't produce jewelry fast enough to suit Mr. Dubois, but he was working as fast as he could. The salon manager wasn't too upset with him; he said the fact that people had to wait for his work kept him in demand and added a certain amount of mystique to his pieces. "That must be a New York thing," David thought with a shake of his head.

His bank account was growing beyond his wildest expectations. He had begun to feel guilty at having the money while wondering if Catherine was in need. Yes, he was saving for a home for them, but he had the rest of his life to earn money and meet their needs. He would feel terrible if he learned she was doing without things she needed while their money was sitting here in his bank account. He didn't know if it would create a problem with her stepfather for any reason, but he intended to send money to her in the next letter.

The bells on the shop door jangled as it swung open. David looked up and to his chagrin, Charlotte Pendleton stood there. Her face was wearing what David had come to recognize as her most seductive smile.

"Hello, David. You don't look very happy to see me," she said coquettishly.

"What a surprise, Charlotte. How have you been?" David asked.

"Oh … so-so, I guess," she said, moving about the shop, looking into cases.

"What brings you to Lexington again?" he asked.

Charlotte came over to stand in front of David and leaning over toward him, batted her eyelashes and said, "Well, David, I can't believe you have to ask me that!"

David could feel the red flush moving upward to his face as he walked behind the counter and tried to ignore Charlotte's comment.

"Don't tell me you're still carrying the torch for *Catherine!*"

Looking her straight in the eyes, David said, "Nothing has changed between Catherine and me, Charlotte."

"That is such a shame, David. You and I could have a good time together!"

Changing the subject, David asked, "How is your father, Charlotte?"

Tossing her head and walking over to another case, Charlotte said, "Oh, Poppy's fine. It was really his idea to send me here again to get me away from Alex. I was hoping I could convince you to come play with me. I'm bored out of my mind!" she said with a pout. Then turning to David with a more serious tone she said, "You know, Poppy really liked you. I think he was hoping that if I came back here you might be more willing this time to associate with me."

"I take it, he's not too happy about your relationship with Alex Caine."

"Truthfully, I'm not either, but when I'm in New York, he won't leave me alone."

"Why don't you just break things off and tell him to stay away?"

Charlotte gave a derisive sort of laugh, "Don't you think I've tried that? Alex is like a wizard's poison … something you know is bad for you, and yet the appeal is too strong to refuse it. He won't give me any rest until I marry him!"

"Do you want to marry him?" David asked her.

Charlotte paused a moment before answering. "I don't know if you can even understand this, David … you're different … you're a *good* person. That's what attracts me to you. Alex and I are not like you. We probably deserve each other. Marriage to him would be a living hell, but more than likely, that's where I'm going to end up. Because nothing stops Alex Caine from getting what he wants!"

"Charlotte," David said softly, "Have you ever considered giving your life to Christ and allowing Him to work out all these things?"

"That means giving up control, David, and I'm too spoiled to having my own way," Charlotte laughed. "And speaking of that, what do you have that's new? Buying jewelry always makes me feel better."

David showed her the few things he'd completed for the shop and she bought some earrings and a bracelet. He walked her to the door and thanked her for the purchase. She stood in the open doorway and patted him on the cheek.

"Remember, sweetie, if you get lonesome, I'm at Aunt Evelyn's," she said.

"Good day, Charlotte," David told her, closing the door as she left.

Neither of them noticed the two men sitting at a table outside the tearoom across the street. The one with the camera was sure he'd taken a good shot of Charlotte patting David on the cheek. That would definitely be one to send to the boss.

*   *   *   *

Martin Pendleton sat in his plush New York office and listened to the report being presented to him by the private investigator, Abner Hawthorne.

"There's a lot of stuff here that's shady, but no proof of outright criminal behavior, not yet anyway. Guys of Caine's caliber eventually evolve to that point, though. They slide by with small stuff and get cocky, thinking they're invincible," Hawthorne said.

"Keep the tail on him. I want to know every move Alex Caine makes, and I'm hoping he'll do something stupid enough to be put away and out of my daughter's reach!" Pendleton said, his face red with frustration.

"I've noticed that Caine has been really restless since your daughter left town. You don't suppose he would follow her to Missouri, do you?" Hawthorne asked.

"It doesn't seem like a move he'd make. He loves wheeling and dealing in the city. I've heard him make disparaging remarks time and again about small towns, and he thinks anything west of Boston is for the uncouth!"

Pendleton rose and walked to look down at the view of New York harbor. As far as one could see in any direction there were buildings that he owned. His wealth was certainly a drawing card for a young man to want to marry his daughter. But Caine wasn't just greedy, he was evil. Martin Pendleton knew that men of his caliber would do whatever was necessary to get what they wanted, and this Alex Caine wanted Pendleton's daughter and his money... the only two things in life that mattered to him! That made Caine a mortal enemy, one especially dangerous to combat because he had no scruples. Pendleton was a shrewd businessman, but honest. Could he maintain his integrity and still defeat a man who had none?

Seeing that the banker was lost in thought, the private investigator laid the report on Pendleton's desk and walked to the door, saying, "I'll get back with you, sir."

Pendleton nodded his response and continued to look out over the harbor. He couldn't understand what Charlotte found so attractive in this demon, Caine. He was too old for her, anyway. Maybe that was the attraction, being able to catch an older man. Well, she had certainly hooked him ... the guy wouldn't move a foot away from her if they were in the same room. Pendleton didn't want to think to what lengths their relationship may have already gone. This was his little girl- his only child - the single object of his affection since his wife had died shortly after

297

Charlotte's birth. He knew he had spoiled her, but that was his only pleasure in life. Now he could see that giving her everything she wanted probably wasn't the best upbringing for her.

There was one thing Charlotte wanted that she had not been able to acquire though - the affections of the young jeweler from Lexington. Pendleton had seen many men fall under Charlotte's charm, but this David Winters had maintained a rigid faithfulness to some other girl that apparently was out west somewhere. This was the kind of man that Pendleton wanted to see his daughter marry. With no son to succeed him, he had hoped to have a son-in-law that he could groom to take over his dynasty. But that would never be Alex Caine! Maybe if Charlotte stayed in Lexington long enough she could eventually persuade Winters to keep company with her. The very idea that some other girl could prevent her from having a young man would be fuel enough to keep Charlotte pursuing him. And as long as she was focusing on David Winters, she wouldn't be thinking of Alex Caine.

"Mr. Pendleton, your board meeting is in five minutes. Here is your list of items to be discussed," his secretary said, handing him a folder.

"Thank you, Clara," Martin Pendleton said, and with a sigh returned to his desk.

*　　　*　　　*　　　*

David worked at the shop until almost eight o'clock. He finished the new necklace, made careful notes and drawings so he could reproduce it the same way, and packaged it to mail to Mr. Dubois in the morning. Locking the shop he walked home, wondering what his mother would have on the stove to pacify his growling stomach.

Reverend Winters looked up from the book he was reading and smiled. "Hello, son, you've had a long day."

David plopped down on the sofa. "I sure did, but I got the new necklace finished and ready to send to New York tomorrow."

"That's good. Your mother had her ladies' meeting tonight, but she left some baked chicken in the oven for you, and there's a letter on the table you might be happy to see," the Reverend said with a smile.

David jumped to his feet. "Is it from Catherine?"

At his Dad's nod, David raced to the kitchen with a whoop of joy. The food forgotten now, he took the letter to his room and closed the door. Trying to open it as quickly as he could, he was still careful not to tear anything. His heart was pounding as he began to read, hearing Catherine's voice in the words:

My Dearest David,

I never believed it would be difficult to write to you, but I've been sitting here for minutes with nothing but the greeting on this paper. Not because I don't have things to say ...it's totally the opposite! How will we ever catch up on telling each other all that's happened since we've been apart? Oh well, I'd better start somewhere ...

David savored every bit of Catherine's long letter as she told him about Baby Jake's birth and the kind lady who helped deliver him, about their

299

arriving at the homestead, and the loneliness of the plains. She relayed their joy in having a good well there and how hard they all had worked to get the wheat planted.

She wrote about how they had saved the life of the Indian boy and meeting his father, the chief, who gave Jeremy some sort of amulet.

When Catherine described what it was like to live in a soddy, David felt guilty being comfortable in his parent's nice, warm home.

> *Since I hardly ever know ahead of time when I will be able to send a letter to you, I have to write it and wait until someone goes to the fort. You cannot know how I treasure hearing from you, My Love, so continue to write. Every day that passes brings us closer to the time of our reunion. Give my regards to your parents and all of our friends at church. Jeremy sends his, as well.*
>
> *David, My Love, I miss you terribly, and I love you with my whole heart.*

> *Catherine*

David carefully folded the letter and placed it with the other mail from Catherine. He savored every morsel of information about her and her life in Kansas. He should get some reading material together to send to her; he'd ask Sarah and Abby what a girl would like.

CHAPTER 20

"Hey, wake up, sleepyhead!" Catherine's eyes opened to see Jeremy's head at the top of the ladder used to climb up to her loft. Since he'd never done this, it frightened Catherine, and she sat up as far as she could without bumping her head.

"What! What's wrong?"

"Relax ... nothing's wrong, except it's February first, and you just got older," Jeremy said.

Catherine fell back onto her pillow and closed her eyes with relief. "Oh."

"Happy birthday, honey," Susannah told her from below.

"I forgot about it being my birthday," Catherine admitted.

"Well, it's a beautiful day outside for a change, and Mama said I could take you to visit Martha and Owen for a birthday present," Jeremy said.

"Oh, thank you!" Catherine said. The thought of getting out of that house was enough to excite her, but to get to go somewhere, especially to visit with Martha, made it wonderful! It was Sunday; maybe Owen would share a Bible study with them.

Susannah had baked a corn cake for breakfast and had placed fifteen candles in it. She lit them as Catherine came to the table, and they sang Happy Birthday to her.

Baby Jake's eyes lit up as he saw the candles burning, and he gurgled and smiled at her.

"I'm sorry that I don't have gifts for you," Susannah said, giving her a hug.

"Getting to visit with Martha will be the best present anyway," Catherine said. "I can't wait to see their dugout!"

"As sunny as it is out there, it's still cold, so wrap up good," Jeremy said. "I'll get Midnight."

Less than an hour later they were on the road. Midnight seemed as excited as Jeremy and Catherine to be out in the crisp air. Since they were riding double, Jeremy didn't want to push him, but the horse was eager to go. Jeremy let him set his own pace as they traveled the roadway that was little more than a wide path through the prairie grass.

There was still snow in places where it had been the deepest, and the sun glinted on the white crystals with dazzling brilliance. Catherine squinted as she looked around. She'd never been any farther than the fields where she'd gathered the buffalo chips, but there really wasn't much difference in the way things looked. Jeremy had said it would take about an hour to reach the Heldman's place. She couldn't wait to see Martha's laughing eyes when she and Jeremy appeared at their door. Catherine had wrapped a small bundle of cookies and sweetbreads she had baked yesterday to bring as a gift for them.

Suddenly Jeremy reined Midnight to a halt, "Whoa, boy!" Then, in a low voice, he said, "Cat, just be quiet!"

Catherine looked over his shoulder to see three Indian braves on ponies blocking the roadway in front of them. Their expressions were not friendly. Jeremy calmly walked Midnight toward them with his right hand on his rifle in the sling. As they came closer, Jeremy nodded his head in greeting. One of them grunted in reply. They moved their horses in closer until they were almost touching Midnight. Catherine's heart was pounding so loudly she was certain they could hear it. One of them reached out and touched Catherine's hair on her forehead that was not covered by her woolen scarf. He laughed and said something to the others, and they laughed too. Jeremy's hand tightened on the rifle. They saw the movement and backed away slightly.

Seeing the wrapped parcel of sweets, one of the Indians said, "Food?" and grabbed it from Catherine's hands. The other two looked all around her. "More!"

Catherine shook her head, terrified, and put up her hands in a gesture for them to see that she had nothing else. One of them grabbed the scarf from her head, freeing her golden curls. With an exclamation of excitement, all three Indians laughed again. One of them pulled out a knife and sat holding it as they made motions as if scalping someone. Jeremy could see that they were taunting them, but he didn't know how far it might go, or how serious it could become. Then he remembered the amulet around his neck that Chief Black Horse had given him. Quickly, he reached beneath his shirt and pulled it out, holding it up in sight of the Indians. There was an instant reaction as the men obviously recognized the significance of the stone on the leather cord. They backed their horses away as one of them said something in their language, then rode off across the prairie.

Catherine and Jeremy watched until the Indian ponies were no longer in sight.

"Whew! I guess it's a good thing we helped Runs Like the Wind!" Jeremy said.

"I'm glad I'm sitting. I don't think I could stand up!" Catherine gasped.

"Come on Midnight, let's get out of here!" he said.

Catherine held on tightly as Midnight galloped the rest of the way to the Heldman's dugout. It was comforting to see smoke rising from the stovepipe protruding from the little earthen home. By the time Jeremy was helping Catherine dismount, Owen had opened the wooden door.

"I thought I heard a horse. Welcome! Martha, Jeremy and Catherine are here!" He came out and shook Jeremy's hand, and Catherine grabbed him in such a fierce hug that he was startled.

"We just had a bit of a scare with some Indians down the road," Jeremy explained.

"Well, Catherine, you're here safely and we have no Indians inside," Owen said, patting her comfortingly.

"Oh, what a wonderful, Sunday surprise!" Martha exclaimed, stepping outside with open arms. "Catherine, I'm so glad to see you! And Jeremy, how are you?"

"Martha, there were Indians! They took the baked things I was bringing to you," Catherine cried, "and my scarf!"

"We're lucky that's all they took. They were really eyeing Cat's blond hair!"

With a quick look all around the horizon, Owen said, "Well, why don't we come inside. Welcome to our dugout."

Just as Jeremy had been impressed with the Heldman's home, Catherine was surprised to see that it felt like a real house inside.

"You have it set up so beautifully. I would never dream we were underground." she said.

"Did the flood do much damage?" Jeremy asked.

"We were fortunate," Owen replied. "The water level stopped just short of the top of the wooden blocks that I'd placed under the furniture; so none of it was damaged."

"The worst were my mud-soaked rugs and getting the floor dried," Martha said. "I will never again take a wooden floor for granted!"

"There was a small stream of water that flowed for days in the normally dry creek bed, so we laid the rugs in there and weighted them with rocks. The movement of the water washed away the dirt in a couple of days, so then we just had to let them dry. It was pretty cold then, so they kept freezing instead of drying!" Martha laughed.

"Tell me about your mother and Pollard and Baby Jake while I put on some coffee," she said, tying on her checked apron.

"Mama seems to be doing better. I think the medicine has helped, but every now and then, she still has the coughing. I feel so sorry for her when it happens. It must hurt." Catherine said in a worried tone. "McCloud is doing fine. Baby Jake is still the sweetest little thing. He's getting so chubby and his hair's growing out on top in light red curls.

"He laughs out loud now and we all act like total idiots to get him to do it," Jeremy admitted sheepishly.

"I think a baby's laugh is the purest sound on earth," Martha said.

"Well, we are so glad to see you two today," Owen said. "Did the pretty weather entice you outside and to our place?"

"I guess you could say that," Jeremy said. "Actually, it's Cat's birthday and since we were blessed with the sunshine, Ma and I decided a visit to you would be a nice present for her. She hadn't been away from the homestead since we got there."

"Well, happy birthday, Catherine!" Martha said. "I think this certainly calls for something special. I'll see what I can whip up here."

"It felt so good to be going somewhere," Catherine said, "and especially to be coming to see you. But if we'd been closer to home when we met those Indians I would have asked Jeremy to go back!" she admitted.

"Did they just take your food and go their way?" Owen asked.

"They left in a hurry when I showed them this," Jeremy said, holding up the amulet necklace. "Chief Black Horse gave it to me after we saved the life of his son. He said that red men would recognize it as a symbol of his friendship with me, and apparently that's true."

"We never know how God will use incidences in our lives. I'm sure you helped the young man out of the kindness of your hearts, but God worked it so that it provided protection for you in the future," Owen said.

"Cat and I were hoping you'd share a little Bible study with us since it's Sunday," Jeremy said. "We have missed our church so much."

"I assure you, he'll be glad to have someone other than me to preach to!" Martha said with a smile at Owen. "Look, dear, your congregation tripled!"

Owen blushed. "Bless her, she does put up with a lot of my preaching to her, but I have been studying some things that I feel the Lord would have us to know ..."

After an hour of Owen's teaching, Martha declared that dinner was ready. The smell of smoked sausage, biscuits and gravy were making it hard to concentrate on Owen's lesson anyway. Martha had opened jars of home-canned tomatoes, green beans and spiced peaches, making a colorful birthday dinner for Catherine. She also brought out a beautiful scarf and gave it to Catherine as a gift to replace the one the Indians had taken. They laughed and visited over the good food and Catherine felt that her birthday had indeed been celebrated.

"I hate to end a good thing, but I'd like for us to get home before dark," Jeremy said.

"Yes, I agree. As much as I'd like to keep you longer, I know you need to be on your way," Martha said. "Tell Susannah and Pollard we wished they'd been here too, and you give that baby a big hug and kiss from his Auntie Martha."

After hugs and goodbyes, Jeremy and Catherine were on Midnight and heading toward home.

"We'll pray for your safe trip back," Owen said.

"Come again!" Martha called with a wave.

Catherine and Jeremy both felt the ride back was the longest hour of their lives. They watched the horizon constantly for any sign of unwanted company. Other than a jack rabbit leaping across the road, however, the trip was uneventful. When they rode into the yard of the little sod house that had looked so desolate the first time they saw it, neither of them had ever been so glad to be home!

*   *   *   *

Pollard McCloud looked out the small window pane, and all he could see was a whirling mass of white.

The vengeful howling of the wind brought a sense of uneasiness about this storm. He could feel its force as the gales blew in gusts against the sod walls. Even the fire in the fireplace struggled to maintain its vigilance as snow blew down the chimney and melted in sputters onto the flames. This was obviously, "*A Big One!*"

Jeremy had brought in as much wood and as many buffalo chips as they had room for in the cabin. McCloud felt they had enough food if they were forced to be inside for days, but they desperately needed Daisy's milk for the baby. They had piled the remaining hay bales around her in the lean-to and he could only hope it was enough to prevent the animal from freezing. As far as the oxen and horses, there was nothing more they could do.

He did need to push open the door occasionally and try to keep a path cleared from the house to the lean-to. They would need to go out to milk Daisy once a day, and if the door was snowed shut, that wouldn't be possible. Every time they opened that door there was a loss of precious heat in the cabin, though. He could only hope this storm passed quickly and was followed by warmer weather.

The barrel of water would last a few days, and the pump would be of no use in below freezing temperatures. They'd have to melt snow for water. Baby Jake's few diapers had to be washed regularly and hung around the cabin. They dried so stiffly that Susannah had to shake them and work the fabric, softening them before putting them on his little body. She hadn't said anything about it, but McCloud could see that the baby needed clothes, too. The few things they had brought from back east were almost too small already, and they tried to keep him wrapped in a blanket to stay warm. Now that he was becoming more active that was difficult to do. They were

308

constantly re-wrapping him, but Baby Jake hated being bound up in that blanket. McCloud didn't blame him. That's how he felt about his entire life. He wanted to move … to do things, but there was always something binding him, preventing him from accomplishing the things he set out to do.

Susannah's medicine was getting low. He would soon need to go back to the fort for more, but he hated being gone. Jeremy handled things well, but since his and Catherine's encounter with the Indians McCloud still felt the need to be close to home.

"Pollard, would you like some coffee?" Susannah asked, bringing him from his reverie back to the small, close cabin. "Catherine made us some biscuits too."

Since there was nothing he could do at the present about all the things that troubled him McCloud thought he might as well drink coffee, eat biscuits and play with his baby son. Everything else would wait, anyway.

*   *   *   *

The blizzard had continued for three days already. Catherine wondered where that much wind and snow came from! Everyone was feeling the effects of "cabin fever." Susannah said she'd read an article back east about people on the frontiers actually going crazy from being snowed in for weeks in small shelters. Everyone was trying to be courteous to each other, but it was especially hard on Jeremy and McCloud because they were used to being outdoors most of the time.

So far, they had managed to milk Daisy and check on the herd. They had not lost any oxen yet, but if this continued, they undoubtedly would. It was impossible for the animals to eat in this storm. Any hay or grain placed before them blew away before they could even see it was there. McCloud knew they could not afford to waste the feed, so the animals would simply have to do without food unto the storm calmed. They needed water too, but it would be frozen before they could consume it. Just how long they could endure in the extreme cold and without food and water, he didn't know. What if they lost the horses? He couldn't bear that thought. He knew that Midnight was more than transportation to Jeremy, just as Flame was to him. Still, the horses were vital to working the farm.

Even the normally happy Baby Jake was fussy. He had begun teething now, and the discomfort was making him irritable.

Catherine was trying to stay occupied by writing answers to the letters she had received from David, Liz and the friends in Lexington. She found it was becoming harder to write about her life here. She knew that none of her friends back home could imagine the bleakness of her existence now and she just couldn't tell them the way things really were. With Liz it was different. Liz had endured hardship on the trail, and things were not easy for her family in Oregon, either. They were struggling through their first winter in a very cold climate too, and like Catherine's family, had not been settled long enough to build all the shelters they needed. At least they had the community of other families who arrived there with them.

Thinking of Liz brought a wave of longing to see her. How Catherine wished for just an hour to share with this sweet friend whose heart had been so quickly bonded with hers. The situations their families faced were in ways similar, and yet, different. The land in Oregon was easy to work, but had to be cleared of heavy timber. In Kansas, the land was hard as rock, difficult to farm, but had no trees at all. In both places men were determined to conquer nature. Some succeeded, yet many lost their families, their finances, and even their lives in the attempt. The settlers in Oregon built log cabins due to the availability of the timber. Liz wrote about how all the neighbors worked together to "raise" a log cabin in a day so that soon every family had a home.

Liz said that she missed Catherine greatly, too. She assured Catherine that she was faithfully reading her Bible. They had enough people there who wanted to join together on Sundays to have an informal church service, and Liz said they were praying for God to send them a minister. She didn't say much about her relationship with Jeremy, only that she missed him and enjoyed his letters.

It was harder writing to David. They had always shared everything, but she just couldn't do that now. His letters were full of excitement about the success of his work. It was difficult for Catherine to imagine that her David was a creator of jewelry that was selling in a fancy business in New York City. From the work he had done on her necklace she could see that he was truly gifted, but the rest seemed like another world. In his second letter he had sent fifty dollars to her as a Christmas present! She felt strange receiving money from him. He told her he had no idea what she would like or might need there, and that was why he sent money, so she could buy something for herself. He told her that he had all sorts of jewelry in mind to create for her, but would wait to make the pieces until she approved them. Catherine instantly had the mental picture of herself performing her daily tasks covered in gold and precious gems.

"Would you prefer to be milked today by diamond studded fingers, Daisy, or shall I wear emeralds? Will the pump flow more freely if I wear golden bracelets that sparkle in the sun? Or would the buffalo chips take on more honor if picked up with hands loaded with rubies and pearls?"

No, she wouldn't tell David everything about her life here, and she didn't need him to give her jewelry.

For some reason she didn't mention to anyone that David had sent her money ... maybe because she wasn't sure how she felt about it. It was a lot of money, and she certainly had no intention of spending it totally on herself. There was no place to spend it anyway. The closest town was Dodge City and they never went there. At any rate, she tucked it away in her journal. What she did tell David was that she was so proud to hear he was teaching the Bible now. The letter from their friends had comments from all of them as to how they were enjoying the class and how much they were learning since David had begun to teach them. She told him that she had been thinking more about what God's plan would hold for them in the future. She encouraged him to pray about that too.

Catherine told David about going to the Heldman's on her birthday and about the incident with the Indians. She tried to make it sound as though it had not been actually dangerous, just unsettling. As always, she assured him of her love for him, and reminded him that their time apart was now half over. She carefully put away his letter with the others and addressed the one she'd written so it would be ready to be mailed at the first opportunity.

*   *   *   *

It was now day four of the blizzard. There was just enough water left in the barrel to make coffee for breakfast. Jeremy had placed a dishpan of snow on the hearth to melt to wash diapers. The wood supply was dwindling as well. They were burning buffalo chips with the wood to make it last longer. Owen had said he had more wood, but it would be impossible to find the way to the Heldman's place.

Jeremy didn't want his mother and Catherine to see his concern, but he knew that they were all thinking the same thing ... how long could they last if this didn't stop?

Jeremy thought of the New Testament story of Jesus and his disciples as they were tossed about by a storm on the Sea of Galilee. Jesus was fast asleep in the boat and seemed a bit perturbed when they woke Him to do something about the storm. He chided them for their lack of faith, indicating that they could have done the same thing He was about to do ... command the storm to be still.

Something began to burn deep inside Jeremy. It was apparent that if people intended to live in this place, they would have to fight, using everything within themselves to contend for survival. He had just realized that there was a tool he had not used in this situation ... his faith. He stood so quickly it startled everyone in the small house. Jeremy reached for his coat and wrapped a woolen scarf around his neck.

"Son? What are you doing?" Susannah asked.

Pulling his hat down firmly he reached for the door handle. "I'm going to speak to a storm!" he said, and went quickly out the door. The only path outside the door was the one they had kept open to the lean-to. As Jeremy made his way through the white corridor the blowing snow stung his face, even through the scarf he'd pulled up to cover everything below his eyes. He checked on Daisy and saw that she was still shivering, but doing all right in her little hay enclosure. Taking the shovel, he pushed snow out of his way until he stood facing the full force of the wind.

"This better not take too long!" he thought as he swayed from the force of the gusts. Then directing his thoughts to the purpose at hand he began to pray, "Father God, I know I'm a real nobody when it comes to people here on earth. But I'm your child, and I'm a disciple of your Son, Jesus Christ. Your Word tells me that Your Spirit lives in me, and will do things through me in Your power and authority. If the disciples in that boat could have spoken to that storm to cease, that means I should be able to speak to this one to stop. Heavenly Father, our very existence depends on this happening, so I'm asking you to work through me, and I will be forever grateful to You. Amen"

Jeremy pictured in his mind how Jesus would have stood in that boat and he squared his shoulders and faced the wind that was freezing his breath as it came from his mouth. With every bit of strength he could muster, he cried out, "You snow storm ...*PEACE! ... BE STILL!*" He became oblivious to the cold and the biting wind. He was at war with a force larger than himself, and yet he could feel confidence rising within him that this force would have to obey a lanky, young guy on a snow covered prairie who believed that God was true to His Word.

Jeremy wasn't sure how long he stood there, but he began to feel peace inside, and turned to walk back to the house, moving stiffly in his frozen clothing. At that moment the howling wind disappeared. Snow flakes still fell gently as he stood outside the door and shook off the ice, but in his heart, Jeremy knew that the storm was over.

CHAPTER 21

"We only lost one ox; that has to be a miracle!" McCloud said. He and Jeremy had just checked the animals now that the snow was melting. The small herd had huddled closely and their unity had saved them. Only the oldest ox was too weak to survive. Water and feed were brought as quickly as the men could get it there, and the animals ate hungrily. The horses looked thinner, but they would be all right, too. Jeremy got his brush and gave Midnight a good grooming to aid in circulation and rid his coat of the bits of ice that still clung to him.

The pump was working again, so Catherine was preparing to do laundry. She had the kettle of water heating on the open fire in the yard. After being closed up in the house for days she didn't even mind the cold. At least it was above freezing so maybe the clothes would dry in a few hours. She went back inside to get the lye soap and clothing, and as she walked into the house she heard Susannah coughing. Catherine had noticed that these episodes had become more frequent in the last few days.

"Oh, Mama, I'm so sorry! Let me get your medicine." Catherine brought the bottle to her and measured out a large spoonful.

Susannah could hardly stop coughing long enough to take the medicine, but finally managed to swallow the

316

bitter syrup. By the time it took effect and the coughing eased she was too exhausted to stay on her feet.

"Just rest, Mama; I'll watch Baby Jake," Catherine said.

When Susannah protested, Catherine insisted. "The laundry can wait until he takes his nap. Just rest."

Susannah sank back onto the bed and closed her eyes. These fits of coughing absolutely drained her. Thank God Catherine was here to care for the baby. Lately, the tiredness just never left. The medicine only soothed the symptoms, but Susannah could tell that it did nothing to remedy the problem in her chest. Soon she would have to face the fear that gnawed at her daily now; the horrible one she kept forcing to the back of her mind. At the moment, though, she just needed sleep ... sweet sleep...

As Catherine rocked Baby Jake and fed him his bottle her heart was troubled. A look at Susannah confirmed that things were not well with her mother. The beautiful face that had always brought peace and comfort to Catherine was now a pale, unhealthy color; even in sleep it showed the strain caused by the illness in her lungs. For the first time, Catherine faced the fact that her mother was not going to get better. It hit her like the force of the storm they had just endured. She wanted to run out the door and across the prairie, demanding it not to be so! She looked down at the baby in her arms. How could he possibly grow up without his mother? Someone could feed and clothe him, but a child needed so much more than that. The idea of Pollard McCloud raising little Jake without Susannah was unthinkable. Catherine could see that he loved this baby, but he knew nothing of the day-to-day care of an infant.

Tears flowed silently down Catherine's cheeks as she realized that Jake's care would primarily fall to her.

The weight of that responsibility settled on her like a heavy blanket. She dearly loved Baby Jake, but her plans for a life with David had not included raising a little brother. How would David feel about this? But then, what if McCloud insisted on keeping the baby? Could she find it in her heart to leave Baby Jake and marry David? The connection with McCloud for Catherine and Jeremy had been Susannah. Would they stay here with him if she wasn't with them? Where would they go if they wanted to leave? How in the world could life go on without her precious Mama?

The questions were endless, and answers seemed to be non-existent as Catherine sat in thought for over an hour, listening to the sound of her mother's labored breathing. Then the scripture Psalms 61:2 came to her mind: *From the end of the earth will I cry unto thee, when my heart is overwhelmed: lead me to the rock that is higher than I.*

"Oh, God!" she prayed silently, "I feel this truly is the end of the earth, and I am so overwhelmed. We need Your leading like never before. Please help us!"

Baby Jake stirred then, awaking from his nap. He opened his blue eyes and looked into Catherine's face. Then his little countenance broke into a smile of recognition. Catherine couldn't help but smile in return.

"Hi, sweet boy, did you have a good nap?" She lifted him up to her shoulder and as he snuggled close, she hugged his soft little body and felt comforted.

      *   *   *   *

Jeremy was headed toward the lean-to to milk Daisy and then to bring the cow out of her little shelter. He noticed that the fire under Catherine's kettle had gone out, and the laundry had not been started. Puzzled, he finished with Daisy and carried the pail of milk inside. Baby Jake was on a quilt with an assortment of things to occupy him. Catherine was preparing lunch and his mother was sleeping. This explained why Cat had not come back to do the laundry. He quietly set down the milk pail. Something in Catherine's attitude brought a sense of foreboding to him. He sat at the table and she met his gaze with a look he couldn't quite interpret. Then he looked at his mother.

Susannah's breathing was still labored. Her face was flushed now and she seemed restless, as though dreaming unpleasant things. Jeremy looked back to Catherine, his gray eyes filled with fear and disbelief. There was no need for conversation. To put into words what each of them was thinking would be too cruel. Jeremy picked up his hat and walked back outside. He went to the corral and whistled for Midnight. The horse immediately came to Jeremy and nuzzled his face with soft lips. It was as though the horse sensed the distress of his young master and was attempting to comfort him. Jeremy laid his head alongside the horse's huge one and stroked Midnight's soft coat. He drew strength from the love of the animal as his mind went a thousand directions, asking many of the same painful questions that had come to Catherine. And like her, he had no answers either.

McCloud saw Jeremy at the corral and thought something was different about the way he just stood there with his horse. He could have sworn Jeremy was crying. He remembered seeing him come from the house just minutes before … throwing down his shovel, McCloud practically ran to the house. Catherine looked up in surprise as he flung the door open and it startled Baby Jake as well. Then

Catherine looked away from him, as though she didn't want to meet his eyes. He picked up the baby who was crying now and patted him awkwardly. Baby Jake smiled through his tears, already happy again. McCloud walked over to the bed where Susannah slept fitfully, and stood looking down at her. She appeared feverish now, not a good sign. He sat down on the edge of the bed, careful not to move it any more than possible. He placed his hand on her forehead and could feel the heat, even beneath his rough, calloused skin. His touch caused Susannah to open her eyes, but they felt so heavy she couldn't keep them open. Coming out of the drug- induced sleep was like pulling herself up out of a deep, dark tunnel, and she was so tired.

"Hi ...," she tried to respond to Baby Jake's jabbering to her. He was smiling, always smiling ... sweet ... baby ... the baby ... he needed her ... have to ... wake up. Pollard looks ... worried.

"How are you feeling, hon?" McCloud asked gently.

Susannah smiled weakly, forcing herself awake, "I'm all right ... But it's really cold in here," she said, shivering. "Did the fire go out?"

The cabin was actually quite warm and the fire was burning normally.

"No, the fire's O.K., but I think you have some fever. We'll put another quilt on you to get rid of those chills," McCloud said, looking to Catherine.

Catherine came and took the baby from him and indicated where he would find a quilt.

"Is there anything you need, Mama? Are you hungry?" Catherine asked.

"Maybe I could eat later, sweetie, but I'm really thirsty," Susannah said.

"Then Baby Jake and I will get you a glass of water," Catherine replied. She returned with the water and handed the glass to McCloud. He helped Susannah sit up enough to drink a small amount of water, and even that bit of exercise tired her so that she was breathing heavily.

"Susannah, I'm going to make a run to the fort and see if the Doctor can come out here to see you, or at least give me a different kind of medicine that will get rid of this fever so you'll feel better." Turning to Catherine, he said, "If you could stick some of that jerky and some biscuits in something, I'll eat on the way." He took money from the dresser drawer and put it in his pocket, pulled a heavier shirt over the one he was wearing, and got his coat.

"Can you take our letters to mail?" Catherine asked, reaching for the letters where she and Jeremy kept them ready to go.

McCloud took them and placed them in his coat pocket. "Take care of her, Catherine. I'll be back as soon as I can." He walked to Susannah and bent down to kiss her on the forehead, patted Baby Jake, and was out the door.

He whistled for Flame as he practically ran to the corral and by the time he reached it, the horse was standing at the gate. Jeremy was sitting on the corral fence and jumped down in surprise to see McCloud running that way.

"I've got to try to get a doctor to come and see your Mother, to get medicine … to do something!"

"I'll fill your canteen and get some feed for Flame while you saddle up," Jeremy said, starting to move.

"Bring a bucket of water for him, Jeremy. I hate that I'm going to have to ride him this hard after he's had to do without food and water for three days in that storm, but I have no choice!" McCloud said, leading Flame to the lean-to where the saddles were kept.

Remembering his own Indian encounter, Jeremy ran to the house and brought McCloud's rifle and handed it up to him as he started off.

"You might need this."

"Take care of things, Jeremy."

Jeremy could hear that Flame was already at a gallop before they reached the main road. This was going to be a hard ride. He turned and walked to the house. Old Pal, right at his heels, looked up at him with concern, sensing something was out of the ordinary. Jeremy bent down and hugged his old friend.

"Yeah, buddy, this is a tough one."

*   *   *   *

When Susannah started to rouse again, Catherine gave her more of the medicine. It might cause her to sleep, but at least she wasn't coughing. Catherine put lunch on the table, but neither she nor Jeremy could eat much.

Jeremy was glad he didn't have important things to get done today because he couldn't keep his mind on work.. Somehow, he'd have to be strong for the rest of his family, for Cat, for the baby, and yes, for his step-father too. McCloud did truly love Susannah; how the man would react to losing her would be anyone's guess.

Catherine would carry the heaviest load in the future, Jeremy knew. She would be the one to care for the baby and the household duties, which she had almost completely taken over already.

For now, all he could do was to keep the fireplace going to warm his precious mother, to be near when she did wake up in case she needed something, and to strengthen his sister as they faced the frightening future.

*   *   *   *

It was early afternoon when McCloud reached Fort Dodge. He was frustrated to find that the doctor had gone to make a call in some situation regarding a soldier. It was probably best that McCloud had to wait for a couple of hours to give Flame time to rest. The faithful horse had given everything he had as McCloud pushed him to the limit to reach the fort. When the doctor arrived he gave more medicine for Susannah, but little hope. He had examined her when they were at the fort before going to the homestead. Listening to her lungs, he knew it was a matter of time before the consumption would progress to this point. He hadn't expected it to be this soon, but settlers often did not have access to most of the foods that properly nourish bodies to ward off disease, and he suspected this was the situation with Susannah. He could not go to their homestead to examine her; it was too far away. He was officially a military doctor and had to be available for soldiers in need of medical care. He suggested that McCloud do what he could to make her comfortable.

"Make her comfortable! Isn't there anything that can be done to make her *well?*" he cried in frustration.

"The medical profession has not yet found a way to stop the deterioration of the lungs with this disease, Mr. McCloud. I am so sorry that I have nothing more positive to tell you, but anything else would be untrue," the physician said sadly. "Try to get nourishment in her, whether she wants food or not. Eating sometimes brings on the painful coughing attacks, so typically, patients with consumption avoid eating, thus practically starving themselves. For your wife to live as long as she possibly can, she must eat, and she must have a will to live."

"I'm afraid she may already have lost that," McCloud said, his eyes misting with tears. "Thank you, Doctor. What will this new medicine do?"

"Probably not much more than the other, slow the coughing attacks, and help with the pain. It would probably be best to limit her contact with the baby for contagion's sake," the doctor said.

McCloud shook his head in agreement. "I need to get started back," he said.

The doctor refused payment for the medicine, as McCloud pulled out money.

"Go be with your wife, Mr. McCloud."

*   *   *   *

Susannah was awake and had eaten some of the soup Catherine made. She couldn't believe she had slept the whole day away. She still felt weak, but Baby Jake didn't want anyone else to hold him now. She rocked him and held him close as he chomped on a small rag toy, trying to ease his teething gums.

Catherine had been keeping the food warm for McCloud, expecting his return at any time. They could only pray he hadn't run into trouble with Indians. Jeremy was pretending to read a book, but Catherine noticed he hadn't turned a page in the last half hour.

Old Pal was the first to alert them to McCloud's arrival as he perked up his ears and stared at the door.

324

Jeremy looked out the window and by moonlight saw him riding up on Flame. Jeremy put on his coat and hat. He opened the door just as McCloud reached it.

"I'll take care of Flame," Jeremy told him.

"I appreciate that, I'm wiped out," McCloud said. Pleased to see Susannah sitting there in the chair he walked over to greet her as Jeremy went out the door. Even though the weather had warmed up, it was still cold enough to send a chill through the cabin as the men came and went. Catherine stoked the fire to increase the warmth in the room.

"Hey, how's my girl?" McCloud asked as he kissed Susannah and Baby Jake.

"I'm all right. We were beginning to worry about you, though," she said.

"The doc was out taking care of an injured soldier, so I had to wait a couple of hours. But he gave me some new medicine for you and he told me it's really important for you to eat and keep up your strength."

"Speaking of eating, Catherine's been keeping supper warm for you," Susannah said.

"Well, I'm certainly ready for food, and a cup of coffee," McCloud said as he shed his coat.

"Oh, I almost forgot, Catherine, you and Jeremy had mail." He handed her two letters, one for her from David, and one for Jeremy from Liz.

Catherine had feared that in his concern for Susannah and talking to the doctor, McCloud would forget to inquire about mail. She was thrilled to see that he had remembered, and she knew Jeremy would be as well. She wished it was daylight so she could go outside to be alone to read her letter. She felt like it was burning a hole in her apron pocket as she sat out the food for McCloud.

Susannah and McCloud went to bed shortly after he finished eating. Baby Jake was asleep too, so Catherine and Jeremy sat and read their letters by the light of the fire. David didn't have much news to tell, just that he was still working really hard on jewelry, and that the Bible classes were going well. As always, he told her he loved her and was waiting as eagerly as she for this next year to pass.

Liz said they were continuing to get settled there in Oregon, adding on to the outbuildings to care for the animals. Her one bit of news was that her brother Billy now had a girlfriend. Her name was Molly, and she loved his crazy songs. Anything more personal, Jeremy didn't share with Catherine.

This day had been mentally exhausting for both Catherine and Jeremy. She could hardly keep her eyes open to finish reading David's letter, so she climbed up to her loft and immediately went to sleep. Jeremy spread his pallet on the kitchen floor and with Old Pal curled up beside him, he was soon sleeping, too.

The sound of Susannah's coughing woke everyone except Baby Jake within the hour. It was really bad this time, but finally eased with the new medication McCloud had brought. As she drifted into the drugged sleep, her children and her husband lay wide awake, their hearts filled with dread of the days ahead.

All of them slept later than usual the next morning. Catherine was awakened to the sound of Baby Jake's crying for his bottle. Susannah got up to fix it, but the activity brought on the coughing again. Catherine hurried down from the loft and went to make the baby's bottle while McCloud tried to help Susannah. She shook her head to his offer of the medicine, and between coughs managed to say that she didn't want to sleep all day again. He could feel that her fever had returned.

"Susannah, it's all right. You're burning up with fever. You need this medicine to rest, so your body can get stronger. We'll see to the baby. Please, I want you to rest," McCloud pleaded with her.

Tears came to Susannah's eyes. "I know I don't have much longer, Pollard. I can feel it, and I don't want to sleep this time away." The coughing seized her again as McCloud held her close, tears running down his face.

Catherine stood frozen, the baby's bottle in one hand, the jar of milk in the other.

The horrible truth was out … the thing none of them wanted to face … or to say aloud. There was no taking it back now. She felt Jeremy take the bottle from her and saw him pour milk into it. He picked up the crying baby and began to feed him. Susannah was crying inconsolably now as McCloud held her, and the sound of her agony filled the cabin and ripped the hearts of those who loved her.

"How do people survive unbearable grief?" Catherine wondered as she sank into a chair and hid her face in her hands.

The next few days passed in a blur for all of them. Eventually, the coughing was so intense and painful that Susannah had no choice but to take the medication. In spite of her family's efforts, she simply could not eat most of the time. In despair they watched her fade until finally, Catherine asked Jeremy if he would go and get Martha and Owen. This was simply too much for them to bear alone.

Knowing what they would face, Martha was still shocked to see the wasted condition of her beautiful friend. Sorrow filled her heart, too, but she would have to shelve her own emotions. This family needed strength from her and Owen now.

Catherine didn't know how to put into words the difference it meant to have the Heldmans there, but she couldn't have made it through this without them. In Susannah's last lucid moments she thanked Martha and Owen for coming and asked them to be there for her family as much as they could. They assured her that they would.

As Catherine sat holding her mother's hand, Susannah smiled weakly at her daughter. "You are so beautiful, my Catherine. Never forget how much I love you. I'm so sorry I couldn't hold on to see you marry David, but when that day comes, just know that somehow, I will be there ... your Papa and I will both be there." She struggled with her own emotions to say what was in her heart. "I don't know what the future will bring with Pollard and the baby. I so hate that this burden will be on you now, but I'm asking you to take care of Baby Jake for as long as he needs you."

"I will, Mama, I'll take good care of him. And I won't let him forget you. I'll always tell him you loved him." Leaning down to hold Susannah close and crying softly, Catherine told her mother how much she loved her.

"I will miss you so much; I don't know how I'll manage without you."

"Just remember that the strength of the Lord will always be present to help."

"Mama ... would you give Papa a hug for me?"

Susannah smiled. "Oh, yes, honey, I'll give Papa your hug.

Jeremy came and Catherine left to allow him his privacy. After a few minutes, Susannah asked to see Pollard and the baby. Everyone left the cabin to give them these last few moments alone. All too soon they heard the heartbroken cries of a man whose grief had no limit, and they knew their beautiful Susannah was gone.

*   *   *   *

Since there was no one else to invite to a funeral service, Susannah was buried that afternoon. McCloud had insisted on digging the grave himself. He chose a place not far from the grave of Dorthea's husband. It seemed that the labor required to penetrate the cold, hard ground gave him an outlet for the fury and pain within him. Several times he stopped and screamed his rage at the heavens. Observing him from a distance, Owen Heldman prayed that somehow this tortured man would find the peace he needed to continue living. He was very concerned about the rest of this family, but especially so, if McCloud's behavior did not become more rational. Owen, in his thoughtfulness, had brought lumber to build a simple casket which he and Jeremy began to put together. Contrary to McCloud, Jeremy was silent as they worked, but Owen saw the tears that filled his eyes time and again.

Martha took over the task of preparing the body for burial. Catherine suggested that Susannah wear the blue dress in which she'd married McCloud. Soon she was laid out on the bed, her beautiful face peaceful now that she was freed from the pain and cares of this world. Baby Jake continued to reach out and to cry for her, puzzled that she gave him no response.

The family chose to allow Martha and Owen to place Susannah's body in the casket after they said their final goodbyes. Jeremy and McCloud carried the casket to the grave, and neither of them had ever felt pain like they experienced as they lowered the wooden box into the ground. Owen read scriptures and prayed a prayer. Then the grave was covered, not just with soil, but with rocks to prevent the intrusive coyotes from digging into it.

Martha and Owen stayed for another day. Martha suggested that they boil the bed clothing to disinfect it. That kept Catherine occupied as it was an all-day job. They aired the cabin and washed down everything that could be cleaned as the loads of laundry boiled. Jeremy remained quiet as he went from one thing to another. McCloud often mounted Flame and rode away furiously. He had refused to eat, and burst out in tears of anguish at least every few hours. So intense was his grief that Catherine and Jeremy felt their own deep sorrow paled in comparison.

Catherine knew that Martha and Owen could not stay, but as long as they were there she could put off facing this new phase of her life. Finally, though, the cabin was spotless; everything had been laundered, and Martha and Owen were preparing to leave.

Martha held Catherine close. "I feel you are my little sister, Catherine. My heart aches for you as though you were my own flesh and blood. You and your brothers will be in my thoughts and my prayers continually!"

"I couldn't have gone through this without you, Martha. I think God sent you and Owen to Kansas just for us. Thank you for everything," Catherine said from her heart.

Owen Heldman reached to embrace her then. "Catherine, remember that we are not that far away. Have Jeremy bring you and Baby Jake whenever you can. We will be praying for you all, and we'll come and check on you again as soon as we can."

Jeremy stepped forward to shake Owen's hand and to hug Martha. He also expressed his gratitude to the loving couple for all their help and support. Baby Jake was asleep and McCloud had ridden away on Flame, so the Heldmans got into their wagon and left. Martha continued to wave with tears flowing down her cheeks as long as she could see Catherine and Jeremy standing arm-in-arm in front of the lonely sod cabin. When she could no longer see them it was as though the dam of her own sorrow broke and leaning on Owen's shoulder, she wept for the loss of her beautiful friend until there were no more tears to come.

CHAPTER 22

"I want a bracelet like this one with rubies for my friend in New York who's having a birthday, and a brooch in your new design for Aunt Evelyn," Charlotte Pendleton said to David. "Can you believe she's going to be sixty-two?"

David grinned, "Well, I guess since we're seventeen, that does sound pretty old. But I don't think you should tell her that."

"I wouldn't dare," Charlotte said, "I'm just glad she still likes to dress up and go places. I would have died here in Lexington if she wasn't one to gad about."

"I can't believe you've stayed here all these months," David said as he wrote up her order.

Leaning over the counter and almost in his face, she put on a sultry look and said, "I'm addicted to jewelry, and you're my supplier."

Backing up to put distance between them, David shook his head, "Charlotte, you are incorrigible."

"Oh, I know," she said flippantly, "But I have no intentions of changing."

"Doesn't your father ever question all the charges to this business?" David asked.

Charlotte laughed. "David, if you only knew what I could run up in New York; Poppy thinks these bills are nothing."

To David's surprise and consternation, Charlotte had remained in Lexington. She was a frequent visitor to the shop, but she was also his most extravagant customer, so what could he do? She still flirted with him and tried to get him to spend time with her, but it was more like a pattern into which their relationship had fallen. He had to remind himself at times that she was not always the person she was portraying here in Lexington, that she could be as conniving and cold-hearted as was needed to get her way.

Today Mr. Goodson was away on business, so David knew he'd have to eat a quick lunch at the tea room and get back to the shop in a half hour or so. Already, his stomach was growling, and even Charlotte could hear it.

"Lunch time, is it?" she asked.

He didn't want to say, "Yes," because he knew she'd use that as an invitation to come with him, but he couldn't deny the loud rumbling of his stomach.

"Yes, but I've got to hurry today. Mr. Goodson doesn't want the shop closed more than a half hour."

"I can't believe you, David Winters. You are the Majestic's most called-for new artist, and you're worried about getting back to this tiny shop in a half hour for your old boss!" Charlotte said petulantly. "You should be telling *him* what you're going to do!"

"May I remind you, Miss High and Mighty, there wouldn't be any David Winters Jewelry at the Majestic had it not been for my 'Old Boss.' He taught me everything I know."

"Well, at least he could let you close up for an hour. That's what everyone else does."

"But see, some of our customers are working people too, and they come in on their lunch hours. Anyway, as fast as I shovel food down, I don't need more than half an hour."

"Where are you going? I'm hungry too." she said.

"Miss Pendleton, may I remind you that I'm grabbing lunch and coming right back here," David said.

"O.K., I'll leave! I'll check on those pieces I ordered in a few days," Charlotte said as she picked up her purse and started out the door.

David pulled the closed sign down after she left, finished his paperwork and locked the door on the shop. Dodging traffic in the street he crossed over to the tea room and ordered one of his favorite sandwiches and a lemonade from the familiar waitress. Just as he took a drink he looked up to see Charlotte smiling down at him.

"I'm starving, David. And look, all the other tables are full. You wouldn't refuse to let me sit with you and make me go hungry, would you?"

David thought, "She's done it again!" But with resignation, he said, "Sit down, Charlotte." It didn't make sense to be rude or unfriendly, so David engaged in conversation with her, wolfed down his food when it came, and went immediately back to the shop, leaving Charlotte eating her own lunch. He thought the man at the table across from them looked familiar, but he was probably imagining it. Lexington was attracting a lot of newcomers lately.

*   *   *   *

"Hi, honey," David's mother greeted him as he came home from work.

"Mmm, something smells good! Is it meatloaf?"

"It is." Mrs. Winters replied. "It will be ready in about twenty minutes. That should give you time to read your mail."

"Mail ... from Catherine?" He asked expectantly.

"Yes, and one from the Majestic," she said. "I put them in your room."

David was already down the hall leading to his bedroom. He laid aside the letter from the Majestic and quickly opened the one from Catherine. As always, he could hear her familiar voice as he read. She told him about going to visit their friends, the Heldmans, for her birthday present ... Oh, no! He had totally forgotten her birthday! How could he have done that? He'd been so busy making jewelry he didn't even send her a card, much less a gift! How could he have been such a dunce? He picked up the letter again and reread that part and then got to how she and Jeremy had encountered unfriendly Indians on the roadway. Somehow, he felt the incident was not quite as uneventful as Catherine made it sound. When she said that the Indians left them suddenly when they saw the amulet necklace from the Indian Chief, he felt that something important had indeed taken place.

Again, he looked up from the letter ... Catherine's birthday was the first of February, on a Sunday. Then it dawned on him ... that was the Sunday he had come home alone from church and had felt such concern for her. Not knowing what situations she might be facing he had entrusted her to God's care and protection. David's heart was filled with gratitude. This assured him once again that God was definitely in the center of his and Catherine's relationship.

He read the rest of her letter. She didn't say much except that her baby brother was really cute and they all enjoyed him. She told him she loved him and reminded him that they were half way through their time of separation.

David folded the letter and placed it back in its envelope. Something was wrong. Catherine's words were guarded. He knew her so well. What wasn't she telling him? He couldn't very well ask her; that would be like an accusation. She thanked him for the money he sent, but didn't say any more about what she would do with it. He was going to have to pray about this.

The letter from the Majestic held another generous check. David was still in awe of how God was blessing him through the jewelry. It sold in New York for twice the prices he charged here in Lexington. Occasionally someone mentioned that they had gone out of their way to come to Lexington to buy his work, knowing they got a better deal here. It didn't matter to David. He was comfortable with his prices, and apparently Mr. Dubois was very comfortable with his big city prices too!

He had to make it up to Catherine for forgetting her birthday, though. It would have to be something special. Thinking back to previous birthdays he remembered giving Catherine a bag of really pretty marbles when she was eight. She had been absolutely delighted with his gift, and they had played for hours. Other gifts he recalled were just as amusing as the marbles. Things were different now. Maybe his mother would have an idea what to send a young lady. She always had answers for him … besides making the best meatloaf in town! Both were good enough reasons for David to head for the kitchen.

CHAPTER 23

For half an hour Catherine had been sitting with a blank sheet of paper in front of her. She couldn't wait any longer to write David about her mother's death, but telling him meant re-living that terrible day herself.

Catherine had learned to keep a handkerchief in her apron pocket. At any time a wave of grief might suddenly come washing over her. All of Susannah's things were still there in the house, so there were reminders everywhere. Catherine and Jeremy wouldn't have it any other way, though. They still needed those emblems of her presence in their lives. Someday they could put them away, along with the tears, but not yet.

With a sigh, Catherine dipped her quill into the ink. Clutching the gold necklace close to her heart, she began to write.

> *My Dearest David,*
>
> *This is without doubt the most difficult letter I have ever had to write. I hope you won't mind if I make it as brief as possible. It is simply too painful for me to go into the whole story now.*
>
> *Our precious mother died four weeks ago. Apparently, consumption had*

been at work in her lungs for a long time. I cannot tell you the emptiness Jeremy and I feel. The one positive thing I can see is that she and Papa are now together again.

Of all of us our baby brother seems to be doing best. My stepfather is so engulfed in his grief that he is hardly aware that any of us, including the baby, are here. His behavior is irrational and sometimes frightening.

David, I must tell you that it will likely be necessary for me to care for Baby Jake in the future. I know this was not part of our plans. I will understand if you wish to be released from your commitment to me. I can't expect you to embrace the rearing of someone else's child, but I can't ignore my responsibility to him. Jeremy and I are all the family he has. I must say that his sweet little smiles are the only joy we have in this household right now.

Jeremy and I are facing many decisions, David. Please pray that we will know which direction we should go. As you share this with your parents please give them my love.

I love you, Catherine

"Is life always so full of changes?" Jeremy questioned as looked out over the prairie. Now that his mother was gone, everything was different.

McCloud was showing no sense of responsibility toward them as a family, nor toward the homestead either. He'd leave for unknown whereabouts, and they never knew when he would return. The last few times he had come in drunk and reeking of alcohol. The stench of clothing he had not changed in weeks was unbearable in the small cabin.

Jeremy was concerned about their finances. They were still living off supplies left from the journey, and he thought those were almost gone. He needed to check with Catherine to see where they actually stood.

Catherine was sealing up her letter to David as Jeremy came inside. She lifted her finger to her lips as he walked in to let him know Baby Jake was sleeping.

"Cat, I've been thinking that we need to take inventory again of our food supplies, and really, our whole situation," Jeremy said softly.

"I can sum that up in one word," Catherine almost whispered, "*BAD!*"

"How are we with food?" Jeremy asked.

Catherine got up to look into the food bins. "We have four potatoes, a few pounds of flour, even less cornmeal, a bag of oatmeal, several jars of home canned vegetables, maybe a couple of pounds of jerky, a small piece of salt pork, some bacon, a little sugar, about ten pounds of beans and a few smaller odds and ends."

"How long will that last us?" Jeremy asked.

339

"Two ... three weeks, more or less." Catherine answered. "Jeremy, this scares me. I'm afraid McCloud is drinking up what little money there was. Anyway, I don't think his head is clear enough to buy supplies, even if he has the money. When he's here, I'm afraid to talk to him about it."

"I think I'm going to have to get a paying job somewhere, Cat. The farm is not going to provide for us with just me to work it," Jeremy said.

Catherine's eyes were huge with fear. "You're going to leave me here alone with Baby Jake?"

"No, no, Cat, I meant we'd all have to go someplace where I can find work."

"But where would we live? It costs money to rent a place."

"I've been thinking I'd sell the oxen. That should bring enough money to support us for a while."

"But what if McCloud doesn't like that? I'm really afraid what he might do."

"Yeah, I know; that worries me, too." Jeremy stood, looking out the window at the planted fields. "We worked so hard getting that crop in the ground, but we can't sit here and starve, waiting to see if McCloud's going to pull himself together. Everything we had is invested in this farm, but it's no more use to us than it was to Dorthea if we can't work it. I can't do that alone. If McCloud comes home in the next couple of days, I'll try to sober him up and talk to him. I'll remind him that although Mama's gone, he still has a child that needs him. If he doesn't make a change very soon, we don't have a choice but to go somewhere else." Jeremy said.

Looking over at the sleeping baby, Catherine said, "Thank God, Daisy is still providing the milk Baby Jake needs." Then she smiled. "I started feeding him some strained oatmeal this morning for the first time, and you should have seen his face when I put it in his mouth! He looked up at me like, 'What are you doing to me?' He spit it out, then tasted the sweet syrup I'd put in it, and decided maybe he liked it after all."

"We'll have to buy him a candy stick the next time we go to a store," Jeremy said.

"He needs clothes, Jeremy. The things he has now are really too small, and soon he won't be able to wear them at all."

"We definitely need money. Mama didn't have any put away, did she? I think I may have about three dollars, and that won't last us very long," Jeremy said.

"Jeremy! I forgot … I have some money! David sent me fifty dollars for Christmas. I never mentioned it because I felt strange about accepting it. I put it away, and with everything happening I forgot about it."

"Oh, Cat, what a Godsend! If we have to use it, I promise I'll pay it back to you someday." Jeremy said.

"David said it was mine to use however I wished, and I can't think of anything I'd rather do than take care of our family." Catherine told him.

The sound of horses' hooves startled them, and their first thought was that McCloud was home. But this was more than one horse. Indians! Fear paralyzed Catherine as Jeremy reached for his rifle and went to look out the window. He stood tensely with the gun aimed toward the curve. As the sound grew louder Catherine's thoughts raced wildly. How would she protect the baby? She'd heard that sometimes the Indians took the babies and raised them, but sometimes they killed them. She'd also heard they weren't always hostile; maybe this group would just want food.

There was no place in the cabin to hide Baby Jake. As Catherine watched Jeremy she suddenly saw him relax, and then his face broke into a smile.

"It's soldiers, Cat! About a dozen of them!" he said.

A moment later Catherine heard a familiar voice commanding the soldiers.

"Company, halt! ... You can take over now, Sergeant."

"Sam! ... Oh, it *is* you!" Catherine was out the door on the run. Barely managing to dismount before Catherine reached him, Lieutenant Sam Rushing was grinning from ear to ear and caught her up in his open arms. Swinging her around to the amusement of his soldiers, he finally sat her down, pushed her away from him to look into her face, then kissed her on both cheeks before hugging her closely again.

"Oh, God, Catherine, it's so good to see you!"

"I can't believe this! Oh, Sam, I didn't know if I'd ever see you again!"

"And I hope that thought broke your heart," he said, his eyes twinkling.

"How did you find us, and what are you doing here?" she asked.

"You mean, what am I doing here, 'officially?'"

"Yes. I doubt that visiting girls on the prairie is on your list of military functions."

Just then Jeremy stepped outside, holding a sleepy-eyed Baby Jake, who smiled at all the activity and faces.

"Oh, I forgot the baby!" Catherine said. "Thanks, Jeremy." She took the infant from him and held him up for Sam to see. "This is our little brother, Jacob; we call him Baby Jake."

"Hey, little fellow," Sam said to Baby Jake, receiving a wide smile in return.

'It's good to see you, Lieutenant Rushing," Jeremy said, extending his hand.

"You too, Jeremy, how are things going for you?" the Lieutenant asked as he shook hands with him.

The initial excitement of seeing Sam had driven the thoughts of Susannah's death and their dire situation from Catherine's mind. Jeremy and Catherine exchanged glances.

"Why don't you come in, Lieutenant, and we'll catch you up on the goings-on around here. Do your men need to water their horses? The pump is right over there; they can help themselves," Jeremy told him, pointing toward the well.

"Let me tell my first officer," Sam said, "then I'll be right in."

"I'll start some coffee," Catherine said, heading toward the house.

*   *   *   *

Soon they were seated at the table as Catherine poured hot coffee for the three of them. Baby Jake lay on the quilt with his bottle.

Sam Rushing looked about the cabin. There was no sign of Catherine's mother, yet he knew the baby had to be the one she'd been expecting. Suddenly, he understood the quiet that had fallen upon Jeremy and Catherine.

"Our mother died a month ago, Sam," Catherine told him.

"I am so sorry, Catherine, Jeremy," Sam said with genuine feeling. "I never dreamed you had gone through this."

"Apparently, she'd had consumption for some time. Maybe it wouldn't have taken her so soon, but she was really worn down from the wagon trip and having the baby, too," Jeremy said.

"And your stepfather? How is he doing?"

"McCloud has practically lost his mind," Catherine said. "We don't know where he is most of the time. He pops in and out and is rarely rational or sober."

"Do you think he's dangerous?" Sam asked.

"We really don't know. We try to keep from having any conflict with him," Jeremy said.

"There have been a few times that he made me uneasy," Catherine said. "He'd sit looking at me … he was calling me, 'Young Susannah.'"

"I try to make sure I'm around when he's here, but soon that's not going to be possible if I have to work the fields," Jeremy said.

"Jeremy, you can't possibly work this place by yourself. If McCloud doesn't get it together, why don't you leave?" Sam asked.

"We were just discussing that when you and your soldiers arrived," Catherine said.

"I don't have any idea what kind of job I could get. I've never done anything but farm work, but I'll have to do something soon. We're pretty sure McCloud is drinking up any money we came here with," Jeremy told Sam.

"Obviously, you're going to have to make some changes soon. What are you thinking? Will you go back east? … Catherine, are you still planning to marry the guy back there?" Sam asked.

344

Catherine blushed. "I just today wrote David and told him our situation here, and that I most probably will have a baby to raise. I guess it's up to him to decide if he still wants me," she said humbly.

"He would not be deserving of you if your marriage depended on that. Catherine, I still mean what I said. If for any reason you don't marry this guy, I'm first in line. As far as I'm concerned that baby would be an added joy, not a burden." Sam told her earnestly.

Catherine was moved to tears at Sam's remarks.

"Sam, I promise you, if something were to interfere with my marriage to David, I will send the troops looking for you! By the way, you never explained what you were doing here."

"As if you don't have enough problems to be concerned about ..." Sam hesitated. "But it wouldn't be fair not to warn you. There has been more hostile activity among the Indians lately, especially since that last bad snow storm. Even the game they normally hunt was killed in those freezing temperatures. Their people are hungry and the government, as usual," Sam said bitterly, "is not doing what they promised to provide them with food. Since the 'Great White Father' is an elusive, untouchable being, they are taking it out on the white men they *can* see and touch. Because activity has increased more in the southern area, we received orders to bring reinforcements from Hays to patrol out of Fort Dodge. I took this opportunity to check on you. Seeing your situation, I can't say that it has eased my mind, though."

Jeremy told him about the incident with the three braves on the way to see the Heldmans.

"Your talisman from the Chief worked that time, but it's possible you'd not even get a chance to show it in time to save yourself," Sam told Jeremy honestly. "Please be careful, and try not to leave Catherine and the baby alone. Keep a gun with you at all times. Since we never know how they are going to act, be friendly if they seem to be, and things may end well. Don't start any hostility yourself."

Rising to his feet, Sam looked out the window. "My men are getting restless and we do need to cover more territory before going back to the fort. As badly as I hate to leave you, duty requires that I go."

"Could I ask a favor of you, Sam?" Catherine asked timidly.

"Anything this side of heaven, my dear," Sam said with a bow.

"Jeremy and I only get to mail letters when someone is going to the fort. With McCloud so unstable, we don't want to give them to him; they would probably never get mailed."

"Ahh, Catherine," Sam said with a groan. "You're asking me to mail a letter to my competition for your affections?"

Catherine just looked at him with her big blue eyes, and said a timid, "Yes."

"I'm telling you, this guy's time is limited. If he doesn't marry you in one year, I am coming to kidnap you! Give me the letter."

"Thanks for coming by, Sam, it's encouraging to know that soldiers are patrolling more frequently, and it was good to see you again," Jeremy said.

They were all surprised to hear a commotion out in the yard. Sam instantly became the officer in charge and hurried out the door with Jeremy right behind. Catherine picked up Baby Jake and stood in the doorway, waiting to hear the cause of the racket. Then she saw McCloud, apparently intoxicated, riding Flame in and out of the soldiers, yelling something about all those soldiers on his property. Sam made his way through the crowd and shot his pistol into the air to get McCloud's attention. McCloud reined Flame to a stop and looked at the lieutenant through bleary eyes. He had lost weight and still had not shaved, bathed, or changed his filthy clothing.

"Well, if it isn't that girl-chasin' Looo-ten-ant Ruuush-ing! Whatcha doin' here at my place, Looo-ten-ant? Oh, I see … You're still chasin' that girl!" McCloud slurred.

"Mr. McCloud …" Catherine could see the red flush rising up Sam's face.

"Well, you can't have her, 'cause she's mine! She's my young Susannah, 'cause my Susannah died … Did you know that, Loo-ten-ant? My Susannah went and died!" He spurred Flame and rode hurriedly to the place out from the house where Susannah's grave was marked with a simple cross. As the entourage of soldiers watched, McCloud threw himself on the grave, weeping uncontrollably!

Sam looked at Catherine, who began to apologize, "Sam, I'm so sorry. I don't think he knows what he's saying!"

Sam placed his arm around her and walked her back to the house, "I'm more concerned that he does. Catherine, never be alone with this man. He is insane. Do you know how to use the gun?" She nodded. "Don't hesitate to use it, if need be. Protect yourself at all costs."

He drew her to him one more time, as Baby Jake squirmed and patted his face. "God, I hate to leave you here! I'll come again to check on you as soon as I can!"

With a kiss to her forehead and one to Baby Jake's chubby cheek he headed for the door.

Jeremy passed Sam on his way out, "Watch that guy, Jeremy!" Sam said, motioning toward McCloud.

Minutes later the yard was empty and quiet again. Jeremy looked over to the grave site where McCloud was still lying motionless. He had apparently passed out from too much liquor and too little sleep. Maybe it was heartless, but Jeremy just couldn't bring himself to haul the man inside the cabin where his stench would sicken all of them. Instead, he carried a blanket and covered the snoring McCloud. As he looked down at the sight, Jeremy thought, "And this is the person our future depends on? … God help us!"

*   *   *   *

It was after midnight when Sam and his soldiers returned to Fort Dodge. It had been a long day, but uneventful other than the incident with McCloud. Sam had thought of little else since he left Catherine. How he wished she'd marry him tomorrow and let him take her away from that wretched place. He'd love the chance to raise that sweet baby, too. What a shame he had such a jerk for a father.

Sam took out the letters to David and Liz to place in the mail drop. He stood looking at the letter to David.

"Just how much does this guy know about what Catherine is going through?" he asked himself. "For Catherine to be so crazy about him, he must be a pretty decent guy. If he loves her one bit as much as I do, he'd be moving hell itself to get her away from there. Maybe it's none of my business, but I feel I have to do something!"

Instead of going to the mail drop, he put the letters back in his pocket and went to his office. Taking paper from a drawer he began to write:

Dear Mr. Winters,

I am Lieutenant Samuel Rushing, a stranger to you. However, we share the acquaintance of a lovely young lady, your fiancée, Catherine Sutherland. It was my honor to be part of the military escort that accompanied Miss Sutherland's family as they left the wagon train and traveled to Kansas. During those long weeks on the trail I became friends with your fiancée and her family and hold them in high regard.

I hope you will not consider this letter as overstepping boundaries into things that do not concern me, but the truth is that I am very much concerned about Catherine and her brother, Jeremy, and now, their infant half-brother.

It was my pleasure to visit this family today as our company was patrolling in the area of their homestead. A more desolate place would be hard to find. I was appalled at the situation in which our dear friends are living. I saw little in the sod cabin in the way of food supplies, and I suspect that they are in dire need in every area.

I brought to the fort a letter from Catherine to be mailed to you. She said that in this letter she informs you of her mother's death. The step-father has become totally irrational with grief, leaving for parts unknown for days at a time and returning in a drunken stupor. I fear for Catherine's safety in his presence, and Jeremy tries to be close at all times.

It appears that Jeremy will soon be forced to find employment to support Catherine, the baby, and himself. Since their homestead is hours away from civilization, that will mean re-locating, which is probably the best thing for them, but presents a whole new set of challenges.

Mr. Winters, if you ever come to this Kansas prairie, you may notice something in common among the courageous women who brave this frontier. It is a look of exhaustion, an expression in the eyes that reveals that dreams have been lost to the incredible difficulties of life here. I saw that expression in Catherine's eyes today, and it broke my heart.

Catherine has told me of your plans to marry her in another year, Mr. Winters. She said that the two of you were waiting for her to be old enough to marry. I am witness to the fact that she already carries the full responsibility of all household chores, and now, the added responsibility of a child. She has fully earned the right to be considered an adult, regardless of her age. Mr. Winters, if you care for her at all, come and take her away from this life before it totally destroys her. I have pleaded for that honor myself, but as highly as she may esteem me as a friend; her heart belongs only to you.

Again, I beg your pardon if you feel I had no right to get involved. I only know that if I were in your place, I would want to know the truth of the situation involving the woman I love.

Yours truly,
Lt. Samuel Rushing
7th Cavalry Unit
Fort Hays, Kansas

Sam put the letter in an envelope and copied David's address from the letter she had given him to mail. Right or wrong, the letter was written and would soon be in the mail. Since Catherine wouldn't marry him, this was all he could do in her behalf. Hopefully, Winters would come and take her out of that despicable place. He winced at the thought ... he certainly never expected to feel good about Catherine's David coming to marry her!

CHAPTER 24

Somehow Catherine's heart felt lighter as she went about her chores this morning. The visit from Sam had been a pleasant surprise. Knowing that he and his men were patrolling the territory made her feel much more at ease.

McCloud had left again sometime in the night without entering the cabin. Neither she nor Jeremy heard the sound of Flame's hooves, so he must have walked the horse until out of earshot. He'd probably be gone for two or three days now; that had been his pattern.

Jeremy entered the cabin carrying the morning pail of Daisy's milk. Setting it down, he said, "Cat, I really need to check on the stock today, but I don't want to leave you and Baby Jake here alone. We can't afford to lose cattle; they're the only asset we have."

"How far do you think you'll have to go?" Catherine asked.

"I don't know; hopefully they haven't gone grazing any farther than a quarter mile. I can see a few of them just over the ridge. Everything looks peaceful out there, but I still don't like the idea of your being by yourself."

"Well, Baby Jake and I can't very well ride with you. Why don't you go one direction for a short while and come back. Then go another one. That way you'll only be gone a few minutes at a time, and you can see that we're all right, too."

"I suppose that will work, but make sure you lock the door after me, and see that the rifle is close by," Jeremy advised.

Catherine did as Jeremy told her, sliding the board across the wooden door. Baby Jake was already back to sleep for his morning nap on the big bed, so Catherine planned to write to Liz. Before she sat down she checked the rifle, saw that it was loaded, and leaned it against the wall. She poured herself the last cup of coffee in the pot and sat down to gather her thoughts. She heard Jeremy ride up on Midnight ... he must have forgotten something. She walked over and unlatched the door just in time for it to swing wide open, almost knocking her down. To her alarm, McCloud stood there, as wretched and foul smelling as the day before, with a sneering grin on his face. She backed away from him in fear.

"What'sa matter, aren't you glad to see the man of the house come home?" he slurred, stumbling inside and closing the door.

Catherine was terrified as he moved toward her.

"Do ... do you ... want something to eat? I'll cook you something," she said.

"It's not food I'm wanting ... I want ... my Young Susannah,"

Catherine could see the crazed, confused look in McCloud's eyes.

"Maybe if I can get him to thinking of Mama he'll go back outside to her grave," Catherine thought, "and Jeremy should be back any minute."

"But Susannah died. Remember? She's buried out there."

"She wanted to die!" McCloud shouted. "She wanted to go be with her Jim!"

Reaching out to grab Catherine by the arm, he pulled her close to him. She almost vomited at the smell and tried to pull away from him.

"I don't need her now; I have you … You're just like her, but you're young!"

Awakened by the noise and sensing the tension in the room, Baby Jake cried out anxiously. Catherine turned and started to get the baby. McCloud reached for her and his hand caught in the chain of the gold necklace David had made for her. The motion intended to pull her back toward him broke the fine gold chain as he held the half-heart in his hand. He grinned wickedly, seeing the distress on her face.   Forgetting the baby for the moment, Catherine practically attacked him.

"Give that to me!" she demanded. "Give me my necklace!"

McCloud was delighted to have something to use as bait. He put the broken necklace in his pocket and held up his now empty hands.

"So you want your preacher boy's necklace, do you? What are you willing to do for it, Young Susannah?" he sneered, coming closer.

Baby Jake was screaming now. The sound tore at Catherine's heart; she'd never heard him cry like that. At the moment, she'd have to concentrate on staying out of McCloud's reach, though.

"Look what you're doing to the baby! He's afraid; you know he never cries like that!" Catherine pleaded.

"So?"… the drunken McCloud said, "I'll make him shut up. Is that what you want? … You want me to shut him up?" He rushed over to the bed and to Catherine's horror snatched up Baby Jake with one hand, holding the terrified baby high as if he intended to drop him. In an instant Catherine crossed the room, grabbed the rifle and pointed it directly at McCloud.

Her blue eyes flashing fire now, she surprised McCloud with the authority in her voice, "Put him down! And gently, or I'll put a bullet in you!"

McCloud stood frozen, not too drunk to realize that Catherine might actually do what she said. He didn't really want to hurt the baby, but who did she think she was to pull a gun on him?

"I said put him down! Now! And do it gently!" Catherine said as she re-aimed the gun at his heart.

"O.K. ... I'm putting him down, don't get carried away there ... See I put him back on the bed ... You can put the gun down now..." McCloud slowly put the crying baby back on the bed and raised both his hands .

"Now, get out of here! Slowly walk to the door with your hands up. So help me God, if you move one step closer to me or that baby, I'll pull this trigger!" Catherine said.

McCloud knew Catherine was an expert shot. He had admired her skill with a rifle as he watched her competing with Jeremy. Unless she was a really good actress, she had full intentions of using this rifle on him if he didn't do as she said.

"All right, I'm going, see? I'm doing just what you said," McCloud moved slowly to the door and opened it. Catherine adjusted her position just enough as he moved to keep him perfectly in her aim. As he walked outside, she followed until he mounted his horse. Jeremy rode up just then, shocked to see Catherine holding a gun on McCloud.

As soon as she saw Jeremy, she tossed the gun to him and cried, "See that he leaves!" and raced into the cabin.

She grabbed up Baby Jake, who was almost blue in the face from crying now. Holding him closely, she talked to him and kissed him, and then practically fell into the rocker as her knees gave out.

"I'm so sorry, baby. I'm so sorry!" The thought that it was Jake's own father who created such terror in him was more than Catherine could comprehend. From now on she would do everything in her power to keep this little one away from Pollard McCloud!

Jeremy came inside and bolted the door. "He's gone now. Cat, I'm so sorry. I shouldn't have left you alone!" He saw that she was still shaking, and Baby Jake clung to her with snubbing sobs. Jeremy knelt and put his arms around both of them.

"Did he hurt you, Cat? Did he hurt the baby?"

Catherine took a deep breath, "No, but he would have. We've got to get away from here, Jeremy. We've got to take Baby Jake where McCloud can never touch him again!"

As she described the incident that had taken place in the cabin Jeremy turned pale at the thoughts of what could have happened to both Catherine and the baby. He didn't dare tell her what McCloud had yelled out as he rode off, "She'll pay for this!"

Suddenly, it dawned on Catherine that McCloud still had her necklace!

"Ohhhh, noooo! Jeremy, McCloud has the heart that David made for me! He broke the chain and put it in his pocket ... He's got my necklace!"

She began to weep inconsolably.

"Cat, I'd go after him, but I don't know which way he went after getting to the road, and I'm not about to leave you again." Jeremy said.

"How will I ever explain this to David? We were going to bring the two pieces together when we marry. Maybe this means we're not supposed to get married. Oh, Jeremy, everything's gone wrong!"

Seeing Catherine's distress, Baby Jake's little bottom lip began to quiver and his eyes filled with tears. From all appearances, another good cry was about to burst forth.

"Come here, little buddy," Jeremy said, taking him from Catherine. "It's all right; everything's all right." He talked softly to the baby as he patted him comfortingly. "How about a bottle of milk?"

Jeremy got the bottle that Catherine had ready. She let him have the rocking chair and then laid down on the bed, pulling the pillow up close. By losing David's necklace, she felt that she'd lost him too. In times past, when things troubled her deeply, she'd go to Mama for a hug and words of wisdom. But this time there would be no warm hug, no advice that was always just what she needed to hear. Mama was gone. Nothing eased that pain. Catherine cried quietly, as Jeremy rocked Baby Jake. Finally, both Catherine and the baby fell asleep.

Not wanting to wake the infant, Jeremy stayed where he was, but the slow movement of the chair was in direct contrast to the thoughts racing through his mind. There were major decisions that he needed to make, and now! He felt so trapped. Trapped by poverty … by Indians … by McCloud … trapped by responsibilities!

357

He had no intentions of living the rest of his life this way. He had to have a plan to get things going in a more positive direction.

"God help me!" he prayed silently as he rocked the baby. "Help me to know what to do!"

*   *   *   *

"I don't think I'll ever feel safe here again," Catherine said to Jeremy as they discussed their situation that evening.

"I can't blame you, but Cat, there's just no direction coming to me as to where we're supposed to go. I need to sell the cattle, and I'm trying to think how to go about doing it. We have the problem of your being here alone if I go anywhere to take care of business. Surely, I can sell them in Dodge City, but I don't think I can herd them by myself all the way to town."

"What if we were to hitch them up to the wagons and drive them in? I know I'm not very good at driving a team, but the animals are so used to doing it I think they'd pretty much follow your wagon." Catherine suggested. "That way, we could take some things from here to set up housekeeping if we can find a place."

"That might work. We could sell the oxen and the big wagon, and keep the farm wagon. Midnight can pull that one when the three of us need to go somewhere. That makes sense, Cat," Jeremy said. "But before we sell these things, I have to ask, do you want to go back to Lexington?"

Catherine thought for a few moments. "As much as I loved our life back there, and David, and our friends … that life is gone. Everything is different for us now. We're not kids anymore. We have a baby to take care of. We don't have a home there, and maybe it's a matter of pride, but I really don't want to go back like this. All of our clothes are practically rags, and Baby Jake hardly has any." Tears came to her eyes and spilled down her cheeks. "I just can't go back all ragged and defeated."

Jeremy reached over to squeeze her hand. "I know, sis. I feel the same way. I hate that things have turned out this way, but it's not the end. God has never let us down, and somehow, we're going to get out of this mess. I'll find work, and we can get on our feet in this next year so that when David comes, you won't have to be ashamed."

"I'm so afraid that things won't work out for David and me now." Catherine admitted, "I'm not the same person that left Lexington a year ago, and if this next year holds as many changes as the last one, I'm afraid we will have grown too far apart for us to pick up our relationship again. Then there's the baby to consider. With caring for him all the time he's beginning to seem like my own. In another year that bond will be even stronger. What if David doesn't want to start our marriage with the responsibilities of a child?"

"Cat, you have to trust God and trust the goodness of David's heart. David loves you and the Bible tells us that "love never fails." And besides, who wouldn't want Baby Jake? Even Sam fell for him instantly ... all he has to do is smile that little crooked smile that lights up his eyes and he gets you right in the heart!"

Catherine had to smile at the thought, "You're right. I'll just leave that to the Lord. There's one other thing, though, Jeremy…"

"I think I know what you're going to say ... we'll be leaving Mama behind," Jeremy said quietly.

"I know that's just her body out there in that grave, but it's so soon. She's probably having the time of her life with Papa in heaven right now. What do you think she would tell us to do, Jeremy? What would Papa say?"

Jeremy didn't hesitate. "They would tell us to leave here, and get out from under any kind of tie to McCloud."

"I believe they would, too. So let's do it!" Catherine said. " … Oh, but Jeremy, we can't leave without seeing Martha and Owen."

"You're right, they were here for us when Mama died; it wouldn't be right to leave without letting them know. O.K., how are we going to fit this in?"

He paused to think, "Cat, what are the things you absolutely have to get done before we can leave?"

"I should go through our belongings and pack up the things we need to take … I can use the empty food crates … I have to wash diapers for Jake and clothes for us, and I need to cook some food to take along" she said.

"How much of that can you do tonight?" Jeremy asked.

Taking a deep breath, Catherine thought, "I can go through things and pack the crates. I'll get up early in the morning and start the laundry. The food should probably be the last on the list before I pack the cooking things."

"I was thinking that I can get the wagons ready while you're washing and hanging out the laundry, and then we could go to Owen and Martha's. I'd like to get Owen's help rounding up the oxen if he thinks it's all right to leave you ladies alone at their place. More than likely it will be too late to start into Dodge by the time all that's done, but we'll have everything ready for an early start day after tomorrow."

Both Catherine and Jeremy felt like a terrible weight had been lifted from them. They could only hope now that McCloud stayed gone until after they left.

*   *   *   *

Catherine had diapers on the clothesline, flapping in the prairie wind, before seven o'clock the next morning. By the time she finished pinning up laundry for her and Jeremy, the diapers were dry, so she brought them in and quickly folded them. The rest of the clothing would dry while they were at the Heldman's.

Packed crates lined the walls of the cabin, ready to be loaded into the wagon. There were things Catherine painfully laid aside because of lack of space; others were too precious to leave behind.

Jeremy had pulled the wagons to the front of the homestead and had gathered into the corral the oxen that were grazing close to the farm.

Soon they were in the wagon and headed for Owen and Martha's. Baby Jake had never ridden in the wagon or been off the farm. He seemed aware that these were new experiences and gazed curiously around at the unfamiliar sights. At times, he'd look up into Catherine's face and smile, as though to let her know that he was perfectly content with the state of things.

Martha and Owen were thrilled to see them. They couldn't believe how much Baby Jake had grown in just a few weeks. As Catherine and Jeremy told them the situation with McCloud and their own desperate need for provision, the Heldmans agreed with their decision to leave.

Owen thought it would be safe to leave the women there at the dugout for a while, so he helped Jeremy round up the rest of the oxen and pen them up. They arrived back at the dugout just as Martha was completing a delicious dinner. She had sacrificed a prized hen to cook a special meal for Catherine and Jeremy to celebrate their going away. There were tears with the good-bye hugs, and promises of letters when Catherine and Jeremy were settled.

As they rode back to the homestead, Baby Jake slept in Catherine's arms. Jeremy and Catherine talked about what lay ahead for them in Dodge City. They knew nothing of the town; only that it was in the stages of being built, which sounded promising for available jobs. Surely there would be a boarding house or hotel where they could live for a while. They would trust God to provide the job Jeremy needed, and maybe there would be someplace Catherine could work and still care for Baby Jake.

Jeremy was hoping to get a good price for the oxen. He knew what McCloud had paid for them, but he had no idea what he could get for them here. It was extremely comforting to know that Catherine had the fifty dollars from David.

Once their plans were settled Catherine began thinking of the things she needed to do upon arriving at the homestead. She hoped Baby Jake's good nap on the ride back wouldn't keep him up later than his usual bedtime; it was so much easier to get things done when he was sleeping.

Old Pal came running to meet them as Midnight pulled the wagon into the drive. Jeremy called to him and he barked and wagged his tail, always glad to see his master.

"I'll take Baby Jake in," Jeremy said as he brought the wagon to a stop.

Catherine handed down the sleeping baby to her brother, and then climbed down from the wagon herself. Inside, she waited to see that Baby Jake was still sleeping soundly. That should give her time enough to go out and gather the laundry.

Jeremy had unhitched Midnight, leaving the wagon close to the house. He began loading the packed crates so they would be ready for their early departure.

Catherine was almost to the house with her armload of fresh smelling laundry.

"Oh, no!" She said aloud, and Jeremy looked up from loading the last crate to look the direction of her horrified gaze.

McCloud was slowly riding Flame toward them. The sneer on his face let them know that he was aware of what they were doing. It seemed that each time he went away and came back, he had slipped farther into the evil that emanated from within him. He hardly resembled the man who loved their mother and had worked so hard to make things better for her. It was as though McCloud needed Susannah's goodness to be that person, and without her there was nothing honorable left in him.

"Goin' somewhere?" McCloud asked mockingly.

Jeremy stepped forward to meet him as McCloud dismounted.

"Yes, McCloud, we are. It's either leave or stay here and starve to death."

"You're not going anywhere. Unpack that wagon!" McCloud ordered.

Jeremy looked down at the ground a moment, and then raised his head to look McCloud squarely in the eyes.

"Ever since you married our mother I have given you respect; not because you deserved it, but because of her. If you were conducting yourself now in a way that was worthy of her, I would continue to show you respect. I would work as hard as I always have to make something of this place. But you have shown no respect for any of us, even your own flesh and blood. Our mother is gone and I'm the head of this family now. I no longer take orders from you. Catherine and I will make decisions together as to what is best for us, and we're leaving." Jeremy said firmly, but in a calm voice.

McCloud's thinking had practically been destroyed through the grief of losing Susannah and the weeks of going without food and sleep. Further deteriorated by his continual state of drunkenness, it was getting harder for him to keep things straight. ...He was confused ... what was Lieutenant Sutherland doing here? Unsteadily he tried to stand at attention and salute.

"Yes, sir! At your command, sir!" Why was the Lieutenant looking at him like that ... why didn't he say something?

"Reporting for duty, Lieutenant Sutherland!" McCloud slurred, still trying to stand up straight. It wouldn't do for the Lieutenant to see that he was drunk. Then a thought occurred to him ... his commanding officer probably had not heard that Susannah was dead.

"Sir, did you know that Susannah is dead?" he said, almost breaking into tears.

"What are you talking about?" The Lieutenant asked with a strange look on his face.

"Our Susannah ... she died ... from consumption ... she just slowly wasted away ... we buried her over there ... the prairie ..."

Catherine and Jeremy stood speechless, listening to McCloud's muttering. There was something authentic in the way he tried to stand at attention … he was addressing Jeremy as his commanding officer, calling him … "Lieutenant Sutherland!"

Jeremy sprang forward, grabbing McCloud by his filthy coat, "Did you know my father? Tell me! Did you serve with him in the war?"

McCloud looked at Jeremy with confusion in his bleary eyes, and then recognition came. The mocking look returned to his face.

"Tell me, McCloud, did you know my father? Jeremy demanded.

"Yes … I knew your blasted, perfect father! How do you think I ended up in Lexington?" he sneered.

"What do you mean by that?" Jeremy pursued.

"You think I just happened to mosey up there and find your pretty mama waitin' to be rescued?"

When Jeremy remained silent, trying to absorb what he was saying. McCloud continued, "You want proof ? I got proof!" Pulling out his wallet McCloud removed the picture of Susannah that her husband had carried to war with him. Holding it out to Jeremy, he said, "Ever see that before?"

Catherine stepped forward to look at the photograph and recognized it as their father's prized possession, the likeness of Susannah when she was fifteen, just before they married. The thought that this man had taken that from their father, dead or alive, infuriated Catherine.

"You beast! You planned the whole thing, didn't you, so you could get our farm?" She beat on him with her fists as Jeremy tried to pull her away.

"Don't touch him, Catherine; he's not worth it!"

McCloud laughed a mocking laugh, "Oh, she'll do more than that; I've been planning this a long time!"

Quickly, he flung Catherine away with one arm, and catching Jeremy off guard, landed a blow to Jeremy's head that sent him reeling backward to the ground. As McCloud tried to regain his balance, he heard the growl just a second before Old Pal leaped at him with teeth bared. Barely missing McCloud's neck, his teeth ripped through the man's clothing, leaving a bleeding shoulder wound. The old dog attacked again, but McCloud moved aside, and pulling a pistol from his pocket put a single bullet into the heart of the loyal pet. Old Pal sank to the ground, motionless as his eyes gave one last look of love to the young man he had adored for years.

Catherine watched in horror, and Jeremy leapt from the ground like a man crazed. His fist connected with McCloud's jaw with a sound of cracking bone. The impact sent the pistol flying into the air and to the ground several feet away.

"That was for taking my mother's picture from my father!" Jeremy said to McCloud. Quickly he hit him again, "This is for deceiving my mother into marrying you!" With another blow … "This is for stealing my farm! … This is for terrifying your own baby! … This is for what you tried to do to my sister, and for taking her necklace! This one's for what you did to my dog!"

McCloud's face was streaming blood from his nose, which was most likely broken, from a cut lip and cuts above both eyes. He fell to the ground, almost unconscious. Catherine ran to Jeremy, who was exhausted, both physically and emotionally. He fell into her arms, sobbing from the release of emotions that had broken free from that place where he had so carefully kept them in check. The full discovery of McCloud's deceit had left both of them shaken. Neither of them noticed McCloud slowly edging his way toward the pistol lying a few feet away from him in the sand.

"Did you really think you'd get away with this?" they heard him say.

Catherine and Jeremy quickly turned to see McCloud standing, though unsteadily, with the pistol pointed directly at them. Pushing Catherine behind him, Jeremy stood to face his enemy.

"Look, McCloud, you got what you wanted. You got our farm, our mother. Now it's all gone. Why don't you just leave and go your way, and we'll go ours. You're obviously in no condition to take care of Baby Jake, but you know we'll take good care of him."

"I'm not leaving until I get what I came after ... my Young Susannah!" McCloud yelled. "She's gonna pay for pulling that gun on me, and you're gonna pay for this!" McCloud pointed toward his bloodied face. He steadied himself and cocked the pistol, firing as Jeremy pushed Catherine to the ground. She watched, frozen in fear, as Jeremy held his hand to the left side of his head and blood ran down through his fingers. His eyes closed and he wilted in a heap on the ground.

"Jeremy!" Catherine screamed, running to him. His white face was still, and blood ran from his head, forming a crimson puddle on the prairie sod. "Oh, God, this can't be happening!"

She felt McCloud pulling her to her feet.

"You've killed him! I hate you! I hate you!" She beat her fists on him as he laughed and dragged her towards the house.

"I'll kill you when I'm through with you, too; then I'll be done with you blasted Sutherlands!" he growled.

Inside the cabin, McCloud threw Catherine down on the bed, waking Baby Jake, who began to cry at the sight of his father. Catherine kicked and fought against McCloud, but she was no match for the strength of a large man. She felt his hands on her body and it sickened her. She thought she would faint from the overpowering stench of this evil man who was determined to destroy her. Her strength was failing and she felt herself slipping into darkness, "Oh, God, help me!" she pleaded silently. She could hear the baby's terrified crying just to her right, but she was helpless to comfort him. "What would McCloud do to the baby after he killed her?"

"Catherine, fight! Fight for Baby Jake!" A voice deep within rose up to bring new strength as she gave a huge push and rolled away from McCloud. Thinking he had totally subdued her, he was surprised and angered as he grabbed her again, striking her on the cheek.

Suddenly, the door to the cabin flew open. To the surprise of both Catherine and McCloud, an Indian brave strode into the cabin. In his hand was a knife held high and ready for use. Instantly assessing the situation with Catherine and McCloud, he gave some command in his language to two braves behind him. The war-painted men rushed over and grabbed McCloud, dragging him away from Catherine and out the door of the cabin. She could hear his screams, even above Baby Jake's, who was even more frightened now at the sight of the Indians. Catherine instinctively grabbed him and tried to quiet him, afraid to look up at the brave still standing there for fear he would take the baby.

"Yellow Cat ... do not be afraid."

368

Catherine looked up, "Runs Like the Wind!" she cried with relief, recognizing him then. He had grown taller and matured. Then she remembered Jeremy. "My mother's husband killed Jeremy! Our mother died, everything has gone so badly! I can't thank you enough for saving me from him!"

"White Brother not dead, Yellow Cat," the brave told her. He stepped to the door and spoke again in his language. Another Indian brought Jeremy inside, supporting him as he walked unsteadily.

"Oh, thank God! Here, Jeremy lie down!" she said, making a place for him on the bed as she picked up the baby.

"Are you all right, Cat?" Jeremy asked weakly, concern in his eyes. "Did McCloud ... hurt you?"

"No, thanks to Runs Like the Wind. McCloud said he was going to kill me, and I think he would have. I have no idea what he planned to do to the baby."

"Man with black heart will hurt no one now! You free from him," Runs Like the Wind said.

Catherine and Jeremy looked at each other. It was not their wish for things to turn out this way, but they were relieved that they would no longer have to live in fear of McCloud.

"What about your head, Jeremy?" Catherine moved so that she could see the side of his head. The blood had already clotted, but there was a red line that began in front of his ear and ended at the curve of his skull. The bullet had grazed his head, leaving a long cut, but miraculously, not a serious injury.

Runs Like the Wind had come closer to inspect the wound as well. He seemed satisfied that it was not severe.

"I get medicine," and he walked out the door.

"Jeremy, what are they doing here?" Catherine whispered. "Are they a raiding party?"

"I think so, but I don't believe Runs Like the Wind knew this was our place. I had regained consciousness and was crawling to get to the cabin door. They rode up, and he recognized me. I just pointed to the door and said, 'Help Cat!'" Jeremy whispered back.

"I'd better wash that wound before he puts his medicine on it," Catherine said. She left Baby Jake sitting there beside Jeremy, looking from one to the other of them.

"Poor baby, he's had a rough few days. I hope this is the end of it," Jeremy said, holding on to the little one.

Catherine returned to the bedside with a basin of water. Even though she was as gentle as she could be, the water caused the wound to sting. Just as she finished cleaning away the dried blood, Runs Like the Wind came in with two small leather pouches. He nodded his approval at seeing that Catherine had cleaned the wound.

He smiled at Jeremy, "White Brother work medicine on Runs Like the Wind ... Now Runs Like the Wind work medicine on White Brother."

Jeremy grinned, "I hope you do as good a job as I did!"

Catherine asked, "Runs Like the Wind, how is your leg?"

He showed them where the scar was still visible, "White doctor say no run, but Yellow Cat pray to Great Father, and now I run," he said proudly. He pulled open the draw string on one of the pouches and stuck his finger into it, drawing out a dark salve that smelled of pine and other things Catherine couldn't define. He spread it gently over the length of the cut. Then opening the other pouch, he took

370

dried herbs and sprinkled them over the salve, pressing lightly so the herbs would adhere to the salve.

"Three days, White Brother, then wash away."

"Thanks, my brother," Jeremy said sincerely. "Please give my regards to Chief Black Horse and Rippling Brook, are they well?"

Runs Like the Wind became serious. "Much trouble in tribe. Many hungry, many sick. White man's leaders no keep treaty. My father want peace, but braves angry, say Chief Black Horse not leader of his people if he not allow them to find food. He send me with raiding party to prevent killing of good people." Runs Like the Wind paused.

"Not all braves honor me. Some people they kill. I am sorry, White Brother ... Yellow Cat ... I am sorry for what red brothers have done."

"Are we going to be safe?" Catherine could barely find breath to speak as she realized the precarious situation they were in.

Avoiding the question, Runs Like the Wind asked one himself, "I see wagon loaded, you go?"

Jeremy answered him, "Yes, we were planning to leave at sunup for Dodge City."

The sound of impatient, angry voices outside the cabin brought Runs Like the Wind to his feet. He stepped outside for only a moment, and when he came back his face was concerned.

"You must go now! Braves do not care you are White Brother to me. I tell them you leave now and take only what is in wagon. They demand cattle for your lives. Red Hawk and I go behind you to protect, but come now!"

There was no mistaking the urgency in Runs Like the Wind's voice. Catherine quickly found Baby Jake's two bottles and filled them with milk. Frantically, she looked around for something to hold the clean diapers. Grabbing a pillowcase, she yanked out the pillow and stuffed in the diapers. Coats … it would be dark soon, and cold….get the white leather blanket for the baby.

Jeremy was moving far too quickly to the liking of his injured head. At times the dizziness overtook him and he'd have to stand still for a moment. The rifle was his first priority … bullets, a few tools… Oh! …the horse… He hurried out the door to re-hitch Midnight to the wagon.

Runs Like the Wind stood protectively in front of the cabin, out of Catherine's way as she hurriedly gathered things. He reached for items as she had them ready and handed them to Red Hawk to put into the wagon. The freshly washed laundry lay in a heap on the ground where Catherine had dropped it when McCloud arrived.

"Our clothes!" Catherine cried, and the brave picked up the lot of them, pushing them into any space available among the crates.

The yelps and war cries of the angry braves were reaching a pitch that was utterly unnerving. Runs Like the Wind would not be able control them much longer. Catherine grabbed Baby Jake and ran to the wagon. Jeremy held the baby while she quickly got up to the wagon seat and then handed him to her.

"No, wait! I forgot the journal! The money's in it!"

She thrust Baby Jake back to Jeremy and jumped down from the wagon. Rushing into the cabin, she climbed up to the loft. Her journal was lying just where she had last written in it. As she reached for it she heard the crash of broken glass and a flaming arrow landed just inches from her on her loft bed. Catherine screamed in terror as flames erupted immediately. She grabbed the journal and practically fell down the ladder, running out to the wagon.

She was barely in her place on the seat as Jeremy, still holding Baby Jake, whipped the reins for Midnight to go.

Runs Like the Wind and Red Hawk rode at the rear of the wagon on either side. Midnight seemed to understand the need for speed, or perhaps he also wanted to escape the shrill noises of the raiding Indians. Catherine's heart was pounding so loudly she was sure Baby Jake could hear it as she took him from Jeremy and held him closely to her.

Looking behind them from time to time, they saw no followers. They had ridden a mile or so when they came to a rise in the road. A glance backward proved that they had left none too soon. The sky was lit with an orange glow and occasional bursts of flames that shot upward.

Their hearts still pounding from their narrow escape, Catherine and Jeremy were torn with emotions. The loss of almost all their earthly possessions was heart-rending, and yet, good memories of the time spent at this homestead were far outnumbered by the negative. Now, there would be nothing left of this season of their lives but a pile of ashes and a wooden cross marking the site of their mother's grave. Certainly the unknown future would be better than the past.

CHAPTER 25

Marion Winters was surprised to see David's mail still sitting on the table when she went in to start breakfast. Two letters had come for him yesterday, one from Catherine and one from a Lt. Samuel Rushing. Knowing that David always came to the kitchen for something to eat after work or Bible Study, she had left the mail there as usual. She and Reverend Winters had gone out making calls on sick parishioners, and David was asleep when they arrived home late. She knew how concerned he had been about Catherine lately, so she was certain he'd want to read the letter as soon as possible.

Maybe she should take them to him now. He had to be at work by eight o'clock, so it might prevent his wasting time on other things. She picked up the letters and took them down the hall, knocking on David's bedroom door.

"Are you awake, hon?" she asked.

David opened the door and continued buttoning his shirt. "I am. 'Morning Mama." He saw the letters in her hand, "Yes! Mail!"

Marion smiled to see the joy on her son's face. He had grown up so much in this past year. Honestly, she and his father had been surprised that his relationship with Catherine had remained strong during this long separation. She was proud of his faithfulness, first to God and also to Catherine.

"These came for you yesterday and I left them on the kitchen table. You didn't go in there last night?" She asked.

"For probably the first time in my whole life ... no, I didn't. It was Abby's birthday yesterday, and we celebrated after Bible study. Her mother had made sandwiches, birthday cake and all the trimmings, so I was stuffed!" David answered.

"Well, you have your letters now; I'll leave so you can read them," his mother turned to go as she heard David read the name,

"Lt. Samuel Rushing? I don't know who that is, but he's from Kansas. Oh well, I'll read it in a minute." He laid the letter aside and quickly opened Catherine's as his mother went back to the kitchen, closing the door behind her.

David sat down on his bed and eagerly began to read, but his anticipation was quickly stifled as he read of Susannah's death. Catherine's beautiful, sweet, caring mother was dead!

It was almost unbelievable. But there was no mistaking the heartache behind the words Catherine had written. David could sense her sorrow. This had happened weeks ago ... no wonder he had been feeling that heaviness in his heart when he thought of her.

She was facing this terrible time without him! Jeremy... Poor Jeremy, he was very close to his mother, so he had to be heartbroken too. And the baby ... he was so young he wouldn't even remember Susannah! At this thought, David burst into tears. Baby Jake would never know what a special person his mother was!

375

David fell to his knees beside the bed, his heart grieved at the news he had received. If it was this painful for him, how in the world was Catherine holding up?

"God, please!" he prayed between sobs. "I feel so utterly helpless! I don't know what to do ... please send someone to help my Catherine and her family! Show me what to do!"

He picked up Catherine's letter and read it again. As she mentioned her stepfather, David felt there was more going on than she could say. David had never felt good about her being around the man. Now with her mother gone, David knew this was a situation he could not ignore. His eyes fell on the letter sent to him by this Lieutenant Rushing ... maybe he'd better read it.

As he sat there on the floor reading Sam's letter, David pictured Catherine, Jeremy and Baby Jake as they tried to survive on the desolate plains without finances to provide even the bare necessities of life. David thought of the bank account that he had been building for his and Catherine's future; he felt ashamed that she was desperately doing without while their money sat in the bank, and he lived in the comfort of his parents' home.

He was thankful to Lt. Rushing for writing this letter. He knew Catherine could never have brought herself to tell him the depth of their need. There were many questions to be answered and things were uncertain for the future, but his priority now was to rescue the girl he loved from this horrible situation. They would settle all the other issues together.

When David walked out of his room a few minutes later, he did so as a man who had mentally taken charge of his family. His parents saw the change as he entered the kitchen and told them he would be going west, using the new railroad that had just completed service to Dodge City. His mother agreed to get clothing together for him as he went to discuss his leaving with Silas Goodson, and to learn the time of the train's departure.

Reverend Winters went to his office to pray. He prayed for God to comfort Catherine, whom they had loved for years as their own daughter, and for her family. When he began to pray for his son, he was at a loss for words. He always knew that this day would someday come. It was the natural progression of life for a child to leave his parents, it was God's plan. He never expected that David's leaving would be so sudden and filled with anxiety, though. Knowing how much his son loved Catherine, Reverend Winters could expect no less from him than to go and help her. This meant not knowing how long it would be before he and his wife saw their only child again, and even though he was a rising artist in the jewelry field and becoming a gifted teacher of the Word of God, he would never cease to be the child of the Reverend and Mrs. Winters.

Dropping his head to his hands, this concerned father began to pray:

"Oh, God, I wasn't expecting this day to come so soon. I know that this is the time that I must release my son into Your safekeeping, and trust that You are watching over him even when I have no way of knowing what surrounds him. Protect him from danger as he goes into situations unknown; give him wisdom beyond his own understanding as he faces things that are new and difficult. May he always sense Your presence near him. Amen."

CHAPTER 26

❝I think we should go to the fort tonight, Cat. We've never been to Dodge City and wouldn't know where to go this time of night," Jeremy said to Catherine after they had been on the road for about an hour. It was pitch dark, and the sound of an occasional wolf or coyote made Catherine shiver and move closer to Jeremy. The noise of the wagon wheels and Midnight's hooves on the hard ground seemed amplified in the night air. That made it impossible to hear the approach of anyone who might be following them.

Thankfully, Runs Like the Wind and Red Hawk still rode right behind them. Catherine and Jeremy knew that these young men had placed themselves in jeopardy by defending white settlers and prayed that the braves' loyalty to them would not create more problems within their tribe.

Baby Jake stirred, sleeping uneasily in Catherine's aching arms. She only hoped she could find a bottle for him when he was ready for one.

Catherine agreed that they should go to the fort. They would be safe there; they would be fed and given a bed for the remainder of the night. In the morning she'd ask if Sam was still at Fort Dodge. She knew he would be extremely concerned if he happened by the farm while on patrol and found it burned to the ground. She wanted him to know that she, Jeremy and the baby were safe.

Jeremy was exhausted and weak from the loss of blood from his head injury. At times dizziness washed over him, and he wanted nothing more than to lie down and be very still. The pain in his head throbbed like the force of a blacksmith's anvil, pounding with every beat of his heart.

But he was alive. And Cat and Baby Jake were alive and unharmed. The past was behind them now, and they could look forward to the future. McCloud was no longer controlling their destiny with his deceitful and selfish decisions.

After what seemed an interminable journey, they could dimly see the fort ahead. Runs Like the Wind rode up beside Jeremy, and he knew it was time for them to go their separate ways. He reigned Midnight to a halt and turned to face his Indian friend.

"Runs Like the Wind, I don't have enough words to tell you how thankful I am to have you as my friend and brother. You saved our lives. You will always be with me in my heart. Please give my regards to Chief Black Horse and Rippling Brook."

Runs Like the Wind took the hand Jeremy offered and shook it firmly.

"You good man, White Brother. Go in peace with Yellow Cat and Little Brother."

"Thank you again for saving me, Runs Like the Wind." Catherine said to him. "I am sorry for the suffering of your people." She reached out to take his hand as he rode his horse to her side of the wagon.

"There is much sorrow for my people, but when I see Yellow Cat smile here," he pointed to his head, "my heart is glad."

"I too, will see you," Catherine said, "I will see you running like the wind!"

That pleased the young Indian and he smiled as he turned his horse to go.

"Red Hawk," Jeremy spoke to the other brave who had stood beside his friend in defending them, "Thank you for your help today. Runs Like the Wind is blessed to have a friend like you." Red Hawk shook Jeremy's hand and nodded in acknowledgement of their appreciation. Glad to be free of the slow moving wagon the Indian ponies leapt into the darkness and out of sight.

Jeremy flicked the reins and though exhausted, Midnight covered the distance to the fort in minutes. Jeremy explained their situation to the guard, who gave the command for the gate to be opened.

Catherine didn't realize how tense she had been until they were inside the fort with the gate closed behind them. At the same time she understood that it was this tension that had been holding her together. She felt she could burst into tears at any minute now that they were really safe. Her mind was playing tricks, alternating between memories of Indians riding wildly around their homestead, and going blank entirely. One glance at Jeremy told her that he wasn't doing much better. He looked as though he might pass out any minute.

As they guided the wagon to the livery stable, Catherine spoke to a soldier there,

"Sir, my brother had a gunshot wound to the head today and lost a lot of blood. Would it be possible to get him to a bed quickly?"

Jeremy was almost swaying now, trying to stay upright on the seat.

"But ... Midnight ... feed ... water," he mumbled.

"We'll take care of your horse, son," the soldier told him. Motioning to two other soldiers to come, he told them, "See these people to quarters and make sure they have what they need. You're going to have to help this young man."

"Would you like me to take the baby, ma'am?" a soldier asked Catherine.

"Yes, please, I need to find his bottle among all this!" She looked in dismay at the wagon load of their belongings. Jeremy had packed the crates neatly, but their clothing was stuffed among them in disarray along with the last few things they had been able to grab. After she handed the baby down to the soldier Catherine located her journal and the pillowcase of diapers. She moved things enough to find a bottle for the baby and decided that was as much strength as she had at the moment. Tomorrow she'd come out and straighten the rest.

Jeremy had practically fallen down into the arms of the soldier who was there to help him, and barely made it to a small room. Sinking down to the bed, he was asleep by the time the concerned soldier pulled off his boots.

"Miss, should we wake the doctor to check him?" he asked Catherine.

"I think morning would be soon enough for him to see the doctor. We've had a very stressful day, and he lost a lot of blood earlier. Sleep is probably more important now than anything. Our Indian friend applied his medicine to the wound," she said.

The soldiers were confused; "Wasn't it Indians that burned your place?

Too exhausted to explain, she just smiled, "It's a very long story!"

Even Baby Jake slept late the next morning. Catherine was extremely grateful for that. Bad dreams had awakened her briefly several hours earlier. Something disturbed her about the dream; McCloud dragging her ... the Indians ... something on one of their horses ... she was too tired to remember. She just knew that she ached all over, and soon went back to sleep. This time she woke feeling the pat of chubby hands on her face and hearing the sweet sounds of Baby Jake's voice. She opened her eyes to look into his smiling face. There were smudges of dirt on his cheeks from their dusty wagon ride, but he had never looked so beautiful to her. He squealed with delight to see her awake and patted her face again. Catherine squeezed him, kissing him under his plump cheeks where it tickled. He giggled out loud and kicked his legs.

"Ouch! You've got quite a kick there, buddy! And you've also got a very wet diaper. We'd better get you changed."

Catherine knew Baby Jake's good mood wouldn't last much longer if she didn't get food for him. It was past his usual breakfast time, and he hadn't eaten for hours. She was thankful to find a wash basin and pitcher of water there in the room where she could freshen up both the baby and herself. A few minutes later she knocked on Jeremy's door. Getting no response, she opened the door to find the room empty.

Walking outside, she saw Jeremy straightening up the messy wagon. Baby Jake jumped as he recognized Jeremy, and held out his arms to him as they came nearer.

"Hey, Jake! How's my little buddy this morning? Whoops! Let's not grab the noggin," Jeremy quickly held the baby's hand away from his injury.

"How are you feeling this morning?" Catherine asked.

"I still have a dull ache on the left side of my head. I saw the doctor already. He said the Indian medicines usually work better than ours, so just do as Wind said and leave it the three days. He thinks I might have a mild concussion from the force of the bullet, and that's causing the headache. He also said that I was a very lucky guy."

"We've all come so close to death, and yet we're still here. There must be a reason God has spared us." Catherine said.

"You know, Cat, if McCloud had continued to do right, like he did for a time there, I feel he'd probably still be alive. But because he chose to go back to his old ways, he died. I only hope that he had time to make things right with God. Hopefully, he listened to the things Owen had to say on Christmas day …" Jeremy stopped when he saw the strange look on Catherine's face as she leaned against the wagon for support.

"Oh, no!" she breathed, and tears filled her eyes.

"Cat! What's wrong?" Jeremy asked in concern.

"Owen and Martha … the Indians killed them!"

"How do you know that?"

"In my dream … I kept having this bad dream last night. I knew something was wrong … I saw something that disturbed me, but when I'd wake up I couldn't remember what it was. When you mentioned Owen's name I remembered … when I ran back into the house to get my journal … as I came out, one of the Indians rode by, and I saw on his horse … tied around its neck…."

"What, Cat?" Jeremy asked as she sat weeping, "What was on the horse?"

"Martha's … blue and white checked apron … and … her … her hair!"

"Oh, no! You're sure, Cat?" Jeremy felt as though a giant fist had knocked the wind out of him, and he could hardly find the breath to speak.

"Yes, I'm sure of what I saw. I know it's possible for someone else to have an apron like that, but there aren't any other settlers anywhere near us, and the hair … it was exactly the color of hers, and long."

"Runs Like the Wind said he hadn't been able to stop the braves from killing people …," Jeremy said softly. "We'd better tell the commanding officer here at the fort so they can send out scouts to see if it's true."

"Oh, Jeremy, their bodies might just be lying there… the wolves, and coyotes… Somebody needs to bury them! And who's going to tell their people? How will they know who to contact?"

Baby Jake had no concept of the sorrow his older brother and sister were experiencing. He just knew that his little belly was empty. He began to fuss, demanding attention to his needs.

"I've got to find something for him to eat, Jeremy," Catherine said. "Surely they have oatmeal here. I'll take care of him while you talk to the officer about Owen and Martha, then maybe we can get some breakfast, too."

The friendly cook was only too glad to feed this family who had so narrowly escaped with their lives. He prepared strained oatmeal for Baby Jake, and gave Catherine milk for his bottle as well. Within minutes she was feeding the hungry baby in the dining hall. It was there that Jeremy found them. Within minutes the cook brought out plates filled with bacon, eggs, fried potatoes and biscuits. The hearty breakfast was a feast to Catherine and Jeremy, and they both felt strengthened.

Jeremy said that a scouting party would go to check both the Heldman and McCloud homesteads to see if there were bodies to be buried. He told Catherine that the doctor had strongly suggested that he spend that day resting as much as possible. From the way he was feeling, Jeremy knew that was good advice. He already wanted to lie down and go back to sleep, and it was just mid-morning.

"Will you be O.K., Cat?" he asked. "I think I'll take advantage of the doc's excuse to be lazy."

"We'll be fine, Jeremy. The baby will soon be ready for a nap too; maybe we'll all just be lazy today … we certainly haven't done that in a very long time!"

They stayed two more days at the fort. Both Catherine and Jeremy found they needed this time … perhaps to transition from life on the prairie to taking the next step into their unknown future, or just to rest after the harrowing experiences of the past few days. Jeremy wrote to Liz and told her of the changes that had taken place. Catherine couldn't bring herself to write to David. How could she write a letter and not tell him something as important as her necklace being stolen by McCloud? He had put his heart and soul into making it for her. It symbolized their coming together at the end of the two years, and now she no longer possessed her part of that symbol. She simply could not bring herself to tell him.

So much had happened, and there had been no time to work through it in her own mind; she wouldn't know how to put on paper the events of that terrible day. How do you describe the pain of the dispute between Jeremy and McCloud, of believing that Jeremy had been killed? She didn't even want to think of the ugliness of McCloud's intentions toward her and how she was saved by Runs Like the Wind and the braves. The sound of McCloud's screams still rang in her head if she thought about it. How could she possibly convey the terror of fleeing for their lives among the raging Indians as their home went up in flames behind them? No, she couldn't write all those things. It was just easier for now not to write at all.

Catherine was disappointed to learn that Sam had been sent back to Fort Hays. That was probably best, though. She was feeling so distanced from David right now, and her whole life was in such upheaval that it would be really easy to lean on Sam. That wouldn't be fair to him, knowing how he felt about her. She wrote a short letter to him, though, letting him know that she and Jeremy and the baby had survived the Indian raid and would be situating in Dodge City within days. She had just dropped it into the mail slot when she saw a group of soldiers returning to the fort. Jeremy went to speak with them as Catherine realized they must be the scouting party that had gone to Martha and Owen's homestead. Minutes later he turned to walk her direction.

"Cat, I talked to the scouts that went to Owen and Martha's," Jeremy quietly broke into her thoughts.

Catherine looked at him, afraid to ask the question he could see in her eyes.

"You were right," he said, sadly.

"I knew it, but I still didn't want to hear that it's true!" Catherine cried.

"Did they say if the dugout was left intact … did the Indians burn up their things like they did our house?"

"No, strangely, they only ransacked the place. The soldiers had no way of knowing what they may have taken, probably a few things as trinkets, but they didn't burn anything. Most of their belongings were left there. The soldiers found information that will enable them to notify their families back east."

"I wish I had that information," Catherine said. "I'd like to write and tell them how much Martha and Owen meant to us. I don't know how we could have made it through Mama's death without the two of them. They were truly God's gift to us."

"Since God already knows the future, Cat, He knew that Owen and Martha would give their lives by obeying Him, and still He had them come here."

"Jeremy, I'm beginning to think there must be something important in His plan for *us*, if God would send people as special as Owen and Martha to see that we made it through our difficult time. We simply have to find the perfect will of God and fulfill whatever He has for us to do"

"Well, the only way I know to find God's will is for us to do each day what we feel He'd have us to do, and I think we've done that. I know we were to leave the homestead, even if the Indians hadn't come. Now there's no way we could stay there … that's behind us.

"Did the scouts say anything about McCloud?"

Jeremy took a deep breath, "They said it was a really ugly scene. They buried what was left of him beside Mama's grave."

"If he wasn't going to continue living like he did while Mama was alive, I'm glad that Baby Jake will never know him. We don't have to tell him the awful things his father did," Catherine said, looking down at the sleeping baby in her arms.

"You're right. I can't see how that would serve any good purpose." Jeremy agreed.

*   *   *   *

Jeremy thought he'd certainly appear more "hireable" without the Indian medicine smeared on the side of his head, and the three days had passed. The doctor wanted to check the wound again before Jeremy left the fort so he had offered to remove the salve and herbs. Because of the contagious nature of Susannah's illness, he also wanted to examine Catherine and the baby while they were there. He was pleased to see Baby Jake so plump and healthy.

"Young lady," he said kindly to Catherine, "You have been working too hard and resting too little. I know that you've not had much in the way of fresh fruits and vegetables since you left your home back east, but once you get settled in Dodge, you need to see if you can't work those into your diet. If you were to get sick, your body has little to fight back with."

Turning to Jeremy he smiled, "Try to put some meat on her bones, big brother! ... All right ... Now let's take a look at that lucky head of yours!"

When the native remedy was washed away, the doctor was very pleased with the condition of Jeremy's wound. It had healed back together with no sign of infection. There were spots of numbness that the doctor said would leave as the nerves were completely restored. He encouraged Jeremy to make sure he didn't take any more blows to the head for a while, but otherwise, he should have no permanent damage.

As they were leaving, the doctor expressed his regrets at Susannah's passing away. He had hoped that somehow she would be able to endure longer. His heart was touched as he watched the children of that sweet woman. Obviously the baby was being well cared for and was definitely loved. The boy and girl were still young, but they now had adult responsibilities.

As the doctor cleaned up from cleansing Jeremy's wound he was wishing he knew what those Indians put in their "cure." That was the best looking three-day-old wound he'd ever seen!

*   *   *   *

Catherine and Jeremy had just placed the last of their belongings into the wagon …arranged much more neatly than when they arrived at the fort!

"Well, Cat, out of two covered wagon loads of possessions this is what we have left," Jeremy stated.

"It's hard to believe, isn't it?" Catherine asked.

"What's really hard to believe is that it's only been a year since we left Lexington. It feels like a lifetime ago!"

Catherine smiled as she climbed up onto the wagon seat, "And we thought we had problems then!"

"I know we don't have a clue what's ahead for us in Dodge City, but somehow, Cat, I feel excited, like it's going to be good," Jeremy said.

Baby Jake squealed and patted Jeremy's face as though in agreement.

"O.K., little buddy, let's get started!" Jeremy handed the baby up to Catherine and swung up onto the seat. As he flicked the reins for Midnight to move forward the large gates of the fort slowly began to swing open.

Catherine had mixed emotions as they neared the gate. They were leaving behind memories of kind soldiers who had been so generous in their care and support these past few days. Catherine's eyes misted with tears as she waved to the dozens of them who had come to wish them well. Midnight stepped briskly as they went through the gates as if all the attention was in his behalf

As Catherine turned to watch the heavy gates swing shut behind them she felt closure of their life on the plains with their mother and McCloud. In an hour or so they would be in Dodge City, entering a new phase of their lives. It would likely be another year before she could expect David to come for her, or was his love as lost to her as the gold half-heart he had given her? There were so many unanswered questions in her future, but Catherine had learned that God was faithful. She did not know what lay ahead, and yet, like Jeremy, she felt an excitement that she couldn't explain.

It seemed that Baby Jake felt it too. Lifting his chubby little hands high he bounced up and down and squealed in pure delight!

"That's it, Jake, "Jeremy encouraged him. "Shout it to the prairie, 'Dodge City, Here we come!'"

EXCERPTS FROM

SEARCH FOR THE WHOLE HEART:
VOLUME II

DISCOVERY

I n his New York City office Alex Caine sat at his desk
with the mail he had just received. He thumbed
through it, looking for a certain correspondence. Here it
was, the large envelope mailed from Lexington, Missouri.
Undoubtedly, it contained information from the private
investigator he'd hired to watch Charlotte Pendleton and
that "jeweler boy" she was chasing. Quickly he tore it open,
not bothering to use the letter opener. Several pages of
paper and a handful of photographs fell out onto his desk.

Caine grabbed the photos, looking hurriedly
through the lot, then slowly at each one individually. His
face was flushed and his expression angry as he threw
down the last of them and picked up the papers.

Bosley, the investigator in charge, had written his
summary of the surveillance performed on Charlotte
Pendleton and David Winters. It gave dates that
corresponded with numbers on the photographs. Most of
them were of Charlotte entering or leaving the small
Jewelry and Watch Emporium. One of them showed

Winters and Charlotte eating at a restaurant. Some of the photographs showed Charlotte at different locations with her aunt or shopping alone. Others were of Winters as he came and went from his home, and at a church building, surrounded by other young people. Charlotte was not in any of those pictures, though.

The one photograph that really sparked Caine's ire was the one where Charlotte was affectionately touching Winters on the cheek as they stood in the doorway of the shop. He noticed that in none of them was there any evidence on Winters' part of physical action toward Charlotte. So he was still the Man of Iron! All the more attraction for a woman like Charlotte. She wouldn't give up until she could break that defense. As much as Caine loved her - if this was love - he hated her too. He hated that she could invade his thoughts and interfere with his business just by absenting herself from him. Yet, when she was in town she couldn't refuse his advances anymore than he could wipe her from his memory. He was used to getting what he wanted, but so was Charlotte, and Charlotte apparently wanted David Winters. That union, Caine knew, was one her beloved "Poppy" would approve!

Caine hated him, too ... Martin Pendleton, one of the most powerful men in New York City and probably, the entire country. His dynasty would have to go to someone when he died, and Caine intended to be that someone. Pendleton was just as determined that it would *not* be Alex Caine and was doing everything he could to influence Charlotte away from him. The banker was probably encouraging his daughter's stay in Lexington, hoping she'd be successful in seducing Winters.

Pushing back his chair, Caine stood and looked down onto the busy street below. He'd been responsible for having some people roughed up to convince them to do things his way, but he'd never gone as far as murder. The stakes were enormous this time, though. Winters had to be removed from this equation before Charlotte was able to spin her web around him. She couldn't entice what didn't exist. Then she'd be all his again, regardless of how Poppy felt about it.

Bosley, the private investigator, had hinted once about knowing people who would do "anything" if he ever needed "anything" done. He thought he could telegraph the private investigator using that word, and Bosley would know what he was talking about.

Now that he had come to his decision, Alex Caine felt pleased with himself and back in control. What a simple solution to this situation that had tormented him for weeks-- kill David Winters! Laughing, he lit a cigar and tilted his head back, blowing smoke rings until the air in his office was polluted with the smell of his foreign tobacco.

*   *   *   *

Catherine and Jeremy's knowledge of cities back east included brick and stone buildings and attractive, stable, wooden structures. Dodge City was a complete surprise to them. Many of the buildings on the main street appeared to have been constructed by amateurs. Most were unpainted, the wood in various shades of aging from the wind and sun. Some boasted tall storefronts, attempting a more prestigious appearance. It seemed to Catherine that almost every other business was a saloon. As they rode by one of them, the swinging doors flew open as a man threw a drunken cowboy out into the street, almost under Midnight's feet.

Just minutes ago Catherine and Jeremy were feeling so confident that God wanted them in Dodge City. They looked at each other now, both questioning their situation.

"Well, this is certainly not what I expected," Catherine said. "Where do we go from here, Jeremy?"

"Good question, Cat," Jeremy said as he reined Midnight around a couple of men fighting in the middle of the street. "Do you think God has visited Dodge lately? Or ever? Maybe He didn't know about all of this when He sent us here," he said, teasing her.

"He could have given us warning," Catherine said.

"Then you wouldn't have come," Jeremy answered.

"You're probably right. Oh well, we're here. Surely there's a place to get something to eat that's not a saloon with men fighting," she said.

The gleaming rails of the new Atchison, Topeka and Santa Fe railroad separated Dodge City by north and south. Jeremy noticed that the north side appeared to be less rowdy. He began to look that direction for a place advertising food. They passed a general store, a shoe shop advertising dead men's boots for ten cents per pair, and a small, but sturdy, building with signage that proclaimed, "We buy gold." Then Catherine saw a sign up ahead, "Aunt Lizzie's Boarding House, Clean Rooms - $.50, Hot Meals- $ .25-.75, No Drunks, No guns, No Foolishness!"

"I think we found our place," Catherine said.

The street was wide, allowing plenty of room for Jeremy to leave the wagon and Midnight hitched to a post just outside the building.

"I'll come around and get Baby Jake," Jeremy said.

The baby woke up as Catherine handed him down to Jeremy. He looked around, his little eyes wide as he took in another new place. Catherine climbed down, holding to Jeremy's free hand. It felt good to be out of that bumpy wagon, and the smells coming from Aunt Lizzie's place reminded her of Mama's cooking.

A girl wearing an apron and carrying a basket of heavenly smelling, fresh bread stopped to tell Catherine they could sit wherever they liked. They made their way through noisy customers, to the only unoccupied table they saw. They were getting settled when Catherine thought she heard someone speak her name. She looked up to see a man and woman seated at the next table. As the beautiful, dark-haired woman smiled at Catherine her mind flashed back to the covered wagon and Baby Jake's birth.

"Miss Emeline! Oh, it's so good to see you," Catherine rose to hug the woman who had come to their rescue and delivered Baby Jake that night on the trail.

Emeline Carter was just as excited to see Catherine, Baby Jake and Jeremy. She hugged all of them while her companion watched with a smile.

"My, how my namesake has grown. Let me have him; I just have to hug and kiss the little angel." Emeline reached out for Baby Jake, and he immediately fell into her arms with a smile. Hugging him to her, Emeline kept telling him what a handsome boy he was. Baby Jake snuggled into her shoulder, and then lifted his head and smiled at her again.

Emeline's attention was totally wrapped up in the baby, so the man with her stood and extended his hand to Jeremy, "If I wait to be introduced, that may not happen. I'm Dwight Harrison, and it looks like my lady's heart has been stolen by that little fellow."

Shaking his hand, Jeremy said, "I'm Jeremy Sutherland, sir. I'm afraid my little brother has that effect. He's quite a charmer."

Catherine stepped over to introduce herself and shake hands with Dwight Harrison. She immediately felt comfortable with this graying, handsome man. There was an air of quiet confidence and strength about him, and his eyes were kind and friendly.

"Hi, I'm Catherine, Mr. Harrison," she said.

"Catherine, I'm glad to meet you. Emeline told me how you came to be acquainted, but please, call me Dwight; you'll make me feel old."

Emeline stopped talking to Baby Jake long enough to take charge;

"Come and join us at our table. We have to catch up on things. Catherine, sit here, Jeremy, you can sit over there. Oh, Dwight, you can't believe how happy I am to see these kids!" she said.

"I think I can, hon. I haven't seen you this excited since you came to Dodge."

"Well, can you blame me?" she asked him. Then to Catherine and Jeremy she said, "Dwight didn't exactly tell me everything in his letters about his wonderful new cow town when he was enticing me to come out here."

"We were shocked when we rode into town, too, Catherine admitted. "I'm not sure what I expected, but it surely wasn't what I saw."

The girl with the apron approached the table and smiled. "Would you like to order now, Miss Emeline?"

"Oh, Tinnie, we haven't even thought about food yet. Catherine, what can we get for Baby Jake ... some mashed potatoes?"

"The only solid food I've given him is oatmeal, but he might like potatoes," Catherine answered.

"O.K., this is my treat today. Tinnie, bring mashed potatoes for the baby, and how about steak with all the trimmings for the rest of us?" Dwight asked. "Lizzie cooks one of the best in town, and this feels like a celebration."

"I can't remember the last time I had steak," Jeremy said, "That's reason enough to celebrate."

Catherine agreed, and Emeline was too busy with Baby Jake to care, so Dwight ordered steaks all around. When Tinnie left to turn in their order Emeline said,

"I've been so glad to see you that I haven't even asked what you're doing here, or about your mother and step-father."

"Our mother died almost two months ago from consumption," Jeremy said.

"Oh, no! I can't believe it. I remember she seemed weak, but I just thought it was from having the baby and the hardship on the trail. I never dreamed she was that ill. I am so sorry; your mother was a precious woman. So the two of you have been taking care of the baby? What about the father, McCloud?"

"That's an unpleasant story, as well. He was killed by Indians four days ago when they raided our homestead," Catherine told her.

"But the three of you made it out alive, obviously. What in the world have you children been through in these past few months?"

"Life has been hard, Miss Emeline," Jeremy admitted. "But Catherine and I are looking forward to starting a new life here in Dodge City. The Indians burned the sod house to the ground. I can't farm the place alone anyway, so we decided to come here and try to find a place for the three of us to live. I'm hoping to find work to support us."

Dwight and Emeline exchanged glances. Emeline said, "I can see there are a lot of things we need to talk about, but for now, why don't we just eat our steak and have a good time. We can work at solving problems later."

*   *   *   *

Down the street at Aunt Lizzie's boarding house Catherine was dreaming of David.

"I love you, Catherine. Can you hear me? I'm sending my love on the wind!"

"Oh, David," she said in her dream, "so much has happened. I'm not the same girl you loved a year ago."

"Has God changed, Catherine? Has His plan for us changed?"

"But I lost my gold heart, David. I don't even know where to search for it; my beautiful heart is lost forever!"

Baby Jake cried out in his sleep beside Catherine, waking her. She comforted the little one back to a sound sleep, thinking of her dream. It was so good to hear David's voice, yet her heart was fearful of what the future held. David's questions rang in her mind as she drifted back to sleep;

"Has God changed, Catherine? Has His plan for us changed?"

400

5423152R0

Made in the USA
Charleston, SC
13 June 2010